The Strange Death of a Romantic

A novel by
JIM WILLIAMS

Print Edition 2014

Licensed by Marble City Publishing

Copyright © 2001 Jim Williams

First published in Great Britain by Scribner, 1999

An imprint of Simon & Schuster UK Ltd

ISBN 10 1-908943-37-8

ISBN 13 978-1-908943-37-8

Praise for Jim Williams' books

The Hitler Diaries

"...steadily builds up an impressive atmosphere of menace."
Times Literary Supplement

"...well written and full of suspense." *Glasgow Herald*

"...the quality of the storytelling is exceptionally high."
Hampstead and Highgate Express

Last Judgement

"...the author journalists read for their next scoop." *Sunday Telegraph*

Scherzo

"Sparkling and utterly charming. Devilishly clever plot and deceitful finale." *Frances Fyfield – Mail on Sunday*

Recherché

"A skilful exercise, bizarre and dangerous in a lineage that includes Fowles' *The Magus*." *Guardian*

The Strange Death of a Romantic

"This is an extraordinarily witty and assured novel." *T J Binyon – Evening Standard*

"...seriously good...technically brilliant...constantly suggestive... dreamy but sinister glamour." *Times Literary Supplement*

To my wife, Shirley

With love – however inadequately expressed

ACKNOWLEDGEMENTS

My thanks go to the usual suspects:

James Hale, my agent, for his unfailing skill and care and the confidence to let me write weird stuff.

Helen Simpson, who provides a second ear on tricky text, copyedits with skill and passion, and who gets the point.

Audrey Hamilton, for valued friendship, encouragement and the hard work of processing the manuscript.

Nick Webb for his understanding and commitment.

Poets are never allowed to be mediocre
By the Gods, by men or by publishers.

Horace

We set our stupidities in dignity when we set them in print.
Are we not trying to impress people by our quotations
rather than by the truth of what they say?

Montaigne

CHAPTER ONE

Anche nello speziale io
1945

Having no thoughts of murder on his mind, Captain Guy Parrot was unconcerned when Colonel Box told him that he was to reconnoitre the location for a new hospital and then establish it. He protested that he was a doctor not an administrator and as qualified to move a hospital as a musician to move a piano. But this was for form's sake. If his orders went unquestioned, the Colonel became anxious that he had made a mistake and inclined to fret. When allowed a modest degree of bullying, he could be touchingly blithe.

For four years Guy had – to a large degree literally – followed the pillar of fire by night and smoke by day in the aftermath of battles in which he never took part, and so had no expectation that the Army would act rationally. He would not have said it was insane. That would be to impute passions it did not possess or – still less likely – an insight into some higher reality. No, the Army was very much of this world: indeed, it seemed imbued with a hyper-ordinariness by which entropy and the dross of material existence had overwhelmed the last sparks of creativity.

Guy understood that the new hospital was to be near Genoa in the north, quite possibly in the American area. Colonel Box, like many others, had a deep animus against the Americans for their late entry into the war and resented their self-confidence and superior resources. He pursued secret campaigns against his opposite number. The lodging of the British Autonomous Hospital within the bounds of

1

US Army territory would, the Colonel hinted obscurely, have a material, albeit minor, impact on the post-war settlement of Italy. Guy was left to imagine it as a useful outpost in enemy territory, like the four-power status of Berlin.

'Of course you're the man for the job,' retorted the Colonel, gamely rising to the objection. 'In Unknown Territory it'll be a Help and a Comfort to speak the lingo.'

Guy nodded in resignation. He did not repeat his past efforts to explain that, for complicated historical reasons, the Italians did not actually speak Italian. To this difficulty might be added that Guy's vocabulary was literary and sadly antiquated and his accent intelligible only in a vaguely delimited area approximately midway between Florence and Genoa.

'It doesn't do to be bashful,' said Colonel Box. 'It disheartens the men. I know you speak the lingo, because you proved it in our fight against the clap.'

His last remark referred to an incident of the previous year. Officially known as the Anti-Venereal-Disease Campaign, it had lasted three months and culminated in 'VD Day' – though, the nature of the illness being what it was, the junior officers such as Guy had had difficulty in imagining the climactic event that would close the proceedings. A service in Naples cathedral, followed by the voluntary adoption of universal celibacy, perhaps? As it happened, the Allies landed in Normandy on VD Day. This coincidence – if that is what it was – gave rise to the rumour, spread by Corporal Long, that the campaign had all along been one of misinformation to fool the Germans.

The origin of the affair lay in the desire of soldiers to sleep with disreputable women. Not that the men would admit to the fact since venereal disease was a court-martial offence. They blamed the insanitary toilet seats and – if Guy correctly understood their confusing references to having a 'J Arthur' or a 'Barclays' – claimed that their sex lives were limited to innocent masturbation. Corporal

Long even went so far as to suggest that venereal disease might in fact be *caused* by abstinence from regular intercourse with the opposite sex. He relied on the proposition that 'Clap and wanking aren't neither of them normal'.

Guy and Lieutenant Jenkins discussed this theory. Corporal Long was a short, amiable Glaswegian, frequently described as 'helpful' in the way of someone who helped the police with their enquiries. Jenkins was responsible for company transport and was Corporal Long's notional superior. He and Guy were walking the lines one night after lights out. The battalion was encamped in wheat fields on the plain somewhere north of Naples and towards the sea. The moon was up, the sky a limpid violet, and the Americans were romantically bombing Bologna. Guy had caught the thrum of their engines which, allowing for the latitude conceded to memory on a sentimental evening of war and Italian moonlight, reminded him of cicadas in the pine brakes of the Riviera. Then, as he was about to say something to Jenkins, they heard an unmistakable catch of breath and a grunt from one of the tents.

'Hark!' said Jenkins. 'I hear the sound of one hand clapping.'

Jenkins was an orientalist and fifteen years Guy's junior, by occupation an assistant bank manager from Morpeth. His level-headed friendliness after so much experience of the Army struck Guy as perverse.

The Anti-Venereal-Disease Campaign was conducted on a corps-wide basis. Because of his supposed command of the language, Guy's role was to lecture those members of the frail sisterhood who fell within the corps area. The Army, with its roots in a shoddy version of realism, conceded that there was no stopping the trade, but required the prostitutes to persuade their clients to use condoms. For their part, the women had no objection to the plan other than scepticism as to its practicality. But, feeling that they had now been granted a kind of official status, they complained at the depressing effect on prices caused by those amateurs who had entered the profession under pressure of war. In this respect, said the women, the Fascists had been more efficient. Even – they said coyly – sympathetic.

Guy delivered his lectures to a script prepared by the senior medical officers at Corps HQ. However, in addition he had to counsel the women and administer medication. His natural diffidence made this difficult, as did his consciousness of the gap between his middle-age and their youth. More problematic was the fact that he was required to discuss things that, in the nineteenth-century novels he had read, young ladies simply did not do. He prescribed vitamins, which could scarcely fail to help, and, when these ran out, laxatives. For deeply cultural reasons the British Army had an inexhaustible supply of the latter as a specific against all ills. Or, as Corporal Long put it in his deep Glaswegian accent, 'They girls will be fine after a good clear-oot'.

Guy ceased prescribing laxatives when they gave rise to a dysentery scare.

At a more philosophical level, he tried to explain that it was immoral of the women to sleep with strangers while their men were away. They admitted the general justice of this point. However, they observed, the men were away for the most part because they were prisoners of the English, and it would be more effective if the doctor delivered husbands rather than lectures. In an egalitarian spirit they also claimed their rights because their men folk, scattered in the remote fastnesses of Wales, were even now sleeping with local girls. Guy learnt that the Welsh were a dark and passionate race, sexually irresistible and much given to magic and perversion. They were preferable only to the English, whose ice-cold maidens caused impotence and whose men were pederasts, facts known the world over and a cause of the British Empire.

In Guy's eyes the Army's ordinariness was this: that, like custard powder, liver salts and cold cream, it was a second-rate product claiming to be something better. Oddly enough, this disappointing perception endeared it to him. For, although the Army was rubbish, it embodied the power and democracy of rubbish, and from its low, muddy plain Guy's modest leaps of imagination and creativity could sometimes seem spectacular.

'Mr Jenkins will organise transport,' said Colonel Box.

Though indifferent to the answer, Guy asked, 'Where shall we be going?'

'North,' said the Colonel airily.

'Is that all he told you?' Jenkins asked later.

'Apparently we're to be given sealed orders, not to be opened before Pisa, which will reveal the final destination.'

'Old Thunder must be off his trolley! Why the secrecy? Doesn't he know the war's over?'

The war in Europe had ended a month before. Mussolini had been hung by his heels from a lamppost in Milan. It was difficult to believe that the Italians had ever been enemies. Indeed Corporal Long, the armchair strategist, asserted that Italy had all along been acting in the Allies' interest, and it was difficult to assert that the farcical Italian campaigns in Yugoslavia, Greece and North Africa had achieved anything for Germany except to consume its forces in secondary theatres.

This theory, like that concerning the origins of venereal disease, was an example of Corporal Long's disconcerting intelligence, for which he had several times been promoted to sergeant. On each occasion, as the Corporal put it, 'It wouldna take,' as if promotion were a form of vaccination. He could not be trusted to have authority without abusing it. But, as he said, 'What's the point o' having power if ye canna abuse it?'

'We'll take Long with us as driver,' said Jenkins. 'And if there are any supply difficulties, he can forage for us.'

This was prudent since they had no knowledge of conditions applying in the north. There were stories of Communist partisans and Fascist war bands.

'In any case it's probably for the best if we put our friend outside the reach of the Provost-Marshal's investigation,' added Jenkins, referring to disappearances of the stock of a new wonder-drug, penicillin. Not that there was any evidence of Corporal Long's involvement.

'Perhaps he'll let us use his Hispano Suiza?' Guy proposed lightheartedly.

The subject of Corporal Long's Hispano Suiza was loosely connected with the Anti-Venereal-Disease Campaign. Certainly, somewhere north of Naples the Corporal had killed a fleeing Fascist *ras*, and, tactfully ignoring the fact that the deceased was shot in the back, the Army had granted him a medal and one of his temporary promotions. At the level of company gossip, however, it was rumoured that he had murdered the official simply to steal his Hispano Suiza motor car. No one admitted to seeing such a vehicle, but it was a fact that the *ras*'s means of transport had never been found, and it was difficult to accept the Corporal's explanation that the man had been escaping on foot, dragging a trunk full of fur coats and silk dresses. Guy had been required to pursue the matter and learned – again by unattributable rumour – that the Hispano Suiza had been sold to a US general. At which point Corporal Long produced a substantial consignment of American-made condoms. Guy prudently accepted the placatory offering and reported to the Colonel that there was no basis for assuming that the Hispano Suiza had ever existed, though in fact he was a little frightened of doing battle with someone of Corporal Long's tactical shrewdness. The supply of more acceptable condoms, together with the distraction of the invasion of Fortress Europe, contributed to making the Anti-Venereal-Disease Campaign a success.

On the night before their departure, Guy went to

church. He was an indifferent Catholic, more religious now in time of war and loneliness than in his piping days of peace, when he attended mass only once a year. The Parrots were neither ancient recusants nor members of the spell-bound horde of Irish immigrants. They were part of that small band who decamped from Anglicanism at the time of Newman and the Oxford Movement, a species of deserter. Guy had difficulty in conceiving the intensity of the point of ritual that had led his grandfather to take such a momentous step, but it had been taken and, like much in life, was irrevocable. Having a passing enthusiasm for his faith during adolescence, Guy made some researches and turned up a reference to an English martyr, Guy of Shoreditch, who had been dragged to the stake under Elizabeth, protesting vehemently that he was ready and willing to denounce the Pope and deny the Real Presence, but been burnt all the same. His final equivocal declaration that 'God knoweth what it is all about, for I am sure I do not' was taken as an affirmation of faith and humility and he was admitted into the ranks of those saints who are decently forgotten. No church was consecrated to his memory, no altar guarded his bones, no miracles were attributed to him that Guy had heard of. Privately he regarded the martyr as the patron of cowards, not having discovered any other to lay claim to the title.

Once he had disposed of more venal sins, cowardice formed the topic of Guy's confessions. It was a difficult subject, since he could not point to any specific act of cowardice he had committed. Rather, it seemed to him that it had insinuated itself into the fabric of his life: that he had so organised his affairs that, avoiding all challenges, no dangers moral or physical confronted him. He was so cowardly that his life gave no occasion for acts of cowardice. It was a hard concept to explain and instead of presenting a brisk shopping list of iniquity containing the usual items of daily use, Guy tended to ramble during confession in the hope of engaging his confessor in moral debate. In this he was opposed by Father Murphy, a Maynooth priest, whose interests were confined to fornication and Irish Republicanism, being against the former and in favour of the latter until the day he was blown up by one of his own bombs while in bed with his housekeeper.

Tonight the silence was profound. Guy realised that he missed the solemn threnody of the American bombers and would never hear it again. The church was an ancient Romanesque structure, crazily shored up against the effect of earthquakes, and standing in a dark alleyway. It comprised a nave, two side aisles with lesser altars, and a chapel to the Virgin. Here stood a statue of Our Lady, looking as aloof and made-up as a fashionable mannequin. She was draped in silver *ex voti* offerings and glass beads, reminding Guy of a shop assistant selling costume jewellery. Yet the effect was to make her more rather than less accessible to his devotions. He had a weakness for poor girls with pale legs ending in cheap shoes, and the tawdry prettiness of the Madonna recalled all the girls, immaculate and fragile, who ran to catch buses in the rain, and passed their humdrum lives in the hope of being visited by an angel.

The priest smoked, counted money and did not speak except to grant absolution. Emerging from the confessional, Guy was astonished to see Corporal Long sitting in furtive prayer – or was he filling in a betting slip? He assumed instinctively that the Corporal's intentions were nefarious and wondered if the man had an eye to one of the altarpieces. Most of the paintings were grimy and torn and displayed sinister Dominican saints in states of terrifying ecstasy. But one, Guy suspected, was a *quattrocento* work of the Sienese school.

'Good evening, Corporal,' said Guy with affected breeziness.

'Evening, Mr Parrot, sir,' replied Corporal Long cheerily.

'Ready for the morning?'

'Och, aye!'

Guy decided further interrogation would be pointless. Corporal Long would only lie to him. All the men lied to him.

'It's a mark of respect,' said Jenkins. 'I wish sometimes the beggars would lie to me. Instead they tell me all their foul secrets as if I were a fellow conspirator.'

'Why "respect"?' asked Guy.

'Because they assume you have principles and feelings.'

'But how can I control the men if they lie to me?'

'Oh, you shouldn't try to control them. Leave that to the sergeants. It's not what officers are for.'

'Then what *are* officers for?'

'To speak good English and die in the first rank.'

Tonight was the last time Guy would see this church, for soon he would be demobilised to England. But first, like a pilgrim to the Holy Land, he would found a hospital for other wanderers.

They set off in the morning, Guy, Jenkins and Corporal Long in the jeep with extra jerrycans, and two privates in a two-ton truck bringing up basic supplies. The privates were called Nick and Jimmy and were reputed to sleep together. Accusations of homosexuality were among the common courtesies of life in masculine institutions, and Guy discounted the rumour.

The main highway was slow with convoys, sappers and engineers attending to damaged bridges and here and there a German tank or self-propelled gun abandoned inconsiderately. But the Corporal was one of those self-confident drivers who know short-cuts through unfamiliar country and Guy was content to let him take them on a tour of the byways of Tuscany.

The sun banished Guy's melancholy thoughts of the previous night. He admired the Tuscan landscape. The emphatic darkness of the cypresses seemed to break it into elements of formal composition, as did the regularity of the vineyards, so unlike the soft, subtle shapelessness of England. The Italians, mostly women working the fields, waved ungrudgingly at their conquerors and Guy returned the gesture while hoping charitably that there was something that could be done for these people.

Guy had not previously seen Jenkins on more intimate terms with the men, but it seemed he was comfortable to converse with Corporal Long and Guy understood now why it was that his subaltern received unwelcome confidences.

When they stopped to fill the radiators at a well, Jenkins said jokingly, 'Well then, Tommy, aren't you glad I got you out of the clutches of the Provost-Marshal?'

'Och, that business o' they penicillin wasna me,' answered the Scotsman, unaffronted by the implied accusation. 'It was Division took that stuff, I know for a fact.'

'Really?' persisted Jenkins. 'Then how is it that no fewer than five witnesses from the town will swear that you were selling the drugs?'

This was the first time that Guy had heard of the five witnesses and he realised that Jenkins, too, hid things from him.

Corporal Long grinned. He directed one of the privates to get more water and, from his own supply, offered the officers cigarettes. Guy knew that in accepting one he was binding himself not to disclose whatever appalling revelation the man was about to make, but he could not be churlish and refuse. Satisfied with his moral hostages the Corporal said, 'It was like this. Since everyone thought I was guilty, I couldna pass up the chance of doing business. But it wasna penicillin I sold 'cos I didna have any.'

'Then what was it you gave them?' asked Jenkins, accepting without comment that the other man was entitled to take advantage of the situation.

'It was they laxatives Mr Parrot hadna any time for.'

'The laxatives!' exclaimed Guy. 'But those would be of no damn use at all in curing infection!'

'I ken that,' said the Corporal complacently. 'But they widna do any harm either.'

Guy was too dumbstruck to respond to this and too compromised by his acceptance of the cigarette. Jenkins, on the other hand, was clearly entertained by the Corporal's imposture and indifferent to its moral aspect. He suggested, half seriously, that after the war the Scotsman should become a lawyer.

They bivouacked near Pisa but not in the city itself where it would be difficult to guard the supplies. They lay up in a field deep in poppies more vivid and abundant than any Guy could remember. Seeing the drab livery of vehicles in such a glory of colour, he was tempted to draw something symbolic from the image, but the symbol – if there were one – was blank of meaning like the emblems borne by unfamiliar saints: the palm leaves and the instruments of their torture. The martyrs carried diminutive replicas of rack and wheel, an exiguous bleeding head or severed breast, and seemed to apologise quietly for these intrusive tokens. Guy considered for a moment that, if he came into money, he would erect a memorial window to his namesake, Guy of Shoreditch. But how would he represent the saint? Presumably with his back to the observer as he tried to run away. And his emblem would be a chamber pot into which he had voided his terrified bladder.

The time had come to open their further orders.

'Best see what Thunder has got for us,' said Jenkins, after dismissing Corporal Long to smoke with the privates.

Guy had tried to persuade his lieutenant, short of giving an actual order, to open the envelope earlier, but Jenkins had refused. Conscious that he had no instinct for the military life Jenkins was incapable of consistently applying the necessary self-discipline. But sometimes, as now, he could be excessively punctilious, rather as an alcoholic in the morning promises to turn over a new leaf and forgoes his breakfast dram.

'It says "La Spezia". Where'n hell's that?'

'On the coast,' said Guy.

'I say, old chap, you don't look so well,' said Jenkins, alarmed. 'Know this place, do you? There's nothing odd about it, is there?'

'Yes, I know it. And no, there's nothing odd about the place. It's just an ordinary Italian town.'

Jenkins rustled the paper and squinting at it said, 'You know, old Thunder's really been quite helpful. He's even suggested a place we might look over. The Villa Esperanza. Know that, too?'

Guy nodded. At the name of La Spezia he had felt his stomach sink, and now, at the mention of the Villa Esperanza, he wanted to vomit. He was surprised, even frightened, at these reactions. He could recall nothing similar, but then, on reflection, he knew that in all the intervening years he had never brought La Spezia to mind. After the events of that summer he had obliterated the name, avoiding any specific connection with that fatal place. And if, *in extremis*, reference were necessary, he had mentioned only vaguely the time 'when I was in Italy', admitting that he knew something of Venice and Genoa, but not La Spezia, of which no one ever spoke.

And the Villa Esperanza? What chance was there that the name should ever have come to him again in life? It was not famous nor in any way remarkable. Princes and Powers had plundered Italy without making a mark on it. Glimpsed on its hill among the pines and cypress, its pink form, hazy in the sunshine, would at most evoke the comment 'That looks pretty.' But on closer inspection the visitor would see that sun and rain had bleached and leached the colour-wash, that wild thyme and oregano had spread through the parterres, and that the spring feeding the fountain was choked; and he would recognise it as one of those picturesque but decrepit houses foisted on the unwary for a season by a dubious agent. Which was exactly how Ambrose Carmody had acquired it, sight unseen.

'Yes, I know it. I have been there,' thought Guy. It was the place where ambition had turned to ashes and life defeated him. There he had acquired the indifference which in his eyes was a sin since it was the armour of evasion and cowardice. There mysteries went unsolved and murder unpunished.

He felt as if he were being dragged back to the stake of a conscience piled high with faggots of forgetfulness. He hoped only that there was merit in the dying prayer of Guy of Shoreditch (if prayer it was).

'God knoweth what it is all about. for I am sure I do not.'

CHAPTER TWO

1945

At first Guy would not go to the Villa Esperanza, which lay several kilometres out of town. He sent the privates with the Bedford truck to take possession and found an *albergo* in the ruins of La Spezia for himself, Jenkins and Corporal Long. He justified it by saying he needed to present himself to the authorities, ascertain the general situation, and establish a telephone link with Colonel Box. This might take some time, since there were unresolved issues about who controlled the area both civilly and militarily, and the Italian telephone system – never the best – was for the present almost non-existent. On the second day Jenkins made an expedition to the site of the proposed hospital and reported, as Guy knew would be the case, that the building would house no more than a couple of dozen patients at best, there was not and never had been a supply of electricity, sanitation was limited to earth privies, and water was flowing in only a trickle from a spring on the hillside.

'Tell Thunder the place just won't do,' said Jenkins.

Guy tried to do exactly that, proposing he investigate the existing hospital facilities in the town and attempt to reach an arrangement. However, here he hit upon one of the Army's rigidities. Perhaps because the new hospital was not strictly necessary, there was no need for flexibility in considering any alternative. At all events, the Colonel insisted that, under wartime conditions, difficulties would be encountered wherever one turned and Guy should therefore deal with them. An instinct of possession meant that no consideration could be given to sharing a building with anyone else – least of all the Americans. In overruling Guy's protests, Colonel Box became quite genial. 'God blast Roosevelt!' he swore gaily, forgetting that, even now, his wish might be coming true, since the President had recently died.

In the meantime Guy wrestled with the problem of writing a letter to Elizabeth. It had been his habit to write each day, collecting the pages and sending them weekly wherever possible.

The problem was that he could not tell Elizabeth he was at La Spezia. It was the place for which he had abandoned her during that terrible summer. The place from which he had tried to write before: letters full of lies and hypocrisy. Naturally, once he had earned his qualifications as a coward, he avoided any mention of that time.

After a week Jenkins said, 'I think we'd better move ourselves to the Villa Esperanza before Tommy gets himself arrested, or we'll have another outbreak of "dysentery" on our hands.'

'Has he been at the laxatives again?'

'Strictly in the line of duty. We've acquired a generator and some cable and fittings. Tommy's found an electrician who'll work simply for food, so we should have power in a day or so. Fortunately we've a good supply of soap and cigarettes. Tommy says he can get almost anything in return for those.'

Guy noticed that Jenkins now invariably referred to Corporal Long as 'Tommy', and that his accent – officer-class assumed for the duration – was shifting to its natural Northumbrian burr. The war was slipping away to memory. The performance over, they were standing impatiently to the National Anthem.

'I hope you'll remember to address Corporal Long by his correct title in front of the others.'

'Of course,' said Jenkins, offended.

Guy relented. 'I don't mind. But if it gets to be a habit you'll let yourself down in front of Colonel Box or someone else one of these days.'

'Thunder has no room to complain. I once heard him call his batman, Daisy, "dear".'

'I expect he was being sarcastic.'

'Daisy didn't seem to think so.'

Guy regretted admonishing Jenkins on the subject of names and ranks. It had become something of a pretence, this belief that they were still in the Army. And, truthfully, the others had all done well. From hints given by Guy they had located the spring and unblocked it and, to their surprise, found the pipes to the house were in good order. Guy had known they would be. He had repaired them all those years ago.

Once water was laid on, it was impossible for Guy to delay his visit any longer. He still had a sense of trepidation, though in La Spezia itself he found the memories less painful than expected: merely flashes of recollection of the days when he and Julia had made shopping expeditions – not the most emotionally charged of their moments together. Please God, it would be the same with the house itself. Perhaps he could put himself into a mood simply to berate its inconveniences and thus avoid any other issues.

'We've acquired a member of staff,' Jenkins announced on the day of Guy's move.

'An Italian?'

'I suppose so, though he's a little fair-skinned for an Eyetie. He claims to be the caretaker – I don't know the Italian word.'

'He speaks English?'

'So-so. Understands it well enough.'

'What's his name?'

'Signor Nessuno.'

Guy laughed. 'I think you've made a mistake.'

Jenkins shot him a sharp glance. 'We're not all Rudolph bloody Valentino speaking the Italiano – *sir*,' he added for effect. Guy let the insult go.

'By the by,' Jenkins continued, 'our Signor Nessuno, or whatever his name is, reacted when your name was mentioned.'

'I doubt it.'

''S God's honest truth, Guvnor,' Jenkins said waggishly. 'He shot up like he'd received an electric shock. What do you make of that?'

Guy racked his brain. Most of the names he had forgotten – they had been only minor actors in the drama. But 'Signor Nessuno' he would have remembered. Except that 'Mr Nobody' was clearly the result of mishearing by Jenkins. Could it be old Enzo? That seemed scarcely possible. He must be dead or in the last stage of decrepitude. In any case, Enzo could not be described as 'fair' by any stretch of imagination. He was dark and simian, one of those wrinkled, sparkle-eyed old fellows admired in Victorian genre painting but repulsive in the flesh: his skin stinking of onion and his breath musty with grappa. Ambrose had referred to him as 'the Troglodyte' and Julia, more tolerantly, called him 'a poppet'.

There had also been a boy, Gianni. Please God it wasn't Gianni!

The Villa Esperanza was not on the shore – an omission not mentioned by Signor Truffatore, the agent. There wasn't even a secluded cove from which to swim. Julia had been furious. 'You'll have to drive us somewhere,' she told Ambrose. 'I'm not going to use the public beaches with all the bloody bedints.'

'Bedint' was Julia's term for the lower orders, more specifically the middle classes. It should have been a code word to put Guy on his guard. But perhaps he was thinking anachronistically from the perspective of wartime democracy. Their language had been peppered with 'wops', 'niggers' and 'Jewboys', used casually and not intended to offend anybody. If one focused on these linguistic markers one would get the wrong impression – or partially so, at least. Of all their sins, surely this one could be forgiven? Though as Guy reminded himself, he wasn't a Jewboy, albeit he was certainly a 'bedint'.

From the small resort of Lerici a road ran high in the hills to a tip where the gulf and the mouth of the River Magra met. A few kilometres beyond La Serra an unmetalled carriageway wound its way up a hill between pines. Guy and Enzo had once hacked back the brushwood at the sides so that it would not scratch Ambrose's Bentley, but in the intervening years it had grown back and was now being broken and scarred by the passage of the truck. It was a secretive route, mostly in shadow and haunted by nightingales; and, because it had to be taken slowly, seemed to go on interminably. It was preposterous to think of ambulances taking the sharp bends and trying to avoid the rocks that slipped from the hillside. Corporal Long, however, relished swinging the jeep round the curves and spinning its wheels like a getaway car's. For a moment he reminded Guy of Jackie Ferris, though it was hard to fix on the point of resemblance. The Corporal was a small man, compact and strong. His hair was black and curly, his teeth white and wicked. His racial type, if it were any longer appropriate to think in those terms, was Welsh rather than Scottish. The Welsh, Guy had been told, were magical and perverse, and that seemed to sum up the Corporal well enough.

Guy had always felt the carriage drive was a trap for the senses, lulling them with dark monotony. When one emerged suddenly from the trees, the sunlight struck the eyes like a blow and the breeze that often scoured the hillside and filtered the colours through russet tints blew scents of thyme and rosemary. Here there rose, on one side, a terrace framed by cypresses and palms, and on the other the slope fell away sharply into neglected olives and oak saplings. It ended steeply in rocks. Only having driven the length of this scorching face did one take the final curve and, rising to the level of the terrace, see the house.

The arrangement was a deliberate and artful device. With no time for English notions of landscaped park, and in any case limited by the topography of the hill, the space before the building was laid out in formal parterres either side of the drive. The latter was tapered, narrower in front of the villa, creating a false perspective and an impression that the house was larger and more distant than in reality. The illusion was the more intense because at most hours of the day the façade was in sunlight and, to the blinded gaze, shimmered uncertainly against the sky.

Approaching the house that first time, in a Fiat taxi hired by Signor Truffatore, Guy, in a shock of delight, had marvelled at the villa's perfections, only to find them as superficial as the reflection of the sun on a still but muddy pond. In addition to the many inconveniences of the interior ('Kinda traditional, kinda old-world,' said Signor Truffatore in English), the fabric and garden had fallen into disrepair. The balustrading round the terrace was dangerous, the urns shattered, the statuary broken, the parterres overgrown with thorny scrub and sinewy weeds. The stucco, which at a distance maintained its original pink, on inspection proved stained with streaks of rusty brown. 'Like a Piccadilly urinal, dear boy!' exclaimed Ambrose, who was apt in most he said.

The heir to Signor Truffatore was Corporal Long, who was chatty in the secure knowledge of undiscovered crime. 'It's as posh as a public library,' he said, with incongruous accuracy. Nick and Jimmy were rolling a drum of petrol to where the generator was hidden. They paused and waved rather than saluted. Jenkins waved back. Guy, after a palsied hesitation over a salute, nodded curtly.

'Where is this fellow Nessuno?' he asked. 'I'd like to meet him.'

'Oh, one can't find him,' answered Jenkins. 'He simply turns up. He drinks – did I mention that? – but he's one of your quiet drunks. He has two or three nests about the place where he flops down when he's had too many. I've told him we can't be doing with that and he must drop down drunk in a regulation spot, Army-fashion. I think he got the message.' He paused. 'I can get rid of him if you like.'

'We'll see.'

'Righty-ho. Well, first things first. Time to see how our billet is shaping up.'

They made an inspection. Guy noted that, in its ruin, the villa had reached a stasis, as if further gradual decay were impossible and it must either be repaired or fall abruptly into total collapse. He noted, too, that it seemed to have become infected by the Army. The rooms, which had once held bad paintings and gimcrack furniture, were now an empty Army-space. The stink of unemptied earth closets had been replaced by carbolic. In the transformation, the interior had lost itself in the general military type and reminded Guy of a sodden hall in North Yorkshire from which a girls' school had been tipped in the second year of the war prior to its infestation by temporary officers including himself. In the Villa Esperanza a tea urn stood on a trestle table in the saloon.

The sun declined in the west over the sea. That limitless view, with no horizon beyond a vague milkiness, was the saving glory of the house. Surveying it, Margot had said, 'Fiddlesticks for the drains! Those at Windsor used to be worse. *They* killed the poor Prince Consort. And as for the furniture, you must go to the Royal Pavilion for true vulgarity.' She was the one who had adjusted most easily to the smell and decoration. 'I was brought up at Fletchitt. Nothing but stinks and flashy tat covered in Boulle work and ormolu. And all those bloody Romneys and Gainsboroughs smiling smugly, as if they owned the place.'

'But there's no *bath*, dearest,' observed Ambrose reproachfully.

'How bedint!'

The image of Margot flickered and died in the sunset.

'I'm getting this wrong,' thought Guy. 'There was more to our group than snobbery.' He suspected his memory of treachery and tried to call up a picture of Margot's bewitching beauty, but it was pockmarked with distillations of bitterness. Perhaps, in the end, the experiences of that summer had all been meretricious, rather like Ambrose's plays, which made one laugh at the time, but were really nothing but froth. Though it was probably too early to say. History sometimes passed odd judgments on the trivial. Fragonard and Watteau had survived. Oscar Wilde looked set to last.

Corporal Long rustled up chicken and vegetables instead of Army rations. They cooked them on a wood fire in the open, after some problem with the Soyer stove. Fortunately Nick and Jimmy had been Boy Scouts. 'I was a Girl Guide, masel',' said Corporal Long. The fire gave off sparks that flecked the night sky. Brushing smuts from his eyes, the Corporal complained, 'They bluidy nightingales is no romantic at all!' Yet often, of an evening, Guy and the others had stood on the terrace listening to them; the men in dinner jackets; the women sheathed in silk; cocktails and cigarettes in hand. Sardonically, Lewis had said, 'We must look like characters on a P&O poster.' The colour of the night had been flat and grainy with stars like a lithograph.

Nick went off to relieve himself and on his return announced, 'That old bugger Nessuno is lurking about.'

'I'll speak to him,' said Guy, getting to his feet.

'I'll come with you,' Jenkins volunteered.

'That won't be necessary.'

Guy went into the house, carrying a storm lantern. In the transient light the walls of the empty rooms seemed to rush away from him. Despite the efforts of Nick and Jimmy, his boots trod on dust. This and the pale frescoes on the walls gave the effect of a mummy's tomb. He wanted to call out, but his tongue stumbled over the name. He couldn't ask. 'Is Nobody there?' He wondered at the

21

absurd confusion. Instead he cried, 'I say! Hullo!' reminding himself of a character in a modern comedy who will wander in through the French window, take the applause of the audience with a knowing but scarcely perceptible pause, and begin the action.

The main door led into a hallway framed in faux marble columns. Either side were lesser rooms of whose original functions Guy was unclear. Above this floor was the *piano nobile*. It contained the large state room painted with baroque frescoes that Guy had learnt to call 'the saloon' and a similar room only slightly smaller. These separated four suites, two each side and extending into short wings. Each suite comprised a bedroom with a withdrawing room and private closet. On Guy's first visit, the saloon had been occupied by a yellow mongrel bitch and her pups, a poor creature which alternately growled and abased herself. Guy remembered her claws tapping across the floor as she slunk to cower under the various items of furniture. One could make a symbol out of such an image, but at the time Guy had been distracted by Signor Truffatore, who was waving his arms expansively and declaiming, 'What a place, huh? Like Giulio Cesare used to live here or sumpin'!'

For no reason Guy inclined to the left. He tried to remember who had occupied the rooms on this side. The memory would come, but not for now. He opened the door and by lantern light saw a figure squatting in the corner, picking at its toes.

'Signor Nessuno?' Guy ventured.

'Si?'

'Captain Parrot. May we speak?' Guy placed the lantern on the floor where they could share the light.

The other man blinked and looked up. 'Hullo, Polly,' he said mildly. 'I thought it was you.'

'Call me, "Nessuno". It's a *nom de guerre* – literally so in my case. Do sit down. You look shaken, old chap.'

Guy did not answer but squatted on the floor. He surmised that this must be one of the other man's 'nests'. He saw bedding, empty wine bottles and other indefinite shapes.

'It must be a shock for you,' said Nessuno. 'It was a shock for me, too, let me tell you. Of course, one knows that these coincidences happen. Do you think they mean anything? I rather fancy they don't. Can I offer you wine? These days I drink – excessively, I'm afraid. I imagine your young boys – Nick and Jimmy, I think they're called? – have told you that. And you also have that Scots fellow. He seems jolly useful. Your Lieutenant Jenkins isn't quite *comme il faut*, is he? Strictly *temporary* officer material.'

Guy decided that Nessuno was drunk. He sensed the doomed struggle to appear normal. He tried not to be uncharitable. The situation was abnormal enough to disconcert anyone. In particular, the familiar voice had issued from the mouth of a stranger. There was something tearful in it and something bright too.

'Cat got your tongue?' enquired his host, adding thoughtfully, 'Odd expression that. Cat's don't eat tongues, do they? I had a cat – Sennacherib he was called – and he liked fish. That's odd, too, because he couldn't stand water.'

Guy saw that Nessuno had lost his hair and that explained much. The remaining features were largely the same, ravaged by the years but not coarsened. Lately, in the shaving mirror, Guy had noticed his earlobes dangling like dewlaps. Nessuno's skin, in contrast, was thin, taut and wrinkled. The effect was peculiarly horrible since the youthful face was still visible behind the mask.

'Have you got time for a chinwag? I hope I'm not keeping you from dinner. It smells delicious, but these days I've not much appetite. I must say, Nick and Jimmy are very decent in offering food. Perfect poppets, as Julia used to say.'

'I heard your broadcasts on the wireless,' Guy said. He

did not mention that he had not merely heard them but enjoyed them. Unlike those of Lord Haw-Haw, they were devoid of any note of triumph. Instead, in their evocation of England, they had reminded Guy of the country columns in the better newspapers: insidious in their rain-soft imagery. Until Rome fell, they had been broadcast daily over the Fascist radio.

Crestfallen, Nessuno said, 'It was dreadfully hard work, keeping up the standard. I had to read pastoral novels and lyric verse – awfully hard to come by when one is at war. It largely put an end to my own work. Hanging me will be superfluous punishment in the circumstances. I suppose they will hang me, won't they?'

'Probably,' Guy admitted. 'Unless you can claim insanity.'

'Oh, I'm not insane, merely silly,' answered Nessuno with a flash of cheerfulness.

They sat in silence for a moment at the thought of death. A moth came in and pestered the lantern. At last Nessuno asked, 'Will you turn me in?'

'I imagine I'll have to.' Guy thought an explanation was needed. 'It isn't personal.'

'Of course not, Poll!' was the stout reply.

'I don't hate you. I did, but I don't now. Have you thought of running away?'

'Too ill. Too drunk. Nowhere to run to. Don't mistake me, old chap. I'm not waiting here with the intention of expiating my sins. Naturally I'm as repentant as you like. But I think that expiation is something only fellows in novels go in for. I have an idea that the rest of us mortals can cope with a lifetime of regret.'

'Why did you become a traitor?' Guy asked suddenly.

'Wine?' Nessuno tendered the bottle. Slowly he wiped the top with furtive experience. 'Quite a decent Barolo,' he commented. 'It's something to be thankful for that one can still get good wine in Italy. Why did I become a traitor? Good question, that. Partly, of course, it was chance – I happened to find myself here. And, then, I never thought of myself as a traitor.'

'But Fascism?'

'Oh *that*! Ridiculous, of course, but no more so than the alternatives. A bad idea in retrospect, I admit. But heroism, community and prosperity – which is what it amounted to in the beginning – are not ignoble ideals. Deciding on these things without the benefit of hindsight is rather like betting on a horse. Similar, in a way, to making one's mind up whether Churchill was right when he put us back on the gold standard. From the aftermath, it seems he was a bloody fool about that one.'

Guy decided that he was not up to the subtleties of guilt. He was content to rely on his moral instincts rather than argument, and trust to forgivingness as a defence against error in blaming others.

Nessuno seemed to have forgotten his treason and was staring dreamily at the moth. 'How's Elizabeth?' he asked.

'Well.'

'Children?'

'We have two. Boys.'

'Really? At your age and with a family, I'm surprised you were called up.'

'I volunteered. There was a need for doctors.'

'How brave!'

Others had said the same, but Guy had looked for the worm of cowardice in the apple of his courage. Yet such was his foresight in evasion that his problems had still been over the horizon when he fled. He suspected complexities in his marriage and the prospect of unreconciled middle age. The Army, like any institution offering a settled routine, was a good place for cowards of the moral if not the physical sort.

Nessuno asked, 'I often wondered what happened to Margot?'

'Surely you read about her in the papers? She married Sir Odo Milne.'

'Of course.' A sigh. 'Forgive my poor memory for detail. I couldn't recall if it was Margot or one of her sisters. They were all beautiful and barmy.'

'Margot and Odo were both interned when war broke out.'

'Yes?'

'She was released last year, just in time to be killed by a doodlebug.'

A flicker of confusion. 'Sorry, Poll, I didn't catch that?'

Guy was surprised, then reflected that the familiar word 'doodlebug' had had barely twelve months of life and could scarcely have reached Italy.

'It's a German weapon. A sort of bomb thing. A' – he made a gesture of wings – 'sort of flying thing. No pilot,' he added for clarity.

'Gosh! How clever of the Germans! Is it true that London's been flattened?'

'Knocked about a bit, but still standing.'

'I'm glad of that. They tell such awful lies here. And Uncle Sammy's? Still there?'

'Yes, but it's changed. It's a club for Latvian officers, or possibly Lithuanians.'

'And that nigger trumpeter, Sammy? Tell me, did he actually own the club?'

'No. The owner was Sammy Solomons, if you remember. I suspect all Negro musicians are called Sammy or Louie. The Sammy you're talking about was killed in the Blitz or joined the American Army – I've heard both stories.'

'Good.' Nessuno shook his head thoughtfully. 'I've often thought of Uncle Sammy's. In a sense, everything began there.'

Guy nodded. Nessuno was right: though, as to beginnings, the classical philosophers used the term 'final cause' to describe not the origins but the outcome of events. There was something to be said for this reversal; for only by the results could one select from an infinity of beginnings. At the time – when all effects were in a fluid and unknowable future – the visit he and Lewis had paid to Uncle Sammy's was an event without significance. Lewis had once said that the trend of contemporary fiction was towards stories without beginnings or ends, but it seemed to Guy that, whatever the objective accuracy of that insight might be, it lacked psychological truth and ignored the desire to understand the pattern of things.

Whether in this room, on this night, talking with the frail Signor Nessuno, or, at another time, with a visit to Uncle Sammy's in Lewis' company, the story *did* begin.

CHAPTER THREE

1930

Fifteen years before his encounter with Signor Nessuno – at a date when war with Hitler was still a distant fear – a younger and more hopeful Guy Parrot ran into his friend Lewis Lockyer. Guy had just qualified at Bart's, and was minded to celebrate, so they agreed to dine and take in a play. They chose the season's sensation, *Imperfect Tense*, a comedy at the Adelphi.

Lewis was Guy's contemporary but had abandoned his studies after a year to do something in publishing. He claimed to 'dabble' in poetry; but whether writing or publishing Guy did not know. 'There's a fair amount of dabbling in both,' Lewis explained.

Lewis's father, Bertram Lockyer, had collected a peerage from Lloyd George. He was a substantial shoe manufacturer with a chain of high-street shops, and owned a house in Northamptonshire, Cloud's Hill, alias Boot Hill, newly built by Lutyens. Guy had stayed there in the vacations and remembered a collection of unfashionable Pre-Raphaelite paintings bought on the cheap and a photograph of Lord Lockyer clasping the hand of the Prime Minister as if slipping him a bribe.

For all that, Lewis seemed to have reverted to some ancestral aristocratic strain. Or perhaps, as Guy sometimes wondered, each age forced its type upon its young men. Lewis had long-headed good looks. He was the image of those idealised youths who had gone to their deaths in the Great War, a fate which he and Guy had missed.

In contrast, Guy was of middling height, with middling brown hair and moustache, better-looking than he was prepared to admit, and the ensemble relieved with youthful enthusiasm. He thought of himself as demotic, rather in the way of one of A. J. Cronin's able and earnest young doctors. Also, in a way, a creature of his time.

He came from Manchester. His father was that anomaly, a moral stockbroker who observed a quiet Catholic piety. Guy's grandfather had found the True Faith in an obscure quarrel about clerical vestments and genuflexion before the altar. Beyond that the memory of man did not run, though the family name, Parrot, was vaguely supposed to be French.

After the performance Lewis said, 'My firm are publishing the piece, but can you imagine it playing in a provincial rep? I can just see some superannuated thespian with false teeth and a wig acting the part of Victor!'

Guy agreed that the play seemed designed for metropolitan tastes. Although he had enjoyed it, the urbane and witty treatment of the theme of divorce had caused a frisson of Catholic guilt.

'Shall we push on while the night is yet young?' Lewis suggested. 'I know a place, not entirely respectable but absolutely fashionable. It has another name, but everyone calls it "Uncle Sammy's". The proprietor holds Continental views about drinking hours and it's considered quite smart to be arrested there.'

'I'm game.' Guy was feeling a touch of afflatus from his recent success but conscious that his allowance was almost gone. 'We shan't need a taxi, shall we? It's just that I'm a little short of tin.'

'This is my invitation.' Lewis squinted unfamiliarly at a familiar street. 'Sammy's is in Long Acre or Seven Dials, there or thereabouts. Well, not exactly *in*, if you understand me. More *off*.'

It resembled an alley except for a discreetly lit door and a pair of prostitutes patrolling an otherwise unlikely byway.

'I'm sorry, squire, this is a members' club,' said the doorman.

'Give the fellow half a crown,' Lewis invited.

'I thought you were paying.'

'Of course. But I only have a fiver.'

'Make it a dollar,' said the doorman. In Lewis's offer he recognised a gentleman. He glared at Guy reproachfully. 'I'll sign you in as my guests.'

Guy fished out two half-crowns and handed them over.

Narrow stairs led to a dark upper room. It was half empty and did not seem very lively. A pianist and a double-bass-player were pulling notes slowly from their instruments as though from a bag. The trumpeter had no head.

'The trumpeter has no head,' said Guy.

Lewis was sitting with his back to the stage so that he could watch anyone arriving by the door. 'How unconventional,' he said.

'Isn't it?'

The trumpeter put his instrument to where his head wasn't and began to play. He had no hands, either.

'Curiouser and curiouser,' thought Guy.

Two girls in spangled dresses came over and sat down.

'Hullo,' said Guy. 'Who are you?'

'I'm Dolores de los Angeles,' said the first, a blonde.

'And I'm Elizaveta Romanoff,' said the second, a brunette.

'The trumpeter has no head,' Guy told them.

'That's Sammy,' said the blonde.

Lewis turned his eyes from the door and smiled. 'Well, Doris and Lizzy, what can we do for you?'

'Charmed I'm sure,' answered Doris. 'I and my friend always drink champagne.'

Lewis ordered a bottle and said, 'There. Now you must promise to be good and not speak unless spoken to.'

'We can dance, if you like.'

Guy remarked, 'I'm not sure I can dance to a trumpeter with no head.' He wondered if he were witty or merely drunk.

'I've told you, that's Sammy,' said Doris impatiently.

The waiter insisted on payment on the spot.

Lewis demurred. 'I still have this problem with the fiver. Be a good chap, Guy.'

'I'm sure they have change. It's a bit thick. I have to keep an eye on my train fare to Manchester.'

But Guy paid none the less.

Lizzy asked the headless trumpeter to play a tune. 'Sammy always plays for me. He calls me his doll. I think that's ever so nice.'

She and Doris began to dance together.

Guy found his eyes had adjusted to the darkness. The trumpeter acquired the head of a handsome African, black to the point of purple. After obliging Lizzy, he suited himself with a plaintive melody.

Guy yawned. 'This is awfully dull.'

'Clubs *are* awfully dull. That's nine parts of their charm.'

'Who are those two dreadful looking tarts over there?'

Lewis eyed them sleepily. 'You didn't call them tarts earlier. The one on the left is Annabelle Croft and the other is Cicily Laforge. They were both in the play.'

Guy was surprised. They looked much older and coarser than he remembered. He wasn't accustomed to women who wore heavy make-up. His fiancée, Elizabeth, used only lip rouge.

Momentarily uplifted by a glass of champagne which he suspected was cider, Guy became annoyed that *his* girls, as he thought of them, were dancing with each other. He forgot he had declined to dance. It was irritating that the trumpeter had got himself a head.

'The chap sitting with Annabelle and Cicily is Commander Jackie Ferris,' said Lewis.

'Oh?'

'He's an American, but he spends his time over here. I don't know if his rank is one of ours or theirs.'

'What does he do?'

'He used to be a bootlegger, running stuff over from Canada in small boats. But the Italians have made a business of it and it's ceased to be fun.'

'And now?'

'He says he's making an attempt on the water speed record. Talks of a boat on Coniston Water.'

'Shouldn't he be there, then?'

'Of course not. Record-breaking is mostly about raising money. Only as a last resort does one take a shot at the damn thing. One can always blame the weather or mechanical failure. In the meantime, it's a wonderful way of cadging.'

Guy examined Commander Ferris and saw a clean-shaven man with light-brown hair. He did not resemble Guy's idea of either an American or a sailor, being too outwardly suave for both. The two women seemed fascinated by him.

Guy fancied that he and Lewis had drifted off to sleep, for another bottle of champagne had appeared. The waiter was calmly rifling his pockets for payment.

More people drifted into the club. A piano was playing a sparkling little ditty and someone was singing in a breathlessly affected voice.

If you want to play the part of a duchess or a tart,
You will find that, at the heart, they're much the same.
Though the duchess finds it funny what the tart will do for money,
Yet the lady plays her own financial game.

For the benefits of rank are like money in the bank,
And we all would like to swank around in ermine.
But while ducal gifts are fine – real pearls from real swine –

Fur looks best when it adorns the backs of vermin.

Guy recognised a song called 'Mrs Earnshaw's Daughter'. It was from a revue, *Lighting up Piccadilly*, by Ambrose Carmody.

The singer rose from the piano to take a bow. He blew a kiss lightly to the audience, then, flicking the tails of his evening dress behind him, skipped down from the stage with dancer's steps and patent-leather shoes, to join Commander Ferris and the two actresses.

'Ambrose can't turn down a chance to "ham",' said Lewis, unfolding his head from dozing on his hands.

'Do you know him?' asked Guy.

'Rather well, as it happens. We were at school together, though he was a senior when I was merely a little tick. Also, as I mentioned, we publish him. Hullo, Ambrose. Excuse me, Guy, while I say hello.'

Bored, Guy sipped his drink. He glanced occasionally and guiltily at the other table, where Lewis was well received and chatting sociably. Guy did not know Ambrose Carmody but had seen photographs of him in the newspapers. They were standard publicity shots, of which the most common showed the writer in a dinner jacket with a hand stuffed jauntily in one pocket, nautical fashion, while the other played with a cigarette in an ebony holder. In all the pictures, Carmody had half-closed eyes and a superior smile.

A minor ruckus at the door made Guy turn. Three men had entered. Two were young and thuggish-looking and seemed uncomfortable in their clothes. The third was in his middle thirties, handsome, assured, black-haired, with a black moustache trimmed narrowly like a matinée idol's. The group took a table and began to give orders noisily.

Lewis returned. 'Sorry, old man. Come and join us. Oh, God,' he groaned, seeing the newcomers, 'not Odo Milne! This could get complicated.'

'Why?'

'It's to do with who is sleeping with whom. I'll explain some time.'

'Who is Odo Milne?'

'Somebody in the Government. I think his title is Lord Remembrancer to the County Palatine of Chester, but what it amounts to is he's one of the Whips. He bleats on about New Politics and writes poetry on themes from Nietzsche. Now do come and join us.'

Guy moved tables. Lewis made the introductions.

One of the women said, 'Parrot? I don't know any Parrots. What do they call you? Polly? Pretty Polly?'

'Annabelle, dear girl, if you are to remain popular and charming, you must learn to tease without cruelty,' intervened Carmody astutely. 'I imagine that Guy has been the butt of that particular joke no end of times.' He smiled and raised an eyebrow, at once tired and amused. His voice was very clipped, airy and wistful as though each sentence were a *bon mot* of such lightness that it would dissolve if examined. Although five or six years Guy's senior, he seemed very young for the success he had achieved, and his blue eyes sometimes looked as if he were dazzled by his own glamour. Guy was struck by his impeccable grooming and the smallness and deftness of his movements, which scarcely made his clothes stir. 'You must call me Ambrose,' said Ambrose. 'Everyone does.'

One of the thugs Guy had noticed earlier, a stocky type with wiry red hair, approached the table. Before he could speak, Ambrose asked his name.

'Harry,' said the thug, disconcerted.

'Join us for a drink, Harry.'

'No, thank you, Mr Carmody. Sir Odo wouldn't like it.'

'Very well, but you do promise not to cause a scene, don't you?'

Harry evidently had a scene in mind but was discomposed by his reception. He confined himself to 'The Guvnor wants a word with you.'

'An invitation? How delightful, dear boy. To your

cottage in the country – or possibly another cottage?'

The quip was enough to despatch Harry to the consolation of his fellow thug.

Sir Odo Milne came over. 'I'm looking for Julia,' he said sharply.

'Have you a particular Julia in mind?' asked Ambrose. 'These days every Minnie and Alice is a Julia. The name is quite devalued.'

'You know very well which Julia.'

Guy looked beyond Milne to where Harry was still trying to decide if he had been insulted. The drink had done something to his eyes and the trumpeter had become headless again.

'She's with Carradine in Tangier.'

'Nonsense!' snapped Milne. 'Carradine doesn't care for his wife – or any other woman, come to that.'

'He says that Julia is the only woman for him: which she is in a manner of speaking.'

'I'll kill any man who touches her!' Milne retorted.

Guy found it mildly odd that husbands were to be killed for sleeping with their wives. But he suspected he had fallen among those to whom it was not odd at all.

Thereafter he remembered nothing. In the way of drink, the last few hours passed as quickly as the first few minutes. It was two o'clock and he was at a tea stall in the vicinity of Shepherd Market. Doris and Lizzy were with him, proposing that he should stay with either or both of them, or that, if he liked, they would make love while he watched. Natural prudence ushered him home.

His last thought before sleep was to wonder who Julia Carradine was, that men might murder for her.

Guy's landlady had no expectations of men. Therefore she oppressed them when they were sober and was tolerant when they were drunk.

She appeared at his door, behind which he was nursing a hangover, and announced sniffily that someone was on the telephone 'and don't be long about it'.

'Hullo?' said Guy gingerly.

'Hullo,' answered Lewis. 'Alive and well, I see.'

'Alive, at any rate.' Guy hesitated, then mentioned the subject that had troubled the lucid moments of his dreams. 'Look, did I behave like a fool last night?'

'No. Not generally.'

'Not generally?'

'Well, you were a little elevated at the end and had to be stopped from tearing the head off the trumpeter. You seemed determine to prove he hadn't got one.'

They agreed to meet in a pub near Bedford Square, a smoke-filled hole frequented by noisy publishers and the occasional fruit porter.

'Let me get you a Bloody Mary,' offered Lewis.

'What's that?'

'It's an American thing, just the ticket if one is under the weather.' Lewis came back from the bar bearing a glass. 'Strictly, it should be vodka rather than gin, and tomato juice not lemonade. Sorry I had to ask you to pay for my treat, but it can be awfully difficult changing a fiver in these places.'

Seated, Lewis asked, 'Do you remember much about last night?'

'A little. Who is Julia Carradine?'

'She's the wife of Hector Carradine, our man in Tangier.'

'Oh, he's a diplomat? I thought…'

'What?'

'Nothing. And Ambrose? I was a bit put off by his manner. Is he an invert?'

'A pansy? Ambrose? Could be, I suppose. He's witty and attractive to women, so it's possible.'

'I hope I wasn't too much of an idiot.'

'Not too much. Everyone was enchanted by your tales of Manchester life.'

'Oh God!'

'Seriously. Sammy's can be dreadfully boring and you provided entertainment.'

'I thought Sammy's was supposed to be chic?'

'It is.'

The glass of gin and lemonade did something to clear Guy's head. He spoke of his forthcoming journey to Manchester to see Elizabeth and confirm arrangements for their marriage and his entering into partnership with her father.

'I see,' said Lewis and surprised Guy by adding, 'Then you weren't serious about coming to Italy with us?'

'Italy? With whom?'

'Initially with Ambrose and me. Though the intention is to keep open house for the summer. I suspected you were talking without much thinking what you were saying. Ambrose wants to retire there for the summer to work on a new play. He's taken a villa near La Spezia – I don't know much about La Spezia except that Shelley died there – and you volunteered to join us.'

'I did?'

'Are you *sure* you don't remember? Ambrose was taken with the idea of having you along. He caught a whiff of gas at the tail end of the war, since when he's been a bit of a hypochondriac. It would flatter his vanity to have his personal physician.'

'I know nothing about mustard gas – I assume it was mustard gas? In any case, I'm marrying Elizabeth.'

'I thought as much,' said Lewis. 'Another drink? Do you think the barman would hit me if I offered him a fiver?'

'I'll pay,' said Guy reluctantly.

Short of money, Guy travelled to Manchester third-class. Elizabeth met him at London Road station. They took a tram to Didsbury, where her father practised from a large Victorian villa. It was built of granite surrounded by laurels and seemed suited to the habitation of a poisoner.

Elizabeth was pretty and lively. Guy thought he loved her. Indeed, when he was with her he knew he did. Apart, he had doubts. They did not concern Elizabeth's worth. Of that he was convinced. Nor did he think he would make a bad fist of being a faithful husband.

His problem was that fidelity was in his nature. It was beyond religious scruple. His sympathy and kindness inclined him to examine the other person's viewpoint and, allowing for a few human lapses, he adjusted his conduct accordingly. It was precisely this – that fidelity and straightforwardness came to him easily – which made him wonder if it were not a virtue but a lapse from the duty of conquering life's moral complexity. Knowing little of her, he wondered about Julia Carradine, who had left her diplomat husband and was pursued by a young politician on the make.

Guy respected Elizabeth's father, a worthy general practitioner, but had been intrigued to learn that Ambrose Carmody's uncle was Sir George Carmody of Harley Street. Sir George was a fashionable physician whose female clientèle had a low birth rate not easily explained by statistics. According to Lewis, Ambrose had offered to effect an introduction. Sir George was looking for a young assistant.

Guy put his thoughts aside. He and Elizabeth kissed chastely, but with enthusiasm.

'How are you, darling?' he asked.

'I'm fine.'

'And your father? Anything I should be warned of?'

'Vegetarianism – macrobiotic diet, specifically.'

'He's become vegetarian?'

'No, not exactly. He's experimenting on himself.'

'Any effects?'

'He farts a great deal.'

Unabashed, Elizabeth laughed. She bounded on to the tramcar, her brown hair bouncing in a counter-rhythm. She wore a pea-green coat over a lighter green summer dress.

Guy tried to imagine her in the long silk sheath that the actress Annabelle Croft had worn at Sammy's – the style he imagined the mysterious Julia Carradine might wear – and failed.

Elizabeth's mother had died in the great influenza epidemic. The house was managed during Elizabeth's absences at Cambridge by an elderly woman whose notions were those of a manse as it might have been thirty years before.

They caught Dr Price on his way upstairs clutching a book.

In a deep Welsh voice, he growled, 'Hullo Elizabeth, Guy. Can't stop. Talk to you later, Guy. By the way, how's your syphilis?'

Guy opened his mouth for an answer, found none and let the moment pass.

Elizabeth said, 'I've bought a gramophone. Do you want to try it out before dinner?'

She opened a door into the drawing room. Among the Edwardian oak furniture and chairs upholstered in cut moquette was a gramophone on a table. Elizabeth wound it and put on a record.

'Let's dance, darling. Show me how London has improved you.'

'I can foxtrot and waltz.'

The music was a foxtrot and they took a turn about the room. Elizabeth spoke of her expectations of a good degree.

'I'm happy for you,' said Guy. 'But it won't make much difference to us, will it? You'll have to give up work when we marry.'

Annoyed, Elizabeth said, 'That's a very old-fashioned attitude.'

'It isn't a question of my attitude. Whatever job you get, they'll make you give it up on marriage.' Guy spoiled the effect by adding, 'In any case, doctors' wives don't work.'

'More's the pity.'

'It can't be helped.'

'It could during the war.'

'This isn't wartime.'

'No it isn't,' mused Elizabeth, and she muttered, 'Damn it!'

Guy felt helpless before this small display of temper. He wondered what it portended. One knew so little about one's partner when one got married. In his case it was made more difficult by the fact that his marriage and career were so bound up together. It was not a consideration that had troubled him before, but now it did. There were other women and other careers in the world. Most likely they, too, would disappoint, but to make an irrevocable choice at this stage was frightening.

A pea-and-ham soup was served at dinner. Guy fiddled with his plate. Dr Price passed in favour of a glass of carrot juice. He was a small, bearded, perky man who wore a tweed suit in preference to black professional garb.

'Syphilis!' he announced with a glance of distaste at his empty glass. 'What's your experience?'

Guy grunted noncommittally. He wondered if Elizabeth's father entertained odd notions about the current morals of medical students.

Doctor Price glared at his prospective son-in-law. 'I come across it often, chiefly among the male casuals, though sometimes the effects, especially on the liver, are masked by drink.'

'How interesting,' murmured Guy.

'Yes! I'm glad you're interested. You'll come across plenty of pox.' Dr Price paused to rinse his mouth with water, coughed and went on, 'The Salvation Army is rotten with it.'

The housekeeper, full of gloom and reproach, creaked over to the table and removed Guy's unfinished bowl of soup. She brought plates of generic meat in brown gravy and a tureen of vegetables swimming in water. Before the

Doctor she placed what appeared to be a mixture of porridge and birdseed.

Guy decided that the Doctor's last remark referred to the condition of the tramps who frequented the Salvation Army's hostel.

'How are your bowels?' asked Dr Price, staring stoically at his plate.

'Father!' interrupted Elizabeth, stifling a laugh.

'Just asking.'

'They're fine, thank you, sir,' said Guy.

'And the stools? Well formed? Pointed at both ends? Good colour? Is there any blood in them?'

'Yes – I mean no, so far as concerns the blood.'

Elizabeth's father whispered, as if casting a druidic spell, 'Do they *float*?'

Off-hand Guy could not remember if they should. He compromised. 'They sort of bob up and down, like a submarine.'

'Why are you laughing, Elizabeth?' asked the Doctor.

'I can't imagine, father.'

The following morning Dr Price took Guy to a hostel in Ancoats where tramps and derelicts obtained occasional shelter. He chatted about his modest but spiritually rewarding practice. He was on the panel of several collieries, cotton mills and friendly societies, and received a capitation fee for dispensing bottles of innocuous brown mixture. He sustained his interest by attempting epidemiological studies of the illnesses afflicting vagrants.

'Hence my interest in syphilis. Treatment has been transformed by the use of arsenobenzol compounds instead of the old mercury. However, I've come across the odd case of *Encephalitis haemorrhagica* and destruction of the liver parenchyma, which may be an effect of dosage. What do you think?'

Guy agreed hesitantly that this might be the case.

The tramps wore dress of extravagant poverty, had

highly coloured faces and wild ways of gesturing. They were beyond Guy's previous experience and he tried to see them as characters in a music hall or pantomime. As the drunks cavorted and made obeisance to the genial Doctor, Guy realised that he was being shown his patrimony. The kingdoms of this world were on offer to him, and they were horrible.

'You seem very subdued, darling,' said Elizabeth later, as they sat together in the drawing room listening to the wireless.

'I'm not certain I'm cut out for medicine,' Guy told her.

She did not chide him for these belated doubts. She said. 'It is sordid, isn't it? But that's where the heroism lies: in its sordidness. My father is a hero.'

Guy reflected that there was another sort of medicine, an unheroic one, practised from the comfort of Harley Street. He wondered what it was like.

Offering Guy a whisky after dinner, Dr Price said with his usual gusto, 'I've been thinking, my boy.'

'Oh?'

'You need a hobby.'

'I have one,' Guy confessed. 'I collect stamps.'

The Doctor pooh-poohed the idea. 'I mean a medical interest! I've cornered the market in pox and clap, but those fine fellows at the mission offer a treasure house of human morbidity.'

'I see. What do you recommend?'

'Skin disease.' He elaborated slowly, as if from a menu of delicacies: 'Psoriasis, scabies, eczema. The last-named divided according to the causative agency, such as contact with aniline dyes, bichromates, bleaching agents or trinitrotoluene; or parasites such as ringworm; or seborrhoeic eczema; or inherent weakness of the derma such as xerodermatous or ichthyotic skin.'

Guy remembered the florid, scabrous complexions of the tramps, their furtive shufflings and scratchings.

'Not to mention our old favourite, athletes' foot! The scourge of the general practitioner's waiting room, but, in my experience, a source of interest and comfort to the lonely when present in moderation. I attribute the rise of Socialism to the increase in clean socks. It diverts the working man from the innocent examination of his feet to the study of books.'

'Is your father trying to put us off marrying?' asked Guy when he and Elizabeth were next alone.

Elizabeth grinned. 'He's just testing you, the mischievous old devil.'

Guy remembered the look of tenderness which Dr Price bestowed on the human flotsam of the casual ward, the manly pat on the shoulder of the despairing former soldiers, the conventional yet sincere words of encouragement to the drunkards struggling with their affliction. 'He's very committed to his patients, isn't he?'

'Yes he is. And you will be, too,' said Elizabeth. 'I know it.'

Her fiancé nodded. He thought of the Saint of Shoreditch, who had found his faith only when tied to the stake. Once his own future was bound to that of the scrofulous poor, Guy did not doubt, that, like his spiritual forebear, he would face his task with dedication and commitment, accepting those moral gifts as life's consolation prizes. But the Martyr had not volunteered for his translation from the realm of sinners. Like a rational man, he had wanted to continue fornicating and cheating his neighbours.

'Are we too young?' Guy asked.

'I expect so,' said Elizabeth. 'One can never be prepared to meet true challenges. Marriage is always an act of faith.'

'We may fail.'

'I imagine we may.'

'And, even worse, we may never realise we have failed.

Life could become tepid and mediocre and we may suppose that that was how it was supposed to be.'

'I think that that sort of failure is preferable to the selfishness of many kinds of success.'

Elizabeth took his hand. For a moment Guy recognised in her the courage to write off conventional success even now at the outset. Then he wondered if she merely lacked imagination. He knew little of her: indeed, there was little to know since so much existed for the present simply as unrealised potential; and those fine qualities which he glimpsed as aspirations might turn to failed actualities. There were many doors into the future and he wondered whether, rather than entering by a single one in an act of faith, it was not wiser and more heroic to batter at all of them, even at the risk that some would lead to misery.

At home that night, while his father sat downstairs reading the financial press, Guy wrote two letters. The first was to Elizabeth, deferring their plans for marriage and releasing her from this engagement if she so desired. The second was to Lewis, reminding him of their last conversation and informing him that, if the offer still stood, Guy would join Lewis and Ambrose Carmody on their journey to La Spezia.

CHAPTER FOUR

1930

It was arranged that Guy should travel first and open the house at La Spezia while the others came down in two motor cars bringing the bulk of the luggage. In the interval before the journey, he met Ambrose only once, at his apartment in Albany in the company of Lewis. The occasion was friendly but concentrated on practical matters so that Guy felt rather as if he were a hired servant, listening while they spoke of people whom he had never met or knew only vaguely.

'Jackie Ferris talks of dropping in on us,' Ambrose said. 'He wants to brush up his sailing in the Med. Says it will help him. Julia has put him in funds, foolish girl.'

'I don't see the connection with the speed record.'

'No, neither do I. But Jackie has other interests.'

'How is Julia?'

'She has a notion to divorce her husband for sodomy, whatever that is. When I explained, she thought it interesting and would like to try it. I'm not certain that she understands entirely, but she may have been being witty. Everyone has become witty since the war.'

'Is Odo still pursuing her?'

'Yes. He has his henchmen posted outside the door day and night. Since he began flirting with Fascism, his love affairs have been conducted like the prelude to a Jacobean revenge tragedy.'

At the frontier Guy expected to be entering the heart of darkness. but the *Guardie di Finanza* and Fascist officials who boarded the train seemed charmed at the notion that tourists were still visiting their country. 'Issa cows by da depression,' explained a despondent traveller in silks. 'Nowbody buy, nowbody sell. Issa terrible!' He exposed his case of samples and Guy studied them good-naturedly as the train rolled along the Ligurian coast towards Genoa. Betweentimes he looked at the sea and, to capture the image, pulled passages of Homer from his memory, though, strictly, these applied to the Aegean. On the landward side was a vista of aleppo pines and mountains clad in oak and chestnut, for which he could recall nothing from Homer, so that they seemed evanescent.

It was curious to be in a strange country in the company of strangers. Of course he knew Lewis, though, on consideration, only slightly. Twelve months as students together and occasional encounters in pubs were not a foundation for anything significant. Especially when one took into account the natural reticence of men concerning anything that touched their inner lives. Ambrose Carmody he was acquainted with from two brief occasions. As to the others who might drop in during the course of the summer, he did not know them at all.

Ambrose's apartment in Albany was very modern, very smart. The furnishings were an artful combination of steel, Bakelite and the finest burr woods, with motifs of sunbursts, clean-limbed figures, and Mezzo-American artefacts. It was an effective piece of self-invention.

Indeed, Ambrose himself seemed an invention, an assembly of mannerisms and affectations in place of a true character. Two points in his appearance fixed this impression in Guy's mind, where it lay not especially pleasantly. The first was the other man's hair, which was exquisitely cut and oiled to a rich honey colour. The second was his cologne, a Hungary water redolent of lemon and rosemary. Guy disapproved of male cologne.

On the other hand, Ambrose's conversation was engaging, affable, witty and malicious. It struck Guy that urbanity was merely a veneer covering vulgarity. Only the middle sort of people – like himself – eschewed coarseness in their speech. Ambrose made Guy feel that the loss was his. This was not an affront but rather a cause for fascination.

Commander Jackie Ferris, Sir Odo Milne, Julia Carradine: Guy picked up their names like a doorman collecting hats as a gay crowd enters a restaurant. At first he thought the intention was to exclude him. Then he realised, with a shock of pleasure, that he was in fact the object of a delicate compliment. For behind Ambrose's casual introduction of his acquaintanceship was the assumption that Guy knew them already. Or, if not that, that Guy would naturally fit into their company and they would like him. They were not strangers, but friends in waiting.

'Issa my card,' said the traveller in silks, pressing a pasteboard into Guy's hand and packing his sample case to leave the train at Genoa.

'It's been pleasant to talk to you.'

'*Si!* Whole worl' one another got to be friens!'

Guy agreed. Friendship did not seem too difficult.

La Spezia was a port. Even before arriving, Guy had glimpsed a sleek liner making its way westward towards the Atlantic and several vessels of the Italian Navy at anchor on the calm bright sea. Now that he was there, he was disappointed. The place was like Portsmouth, a civilian and naval harbour backed by arsenals, depots, marshalling yards and dreary commercial buildings relieved only by sunlight.

Here the officials were more insistent as to Guy's identity and motives, presumably because of the presence of the fleet. Did he have a camera? Yes, as a matter of fact he did, a Kodak. Was he a spy? No, on reflection he didn't think so. *Scusi?* His interrogators were not used to the subtle evasiveness of English speech.

'No, I'm definitely not a spy,' said Guy.

The official was satisfied and ticked off the not-a-spy

entry on his sheet of questions. Guy supposed that had he indeed been a spy he would be additionally guilty of causing a form to be completed incorrectly.

On a shaky international telephone line, Guy had spoken to the agent chosen by Ambrose to arrange the villa and see to its appointments. The number was that of a rowdy bar and the agent seemed to be an exotic American, though his name was Italian. At La Spezia railway station Guy waited for this person to make himself known.

A loping, skinny man came bounding to meet him. He wore a brown woollen suit, too hot for the weather, and a greasy felt hat which he raised to mop his forehead. His face was at once classical and feral, as if a Roman had mated with a weasel and their offspring had forgotten to shave. A pungent cigarette dangled from his lips and his breath smelt of spirits. He pumped Guy's hand.

'Whaddaya know, whaddaya say? You gotta be Porridge, am I right?'

'Parrot.'

'Porridge – Parrot – whatever. Mine's Truffatore, but you can call me Joe.'

'Guy.'

'I know you're a guy.'

'My name is Guy.'

'You don't say? Crazy name, but your mamma gotta know what she was doing, am I right?'

Signor Truffatore made small talk as they searched out a taxi.

'I gotta brudda. You gotta brudda? Name of Cesare, lives in Detroit, you probably know him.'

'Cesare? No, I don't think so. Have you been to America? Is that where you learnt English?'

'Nope. I worked the boats as a stooward. You meet a lotta classy dames, working the boats. Learn you English right. Here, this one. Give the guy your bags, Guy. You sure you called Guy? Don't seem right.'

The taxi had been scoured to indeterminate grey by the

weather. Signor Truffatore argued furiously with the driver before ushering Guy inside.

'Sunnabitch is a crook,' he said cheerfully. 'All goddam Wops is crooks 'ceptin' me.'

'And your brother.'

'And my brudda.' Truffatore grinned and punched Guy on the shoulder. 'You're a kidder. I like that. You and me are gonna get along fine, Guy.'

'I'm glad about that – Joe. Do we have far to go?'

'A ways.'

Guy had studied La Spezia only enough to know that it lay at the head of a narrow gulf. Their route took them along the shore to the east side. Westward, across the placid sea, a peninsula blocked the horizon. This was Porto Venere on which stood the Church of San Pietro, at the foot of which were rocks and the cave where Byron was inspired to write *The Corsair*. For the present Guy meditated on the effect of light and haze and the prospect of distant lands forever beckoning.

They passed vineyards, olive groves, cypresses and umbrella pines. The hills fell precipitately to the sea. Guy, who had travelled to nowhere more exotic than Polperro, was surprised that the country should be as he imagined it and unsure if he were disappointed or not.

Passing Lerici, Signor Truffatore expounded on his services as a guide, which he was prepared to offer at moderate rates. Remembering that he was usually to be reached in one of La Spezia's bars, and that he wore a woollen suit and felt hat in this heat, Guy doubted his claim to have explored the Ligurian hinterland.

'You don't believe me, am I right?'

'I didn't say that, Joe.'

'I can tell.'

A villa by the shore flashed past. Signor Truffatore cocked a thumb over his shoulder.

'Casa Magni. Thassa place where some Limey poet lived. Hunnerd, maybe two hunnerd years ago.'

Guy remembered a remark by Lewis and something learnt at school. 'Shelley?'

'Nope. Not Shirley.'

'Are you sure?'

'Sure I'm sure. It was a *guy*,' said Signor Truffatore condescendingly.

'I see. And do you know anything else?'

'He was murdered.'

'Murdered!'

'God's truth.'

'I can't believe that.'

'Hey, whadda *you* know? You thought the guy was a dame.'

'That's true. Well, what happened?'

'The usual.'

'I don't follow you, Joe.'

Signor Truffatore turned in his seat and his eyes fixed Guy's earnestly. 'Look, it's the same the whole world over. It coulda been Chicago and Lake Michigan, but it happened to be here.'

'Yes?'

'A coupla guys invite the other fella – the Limey – to a day's fishing in their boat. They go out a ways. Catch a few fish. Sink a coupla beers, nicely nicely. And then' – he mimed a gun to his temple and pressed an imaginary trigger – 'blam! They bump him off. They throw the stiff overboard. It bobs around a whiles. The fish breakfast on it. A few days later it lands onna beach at Viareggio. *Basta! Finito!*'

'Good Lord! And was anybody caught?'

'Nope. No evidence. A professional hit. They sink the boat. They burn the body.'

Guy thought it an intriguing version of the death of Shelley. It made the poet sound like a bootlegger such as Commander Jackie Ferris had been and, for all Guy knew, still was.

The Villa Esperanza and its garden melted in sunlight. The surrounding pines, their dusty tops like sombreros, nodded somnolently in the faintest breeze. Signor Truffatore's natural walk was a coolie trot. He followed an amazed Guy, picking up cues like small change.

'Nice, huh? Classy, am I right? Kinda ancient or Roman or sumpin'.'

'It's astonishing!'

The door, with its foot in a drift of bronze pine needles, was unlocked but required forcing against the warping of the wood. The two men entered and deposited their bags on the dusty tiled floor between the *scagliola* columns.

Guy beamed at his new friend, 'You've done us proud, Joe.'

'I have? Oh, yeah. Sure.'

Only gradually did the inconveniences of the house become apparent. The lack of power or a water supply, the earth privy, the single hip-bath discarded in an out-house, the wood-fuel cooking range.

After the tour, they perched on their cases in the largest room, the saloon, where a stray yellow bitch had made a home with her pups. It was furnished with various items of flimsy painted furniture, mostly a suite of upright chairs to allow ladies to sit down between dances. On the seaward side, windows gave on to a shaded loggia, though for the moment this view, like any other, was barred by shutters.

'The house is lovely,' admitted Guy, 'but it won't do as it stands. I suppose we can manage with oil and candles for power, but we must have water. The place needs cleaning. And we must have staff: a cook, a skivvy and a man or two.'

'Hey, no problem.'

'Unfortunately I haven't much money.'

'We gotta problem.'

'I'd assumed – Signor Carmody assumed – that the villa would be more or less ready to move into.'

'He got plenty of dough, this Carmody guy, Guy?'

'Oh, yes. He's a very successful playwright, actor and composer. In England he's world-famous.'

'Is he world-famous in Italy?'

'The Americans love him.'

'You don' say? I betcha he knows my brudda, Cesare.'

It was settled that Signor Truffatore would go into Lerici and La Spezia and purchase supplies with the little money Guy could give him, and raise credit on the reputation of the world-famous Ambrose Carmody.

'I can't tell you how grateful I am, Joe,' Guy confessed.

'I know,' said a reluctant Joe. 'I'm a pal.'

Guy went to bed hungry and a little light-headed. He chose a first-floor apartment. It had been occupied by a lady and was decorated with some mildly erotic eighteenth-century prints, now discoloured and foxed. He opened the shutters.

It was strange, he thought, how refreshed he felt in the circumstances. Although the house posed some severe problems, they were of a practical not a moral nature and did not involve mental agony and difficult choices. In fact, he looked forward to the hard physical labour involved. And the Villa Esperanza with its views down the hill (or was it a mountain?) was so beautiful. He cut a sprig of oleander to decorate his room and watched it glow dimly by moonlight. He slept contentedly.

In the morning, as Guy's belly grumbled over an absent breakfast, Signor Truffatore appeared bearing bread, cheese, cold meats, olives and a bottle of wine.

'You're a good friend, Joe.'

'Sure. I'm a real prince.'

Signor Truffatore was still wearing his brown woollen suit and felt hat.

'Why do you wear those clothes in this heat?' asked Guy.

'In this country you gotta show class. The Wops don' respect you if you got no class.'

In the cool hour after sunrise Guy had walked the property searching for the water supply he knew must exist. He showed Signor Truffatore what he had found.

'There's a spring here. The flow is stopped by rocks, but I've tried the water and it tastes fine.'

It rose high on the hill where the pines gave way to oak and chestnut. From here the shore was hidden by trees but the further reaches of the sea could be seen, Porto Venere, the sails of caiques and yachts, and ships steaming up the gulf to La Spezia.

'There must be pipes down to the house. I've found traces of a cistern, and there's an outlet in one of the sheds or whatever one calls them. And there's something else I want to show you.'

Further down the slope to the side was a clearing which had once been gravelled but was now invaded by thyme and oregano. A nightingale occupied one of the trees and was singing extravagantly. At the upper margin, with a view of the sea, stood a grotto with a stone bench long enough to recline on but covered in vines. In the centre of the clearing was a dry fountain with a group of statuary. It comprised two naked figures.

'Who do you think they are?' asked Guy.

'Cupid and the other guy – Venus.'

Venus bore the usual male appendages.

'Are you certain?'

'Who lives in this country, me or you?'

'That's true.'

The figures were of a man and a boy. The man's left hand lay lightly on the boy's shoulder. Each gazed into the eyes of the other, their postures relaxed, contained in self-absorption. Vines had crowned the man with a wreath.

Guy contemplated the statues in silence while his companion fanned himself with his hat.

'This fountain could be made to work,' Guy said. 'We're downstream of the spring. No, that won't do – not enough pressure to drive the jet.'

Signor Truffatore was blowing away the insects that tried to settle on him.

'Of course!' exclaimed Guy. 'That explains the cistern. When it fills, there's enough head to operate the fountain.'

'Whatever,' remarked Signor Truffatore. Seeing that Guy was not disposed to leave, he directed his attention to the two figures. 'Those Romans were small, know what I mean? Small where it counts with a guy.'

In fact the carving was consistent with the ease and overall harmony of the group. The sculptor had indicated their masculinity, but his interest had been to convey that enigmatic exchange of glances.

'No wonder they lost their goddam empire,' said Signor Truffatore.

Guy was left alone while his companion went to search for staff. He found a pick, returned to the spring, and levered out the rocks that hindered the flow. For the present it was impossible to free the pipes, which were buried and blocked by silt, but the spring gave enough water to fill buckets at will. Guy did this and passed the day cleaning several of the rooms, interspersed with further pleasurable expeditions up the hillside to renew his supply. In the middle of the day he took a nap.

At nightfall Signor Truffatore returned with an ancient creature in tow. It was a wizened old man shod in tyres tied with string that was cross-banded around his calves. He carried a shotgun.

'His name is – what the hell, call him Enzo. He don' speak English too good, but he used to work here for the last owner.'

'Excellent,' said Guy. 'I'm pleased to meet you, Signor Enzo. What happened to the last owner?'

'He was murdered,' Signor Truffatore answered for the old man. 'A coupla guys…'

'There seem to be an awful lot of murders around here.'

A shrug. 'It's the country. We been doin' it ever since

Giulio Cesare got his.' Signor Truffatore indicated the gun. 'Blam!'

Guy saw Julius Caesar fall to the ground, surrounded by his fellow mobsters.

The following day Guy began work with old Enzo, who confirmed the existence of the pipes leading from the spring to the house and also to the fountain. They were, he managed to convey, a perpetual problem and, unless regularly maintained, filled with soil and gravel in a year or so. He pointed out the line, and, section by section, they began to uncover the pipe and clean it. Guy reserved the fountain for future operations. The mystery of the grotto intrigued him and he decided that his task for the summer would be to restore it. But first, he suspected, he would have to dig out and possibly reline the cistern, which had been filled by a small landslide.

During their conversations, Guy learnt from Enzo that there was some truth to the story of the murder of the former owner of the Villa Esperanza. At the time of the Matteoti killing, the local Fascists had called at the property and taken away the owner, who had never been seen since. No-one knew if he was dead or alive and no-one cared except a firm of lawyers in Genoa who let the villa and stole the rent. Because of the economic depression, there had been no visitors for a year.

Guy toiled for four days with enthusiasm touched by sunburn. Enzo worked in the mornings and, by tacit consent, got drunk and slept away the afternoon. Signor Truffatore put in brief appearances to deliver food and stand over the excavations to no particular purpose. He went away, claiming mysterious errands.

'I gotta see a coupla guys,' he explained.

Guy imagined the gulf of La Spezia slowly filling with bodies.

It was evening. By candlelight Guy was writing a letter to Elizabeth. After three days it was unfinished. What should he say? He knew he had treated her shabbily. He examined his conscience for guilt and found a space where it had been, like something left behind in England. He decided that the obstacle to remorse was the well-being he felt at the Villa Esperanza. The beauty of the surroundings, the simple food and hard exercise had given him a new form of consciousness, almost earthily pagan in its absent moral content. It was odd; even disconcerting. Guy decided that, come Sunday, he would find a quiet local church and make confession. Perhaps he could not make a true act of contrition but this substitute would keep alive the glimmer of his duties. Poor Elizabeth, he thought.

He heard a door open, footsteps in the hall and voices.

'I gotta brudda in Detroit. You probably know him.'

Grateful for the intrusion, Guy called 'Joe!' and rushed out with the candle, knowing the hall would be in darkness.

He interrupted three men in conversation and Signor Truffatore saying, 'There was this coupla guys...'

'Guy – excuse me, Joe – is that you?' Lewis was shielding his eyes to see behind the candle flame. 'Where is the light switch?'

'I'm afraid there isn't one,' said Guy. 'The facilities are pretty primitive, but you shouldn't let them put you off. Is that Ambrose with you?'

'Verily it is, dear boy.'

'Hullo, Ambrose. Good to see you. Wait a moment while I get more light.'

Guy had provided a supply of candles in each room and now lit one of them. It revealed his two friends, travel-stained and weary.

'Give us a hand to bring in our kit, there's a good fellow,' said Lewis. 'Joe would help, but he says he can't stay. He has to meet two men in town.'

Guy went outside with Lewis, where a green Bentley filled with luggage was parked. Ambrose remained in the hall, having subsided on a chair.

'Is Ambrose ill?'

'A little under strain.'

'Where's the other car?'

'We had a breakdown somewhere in Switzerland. We transferred the bags and pushed on. Fred stayed to sort out the damage. He'll be here in a day or so.' Fred was Ambrose's driver and dogsbody.

They heaved a trunk inside.

Guy said, 'I've fixed some rooms for you both.'

'Good man. I'm sure they'll be fine. All we need is a hot bath to set us right.'

'I'm sorry, but there'll be no hot baths. In fact, no baths at all for the moment.'

Ambrose groaned. Lewis asked, 'Are things really as primitive as that?'

'Afraid so. But there are compensations. The place is lovely.'

'Is the swimming good?'

'I haven't checked. No time.'

'Food?' Lewis laughed. 'Please God there's food.'

'I can offer you something cold. I haven't seen to the stove yet. It burns wood. I should get to it tomorrow or the day after.'

'Then how've you been spending your bloody time if there's no food, no baths and no bloody lights?' bellowed Ambrose from the gloom.

'Look, I didn't book this property, you did. I've spent four days simply getting a supply of running water.'

The answer was truthful and Ambrose's reproach unjustified but Guy felt responsible for the deficiencies.

Lewis touched his shoulder and shook his head. 'The journey has been perfectly awful.'

Guy had set up a table in one of the apartments. The atmosphere was chill. Guy tried to enliven it by explaining that, according to Signor Truffatore, Percy Bysshe Shelley had been killed in a Mafia assassination.

Ambrose glanced dully at Lewis. 'I'm not surprised. He

was a poet, after all.'

Guy put his knife down. 'Am I misunderstanding something?' he asked. He looked to Lewis, whose lips formed a tense but resigned smile.

'The fact is that Ambrose and I have argued our way through three countries.'

'We didn't argue in Belgium, where you ran over a dog,' retorted Ambrose.

'No, I admit that was amusing. But Belgium is a very small country and it was a very small dog. We should have had to slaughter them by the kennelful to get through Germany.'

'I see,' said Guy, not seeing at all. 'What did you argue about?'

'Writing – plays, poetry and so forth. It's too tedious to explain.'

'I suppose you like poetry,' said Ambrose, 'even write the bloody stuff.' His 'bloody' had none of the casualness of ordinary profanity but was delivered like a piece of ripe fruit.

'I like it, certainly,' answered Guy, uncertain if he did, except that he remembered some learnt at school.

Ambrose snorted. 'I know the sort of poetry your kind appreciate. I saw the poor innocents packed off to war with a volume of it for comfort in their knapsacks. How does it go?'

He cleared his throat.

> 'Outside the gaol in Ludlow town
> Poor Jack, who once with Tom went down,
> Stiffens as the bell is rung,
> And knows that Tom's well hung.'

Guy supposed this was a challenge. Lewis took it up.

> 'Lads go to war from western shires.
> Friends, fused with friends by manly fires,

Enter the breach: in long ranks serried,
Each with his manhood buried.'

He glared across the table.

Ambrose chewed in silence, then made an observation about olives which Guy did not catch. Then, to Guy's astonishment, his eyes filled with tears and he broke into hoots of laughter.

Guy worked on the stove. Old Enzo chopped wood. Signor Truffatore delivered a fat cook named Maria, and then had to leave urgently to meet two friends.

Lewis and Ambrose had composed their differences. In the morning, dressed in flannels, they knocked a tennis ball about the parterres. In the afternoon they went searching for somewhere to swim. Guy did not mind. The intricacies of the stove and the necessary improvisations to replace the broken parts fascinated him. He put aside the letter to Elizabeth under a new interpretation of his situation. He would not think of her. This was not an act of cruelty. Here in Italy he was finding calmness and a new balance. When he returned to England he would approach her with fresh sincerity and commitment.

Scarcely had the returning Bentley stopped when Ambrose sprang from the passenger seat. He was jaunty. Rolling his R's he asked, 'What chance of gr-r-r-ub, dear boy?'

'The stove is mended and we have a cook.'

'Where is Joe? Has he gone Bunburying? I must meet his charming business acquaintants. Did he really say Shelley was murdered? I suggest we eat on the terrace this evening.'

Lewis brought the bag containing damp swimming costumes. Guy asked, 'How did it go?'

'Marvellously.'

'You and Ambrose are friends again?'

'It was only a tiff.'

'So we're all in a good mood?'

'Yes. Strange to say, I hit another dog, a yellow one lurking near the house. That seemed to jolly Ambrose up a bit, though I only clipped the brute. Still I must be careful or people will begin to talk.'

'And the swimming?'

'There's nothing nearby, but we found a lovely beach at Fiascherino. Ambrose swims magnificently. He's always in excellent form afterwards. When he went to Turkey. he swam the Bosphorus.'

'I believe Byron did the same.'

'Byron?'

Fearing to be contradicted, Guy explained, 'I recall that he was also at La Spezia – in fact, at the time Shelley died.'

'It's a small world,' said Lewis.

At dinner Guy thought: I haven't left the villa since I arrived here, not even to swim. How many days is that? I wonder what it means?

Maria cooked a dish of veal. Guy could not put a name to it. He added to his resolutions that he must learn Italian.

'Where on earth is Fred?' Ambrose complained. In the transfer of luggage, the cocktail-shaker had been left in the Alvis. Ambrose had had to prepare martinis in a jug. In any case there was no ice, a deficit beyond remedy.

Guy looked out to the sea as if he would see Fred arrive from thence. The water was turquoise. The last boats making for harbour had orange or indigo sails in sun and shadow.

'What do you both intend to do while we're here?' he asked.

Lewis waved a hand, cooling himself or beating away a fly. 'I shall write poetry.'

'I have to make arrangements to transfer *Imperfect Tense* to New York.' Ambrose put down his glass and groaned: 'Dear God! There's no telephone!'

'You can probably phone from Lerici.'

'*Thank* you, Guy. I shall enjoy myself immensely, trotting back and forth like a native messenger.'

'No doubt it will do you good,' Lewis suggested curtly.

'You wouldn't say that if you suffered from my health.'

'I *do* suffer from your health.'

'Cruel boy. And you, Guy? What will you do?'

Guy explained his ambition to restore the fountain to its glory. His effort at description failed. He sounded like a meddlesome plumber.

Making his excuses, he went to the clearing. He had not seen it by twilight. In fact, there was no twilight amid the trees, merely a view out of a darkened arena to a western sky and the red sun lingering briefly on the horizon. Bats were already flying, and, below him, Ambrose was calling for candles to be brought.

I should like to bring Elizabeth here, he thought. He was aware of the stone figures behind him, like two friends conversing in quiet tones about a third. It occurred to him that, assuming he were right and Venus had not changed her accustomed sex, they might represent Hadrian and Antinous. An indelicate notion but, on reflection, he doubted that Elizabeth would be concerned. Had Byron and Shelley not been friends without imputation of scandal – at least, not on that count?

Guy began his descent.

Down below, Ambrose called, 'Matches! Any bloody matches?'

'Here's my lighter,' drawled Lewis. 'I told you you should have bought fuel for yours.'

A car was making its way up from the road. Fred, perhaps.

The girandoles in the saloon had been lit and threw a glimmer to guide Guy. As he drew nearer to the terrace, he saw candles on the table where they had dined and a roadster parked nearby. He recognised Ambrose in his smoking jacket, Lewis in flannels and the pullover he had

61

put on as evening fell, and a third man, presumably Fred. But who was the woman?

Ambrose exclaimed brightly, 'Guy! You seem to have ambitions to be a labourer. Be a dear fellow and give Fred a hand with his traps.'

'I'd be glad to.'

'Margot, hand that hatbox to Guy.'

'Here, *Guy*,' murmured a female voice with a hint of laughter in it. Its owner was blonde, svelte and only darkly visible. 'And will you take this, too, *Guy*?' Guy was not used to hearing his name caressed.

'Stop flirting, you trollop,' said Lewis.

'Oh, darling! *Guy* doesn't mind, do you, *Guy*?'

'Not at all.'

'And what about my bags?' said a second unfamiliar voice.

'Oh, I'll come back for those,' Guy volunteered cheerfully, once he had recovered from his surprise at another woman emerging from the shadows. This one had spoken more directly, less flirtatiously. Only later did Guy appreciate how very feminine the voice was, even in that first brief exchange.

He hopped to deposit the packages in the hall and returned to find cigarettes being smoked and one offered to him. The donor tendered the candle to light it and by the flame he saw the face of a dark-haired woman somewhat older than himself, one whom at first he classified only quickly as 'a beauty' – an expression taken from the Society pages of the newspapers, signifying little. She smiled and seemed to regard him with an amused squint from the one eye that was not obscured by the tilt of her hat. After the cigarette followed the hand itself. It did not shake Guy's but was placed on his palm like a gift.

'Hullo, Polly,' she said. 'I've heard so much about you. My name is Julia Carradine.'

Guy found it odd to be the object of someone else's story.

CHAPTER FIVE

1930

Guy found Margot lounging in beach pyjamas over breakfast on the terrace.

'Oh, hullo, Polly – or do you prefer to be called Guy? Would you like some coffee?' She offered a hand. 'At this stage we should shake. Tomorrow you'll know me better and we'll be friends, and then you may kiss me. Maria!' she called. '*Un caffè per il signore.*'

'You speak Italian?'

'Not a word. I make it up. The language is so theatrical I'm convinced everyone makes it up.'

'You look very refreshed this morning.' In fact Guy thought she looked lovely. Her blond hair had been shaken out but not dressed and stray locks gave her an artless air.

'Have you seen Signor Truffatore today?' Guy asked then corrected himself. 'I'm forgetting you probably don't know him. He's Ambrose's agent.'

'Oh, I know Joe,' answered Margot gaily. 'We met earlier. He brought some bits and pieces and we had a chin-wag. Then he had to leave suddenly to see some people.'

'A "coupla guys"?'

'Yes, that's what he said. Isn't it extraordinary what a small world we live in!'

'What do you mean?'

'That I should happen to know Joe's brother.'

'Cesare? From Detroit?'

'I can't swear it was Detroit, I rather think it was Chicago. I'm sure it was Chicago. I was there with Davenant – my husband, Raymond Davenant.'

'Do go on. You met Cesare Truffatore?'

'He was definitely called Cesare. I can't swear to the Truffatore.'

'And what line was he in?'

'He said he was an importer. I don't know what of. If you're interested, you should ask Jackie Ferris. He used to be an importer, too. They did business together.'

Lewis emerged from the house. He gave Margot a perfunctory kiss and took a seat. Guy, assuming he kissed Margot at all, could not imagine being so passionless. He had concluded she and Lewis were lovers, because the previous evening she had asked for her bags to be placed in his rooms and, Guy supposed, had spent the night there. He wondered if, perversely, this intimacy explained their mutual casualness.

Margot said, 'I must go inside and see to my hair. Guy is too sweet to say I look a fright. Shall we go to the beach this morning?'

'There isn't one,' said Lewis.

'Then you must find one. And it must be away from all the bedints.'

When Margot had gone, Guy raised a subject which was troubling him.

'I hate to mention it, Lewis, but we have to come to an arrangement concerning Signor Truffatore's expenses. I've laid out about fifty pounds over and above whatever Ambrose may have paid him.'

'Oh?' answered Lewis indifferently. 'I don't see that it's my business.'

'But I understood that you and Ambrose were paying for everything.'

'Ambrose, perhaps.'

'I don't want to sound brutal, but I haven't a lot of money. I'm still living on my allowance until I start in practice.'

'Believe me, I'd love to help. Fact is, all I have is a draft for a thousand pounds. I know it's a lot, but I expect a devil of a job in trying to cash it.'

Guy decided there was no point in pressing. Disconsolately he went for a walk. He would examine the state of his excavations, visit the grotto and then, perhaps, search out old Enzo to discuss hiring a boy to help them.

It was still early enough for the grotto to be in shade. A woman was there, examining the statues thoughtfully. Moving lightly around them, she seemed to change the composition of the group, creating a suggestion that the relationship between the two male figures, though carved in stone, was not fixed.

'Julia?' Guy was not certain it was she. He had seen her only briefly and, like Margot, she was now transfigured by morning. She turned and smiled.

'Hullo, Polly.'

They did not shake hands, but Guy felt there was more friendship in her smile. His first impression was confirmed. She was indeed beautiful. So, of course, was Margot, but Julia's beauty was darker and more intriguing. Guy refused to speculate further. He thought of Elizabeth but only briefly on this bright morning.

'Do you suppose they're father and son?' asked Julia, turning to the statues. 'Lovely, aren't they?'

'I had an idea they might be Hadrian and Antinous.'

'Romans? Do you know about that sort of thing?'

She was wearing a very simple dress. It was pale green and very fresh among the trees and the first bars of sunlight.

'You don't intend to go to the beach?' Guy asked.

'No, I thought I'd do some shopping in La Spezia. By the way, do you know what a "currant porpoise" is?'

'No.'

'Apparently we've got one – or, at least, we have everything we need to make one. Signor Truffatore told me.'

'Really?'

'Yes. He said we have everything we need for our

"currant porpoise".'

'It sounds like a cake. I should speak to Maria.'

Julia looked at her watch.

'I think I shall go now, while the day is still cool. If Fred is free, he can drive me.'

'I could drive you,' Guy volunteered.

'Could you? Lewis said you were a kind person.'

Was she making fun of him? wondered Guy. Although, in the ordinary way, he was pleased to be considered kind, here among these people it seemed inappropriate. Julia's manner, however, was disarming and his own mood excellent.

The others had gone to the beach in the Bentley. Guy took the smaller car. Where the road passed above Lerici he halted so that Julia might look down on to the town. This early in the morning it was still partly in shade though the fortress upon its rock stood out in sunlight. The same light had flickered on the aleppo pines along the shore of the gulf. Here the flow of pines, which seemed to billow down the hillside, was broken by the roofs of villas and ornamental cypresses.

'Shelley was living here when he drowned in a boating accident,' Guy said. 'According to Signor Truffatore, he was murdered.'

Julia did not laugh.

'You don't find it strange?'

'Not especially.' She looked out of the window rather than at Guy. 'Isolated among foreigners – living on top of each other – I imagine that tensions in that little group ran high. Naturally I've no idea whether Shelley was murdered, but I don't find the notion too implausible.'

Guy felt flattened by the failure of his attempt at humour. His spirits were raised as Julia gave his hand a quick, comforting pat and blessed him again with her radiant smile. He ventured: 'I believe that, in Shelley's time, La Spezia was little more than a village. Nowadays it's an arsenal and port for the Italian Navy. I shouldn't think the shopping is up to much.'

'That's all right. I don't like shopping.'

'Then why are we bothering?'

She looked at him, a little surprised. 'You really don't understand women like me, do you? Shopping is what we do to waste the daylight hours. A visit to Derry's is a religious obligation, almost like going to mass.'

'You're a Catholic?'

'I think so. I converted for Hector's sake. His family were Catholics before Christ. It seemed such a small thing to please him.'

'But you're no longer sure you are Catholic?'

Julia patted Guy's hand again. 'I don't want to embarrass you, but you must realise I'm unfaithful to Hector. So I suppose I ought to stop being a Catholic. It's rather like returning the wedding presents.' She laughed, and her laughter was so limpid and free of bitterness that Guy could not consider her last remark cynical, though it was hard to attribute any other meaning.

'Dear Guy,' she went on. 'We are such dreadful people. We have absolutely no shame.'

Starting the car again, Guy remarked, 'Lewis is the only one of you I know well. He seems very decent.'

'Lewis! Oh, forgive me, I mustn't giggle. Lewis is a perfectly charming monster. But he hasn't a decent bone in his body. Yet...' she mused, her voice dropping lower and becoming thoughtful.

'Yes?' Guy turned his eyes from the road. He tried to catch her expression. It was of fleeting sadness.

'I keep hoping that somewhere in the trash and tinsel of our existence, there is something – a spark of something that might be redeemed. I don't know how. By love, I suppose. When you know me better – as I hope you will – you'll realise I'm a sentimental thing. I do believe that love has a redemptive power. Oh, do watch your driving! You're not another dog-slaughterer, are you? Lewis seemed to have a positive fetish about killing them.'

On the approach to La Spezia, Guy took vague account of the moles that stretched across the gulf, warships in the harbours and repair yards. The city confirmed his first impression. It was modern and industrial, with factories everywhere concerned with fitting out the fleet. The effect was of purposeful griminess. He wondered if Fascism were as threatening as it was sometimes depicted. So far as La Spezia was concerned, it lacked the glamour of the newsreels, displaying merely a few posters proclaiming '*Il Duce ha sempre raggione!*' and others concerned with growing wheat and raising children. There were more soldiers and policemen than one would expect in an ordinary town, but they slouched and looked as bored as they did everywhere else. The only sign of Fascism militant he had so far seen was a squad of young men. He supposed they were conscripts. He had noticed them running along the beach at Fiascherino one early morning. They were disciplined and chanted slogans and did not look especially happy.

Guy found the centre of town and parked the Alvis in the Piazza Cavour, where there was a market.

'I fancy this was a mistake,' said Julia. She had acquired a girlish gloominess, and seemed young, very pretty, very sad, kicking her toes on the pavement while Guy took her bags from the car.

Guy said nothing. He did not know if her response would be light and laughing or if she might snap at him again. He noted only that her simplicity looked like elegance against the backdrop of widows, matrons and girls in cheap fashions.

To Guy's surprise Julia shopped for groceries rather than luxury items. She sniffed at cheeses, pinched chickens and tested the crusts of bread. She was at ease with the Italians and spoke the language.

'Where did you learn?' he asked.

'Hector is in the Diplomatic. We did a short spell here before he was posted to Tangiers.'

Guy wanted to ask why she had not gone to Tangiers.

'Was your marriage happy?' Immediately the question struck him as fatuous.

'Perfectly, for so long as we interested each other – which was about two years. You ask the oddest things. Have you got anyone?'

'A fiancée, Elizabeth.'

'What is she like?'

'Intelligent. Good-humoured. Dare I say attractive?'

'Go on. I shan't mock. She sounds very nice.'

'She is very nice,' said Guy with more enthusiasm than he had recently felt.

Julia looked sad again. 'Then go and marry her. I'm sure you'll be very happy.' Unexpectedly she added, 'Leave La Spezia. There's nothing here for you. Ambrose, Lewis, Margot and I are not in the slightest bit nice. We can be very cruel. We don't mean to be, but we're spoilt and dreadfully selfish.'

'I've come to La Spezia in order to have time to decide whether to marry.'

'Really? I got married in a passion. I do everything in a passion.' She hesitated. 'That sounds more exciting than it is. When one isn't in a passion, one is always repenting. I spend more time repenting than most nuns.' She smiled again, took Guy's hand and held it as they walked. 'Don't let me ruin you, will you? I should hate that.'

Browsing in the market, they were for no obvious reason stopped by a *carabiniere*. He was civil to Guy, flirtatious to Julia, and asked for their papers.

'You are tourists, no?'

'Yes.'

'La Spezia is not very touristic.'

'We've taken a villa near Lerici, which is very touristic.'

The papers were returned. 'May I look in the Signora's bag?'

'Yes, of course,' said Julia. She was insouciant and returned the policeman's flirtations.

'You have a camera.'

'That's right. Do you want to look at it? I can show you how it works, if you like.' To Guy she said, 'Did I also tell you that we are all very clever, even Margot in her own way?'

'You are not near the beaches,' said the policeman more solemnly. Guy began to feel uncomfortable. Julia, still careless in her self-assurance, answered, 'We didn't see any beaches. We're shopping.' Recklessly she added, 'Is it money that you want? Polly, I do believe this handsome fellow wants a bribe.'

At once they were surrounded by civilians who, on inspection, were not civilians. Two unshaven men in leather jackets had come alongside and were conversing with the *carabiniere*.

'Don't look now,' whispered Julia, 'but I think we're going to jail.'

'Oh God.'

Julia shot Guy a glance. 'Don't let me down. You haven't been to jail, have you? When I was a giddy young thing, I was always going to jail. It isn't so bad. The turnkeys are so used to drunks and burglars that when they see a pretty girl they can be awfully jolly.'

'I'm not a pretty girl,' said Guy.

'You don't have a very positive attitude to life, do you?'

One of the plainclothes men went to summon a car. Reconciled to her arrest, Julia offered cigarettes, which were accepted. Guy calmed himself by studying the sky.

When the car arrived, Julia said, 'Here goes. Don't be glum, Guy. I'm sorry for getting you arrested. I hadn't realised you had a prejudice against prisons.'

Guy decided he was annoyed with her. 'Don't you ever think of others?'

'Often. But probably not in the way you imagine.'

'You don't care what effect your actions have on them.'

'I care what they think about me. Sometimes that even makes me virtuous.'

'You have absolutely no morals.'

'How bedint!'

Guy was to discover that Julia had the self-confidence of the habitually guilty. In the police car she placed her hand on his and said gently, 'I forgive you.' He was too taken aback to protest.

At the station the brutal Fascists proved to be chivalrous. The prisoners were given coffee and, as the day wore on, a plate of pasta and a glass of wine.

'Is it always like this?' asked Guy, reluctant to admit that he was starting to enjoy himself.

'Usually. Naturally, lunch varies.'

'I can see that.'

Julia hitched her skirt and examined her legs, turning each slowly.

'I wish you wouldn't do that,' said Guy.

'Damn it, I've got a hole in my stocking. In the old days I used to carry knickers and stockings in my bag against the off-chance of winding up in chokey. Becoming a diplomat's wife has rather broken me of the jail habit. Hullo! Someone's coming.'

The door opened and a small, bald, elderly man with waxed moustaches resembling the late Kaiser's entered. He wore a dove-grey suit that Guy would have described as 'natty'.

'My name is Lady Julia Carradine,' Julia challenged, 'and this is *Doctor* Guy Parrot. To whom have I the pleasure of speaking?'

The newcomer smiled benignly and took a seat. 'I am Inspector Ercole Porrello, and I know your names already, Lady Julia, and that you are living at the Villa Esperanza at Lerici.'

'Then you must know that I am the wife of a diplomat.'

'*Si*. But not in Italy. Here you are a private citizen, subject to the ordinary laws.'

It occurred to Guy, then, that this was perhaps not the case for a five-bob fine and a ticking-off from the magistrate.

'Who are your friends, Signor Carmody and Signor Lockyer?' asked the Inspector slowly. Guy noticed that his eyes were damp with age or amusement; it was impossible to tell. His manner remained mild.

'Signor Carmody is a very famous playwright, lyricist and actor,' said Julia grandly. 'Signor Lockyer is a poet – also very famous,' she added more doubtfully.

'I see. And you are spending the summer here in La Spezia like Signor Shelley and the Cavaliere Byron in long-ago times?'

'Yes.'

The eyes twinkled, and to Guy's surprise the Inspector said, 'Signor Shelley was murdered.'

'So I've heard,' said Julia. 'I'm sure that was very wrong of him.'

'Who committed the crime?' asked Guy, unable to resist his curiosity.

Inspector Porrello shrugged, suggesting by the gesture that, had he been around at the time, the mystery would have been solved. He returned to the matter in hand. 'You must understand, Lady Julia, Signor Parrot, La Spezia is full of military installations. It is not a place where one can wander freely, waving the camera.'

'No, I'm sure not,' said Guy.

'Nor is it the place where bribes should be offered to honest but poorly paid policemen. We are not the greasy Wops you are imagining.'

Even Julia was deflated by this last observation.

'Still,' concluded the Inspector, 'you may go. Conduct yourselves well. Enjoy your holiday.'

During the return journey, Julia dabbed her eyes and said

with some emotion, 'Do you know, that fellow made me feel ashamed for trying to bribe the *carabiniere.*'

'So you should be,' said Guy. He found it difficult, however, to disapprove of an experience that was so interesting.

'Now you understand what I mean about acting on the spur of the moment and regretting it afterwards. I'm sure I shall be sorry for a whole hour.'

Guy laughed. 'You are the most dreadful woman I've ever met.'

'Yes I am,' agreed Julia. Guy glanced at her and saw that she was not joking. 'And I do so wish I weren't.'

However, by the time they reached the Villa Esperanza, she was perfectly cheerful.

They found the others in the saloon. Margot was reading a magazine. Ambrose and Lewis were having a drink with Signor Truffatore.

'Julia! Guy! My dear children!' Ambrose was a little elevated. 'Joe has saved our lives. He's brought us an ice-box, you know, one of those old-fashioned things that one insulates with straw, no need for electricity. He'll bring us supplies of ice every week – how often, Joe?'

'Coupla times,' said Signor Truffatore.

'Coupla times,' said Ambrose.

Guy accepted a whisky and soda. Signor Truffatore sloped off to see his friends. Guy asked, 'How was the bathing?'

'Wonderful,' enthused Margot. 'Except that Lewis ran down a dog.'

'I did not,' retorted Lewis. To Guy he explained, 'It was that yellow bitch which lurks about the premises. I merely gave her a fright.'

'I'm afraid I've been feeding her,' confessed Guy. 'That's why she stays around. She has pups.'

'So that's why I keep seeing yellow dogs everywhere. I was starting to think I was becoming deranged in the canine direction.'

By now the night was falling very quickly.

'And how was your day?' asked Ambrose.

'We whiled it away in prison,' Julia told him.

'Decent jail here?' Lewis enquired.

'Not as nice as the cells at Bow Street.'

'Ah, dear old Bow Street!'

Drinks were finished and candles lit in the girandoles. Ambrose ordered Maria to serve dinner in the saloon, since a sudden squall had got up and the terrace and loggia were being peppered with sand.

'An unforeseen storm like this did for poor Percy Shelley,' commented Ambrose as they ate.

'Our new friend Inspector Porrello – who mustn't be bribed, by the way – agrees with Joe that Shelley was murdered,' said Julia.

'Really? Did he say who bumped him off?'

'No, but I got the impression he has a suspect.'

'Well, I shouldn't be surprised. Byron and the Shelleys were appalling people.'

'You think Byron did it?'

'Possibly, though he had such a crowd of disreputable hangers-on that anyone might have.'

When dinner was over, Guy volunteered to clear the scraps to feed the dog. He took a bowl from the kitchen and placed it outside. The storm had blown over and the dust-veiled stars glimmered faintly. Taking a lantern he decided to walk to the grotto, where the leaves rustled as if the statues were whispering. He tried to imagine it with the fountain playing and the water catching starlight.

Then Julia was at his side. She had come up silently, wearing a thin shawl draped to cover her hair like a woman going to take communion. Guy saw her tremble in the evening chill. The effect was intensely physical but not sexual, being too innocent.

She said, 'On closer inspection, you don't like us, do you?'

'You're very different from the people I know well, but

I wouldn't say I don't like you – I don't know when I've felt so merry.'

'We're perfect shits.'

'Why are you so hard on yourself?'

There was no reply.

'Do you want to walk on?'

'No, I'm too cold. Put your arm round me.'

Guy did so gingerly, wondering if this were an invitation to kiss her. But her face was turned away, bidding farewell to the statues. When she looked again at Guy, it was simply to ask that they should walk back to the house.

The others were still in the saloon.

Ambrose said, 'The nights promise to be terribly long and dull if we don't find something to do. Did you happen to see a casino in town?'

'No,' said Julia.

Margot put down her magazine. 'I've asked Joe to get us a gramophone and some records. Then we can dance.'

'You may dance if you wish, dear. I require something to stimulate the mind. Theatre or baccarat, I don't mind which.'

'At Fletchitt, when we weren't killing foxes, we used to tell stories.'

'You interest me,' said Ambrose. 'Were they good?'

'Don't be silly. We're speaking of my family. They've never done anything that wasn't dull.'

'Byron and the Shelleys used to tell stories,' Guy recalled.

He wondered if he should have spoken. The others were looking at him with curiosity.

'Ghost stories, I believe.'

'And murders?' asked Lewis.

'I imagine so. Anything that was different and mysterious. They began at –'

'Diodati.' Lewis laughed. 'So they did. That's how the

story of Frankenstein was born. Around the fireside at Diodati, during a storm over Lake Geneva. Ambrose?'

'I wasn't there but I vaguely remember its being mentioned. Very well then, stories it shall be. And Guy shall begin, since it was his idea.' He looked at Guy.

'Good God, I can't tell stories. In any case, the idea was Margot's.'

'What a cad you are, Polly. On this occasion I do believe a gentleman would go first.'

'I know nothing about storytelling.'

'Pish!'

Guy opened his mouth to protest further, but found himself the object of some hard-eyed stares. Even Julia, with her vagrant mood swings, was unsympathetic. It occurred to him then that they understood quite well that his sense of ineptitude was genuine, and it was, to them, a matter of no importance. His reaction was an object of amusement and a species of test.

'Oh, very well,' he agreed. 'But not tonight. I have nothing prepared.'

'Then shall we play a rubber of bridge?' asked Ambrose indifferently.

CHAPTER SIX

1930

Guy slept badly. He dreamt of story-telling, of the death of Shelley, and of Julia Carradine. They were not pleasant dreams. Perhaps in the others' world it was a casual matter to tell entertaining stories, but he felt it was grossly unfair to impose on him the task of keeping them amused. It smacked of malice and humiliation and, what was worse, Julia had allied with Ambrose, Lewis and Margot against him as if no intimacy had been established between them during their trip to La Spezia.

In the morning he saw things differently. If story-telling were their notion of relaxation, it was natural that he should be asked to contribute. Though he did not like the idea, Guy decided that, if he applied himself, he could make an adequate fist of it.

Today, he told himself, he would make a start on clearing the cistern. The sun was no sooner risen than he strolled up to the spring. He removed some stones which had been dislodged by the previous evening's storm and then sat on the grass, breakfasting on stale bread, an onion and a flask of wine and water.

In due course old Enzo arrived, emerging through the trees like a hedgehog out of a pile of leaves. Guy led him to the cistern and indicated his requirements. They worked for an hour, lifting rocks and digging out the loose spoil. At last they reached a rock too large for them to manhandle.

'No good,' said Enzo in simple resignation.

'Perhaps we could blast it?' Guy speculated.' Boom?'

Enzo rolled his eyes.

'You're right. I don't suppose there's much use asking the local Fascists for the loan of any spare bombs.'

He examined the monstrous object. He did not relish the thought of trying to break it with picks. Dimly he recalled that stone could be split by alternate applications of fire and cold water, but this struck him as one of the implausible techniques in which only engineers and Boy Scouts were expert.

'Well, it looks like we're finished for today,' he admitted. 'Time for wine.'

Guy ambled back to the house, where he found Ambrose sitting in the shade of the loggia, knitting.

'You're knitting,' he said.

'Perspicacious fellow.'

'What are you knitting?'

'Socks.'

Guy wondered if he were suffering from a mental aberration brought on by heat and exertion. He looked for a book or newspaper. At last convinced that Ambrose was indeed knitting, not reading, he grunted and went inside to get a glass of water and a straw hat.

'Do you often knit?' he asked on his return.

'It soothes the troubled breast.'

'I see. And do you make many things?'

'No, only socks. Some of the fellows made balaclavas, but I could only manage socks. I suppose I could knock up a scarf, too, but I don't see the challenge in scarves.'

'You learnt in the Army?'

'Most British officers can knit. It was something to do in the trenches.'

'I didn't know.'

'You wouldn't. It's a bit of a secret. The War Office never cared to advertise the fact. They thought it would be bad for morale if it were known that we spent our time knitting instead of sharpening bayonets and dreaming of throat-cutting.'

Lewis came out.

'Ambrose is knitting socks,' Guy told him.

'Yes,' said Lewis indifferently. 'He often sits in the wings and knits during the performance of his plays. It takes his mind off the critics and makes him popular with the girls.'

'Why?'

'He does their darning. I say, does either of you chaps want to play tennis?'

'What about the women?'

'Our darling sluts are still in bed.'

'Ambrose wears silk socks,' Guy persisted.

The older man put his handiwork down and said testily. 'Look, if a fellow can't knit in peace, I'll go inside. And for your information, Guy, *my* socks are for knitting and not for wearing.' He went into the house.

Guy was alone when a few minutes later Julia approached. She came unexpectedly up the hill from the direction of the road.

'I understood you were in bed,' he said.

Her face was attractively flushed and the sun had touched her forearms. She settled gracefully in a chair and fanned herself with her hat.

'I've been for a walk. I watched the lovely soldiers on their morning run. May I share your glass of water?' She took it and imprinted her lips on the side. She blinked and shaded her eyes with her hand, giving the impression of looking for something remote and uncertain. Now touching Guy's hand she said, 'I believe that we all owe you an apology for last night.'

'I don't know what you mean.'

'Yes you do. Let me go on. I'm not very good at apologies and, if you insist on being a gentleman, I won't be able to make this one. We were perfectly foul to you.'

'I understand.'

'Do you? I'm surprised you can bear to speak to me. I pretended to be your friend – no, I *am* your friend – and yet I let you be embarrassed by that business of the stories.

You don't have to make up a story for our benefit, if you don't want to. It was thoughtless of us to suggest that you should, but it never occurred to us that there would be a difficulty. You see, for us story-telling is easy.' Her eyes had turned away from the western horizon and now looked at Guy's with a tender puzzlement, as if he were as great a mystery to her as she to him. 'It comes quite naturally, because we're terribly over-confident and such thorough liars. Have I shocked you?'

'A little,' said Guy. 'But, really, I don't mind giving story-telling a shot. I just don't know how to go about it.'

Julia smiled and said gaily, 'It isn't so hard. Most stories are trivial and are told by trivial people. Bear that in mind and you won't be intimidated.'

'I should like my story to be good.'

'Then model it on something you've read. Hugh Walpole, perhaps. Ah, I see you don't know Hugh Walpole.'

'No. I'm afraid I don't read very much. I'm a doctor.'

'How about *Gray's Anatomy*? A ghost story based on *Gray's Anatomy* would be dreadfully witty and extremely modern, but possibly a little adventurous.'

Guy grinned. 'Not *Gray's Anatomy*. But I'm sure I'll think of something.'

Julia was laughing – *with* him, not *at* him, thought Guy. She said, 'Oh, I can't tell you how relieved I am that we've had this conversation. I felt so guilty, and I do want to be friends with you.'

'Why?'

'Why?' Her voice fell. 'That is a good question,' she said. 'I suppose because you're the first good man I've met in such an age. Don't blush and don't be vain. "Good" is such an inconvenient thing to be and, for some reason, a little sad. I don't know why it should be sad,' she mused. Then: 'Let's not talk about it any more.' She reached beneath her and pulled out a ball of wool. 'What have I been sitting on?'

'Ambrose was here earlier. Did you know he knits socks?'

'Yes. It's the most human thing he does. He knits them by the dozen, doesn't know what to do with them, and leaves them lying around everywhere for his friends to trip over. I don't knit or do anything useful. Shall we walk?'

'You've just been for a walk.'

'Up the hill. You've been working there. Ambrose and Lewis think the sun has affected you.'

'Do you want me to show you?'

'Please.'

Guy took her hand and they strolled together: or, rather, he strolled and, to keep up with him, Julia took long, girlish strides. This morning she was not wearing stockings.

'This is it,' Guy said as they stood by the cistern. 'Nothing much to look at. Enzo – that's the old man – and I have to work out how to remove that great boulder.'

'What's the point?'

'The cistern feeds the fountain, the one in the grotto. I intend to get it working.'

Julia stared silently into the excavation.

'It looks like a grave. I mean a stone sarcophagus like the Etruscans made.'

'It isn't. It's simply a cistern for holding water. But it may be very old – older than the house, I suspect. Roman, perhaps.'

'Still, it's very melancholy. Almost haunted.' She was looking now at the trees. They were dry and dusty and threw a jumble of light and shadow. Julia said, 'One moment I'm up and another I'm down. I'm afraid you'll have to get used to that. Whenever I think, I grow sad.' Her lips became tight as if she were being brave. 'So I try not to think.'

From the small drawing room attached to his bedroom, Guy could look down on the terrace and across the tops of pines to the sea and Porto Venere. Margot was lounging in her beach pyjamas like a lizard on a rock. The others had retired from the afternoon heat. Today the sky was full of swallows and the yellow bitch had come forth to lurk, watchful and exhausted, in the shadow of a deckchair.

There was a lady's writing table. It was painted pale blue with swags and sprigs of flowers. In it Guy found some steel-nibbed pens, a pounce-box filled with dry sand and several sheets of faded lilac writing paper. In a drawer where he had put his shirts he came across a peach silk stocking. From the floor he picked up the corner of an old photograph lodged between the boards. These scraps of another person struck him as fragments of memory or clues to a mysterious death in a strange land. Yet he must suppose they meant nothing.

Taking his pen, Guy wrote: 'I have dreamt again of Diodati.' The words seemed luminous, like something read before. He hesitated over the next sentence, wondering whether originality mattered. Presumably it did, though he was not certain why. For the everyday practitioners of science it did not, or there would be no predictable outcomes to their work, and possibly the same was true of artists if they hoped to meet the expectations of their customers.

He tried another sentence. The main thing was to knock off a little tale of Byron and the Shelleys. He would make an effort to recreate their world imaginatively, but in the end it did not matter. The result, however vivid, would be merely something he had dreamt up, and, put like that, of no importance at all.

He began to write.

A breeze from the sea blew insects over the terrace. 'Disgusting!' exclaimed Margot, fishing mosquitoes from her drink. They abandoned the notion of dining outside and set a table in the saloon. Maria served octopus, black and glistening with ink.

'How was the swimming today?' asked Guy.

He failed to catch any interest.

'The weather is too damned hot,' Ambrose remarked tersely.

'Do you think we'll have another storm?' said Lewis.

No-one answered. Maria tottered in to remove the uneaten dishes.

'Is it fun, being arrested here?' Lewis asked. He glanced at Julia. 'Is it something I should try if I get bored?'

'Raymond has written to me,' said Margot. 'His creditors have decided he's still in love with me and want me to mortgage the London house.'

'Will you do it?'

'I might. It's the most romantic proposition I've had in ages.'

Maria brought zabaglione in small glass dishes.

'I've had a letter from Odo,' said Julia. 'And another from Jackie, who wants more money for his boat.'

Margot stirred her pudding. 'Damn! I was hoping for junket like we used to have at school. I wouldn't write to Odo. He actually *is* in love with you, which isn't romantic at all.'

'Will you reply to Raymond?'

'No. He'd be too shocked. I did pen a little missive to his solicitor when he enquired into my affairs. I was madly passionate and volunteered to have his child. He pretended I was referring to Raymond, which is absurd.'

Guy laughed, and the others looked at him strangely.

When dinner was ended, they followed Ambrose to the small parlour attached to his bedroom. He carried a candle, like a figure from Poe, and lit two wall sconces, casting a fitful light on what had once been a masculine room. Some hunting prints and brassbound travelling furniture remained.

'Cards again, I suppose?' he said wearily. 'By the way, Polly, could you run to some veronal? I'm not sleeping very well. The nights are too oppressive.'

'Guy has been working on a story to entertain us.' This remark came from Julia. Guy looked at her reproachfully, but she seemed not to notice.

'Have you, Guy?' asked Lewis. He sounded surprised yet respectful. 'We were only ragging you last night. I thought you understood that.'

'Polly isn't as frivolous as you are, darling,' said Julia acerbically. 'When other people speak, he thinks they mean what they say. And when he makes a promise, he tries to keep it.' She turned her eyes on Guy, who was at a loss since it seemed to him that, in raising the subject of the stories she had betrayed him again. Yet her expression was kind, even hopeful.

'I've put together a little something,' he admitted.

'Then you must let us hear it,' said Ambrose.

'It's in my room.'

'I'm sure we can wait.'

Guy looked at each of them. 'All right, I'll get it,' he said.

Returning to his room, Guy had occasion to glance back. He saw the others still sitting silently by candlelight. It was the effect of a moment, for, as he crossed to the staircase leading to the upper apartments, he heard conversation and laughter. Ambrose was singing.

CHAPTER SEVEN

Diodati

(A Tale of Byron and the Shelleys)

by Dr Guy Parrot

I have dreamt again of Diodati. I came by boat across the long low level lake, and for a while it seemed I could make no headway against the current. Either side the moonlit mountains rose and lightning flickered between the peaks, but there was no noise except the creaking of the rowlocks, and the splash of oars like the telling of a clock.

All at once, as is the case in dreams, my little boat was nudging the jetty. But it was not the jetty as I remembered it, small, neat and welcoming. Rather it seemed to have grown, or I had shrunken, and it formed a towering portal to my former realm.

When I disembarked, I found my feet touching rotten planks. The verges, which once were clipped and sprinkled with delicate bindweed, had grown wild. Sedges had invaded them, and the fine tendrils of the bindweed had turned to sinews that wrestled over the jetty. All was wild, and the sinister pines of the high Jura had descended to exercise their sway over the lake.

So to the path that led to Diodati. Surely it would remember me? It could not be so cruel as to forget! Alas, it could. The hill I had trod so lightly was become a mountain and the grass that once caressed my ankles was turned to nettles. The silent lightning flashed and the sad sentinel of night played her pale games in the shadows. And there, oppressed by shadows and moonlight, was our own dear Diodati where once we were so happy!

The cottage was ruined and its fires dead. Broken were the shutters and broken the little panes. Yet it seemed for a moment that Diodati still lived. A trick of light lent life to the house, a shard of broken glass recalled a vanished goblet, a dying fire set by trolls or vagabonds wafted the remembrance of manlier smells.

Foolish and inconstant dream! Diodati was dead as a grave in a sad cemetery. If life there were in this dull desolation, it would be an animal grazing the thin grass among the shattered stones and a goatherd sitting on a broken throne, piping a lament. And I would ask him where I might lay my wreath of laurel and star-shaped flowers.

My life at the Casa Negroto is full with small things. I sit by the open window and do my needlework by sunlight. My darling sleeps until noon. When he awakens he comes to me, kisses my forehead and asks, 'How is my little Goose today?' For so long as he asks, his little Goose is well.

In the afternoon he writes his poetry and in the evening brings it to me to make a fair copy. When I have finished he enquires perhaps, 'Well, Goose? What do you think? Has the Gander laid an egg?' Or, if the writing has been hard, he smokes a cigar while I work, only to say before he retires, 'I'm afraid your old Gander hasn't been much fun today.' And I smile.

How different things might have been if Percy and I had never met Lady Leaper, or she had not claimed the high regard befitting the wife of an Irish peer with an ancestor who brawled in the barn of a ruffianly Celtic king and a medal blessed by the Pope.

We were staying at the Hôtel d'Angleterre on Lake Geneva. Percy's father disapproved of me: I was too shy, too gauche, to grace his family name. So we had fled England to live in cheaper countries on Percy's reduced allowance; he wrote and I attended on him, making his happiness mine as good women do.

And, for so long as we were left alone, we were terribly happy. To write, to read, to stroll and take a single glass of wine and water, these are enough when one is in love.

The hotel was inhabited by English people taking the Alpine air or making their way to Italy. For all her great ancestry, Lady Leaper perhaps suspected that they would not welcome her society, or even snub her. She said the reserve was on her part. 'An Irish baronet ranks equal to an English earl – at least so far as concerns earldoms created after Henry the Eighth.'

Her wealth came from her second husband, Captain O'Brien. 'We agreed I should keep my title,' she said. 'The Captain was a naval man.'

'In the Royal Navy?' asked Percy.

'No, the Emir of Tangiers. It's a very old family.'

Percy's good nature would not allow him to reject Lady Leaper's advances. 'She's an original,' he said. And when I suggested meekly that I did not like her he answered, 'My poor country mouse. You must get used to the world's ways.'

We played cards, the three of us. She spoke throughout our games. She had a vulgar preoccupation with money. 'These days there's none to be made out of slaves. You feed and water them and still the brutes remain ungrateful.'

Day after day our poverty, Percy's amiability and my terrible shyness forced us to accept her hospitality, endure her loud-voiced tactlessness.

One day she said, 'You do know, don't you, that Lord Byron is in this neck of the woods?'

'I wasn't aware,' answered Percy.

'You don't suppose he'll drop in here, do you? I don't see why not. This is where the British hang out. Have you heard anything that's said about him? Of course decent folks can only talk of him in whispers. He's had to flee England.'

'Then, if he does visit the hotel, you won't be able to receive him.'

Lady Leaper pulled a face and adjusted her false red curls. She said, 'I'm not sure but I mightn't acknowledge him. My husband – I mean Sir Patrick, not the Captain – knew his family. And the precedence question is different for the Scottish peerage. Also, despite being very rich, he's an unfortunate creature and Christian duty demands that I recognise him. So all in all, I think it'll be all right.'

For poor Lord Byron's sake I wished that he might call anywhere except at the Hôtel d'Angleterre.

The next evening we were taking coffee and playing cards in the hotel lobby, where Lady Leaper liked to post herself to see and be seen. There was a flurry among the porters as a boat arrived at the dock, and some moments later two gentlemen entered. The first was not above thirty, a tall, dark-haired, elegantly dressed man who seemed tired, drawn and aloof.

'Oh my!' exclaimed Lady Leaper, putting down her cards. 'That's Lord Byron! I recognise his picture from the engravings in the newspapers. Also I saw him as a boy at Byron Hall.' She raised a hand and waggled her fingers coquettishly. I blushed and twisted my handkerchief in embarrassment.

The newcomer approached us. His face seemed older than his years and, although his expression was of perfect civility, there was in his eyes such a hint of wildness that, in contrast, I felt inexperienced and very young.

'Madame,' said Lord Byron, kissing Lady Leaper's hand as if she were perfectly known to him. He introduced his companion as Dr Polidori, his personal physician.

'Well,' said the old lady, 'if you have the time of day, what say you pull up a chair and join us, my lord?'

I caught a flash of weariness and pain, but, politely, he said he was much obliged. He summoned a porter to bring chairs.

We chatted, or rather the others did, for I said nothing. I

felt like an idiotic schoolgirl. I imagined the situation. Lady Leaper would make some appalling error of tact and Lord Byron would lose his temper. No, he would not do that. He would simply stand up and, with his superb manner, explain in chilling tones that he was glad to renew the connexion but he must be going. And that would be that. I should never see him again. If he ever thought of me afterwards, I should be the plain girl in a shabby dress who had watched as he was insulted. Or, still worse, we would meet and he would vaguely recognise me, think I was a servant, and bestow a kind word or a tip.

In fact he behaved splendidly, even while Lady Leaper imposed outrageously on their supposed acquaintance.

In an interlude while she paused for breath, his lordship leant towards me and said, 'You seem very hot. Or you have eaten something disagreeable – Irish stew perhaps?' He smiled wearily. 'What is your name?'

'Mary,' I stammered.

'Such a simple name,' he murmured as if in tender regard for something inanimate, a flower perhaps. Yes, I thought, he will understand the language of flowers. Despite his passionate nature he was a man of exquisite sensibilities. But he was merely being kind. I was too insignificant for his notice. He was taking a moment's relief while Lady Leaper marshalled for her final assault.

'Say, Lord Byron,' she boomed in her excitement. 'Is it true, all that stuff they write about you in the newspapers?'

I writhed in agony of embarrassment and shame.

Lord Byron, however, merely raised an eyebrow. He said, 'I am not acquainted with the articles in question. If they are flattering, you may be certain they are lies. If, on the other hand, they abominate my character, they are assuredly true.'

'Oh my!' exclaimed Lady Leaper.

'And now, if you will forgive me, I must retire. Come, Pollydolly.'

He rose and his companion with him. In the confusion

of collecting cards and wraps and signing the bill, he spoke to me again. 'You must call me George,' he said curtly.

'I couldn't.' I said in confusion.

'Don't be a goose!' he snapped, immediately adding, 'Forgive me, forgive me. I am indeed tired. Still, you must call me George, since already I've grown awfully fond of you.'

Two days later Lord Byron accosted us as we walked by the lake. He was with Dr Polidori, who seemed a dull pompous fellow of the kind who would be considered a good sort.

'I have taken the most dreadful liberty,' his lordship began directly. 'But I must get you out of the clutches of that damnable woman. I've rented a cottage for you. Its name is the Maison Chapuis. It's on the other side of the lake near the village of Montalegre. I'm negotiating the lease of the Villa Diodati, which is just above. There, I don't doubt, we shall all be very jolly.'

Elated and grateful, Percy and I returned to the Hôtel d'Angleterre to pack our few possessions. But already, as if by alchemy, our news had reached Lady Leaper and she was waiting for us.

She said, 'Well you're a dark horse, aren't you, dearie, snatching Lord Byron like that? I don't bear grudges, but I can tell you nothing good will come of it. Men like Byron see nothing in chits like you except youth and freshness, which is soon used up. At heart they're monsters and your bloodless affections are no good to them.'

'I appreciate your good wishes,' I answered and left her. But if only I had listened to her, what would have happened?

It was the dearest, sweetest cottage. Delphiniums, hollyhocks and lupins grew in the garden; pots of geraniums stood in the windows. Already I could see how I would spend my summer. We would pass our days in perfect friendship. Percy and George would ride, or sail upon the lake, and when they returned they would see the candles at the little windows, see the glow of warmth at the open door, smell the new bread of my own baking. When our meal was finished I would prompt them: 'Read to me.' Laughing they would say, 'No. No, we're too tired.' But good, stout Pollydolly would pause in the mixing of a punch and encourage one of them. 'Be a sport, old man, and do it to please the little woman.'

That is how it would be.

The morning after our arrival broke with a freshness as of spring, redolent with forest scents and the cool vapours of the lake. I heard George's voice calling, 'Hullo there! May a pair of hungry corsairs board your craft?'

Percy ran down to the jetty, razor in hand and his face still flecked with foam. He brought them to the house, where I was cooking eggs I had only that morning collected.

Smiling at me, George said, 'I thought our little goose might trust her goslings on the water. Indeed, she can come with us for a spin up to Meillerie.'

'That sounds a splendid idea,' answered Percy. 'What do you say, old girl?'

I said I thought it was splendid, too, but excused myself. I was nervous of the rough and tumble of three fine young men in a small boat. I would walk in the woods. There I had seen a narrow path. I would follow it through its border of azaleas and rhododendrons, and gather blooms of salmon, white and gold, delicate and graceful and waiting to drop their petals in the soft summer rain.

As afternoon wore on a storm broke distantly across the lake where the men had sailed. I told myself I would not think of it, but my fingers trembled as I arranged the flowers. And I whispered to them that I was a silly fool to think they could not manage the boat.

Night fell. I set the table and lit the candles. Casting my

shawl about me I made brief dashes to the jetty, and, as a fisherwoman in trepidation must look for her husband on a stormy night, I peered across the black waters, hoping that each flash of lightning would reveal the frail craft. My heart beat wildly and I reproached them for the agony they caused to me, and then reproached myself for my reproachful thoughts.

The candles flickered, and as each went out I replaced it. Then a knock came at the door. It was such a small, ordinary knock, one that a polite neighbour might make. I opened and there they stood, all three, soaked to the skin, grinning like cheerful vagabonds who have just escaped a hanging.

Over dinner, which they attacked ravenously, George explained the terrors of their voyage. Some way short of Meillerie a wind had blown up and stirred the lake as if it were a great ocean.

'We had our work cut out to get the sails down and hold her against the waves, let me tell you. Pollydolly was no use at all – you'll forgive me for saying that, won't you, old fellow? But Percy was a brick, though at one point I thought we'd lose him overboard.'

I shuddered for I knew that Percy could not swim. Gently I had warned him of the dangers he ran with his inexperienced delight in sailing. His answer was always the same. 'True sailors can't swim. It's of no use at all if one goes down in the Atlantic. One must trust to God.'

Oh, if only God had been present at La Spezia!

After dinner, we settled to amuse ourselves, my three bluff pirates and I. How comfortable and comforting George and Percy were as they toasted their stockinged feet against the fire, smoked their cigars and bragged in good fellowship about the day's exploits. I thought how noble they looked, fired and ready for a brigand existence: fierce as *banditti* who, independent in their mountain eyrie, are alert to commit outrage on their stolid neighbours or equally, out of extravagant caprice, to do delicate honour to a lady. Their lofty spirits were armed for great and terrible deeds, indifferent to the world's praise or condemnation. Their souls were fit, as their wills would drive them, for the heights of heaven or depths of hell.

'Well,' said George at last, 'what shall we do now, my bullyboys? Fight a duel? Play cards? Kidnap a fair maiden? Or perhaps our little Goose will sing a rondelay to soothe her savage warriors while we smoke and count our Saracen gold?'

Just then we felt the gale buffet the window glass and the whole house creaked and stammered. The storm was upon us and its gods were casting thunderbolts about the high Jura.

'Why do we not tell stories?' I suggested. 'Stories of knights and their ladies.'

'Nay, not that!' exclaimed George. 'Rather let us affright ourselves this eldritch night with legends of ghosts and goblins, spirits sprung from the chasm, fell deeds and unquiet dreams, horrors and undiscovered murder! And,' he continued pointedly, 'the lovely Mary shall not be excused. She shall contribute some bones to the charnel-house of our tale. What do you say, O Goose? Shall we hear of virgins immured by jealous parents in the dungeon of a ruined *castello*? Of shepherdesses kidnapped by robbers? Of a lady snatched from her dulcimer and forced to soothe the passions of a barbarous sultan?'

'I could not do that,' I murmured. In George's eyes I saw that sultan: and, too, the robber and the jealous parent, with a thousand other men all wild and terrible and apt for deeds of horror and glory.

Then it came to me with a lightning flash. Their modest mouse, trembling at the boldness of her own thoughts, could yet tell a tale to make the world fearful and, amazed. Indeed I could, for was not the material here before me?
I would speak of monsters. And of the monsters who create monsters.

CHAPTER EIGHT

1930

'*I have dreamt again of Diodati.*'

Margot clapped. 'How very witty, Guy! It sounds like one of those romantic novels written by ladies who wear sensible shoes and live with female companions.'

'I didn't intend it to be witty.' Guy remembered the book Elizabeth had lent him and which he used for the basis of his tale. He was sure it wasn't intended to be witty. Perhaps he had missed the point?

Tactfully, Julia asked, 'Why did you choose the theme of Byron and the Shelleys?'

'I thought there was a similarity to our situation. All of us on holiday together, telling stories to while away the evenings, just as they did at Diodati.' In fact Guy considered that, on this point, he had been quite clever and he half expected the others' admiration. Apparently he was mistaken.

Lewis lit a cigarette at one of the candles. To Guy, his expression looked more solemn than the story merited.

'You hint that the relationship between Mary and Byron was very intense and that something sinister happened at La Spezia.'

'I didn't have anything particular in mind. I was aiming for suspense, just to sustain the storyline. After all, Shelley did die near La Spezia.'

'That event was tragic but not sinister.'

'Then I don't know,' said Guy.

'Perhaps you had Joe's tale of murder in mind?'

'It's possible, I suppose.'

'And then? What happened next? Who was the murderer?'

'I don't understand?'

'Who murdered Shelley?'

Guy was uncertain how to answer. 'There was no murder.'

'In the story!' Lewis pressed him impatiently, and Guy could only stammer that there was no murder.

'The story stops where it stops, and there is nothing afterwards.'

Ambrose intervened. 'You are being very trying, Lewis, dear, after Guy's valiant effort. However, Guy, before you preen yourself, there are certain points of inaccuracy in your story which should be brought to your attention.'

'Really?'

'Yes, really. For example, as I recall, Mary had a small child, a brat yclept William, fathered by Shelley. Not very important, perhaps, but it challenges the whiff of virginal innocence that hangs about your version of the mother.'

'I'm sorry, I'd forgotten.'

'No need to apologise,' said Ambrose indulgently. 'Lewis, do stop pacing the floor like a detective in American pulp fiction. Where was I, Guy? Ah, yes, the evening at Diodati when all the story-telling began. It seems you have omitted another of the *dramatis personae*.'

'I have?'

'You have. I speak of Claire – Claire? Step-sister to Mary and mistress to Byron, who soon learnt to despise her. I don't think we can do without Claire. Her presence would have entirely changed the pattern of tensions within that little *ménage*, don't you think?'

'Yes, I can see that it might have,' said Guy. Trying to salvage his efforts, he added, 'But it is only a story I made up, Ambrose. It doesn't have to be accurate, does it?'

'How very brave you are.' Ambrose smiled. 'Let me

inform you, dear boy, that notwithstanding the licence you arrogate to yourself as an author, your copy-editor will want to drink blood from your skull; critics will slander you for failing to command your subject matter; and private pundits will sharpen their swords in the inglenooks of Tunbridge Wells and set mantraps about the byways of Guildford. It is astonishing, the depth of learning possessed by the literate inhabitants of Guildford. You'd think they would have better things to do than waste it on the rubbish scribbled by authors. No, no, Guy, if you wish to be taken seriously, you must get the minor facts right. Then you may tell the most pernicious lies about everything else.'

It was decided that next day they should go to Porto Venere. They would take the Bentley, leaving Fred to bring up supplies in the Alvis. In the event, Margot remained behind, complaining that the sun had made her unwell and saying that, as part of her campaign against her estranged husband, she would write another torrid love letter to his solicitor.

'Will she?' asked Guy.

'Of course not,' said Lewis. 'Margot is a hard-nosed businesswoman. Her family made its pile from slaves and coal.'

The road took them through La Spezia, skirting the arsenal, the naval yards and a large basin enclosed by breakwaters where a number of warships were at anchor. Guy half expected to be stopped and interrogated, but the *carabinieri* and militiamen either ignored them or gave a cheerful wave.

Before the village itself were a narrow strip of sand and a collection of hotels glittering gaily with sunlight, and an ancient steam ferry was beating its way northward in a brilliant plume of white smoke.

Ambrose halted the car. 'I suggest we don't drive further, where I'm told the streets are very narrow. I propose to sit here in splendour, drink champagne, swim a little, and take gracious notice of the natives. You may do as you choose.'

Guy said he would like to see Porto Venere.

'I shall go with Polly,' said Julia. She slipped her arm through his and smiled mischievously. From her repertoire of dresses she had selected one that looked as if it had been bleached sky-blue by the sun. Guy knew that the simplicity was artificial – she was wearing crimson lipstick – but she conveyed the charm of a Columbine, a knowing innocence and tender excitement. The truth was that Julia delighted and troubled him in equal measure.

They scaled the narrow streets and steep alleys, hand in hand, their faces to the shadows and backs to the sea, where boats bobbed at the quay in twinkles of colour. They climbed steps and passed under arches, stumbled and blinked in sudden splashes of light, until in the shadow of a ruined Genoese fortress they paused to take a drink at a café.

Fanning herself, Julia said, 'May I ask you: why did you choose to tell a story of Byron and the Shelleys?'

'I thought I explained.'

'You weren't trying to comment on us – I mean our group? That would have been very clever.'

'I'm not clever.'

'In some respects Byron and Ambrose are alike: utter swine, both of them. Lewis claims that Ambrose, too, is a genius. Do you think that's likely?'

'No.'

'Are you sure you're not being clever? The appearance of ingenuousness can be very attractive.'

Guy was amused. 'I'm quite sure.'

Julia laughed. 'When I'm with you I feel virtuous – or, at least, full of good intentions. Let's go and look at a church.'

They found a square. Julia let go of Guy's hand and skipped across it, spinning now and again as if by her passing glance she could sweep him up and bear him after her. The square gave a view over the sea to an island which seemed to cruise slowly in a creamy haze. Nearby stood an ancient church built partly of black and white marble, dilapidated and undergoing restoration. Julia halted. When Guy caught up with her, she was subdued.

'We can't go in. It's closed.'

'There's another one, San Lorenzo.' Guy waved vaguely. 'Up there, near the castle. You can see the tower.'

'No. It's a sign. I'm not meant to go in. In any case I have no scarf, my hat is in the car and my dress has short sleeves. So, you see, God doesn't want me to pay him a visit.'

Guy thought of his namesake of Shoreditch. 'God can be very forgiving.'

'Don't be pious with me!' Julia snorted. Her eyes grew moist. 'You aren't clever at all, are you? You really are ingenuous.'

'I never said otherwise.'

'You should have pretended.' She was angry and distressed. She turned on her heel and fled.

Guy followed at a walking pace and lost her in the labyrinth of steep narrow streets. He tried not to think harshly of her, but she was, for the moment, the most infuriating woman he had ever met. Yet when he reached the shore, he saw her by the Alvis chatting amiably with the driver.

Turning to Guy she said brightly, 'Do you know Fred? He's a mine of the most fabulous stories.'

'Fancy a drink?' asked Fred. He was a grey-haired Londoner of middle height, slightly paunchy and red-faced. He and Julia were sharing a bottle of champagne. 'If you want the boss he's out there on the rocks. Where was I? Oh yeah, I says to the boss, "Let me tell you –"'

'Fred says he gave Ambrose all his best ideas,' exclaimed Julia as if this were something Guy must hear.

'Not *all*, I said *some*,' Fred corrected her complacently.

Lewis was sitting reading in the shade of a stone pine. Ambrose, his face flushed, was scampering up and down the rocks, carrying children on his back while their mothers watched approvingly. Guy had not seen him before in this attitude of innocent playfulness. When the children squealed, he squealed. When, in excited voices, they tried to speak to him, he called back, 'Spaghetti! Linguini! Macaroni!' which was much appreciated.

Behind Guy a cockney voice said, 'Jus' before the battle of the Somme, General Haig says to me, "Fred..." '

Margot was very merry at dinner.

'You are being secretive and most provoking,' Ambrose rebuked her. 'Next time you claim to be ill, please have the decency to look pale and wan instead of positively blooming.'

'I have a surprise for you.'

'You are reconciled to your husband?'

'I said a surprise, not a miracle. I've written something to amuse you. It's a play.'

Ambrose placed his knife and fork down carefully. 'You intrigue me. I thought plays were my forte. A comedy?'

'I'm not sure. Life is so odd that one can be funny while being frightfully realistic.'

'I trust it isn't a parody of my own work? I do so hate parody and criticism. They're such cheap ways of raising a laugh. Moreover, what's the point? The audience learns nothing from the former and the writer learns nothing from the latter.'

Guy was puzzled. 'Surely you learn something from your critics?' He noticed that Lewis had put down his own cutlery and was holding a napkin to his mouth. 'Don't you?'

'I make it a point of principle never to do so,' said Ambrose. 'By ignoring them I contribute to the relief of unemployment. Not that I care for critics, but they do have

100

mothers. I once knew a critic's mother.'

'You claim to know the most exotic people,' said Margot.

The subject of the play came up again later that night when the men were smoking in the loggia. Margot emerged from the house with a sheaf of papers.

'My play!' she announced. 'I've written out the parts. Ambrose, you can be George.'

'Byron?'

'And Lewis is Percy.'

'*Grazie*. I assume you refer to Shelley?'

'I shall be Mary and Julia will take the part of Claire – I've corrected your omission, Guy, and introduced her. Ambrose was right. The presence of Claire alters *everything*! You're not offended, are you?'

'Not at all,' said Guy good-naturedly.

By moonlight, Ambrose was scanning those pages given to him. He grimaced. 'This script contains only my part and the cues to speak. It gives me little idea of what the others will say.'

'Do be reasonable,' answered Margot, pouting. 'I can't be expected to write the whole thing out five times. And where would be the surprise if everyone knew everything?'

Guy asked, 'Is there a part for me?'

'Oh yes!' Margot handed over two sheets. 'You're the linchpin of the whole thing. You know? Like the Bloody Serjeant in *Macbeth* – or someone equally bloody if not exactly a serjeant.'

'Thank you.' Guy accepted the pages and was pleased, though he could not recall which character had played the crucial role in the relations between Byron and the Shelleys.

'You're the Hotel Manager,' said Margot.

CHAPTER NINE

Past Confusion

A Romantic Comedy

by

Lady Margot Davenant

The Characters	*The Players*
Mary	Lady Margot Davenant
Claire	Lady Julia Carradine
Percy	Mr Lewis Lockyer
George	Mr Ambrose Carmody
Hotel Manager	Dr Guy Parrot

The action takes place in the suite of an hotel somewhere terribly chic where Byron and the Shelleys might have stayed.

ACT ONE

The drawing room, which is elegantly furnished with Hepplewhite gramophone, Sheraton cocktail-cabinet, et cetera. MARY *is ready for the theatre.* PERCY *is dressing and his shirt is still collarless.*

PERCY: Make me a drink, darling, while I find my collar stud. If there's no ice, call room service.

MARY: It's too bad of you. Claire will be here any moment and George won't be far behind. By the way, why are you so late?

PERCY: I shouldn't be if I hadn't lost that stud. Do you know where it's gone?

MARY: I haven't a notion, and you know I hate mysteries.

PERCY: It's only a collar stud.

MARY: That's the worst part. If it were a murder it would be different. There are a limited number of solutions to murders.

PERCY (*striding to* MARY *and kissing her*): Darling Mary, I love you! You've hit on it!

MARY: I have?

PERCY: Yes. The answer was in that word 'solution'. I distinctly recall putting my stud down next to the bottle of seltzer I opened when I was feeling seedy. By the way, what were we doing last night?

MARY: It was a perfectly ordinary evening. We listened to poetry and then pushed on to a nightclub.

PERCY: Poetry? No wonder I got drunk. (*The doorbell rings.*) Answer that, will you? I'll see to my collar. (*He grabs his drink and exits.* MARY *opens the door. Enter* CLAIRE.)

MARY: Claire!

CLAIRE: Mary, darling! (*They exchange kisses*) How divine you look. Is George here?

MARY: Not yet.

CLAIRE: Percy? (MARY *nods towards the bedroom.*) Too much poetry again?

MARY: I'm afraid so.

CLAIRE: Poets will be poets. Are you going to offer me a drink? I wonder when George will arrive. He also tends to overdo the verse.

MARY: Martini? Ice? Olive? You seem very interested in George.

CLAIRE: I'm in love with him.

MARY: He's married to Annabelle.

CLAIRE: I shouldn't be interested in him if he weren't. To be the wife of a poet is to be a mere bedwarmer.

MARY (*with a touch of indignation*): I am Percy's wife!

CLAIRE: Don't be angry. I promise not to tell.

MARY: I'm not angry. (*She mixes the drink and lights a cigarette.*) By the way, are you having an affair with George?

CLAIRE: Have you heard something? (*She hesitates, then confesses.*) Very well, I am.

MARY: Does he know? Ha, Ha! How ridiculous! He must know – or at least suspect.

CLAIRE: Are you trying to provoke me? I tell you I am having an affair with George. He simply adores me. (*She stubs out her cigarette.*) And now, if you don't mind, I'll powder my nose before he arrives. (*Exit* CLAIRE *to bathroom.*)

MARY: Damn! (*She moves to fix herself another drink.*) (*Enter* PERCY *from bedroom. He is wearing a collar but no tie.*)

PERCY: I say, another mystery!

MARY: What now?

PERCY: I can't find my tie.

MARY: Oh, God! It's like the second murder in one of those stories one reads – you know, the murder that no one is terribly interested in. By the way, Claire is here. Did you know she's having an affair with George?

PERCY: You seem angry, darling.

MARY: I am. When the man one most admires is sleeping with one's sister, surely that counts as incest?

PERCY: Only among strict Catholics. (*He pauses.*) Just a moment, I thought *I* was the man you most admired?

MARY: Don't be silly, darling. We're married.

PERCY: Can't a wife admire her husband?

MARY: I suppose so. But she must never admit it. She would appear too ridiculous.
(*The doorbell rings.*)

PERCY: Hullo, it must be George.
(PERCY *answers the door.* GEORGE *enters.*)

GEORGE: Evening, Percy. Mary, my sweet, you look delightful.

PERCY: Can Mary get you a drink while I search for my tie?

GEORGE: Gin and It. How are you? Everything all right in the poetry game?

PERCY: Can't complain. And you?

GEORGE: Much the same.

PERCY (*to* MARY): I'll look in the bedroom again for that tie. (*to* GEORGE) You'll entertain Mary for me, won't you?

GEORGE: Delighted to.

(*Exit* PERCY. GEORGE *and* MARY *look at each other with a degree of embarrassment.*)

MARY: You still haven't got a drink. Gin and It, wasn't it? (*She pours the drink.* GEORGE *takes a cigarette from the box on the table.* MARY *takes up the lighter from the table. She produces a flame and holds it in cupped bands. They linger over the act. Then* GEORGE *pulls away abruptly.*)

GEORGE (*thoughtfully*): Don't you hate the stock gestures of conventional theatre?

MARY: Don't carp. You make your living from them, or from the usual poetic sentiments, which amounts to much the same thing.

GEORGE: They are very clear in conveying meaning.

MARY: Yes, they have that advantage. (*She turns to stub out her cigarette.*) Do you remember that evening at Diodati?

GEORGE: Yes. You told us all a story. Of monsters.

MARY: My monster was based on you.

GEORGE (*pleased*): What a sweet thought.

(*The bathroom door opens.* CLAIRE *sticks her head out.*)

CLAIRE: Mary – oh (*flustered*), George, it's you!

GEORGE: Good evening, Claire.

CLAIRE (*recovering from her surprise*): Mary, darling, can you give me a hand? Excuse us, George, this is a matter between two women. Help yourself to another drink if you feel like it.

GEORGE: By all means take your time.

(MARY *exits to bathroom with* CLAIRE. GEORGE *hums a tune, finishes his cigarette and fiddles with a bottle. Enter* PERCY, *wearing tie.*)

PERCY: Hullo, George. Has Mary seen to you? I was trying to find my tie. Do you have that problem, finding your tie?

GEORGE: Socks. I can never find my socks. I mean, not a matching pair.

(PERCY *pours a fresh drink.*)

PERCY: Where are the girls? In the bathroom? Socks, you say? You interest me.

GEORGE: As it happens I have a theory. Observation has convinced me that the sock is by nature a migrant and solitary animal, living in pairs only by dint of human compulsion.

PERCY: I'll accept that. And studs and ties? Much the same thing I suppose. Except that ties don't live in pairs.

(*They raise their glasses and look away for a moment in silence, then speak simultaneously.*)

PERCY: Look, about this tie business –

GEORGE: I was thinking of murdering Claire –

PERCY: Pardon?

GEORGE: No, you first. I thought you were going to say something interesting.

PERCY: Was I? It's quite gone out of my head. I think we'd better talk about murder instead.

GEORGE: You don't mind?

PERCY: Not at all. But keep it short since those two are bound to come out in a moment. Do you have a reason, or do you intend to slaughter Claire on general principle?

GEORGE: We've been having an affair.

PERCY: Good Lord! (*puzzled*) And that's the reason? Claire is your mistress, ergo you want to kill her?

GEORGE: That's pretty much it.

PERCY: Righty ho. (*pause*) There are some gaps in the logic, don't you think?

GEORGE (*testily*): I was keeping it short. You can fill in the details from your imagination.

PERCY: That does leave one rather spoilt for choice. (*cautiously*) But why are you telling me? Are you looking for sympathy? I sympathise terribly.

GEORGE: I was hoping you'd lend me a hand.

PERCY: To murder Claire? (*pause*) I'd better have another drink.

GEORGE: Be careful not to get tight.

PERCY (*hesitating over the cocktail cabinet*): Is it a problem if I get tight? I mean, do you intend to kill her off tonight? – by the way, should one say 'knock her off' or 'bump her off'? Americans have such flair with language.

GEORGE: I prefer to say 'murder'. My intentions may be felonious but they are never vulgar. Well? Are you with me? To help a friend?

PERCY: I might in the general way. But I fancy that murdering one's sister-in-law is a special case. It's probably illegal and, for all I know, immoral. Certainly it shows a lack of proper family feeling. (*The bathroom door opens.*) Hush, they're coming.

(*Enter* MARY *and* CLAIRE.)

CLAIRE: Percy, darling! (*They kiss.*)

MARY: How are we for time?

GEORGE: We should be pushing on to the theatre.

PERCY: I'll go downstairs to get a taxi.

CLAIRE: I'll come with you. I left my fur coat with the concierge.

(*Exit* PERCY *and* CLAIRE. MARY *and* GEORGE *look cautiously at each other.*)

MARY (*curtly*): You should finish your drink.

GEORGE: Don't snap at me. Anyone would imagine we're in love.

MARY: Preposterous! I've already told you I think you're a monster! Not to mention vain, arrogant and a selfish brute!

GEORGE: Your degree of insight would do you credit if we were married.

(MARY *hesitates in putting on her coat. She stares at* GEORGE.)

MARY: Do you really think we could be married?
(*impatiently*) No, of course not, you're married already – to Annabelle.

GEORGE: I could murder her.

MARY: But there's Claire to consider.

GEORGE: I definitely intend to murder *her*.

MARY (*admiringly*): Oh, George, you are impossibly romantic!

GEORGE: Mary, my darling, do you think that a man so unprincipled as to write poetry would hesitate to murder his mistress?

MARY: You would make that sacrifice for me?

GEORGE: I would sacrifice *anyone* for you.

MARY: Oh darling!

GEORGE: Mary!

(*They rush into each other's arms and embrace at length. Amidst murmured endearments* MARY *breaks off.*)

MARY: Oh damn!

GEORGE: What is it, dearest?

MARY: If I'm to be free to marry you, I shall have to kill Percy!

CURTAIN

ACT TWO

The same room later that evening. Enter MARY *and* GEORGE. GEORGE *mixes drinks and* MARY *lights two cigarettes, passing one to* GEORGE.

MARY: What an absolutely dreadful play!

GEORGE: I agree. The setting wasn't chic, the characters weren't debonair and the dialogue wasn't witty. In fact, there wasn't a single note of realism. (*He accepts the cigarette.*) Thank you. How long do you think Percy and Claire will be?

MARY: I'm not certain. It was awful bad luck that she slipped and twisted her ankle in the restaurant. She said it was on a prune.

GEORGE: Prunes can be so cruel.

MARY (*businesslike*): I think we should take the opportunity to discuss how I am to kill Percy. It's more difficult for a woman to murder her husband than for a man to murder his wife and mistress. I'm sure there must be some sort of skill to it, like plastering walls or mending cars. (*She considers the point; then, relieved*) I think I shall ask the hotel management.

GEORGE (*surprised*): Do hotels arrange murders?

MARY: This is a very good hotel. They may have a murderer on the staff. (*She goes to the telephone.*) Hullo? ... Signorina, this is room four-four-seven. I should like to speak to the manager ... About what? I want someone to murder my husband ... No, I am not American! (*She puts the receiver down.*)

GEORGE: Will he come?

MARY: Probably. The operator was not convinced this is an emergency, but, naturally, she was sympathetic.

GEORGE: Would you like to dance? (*He looks around for the gramophone.*)

MARY (*faintly*): No. The thought of murder is making me inexplicably tense. It's all right for you. You're a writer. You probably murder people all the time. (*They stare at their drinks again.*)

GEORGE (*casually*): It was very gallant of Percy to volunteer to help Claire. (*hopefully*) Do you think she may be setting her cap at him? She may leave me?

MARY: Possibly. One poet is much like another, once one has stopped listening to them. In any case it wouldn't solve our problem if Percy and Claire fell in love.

GEORGE: It wouldn't?

MARY: I should still have to get rid of Percy in order to marry you. And, God forbid, Percy might murder me in order to marry Claire. (*She sobs.*) Oh, darling, why can't the course of true love run smooth! (*They embrace. There is a knock on the door.*)

MARY: That will be the manager. Give me a moment to collect myself. Killing people must be very wearing on the nerves and, like getting tight, one might regret it in the morning. (*She dabs her eyes. The knock is repeated.*) There. I feel better. Let him in. (GEORGE *opens the door. The* HOTEL MANAGER *enters and nods to both. His manner is suave, bordering on obsequious.*)

MANAGER: Signora, Signore. How may I help you?

GEORGE (*to* MARY): Fire away, old girl.

MARY (*bright and winningly*): I want to murder my husband.

MANAGER: Ye-es?

MARY (*impatiently*): Is that all you can say? Don't you offer a service for this sort of thing?

MANAGER (*shaking his head*): Sadly, you are the fourth lady I must tell we have no demand for such service.

MARY: The fourth? You said the fourth? (*appalled*) Do women always want to murder their husbands when staying in your hotel?

MANAGER (*thoughtfully*): When on holiday, spouses

usually wish to kill each other. It is only natural.

GEORGE: But you disapprove?

MANAGER (*shrugs*): It is not for me to decide. But holiday murders are like holiday romances: the passion rarely lasts.

(MARY *paces the room. She comes to a decision and confronts* MANAGER.)

MARY (*coaxingly*): Surely there is someone on your staff who would do this little thing for me? Naturally I'd be prepared to tip.

MANAGER: You are too generous, but, alas, Signora, the quality of staff has declined since the war.

MARY (*angrily*): Can you believe we are in an economic depression, when one can't get murderers even for money!

GEORGE: (*To* MANAGER) We apologise, Signore, for taking up your time.

MANAGER: It is I who should apologise. (*He turns to leave, hesitates and turns back.*) I have one request. If you decide to proceed, I should be grateful if you would not leave the body in the hotel. (*He smiles agreeably.*) Speaking personally, I should be pleased to remove any of the Signora's victims, but the hotel owners have a strict policy. They do not allow bodies or food to be brought from outside on to the premises.

(MANAGER *bows and exits.*)

MARY (*still angry*): I shall never recommend this hotel to my friends.

GEORGE: I need another drink. By the way, we're running out of ice. (*inquisitively*) Have you many friends who want to murder their husbands?

MARY: I've never asked. It's one of those small points about women that one simply assumes. No one has ever told me that she doesn't want to murder her husband, and that must mean something.

(GEORGE *pours* MARY *a drink. She takes a sip, sighs and calms down.*)

MARY (*smiling tenderly*): Thank you, George, you are being awfully decent. (*They clink glasses.*) Chin chin. (*They take another sip.*) A propos, are you implying that most men don't want to murder their wives? An awful lot do.

GEORGE: Yes, but brutally and without premeditation. I suspect it's part of the carelessness that causes us to lose our collar studs and ties – or, in my case, socks. (*There is a knock at the door.* MARY *opens it.* PERCY *and* CLAIRE *enter.* CLAIRE *is limping.* PERCY *kisses* MARY *and takes off his coat.*)

PERCY (*puzzled*): Do you know, I just ran into the hotel manager, and the fellow had the cheek to ask if I cared to settle my bill. We're not leaving, are we?

GEORGE (*evasively*): We have talked of going to La Spezia.

PERCY: That must be it. What is it that people say about the place? 'See La Spezia and die.' Or do I mean Naples?

MARY: I think it may be La Spezia.

GEORGE (*looking at the wall clock*): Good Lord, look at the time! I must leave if I'm to feel fresh in the afternoon. Percy, Claire, Mary, I bid you adieu.

PERCY: So long, George.

(GEORGE *kisses the women, shakes Percy's hand, collects his coat and exits.*)

MARY (*who has been staring through the door at George's back*): I must go to bed. I'm feeling tired. Claire, darling, I'll see you in the morning at the hairdresser's.

CLAIRE (smiling): Of course, darling.

(*They kiss.*)

MARY: Don't stay up too long, Percy.

PERCY: Righty ho. Sweet dreams.

(MARY *goes into bedroom.*)

PERCY (*calling after her*): Would you awfully mind searching for my pyjamas? I seem to have mislaid them.

(*The bedroom door closes.* PERCY *and* CLAIRE *look at each other meaningfully.* PERCY *goes to the cabinet for drinks.* CLAIRE *takes off her shoes.*)

PERCY: Damn it, there's no ice!

(CLAIRE *comes up behind* PERCY *and kisses him on the neck.*)

CLAIRE: Are you sure Mary can't hear us?

PERCY: Positive. She'll go straight to bed and sleep like a log.

(*They embrace passionately. A voice comes from the bedroom. They stop immediately.* PERCY *looks nervously at his glass.*)

PERCY: Look, I say, is it absolutely necessary for me to kill Mary? After all it's not as though, afterwards, I could marry you. That would be incest.

CLAIRE: Only among Orthodox Jews.

PERCY (*unconvinced*): I shouldn't mind so much if you told me you loved me.

CLAIRE (*archly*): I couldn't possibly do that. I respect you too much.

PERCY: But I want to be loved!

CLAIRE: No, you don't. You're a man. You want to be admired. Love is a sort of consolation prize. Come, kiss me.

(*They kiss.*)

PERCY: Now let me understand this. I am to murder Mary?

CLAIRE: Yes.

PERCY: And you are to murder George?

CLAIRE: No.

PERCY (*surprised*): Oh? And why not?

CLAIRE: I've explained already. George isn't my husband, merely my lover. There would be chaos if one started killing people to whom one owed no obligations. One couldn't walk safely down the street. We are discussing murder, not mayhem.

(PERCY *sits down and puts his head in his hands.* CLAIRE *regards him disdainfully and lights a cigarette.*)

PERCY (*plaintively*): I feel so terribly inexperienced! I need professional help.

CLAIRE: I suppose we could ask the hotel management.

PERCY (*relieved and surprised*): Could we? I shouldn't have thought that a respectable hotel would arrange murders.

CLAIRE: This is a very bad hotel.

PERCY: You're right. I'll do it.

(PERCY *goes to the telephone.* CLAIRE *sits down and massages her injured ankle.*)

PERCY: Hullo, this is room four-four-seven. I want to see the manager … What do you mean, again? … Never mind … He'll come? … Grazie.

CLAIRE: Is he coming?

PERCY (*puzzled*): I'm not sure. The operator seemed rather surprised when she heard my voice.

CLAIRE: Well, we'll give him a few minutes.

(PERCY *sits down beside her, tries to embrace her and is pushed away.*)

PERCY (*annoyed*): Sometimes, darling, I suspect that you're doing this – egging me on – just to make George jealous.

CLAIRE: Nonsense, George is far too vain to be jealous. (*She kisses him.*)

(PERCY *runs his finger round his collar uncomfortably.*)

PERCY: Look, if I were to take my collar off, would you make a note of where I put my studs?

CLAIRE (*stand-offishly*): Suddenly you're becoming very intimate.

PERCY: Oh, I don't mean to presume. It's just that I'm always losing my studs. George loses his socks.

CLAIRE: I know.

(*There is a knock at the door.*)

PERCY: Good-oh. That must be the manager. I'll get it. (PERCY *answers the door. The* HOTEL MANAGER *enters. He glances at* PERCY *and* CLAIRE *in surprise. He checks the door number, sees it is correct and smiles.*)

MANAGER: Signora, Signore, how may I help you?

PERCY (*reluctantly*): I say, I don't know how to put this, but I was wondering…

MANAGER: Yes?

PERCY: …if the hotel could help me to murder my wife?

MANAGER (*Hesitates, then smiles again.*) Certainly.

PERCY: You could? You will?

MANAGER: Of course. It is a service we have recently introduced. There is a great demand for it.

PERCY: Recently? How recently?

MANAGER: Very recently.

PERCY: But … I mean … you have the necessary experience?

MANAGER: This is Italy, Signore!

PERCY (*relieved*): Of course. I'd forgotten.

(MANAGER *turns his eyes on* CLAIRE.)

MANAGER: May I ask a sensitive question? The Signora, is she, perhaps, the intended victim? I ask because I understand that in America these things are sometimes provide for in the marriage contract.

PERCY (*surprised*): Good God! Well not in England. I wouldn't dream of discussing her future murder with my fiancée. It would show a lack of faith in marriage.

MANAGER (*bowing*): *Che delicatezza.*

(*He waits. There is an embarrassed silence.*)

CLAIRE: What are you waiting for?

MANAGER: I thought the Signore might want to make the arrangements straight away.

PERCY (*to* CLAIRE): Gosh, this is all rather quick! He's like a man selling you life insurance.

MANAGER: Yes, it is something like that. If we make arrangements immediately, we reduce the risk that our client will himself meet with an accident.

CLAIRE: Do you often have accidents here?

MANAGER: In the street, or in the hotel, accidents happen everywhere. (*He pauses and looks pained.*) You will excuse me, please. May I use your bathroom? I have eaten something disagreeable.

PERCY: Feel free.

(MANAGER *bows and exits to bathroom.*)

PERCY: Well he's a rum cove! Anyone would think that *I* was the intended victim.

(*The bedroom door opens.* MARY *enters in her nightgown.*)

MARY: Don't mind me. I need to use the bathroom.

(MARY *exits to bathroom. Silence.* PERCY *and* CLAIRE *stare aghast at each other. There is a knock at the door.*)

PERCY (*surprised*): Who can that be? You don't suppose it's an assassin already?

CLAIRE: Don't be silly. Answer it.

(PERCY *opens the door.* GEORGE *enters. He is barefoot and half-dressed.*)

GEORGE: I know this will seem an odd question, but did I by any chance leave my socks here?

(PERCY *opens his mouth to answer. The bathroom door opens and* MARY *enters.*)

CLAIRE: Is everything all right, Mary?

MARY (*brightly*): Oh, yes! Marvellous. Absolutely marvellous.

(CLAIRE *stares at* PERCY. MARY *stares at* GEORGE, *gestures at the bathroom door and makes the sign of throat-cutting.* GEORGE *and* PERCY *both start for the bathroom.*)

GEORGE: I'll just check if I've left my socks…

PERCY: I think I've mislaid my … my … my toothbrush!

MARY (*almost screams*): No! No! Don't go in there!

(*They all look at her. She is horror-struck, at a loss for words, and finally sheepish.*)

MARY: The … the floor is wet! Whoever goes in there might meet with (*hushed voice*) an accident.

(*The bathroom door opens. The* MANAGER *emerges with his back to the others, closes the door and turns.*

He sees all four, raises an eyebrow and, as always, smiles.)

MANAGER: Signore and Signori, how can I be of service to all of you?

(*In turn* MARY, CLAIRE, GEORGE *and* PERCY *look at each other, first with horror, then with realisation, and at last with amused resignation.*)

GEORGE: What a relief. You're just the fellow we all need! (*He spares the others a final smile.*) Would you believe that we've run out of ice?

(MANAGER *bows.*)

CURTAIN

CHAPTER TEN

1930

The boy was beautiful, one of those rare creatures so striking that people, on first seeing them, feel obliged immediately to voice their admiration.

Ambrose put it quite simply. 'What a beautiful boy!'

Lewis said, 'I've just seen the most good-looking lad.'

Julia asked Margot, 'Have you seen that perfectly lovely child?'

To which Margot answered, 'Yes. In fact he's such a darling I swear I felt a Sapphic pang – which I'm sure isn't the correct reaction at all.'

Signor Truffatore brought him one morning before breakfast along with groceries, a wind-up gramophone and some records.

Fred broke the news. He said, 'Joe's jus' tipped up with somebody's little lad. You should see him. He's as gorgeous as a Shepherd's Bush tart.'

'The kid's name is Gianni,' said Signor Truffatore. 'He's the son of a guy I know. I don't mean Guy. I mean some other guy. Guy – your Guy not my guy – asked for some help about the place to give Enzo a hand.'

'Enzo is the old fellow?' asked Lewis.

'That's the guy.'

Guy and old Enzo had gone up the hill to study the problem of the boulder that blocked the cistern. They had already attacked it with picks to no effect. The alternative of applications of fire and water had been discarded because of the risk of a conflagration among the dry brushwood.

'What you need,' said Fred, 'is to build an A-frame

over the hole. Then you can lift it out using a block and tackle.'

Guy was impatient, as if Fred, too, were keeping secrets. 'You've been watching me for two days. Why didn't you suggest it before?'

'It's like I said to General Haig: "You've got to study the problem first." And do you know what he said? He said, "Fred, you're *right*." '

Guy went down to the house to wash and have breakfast. He found the others lounging at the table in their night attire, offering pieces of fruit to the boy, who sat still and solemn as an icon.

'With a face like that, he could sell make-up in Selfridges,' prompted Fred in a whisper.

The boy's skin was very smooth, a pale bronze. His lips were large, the colour of bruised plums. He sat bolt upright but at ease, looking directly ahead as Pharaoh might have looked.

'Does he speak English? Do you speak English?' Guy asked. A pair of brown eyes scanned him impassively.

'The kid gotta few words but he don' speak too good.' Signor Truffatore tapped his forehead. 'He's kinda slow. You don' like him, I get rid of him. Jus' say the word.'

Guy was reminded of how an owl turns its head. The body remains motionless, the head rotates, the face remains expressionless except that the eyes blink. The boy did this now.

'I'm sure we can give Gianni a try,' said Ambrose.

'Absolutely!' enthused Margot.

'He can help Maria in the kitchen and the house, and in his spare time give Guy a hand in burying his victims or whatever it is he does up on the hill.'

Ambrose patted the boy's hand. Gianni responded by glancing down as if he had received a small insect bite that did not trouble him much. Signor Truffatore addressed a few words to him in Italian and he rose to follow the older man into the house. He was taller than Guy expected, lithe

119

and easy in his movements. Guy guessed he was about fifteen.

Margot smiled. 'I feel deliciously faint and rather damp.' She looked to Lewis. 'Darling, I want you to take me shopping. If it would amuse you, you may get us both arrested. Guy, you're very practical. What is the exchange rate?'

'Ninety lire to the pound, I think.'

'Does one get lots of colourful bank notes?'

'Quite a few.'

'Wonderful! I love the feeling of being terribly rich.' Margot giggled. 'Of course, I am terribly rich. How shameful!'

'I'll come with you,' said Ambrose. 'Fred, you can drive. I have some cables to send to my agent in New York. Joe, do you want to come with us and be our guide?'

'I'll take a powder, if that's okay by you.'

'You gotta see a coupla guys?'

Joe gave a thin smile. 'Sumpin' like that.'

With Enzo's help, Guy began to clear the overgrown brushwood that intruded on the path and made access from the road to the Villa difficult. Beneath the pines was a growth of juniper, buckthorn and myrtle, dry and fragrant.

Seeking at the outset to understand Italy, Guy had bought some second-hand books in a shop in Charing Cross Road. They included a guide by someone who loved Italy but hated Italians, regarding them as a verminous infestation of the country. The author held to an obscure theory according to which the English were the true heirs of the Romans and, apparently, of the Jews, too. Wrestling with these ideas and an Italian primer, Guy whiled away the afternoon reading.

Julia came padding out of the house barefoot and smoking a cigarette. Seeing Guy she muttered, 'Oh God, I must look like a Neapolitan washerwoman.'

'Can I get you a drink?'

'Hmm, hock and seltzer. I have a headache. I've been sleeping.' She looked about her and slumped into a chair, eyes closed.

Today Guy saw another facet of her. She was slatternly. Her hair was awry. At the clink of a glass, she opened a cold, louche eye, stretched out a hand and took it. She bore the bravery of those bold sluts with brassy looks, mouths like wounds and stockings rolled in bandages around their ankles. Guy knew them well. They stood on the poor street corners of Manchester and gossiped like veterans at a reunion.

At his next glance, Julia had folded her legs under her. Her hands were pressed together as if in prayer and her head rested on them. Dark eyelids flickered; her mouth, set in a pale bud, trembled. She resembled a faery curled upon a leaf.

It occurred to Guy then that he had never seen Elizabeth asleep. Only now did he recognise this lacuna in his ability to grasp her complete physicality, their mutual entrapment in a surface of polite appearances and conventional words. How sad it was for both of them that their courtship was little more than a pious fraud redeemed only by sincerity of intention. The truth was that, though Julia seemed in her caprices to be deeply unknowable, yet he felt he knew her better than he did Elizabeth. Julia, for all that she had secrets, was unguarded. But Elizabeth, who probably possessed few secrets, was hidden from him in the purdah of English good manners.

Julia stretched and shook her hair. She stared at the sky, where swifts were screeching after flies. She looked at Guy with gentle thoughtfulness.

She asked: 'Have the others come back?'

'No.'

'They're late.'

The sun was low, sinking towards Porto Venere, picking out the silhouette of the fortress and splashes of colour from the houses scattered among the grey pines.

'Perhaps they've had lunch with Inspector Porrello.'

Julia smiled. Guy had never before seen her looking contented. He sensed a feline inwardness.

'Is Lewis in love with Margot or she with him?' he asked.

'I doubt it. Lewis is a Narcissus and Margot is quite splendidly selfish and has no shame.'

'Is Ambrose attracted to you?'

Julia started and answered sharply, 'What makes you ask that?'

'I'm sorry. I don't mean to pry. But you have travelled together as a group. You are here and not with your husband in Tangier.'

'My husband is none of your business. Nor, for that matter, is Ambrose.'

'I see I'm making a mess of this,' said Guy.

He went for a walk. He found the yellow bitch snoozing under a bush and gave her a stroke. He saw Gianni hanging out washing in the drying area behind the house. Guy waved, but the boy did no more than return a noble, half-witted stare. Beneath his feet Guy heard the spring water trickling through the pipe and felt a touch of pride that this was his handiwork. Some day soon, he was sure, there would be the fountain.

He went to the grotto to see the statues. He suspected that, by his frequent visitations, he was testing their reality. The grotto conveyed a strangely powerful feeling that the two figures were instinct with life and that, over the slow centuries of their immortal time, they would move in barely perceptible gradations towards a greater expression of love.

Turning, he found that Julia had followed.

'I knew you'd be here.' She was still barefoot and her toes curled under the prick of pine needles. The tenderness with which the statues had affected him must have shown in his face, for she went on, 'You have a kind and forgiving nature, haven't you, Guy?'

'Have I?'

'And so modest, too!'

'Now you're making fun of me.'

'I don't mean to. I joke only because I'm feeling guilty. The others, too. We feel guilty all the time, and so we're bright and shallow, gay and thoroughly miserable.'

Cautious and hopeful, the yellow bitch had come cowering and sniffing.

'I've forgotten to feed her,' said Guy.

'I'm not in love with Ambrose and he isn't in love with me. We're bound together by … other things.'

Guy remembered something. 'What were you quarrelling about while you were travelling through Germany?'

Julia seemed relieved. 'Oh, that was mainly between Lewis and Ambrose.'

'What was it about?'

'Art and writing. You must speak to Lewis if you want to know more. As far as I can tell, Lewis thinks Ambrose is squandering his talent on vain, frivolous things.'

'Is he?'

'Who knows? Frivolity has its place – especially after the horrors of the war. You should understand that, no matter how he may appear, Ambrose is like you: very modest.'

'I find that difficult to believe. I heard the way he dismissed the opinion of critics.'

'Oh, that! It was an affectation. Of course Ambrose reads the critics. When they praise him he's childishly delighted, and when they don't he sulks and can't bring himself to write.'

'Then why did he say otherwise?'

'Because it's shameful to have so little integrity that one is blown hither and yon by the praise or blame of others. I have warned you against taking what we say at face value.'

'Does that include you?' Guy asked.

'Oh yes,' said Julia.

They ate indoors because of a breeze. Gianni helped Maria to serve dinner. Barefoot he bore each dish. Between times he stood without motion in his expressionless beauty.

'Do you think the boy is an idiot?' asked Ambrose.

Guy suspected he was.

'Not idiotic, elemental,' Julia suggested.' Think of fauns and dryads: playful spirits who have no more than an animal intelligence.'

'I wonder if he smokes?' Lewis offered the boy his cigarette case. Gianni took a cigarette and accepted a light. He smoked indifferently, without sign of pleasure or disgust.

'I think he's divine,' said Margot.

Divine or not, the boy's impassivity could not sustain their interest and they fell to talking of other things.

Guy asked Ambrose, 'Have you settled with Joe? I hate to think how much he's owed.'

'You should consider, rather, how much I am owed. Agents, theatre managers, publishers – sometimes I weep for my creditors.'

'It's just that I've been put in a false position. Because he took his first orders from me, Joe expects me to pay him.'

'You seem to have a vulgar interest in money,' said Lewis.

'Have you exchanged your banker's draft?' Guy retorted.

Lewis shrugged. 'The bank in La Spezia wants to make enquiries. They have a problem in handing over large amounts of cash simply on the say-so of a bit of paper.'

Margot had a solution. 'Can't you hock something, Guy? My father popped everything in order to marry my mother. The pawnbroker even provided ushers for the wedding, so that he could keep an eye on his investment. It's considered perfectly good form.'

'I don't see why I should go into debt, even if I had something to pawn.'

'Well, I'm sure you know best. The morals of the middle classes have always been a mystery to me.'

Guy looked to Julia, hoping for support, but she had evidently lost interest in the conversation. He realised then that it was pointless to have any expectations of her: that her shows of affection were as spurious as those of a cat; merely a self-centred imitation of concern.

'I shall smoke outside,' he said, and was embarrassed by the pettiness behind his words; not that the others remarked on it.

The breeze had dropped. Bats flitted in the pine tops, a nightingale sang, and out over the darkened sea a steamer sounded a melancholy horn like a cow that wanted to be milked.

Again he found Julia at his shoulder, holding a cigarette and a cocktail glass.

'What has upset you?' she asked.

'I didn't think you'd noticed.'

'I didn't, not at first. You have no idea how incomprehensible you are to us. How mysterious.'

Guy was startled by the oddity of this notion.

'Are you laughing?' asked Julia.

'No ... no.' Then he realised he was, and Julia, too. 'Me, mysterious? It's too much!'

'I don't see why. Stop laughing, Guy. You're making me cry. I don't see why you shouldn't be mysterious.'

'It's absurd.'

'No, it isn't. Well, maybe a little strange – no! It isn't strange at all. Do stop laughing.'

She took Guy by the forearms to make him face her. She was still holding her glass and its contents trickled over his hand. Guy felt a physical shock of intimacy that put an abrupt end to laughter. Julia's face was turned up to his with an expression of self-doubting expectancy, and for a moment Guy thought she would kiss him, or even that he might kiss her. In that hesitation he looked beyond her and saw, in the shadows, Gianni waiting in patient silence with a tray of drinks and, still further, at a dimly lit window, Lewis staring vacantly into the night, perhaps watching them or perhaps not.

It was enough to inject a spark of realism into Guy's thoughts.

'I'm out of place here,' he said. 'I should leave.'

'I did warn you.'

'The others don't want me here.'

Julia shook her head. 'That's where you're mistaken. More than anyone, you are the star of our little firmament.'

'You're flattering me. Why should you all want my company?'

'You intrigue us. We know each other too well – despise each other too much. I do believe you want to be flattered!'

Guy was amused by that accurate insight. The idea of being mysterious was, though incomprehensible, very attractive and only his common sense prevented its going to his head.

Presently Julia said, 'In any case, it's too late for you to leave, isn't it?'

Guy was left to interpret that remark.

The window into the loggia opened and Lewis called out, 'Guy, we need you to make a fourth at poker.'

'Who's playing, besides you and Ambrose?'

'Fred. He says he used to play with Haig and Marshal Foch.'

The door closed and the night made itself whole again. 'I'm going to smoke another cigarette,' said Julia.

Join me in a drink?' Guy took two glasses from the tray. The boy remained stock still. Thinking of Julia's remark – was she being flippant? – that the others despised each other, Guy asked her, 'Was Margot having a dig when she wrote her play? Ambrose was uncomfortable opposite her Mary Shelley. Is she setting her cap at him?

Perhaps trying to make Lewis jealous?'

'Margot was being mischievous.'

'I imagine she was. My question, however, was how much truth there was in what she wrote.'

'Let me see. Have I got this right? Mary – that is to say, Margot – is married to Percy – otherwise Lewis – but in love with George, alias Ambrose. I, in my disguise as Claire, am the mistress of George/Ambrose, but make a pass at Percy – or do I mean Lewis? – in order to make Ambrose – or George as the case may be – jealous. In consequence of which, everybody proposes to murder everybody else.' Julia looked aslant at Guy. 'Well?'

'It does seem unlikely,' he admitted.

'Doesn't it?'

Over cards, Fred revealed he had had an interesting war.

'We was playin' poker, me, Sir Douglas, Marshal Foch, an' some staff officer or other whose name I forget. This was jus' before the third battle of Wipers – Passchendaele to you and me, settin' the record straight.'

'You have a commendable regard for history,' said Ambrose.

For poker Ambrose insisted they remove their ties and roll up their sleeves. 'In the interest of atmosphere, dear boy.' Fred had already obliged.

' "What I want to know," says Sir Douglas to the rest of us, "is should I or shouldn't I 'ave another crack at the Boche? What do you think" – and he looks me in the eye – "*Fred*?" '

'And what did you think, Fred?'

Guy was drowsy with whisky. The air was tepid and visible in slow coils of smoke. Lewis was nodding. Ambrose, half alert, fumbled the cards in an attempt at a gambler's shuffle.

'So' – Fred had an amateur actor's sense of timing, with pregnant pauses, frequent emphasis – 'so, I says, "I'm telling *you*, Sir Douglas, you've got *no* chance." Enough said.' Fred beamed knowingly.

'And what was the outcome?' asked Ambrose.

'Very democratic. We took a vote on it.'

'On whether to fight the battle of Passchendaele?'

'Sir Douglas an' the staffer, whatsisface, votes for bashin' the Boche; your Uncle Fred votes agin'; an' Marshal Foch abstains, though it was clear 'e was on my side. To cut a long story short: the "ayes" 'ave it, we fight the battle, an' the rest is 'istory.'

This impossible tale seemed to satisfy everyone except Guy. Sensing that it might be a breach of etiquette he still asked, 'You were very close to Field Marshal Haig?'

'I was 'is *driver*, Mr Parrot,' Fred answered solemnly. Seeing the explanation had failed to convince, he added, 'It's a position of *trust*. An' 'oo else was Sir Douglas to turn to, to get the opinion of the ordinary Tommy?'

Who indeed? Fred seemed proud of his sacerdotal role as the conscience and common sense of the British Army.

The records brought by Joe contained dance music. While the men continued their poker, Margot and Julia circled round them in a slow foxtrot, Margot taking the man's part. In Guy's experience, women in such circumstances normally held each other apart and moved as though pushing a pram, but Margot had Julia in a close embrace. Their cheeks touched. Margot clasped a cigarette between the fingers of her right hand. Once she kissed Julia's ear, provoking no more than a smile. Julia danced as if dreaming.

'I'll take two,' said Ambrose, exchanging cards. He struck an attitude, holding them close to his chest, allowing his eyes to close to slits, a cigarette dangling from his lips. Interpreting a glance from Guy he relented and said disarmingly, 'Oh, dear, am I overacting again?'

'You're always overacting,' Lewis observed coolly.

Ambrose put his cards down. 'The Poet speaks!'

'Overacting, posturing and wasting your life as a mountebank who at heart hates himself.'

Ambrose did not answer directly but turned to Guy and, as if he were a dowager with a hearing problem, said with the confidence of the truly tactless, 'Did you know, dear boy, that Shelley used to din this same point into Byron's ear as they tootled around in boats? He claimed that George was trivialising himself. *The Corsair*? Piffle! *Childe Harold*? A trifle!' His voice lowered. '*Entre nous*, dear Percy's poetry was a total failure in his lifetime. Only the energy and simpering of his widow rescued him from a just obscurity. Can you therefore imagine what George's relief must have been when our boy failed to return from his boating trip? I say no more. I make no accusations …

'Lewis, what do you want of me? Is it *my* fault that I did not join Our Glorious Dead? Would it suit your tender soul to stand at the Cenotaph while the band plays a tune on the big sassoon and weep at the blue-eyed, poppy-lipped boys Who Shall Return No More? For, alas, some of us *did* return and – wonder of wonders! – we were ugly, unheroic and ignoble, and our youthful promise turned out to be unpromising. Contrary to popular supposition, there is no wisdom to be got from the experience of war, merely sentiment. Our shame and horror make us no more fit to prevent the next war than our fathers were to prevent the last.'

Evidently Lewis had heard much of this before, for he replied calmly, 'I haven't asked you to write war poetry.'

'Nor do I. I write rubbish, which makes me inordinately proud and not a little *rich*, though – I am speaking to you, Guy – inexplicably short of cash at times to settle with the likes of Joe. Frankly, Lewis, I do not believe you. You fail to understand that my triviality and cynicism are the true and perfect expression of such wisdom as there is to be had out of the late hostilities. Instead, you want pathos and gruesome realism.'

Ambrose stood and began to recite.

'Today we have naming of parts. Yesterday
We touched on "erogenous zones". And tomorrow
Is fucking – the do's and don'ts. But today,
Today we have naming of parts. The howitzers
Roar and brag as they shell the forward trenches,
And today we have naming of parts.

'This is your ugly mug. And this
Is your stupid brain, which is totally useless
In the barracks or the brothel. And this moist spot is the cunt,
Which in your case you have not got. The enemy
Stumbles in blindness across the erogenous zone,
Which in our case we have not got.

'This is a woman's tit, which is always stroked
With a gentle graze of the palm. And please do not let me
See anyone squeezing the nipple. You can do it quite easily
If you have any softness of touch. The shellfire
Scours the bomb-proofs and the dug-outs, grazing on lives
Without any softness of touch.

'And this, my lads, is your finger. The purpose of this
Is to open the crack, as you see. We can slide it
Firmly backwards and forwards: we call this
Greasing the way. And firmly backwards and forwards
The bayonet is thrust and withdrawn from the enemy:
They call it greasing the way.

'They call it greasing the way: it is perfectly easy
If you have any softness of touch: like the face
And the cunt, and a woman's breast, and the chance to love,
Which in our case we have not got; and the guns' barrage
Ceasing on start of the attack as the bayonet thrusts
Backwards and forwards.
For today we have naming of parts.'

When Ambrose finished, there was a stillness broken
only by the last phrases of song from the gramophone.

Then Fred, emboldened by encounters with field marshals and regimental sergeant-majors, spoke. 'I think that was quite out of order, Mr Carmody. All that effing and blinding in front of the ladies, and taking the piss out of Our Departed Heroes, if you'll pardon my French.'

'Do be quiet, Fred,' Ambrose answered sternly.

There was, in the room, a ukulele. It was one of those odd objects brought for obscure purposes, like Lewis's cricket bat. Ambrose took it now and started to sing.

'The dreaming spires of Oxford reach up unto the stars,
But I, who am more earthly, prefer the local bars,
Where the price of sin is a glass of gin, and the true sin moderation,
And the wise man mocks at the dose of pox he may get from fornication:
For a soldier out of luck
Will always want a fuck.

'Annabelle and Mirabelle, Dorabelle and Clara,
Mary, Magda, Millicent, Margaret and Sarah:
Do I love them? Yes I do.
And bless their wanton hearts,
For today we have naming of tarts.

'The stately homes of England are strictly for the bores,
Unlike the humble cottage, beloved of humble whores,
Where "the air like wine" smells of stale urine and there are no likely wenches,
And we take our fun from a private's bum as we used to in the trenches:
For the urgent needs of war
Have brought our morals far.

'Fred and Ted and Joe and Sam, they and many another,
Albert Frith from Hammersmith, his cousin and his brother:
How I loved them! Yes I did.

And all their wayward arts,
For today we have naming of tarts.'

His face sweating at the final crescendo, Ambrose cried, 'Hay thaynk yew!' like a music-hall turn, bowed and burst into tears.

CHAPTER ELEVEN

1930

Guy woke in the small hours feeling dehydrated and crapulous, and lay for a while in darkness with the smell of a chamber pot, the crepitation of roof timbers and the hooting of an owl somewhere among the pines and chestnuts. Then, having, in his fuddled state, forgotten the carafe of water he usually took to his room, he decided to make an expedition down to the kitchen to slake his thirst.

By night and moonlight, the saloon was an aquaeous green, like water whose even colour is stirred by the shadows of passing clouds and bounded only by haze and reflections. Or (so Guy thought from the agonised confessions of a former soldier) like a trench filled with the tremulous yellow-green air of a gas attack.

Forgetting his thirst, Guy dropped on to a couch by one wall and watched the others shift uncertainly in patches of opalescence and lividity. He heard a cry. He supposed at first that it was a night bird, but the note of fretful horror was not a hunting call: rather the whimpering shriek of sleep terrors. Beyond the further wall, Julia was turning in her bed and mewling with infant fright.

There was nothing to be done, Guy told himself. He could not intrude on her sleeping. That same soldier had told him that one of the peculiar horrors of a gas attack was its loneliness. Objects lost their common form or vanished altogether. Extraneous noise was suppressed in concentration on one's own breathing and motion reduced to a muddy swimming under the cover of a clinging gas cape. Thought was limited to the terror, memory and repentance of a sinner called to judgment.

In glaucous light and loneliness, Guy struggled to grasp imaginatively Julia's interior world, doing so with an intensity he had never applied to his study of Elizabeth. He was discovering the inadequacy of the mental model by which he valued others: his assumptions of their kindness and decency. Not that he doubted for a moment that Elizabeth was kind and decent, but – so he now thought – she must be much more; and it was infantile on his part and a source of his present dissatisfaction to have ignored her depth and richness. It was odd that he should get this insight from Julia, for whom kindness and decency were evidently a struggle against the obscure agonies that troubled her soul.

Guy decided to take his early-morning walk by the sea. The path to the shore led through the pine woods past the villas scattered on the hill above Fiascherino. At this hour it was still shadowed with blues and greys. The shore was a raw umber, and the sea a wash of slate and indigo fading to turquoise and blue on the far horizon.

The young militiamen, chanting praises of Il Duce, clattered past as they did each morning. When they had gone, they revealed Lewis standing in thought by the water. To Guy, his handsomeness was startling. He had been swimming. He had dressed, but a towel was thrown over his shoulder and his blond hair was wet. He stared over the sea, his posture lithe and athletic.

He turned. 'Hullo, Guy.'

'Hullo.'

An eye was cast lazily after the retreating young men. 'Who are those boys?'

'I don't know,' said Guy. 'Conscripts or militia, I think. They come past every morning.'

'I see. Well, at least Mussolini has made his runners train on time. Do you care for a walk?'

'That's what I had in mind.'

They followed the shoreline, passing only the

occasional peasant with a basket or a mule piled with faggots.

Lewis asked, 'Did you enjoy Margot's play the other night?'

'Yes, I thought it amusing. But I rather wished I hadn't begun this business of Byron and the Shelleys.'

'Why not?'

'Because their situation was similar to ours. Byron was a genius and Shelley a poet. Ambrose is ... if not exactly a genius, something close to one. And you turn out poems, I believe.'

'I'm no Shelley,' Lewis confessed modestly. 'And who are you?'

'A nonentity, like Polidori.'

On a patch of rock a gull was tugging determinedly at something lodged in a crevice.

'The affair at La Spezia ended in tragedy,' Guy commented.

'Shelley drowned.'

'Or was murdered, if you believe Joe.'

'Exactly. And now Margot has introduced the theme of murder into her play.'

'She heard Joe going on about it, and the idea is quite amusing. I shouldn't take it seriously.'

'Do none of you take anything seriously?'

'Oh, we're *very* serious people.'

'Julia is trying to persuade me you're all perfectly horrible.'

'I suppose we are.'

Guy remembered Ambrose's distress the previous night when he recited his appalling poem. Guy felt a shudder of disgust at the sacrilege, the cruelty and tastelessness. Yet it was clear that Ambrose had not acted out of simple mockery.

'Is Ambrose a genius?' he asked.

'I think so – or, at least, potentially so. To date he's produced nothing but reviews and some frivolous plays.

But I do believe he has within him the capacity to express perfectly the spirit of our age.'

'And what's that? What should Ambrose be writing?'

Lewis smiled. 'I have absolutely no idea. Only Ambrose can tell us. His task is not to work to a goal set by others. He has to define it for himself and, if he does it right, it will be clear to us and we shall *know*.'

Guy glanced at him and caught a curious gleam in Lewis's eye, which he was put to some difficulty to interpret. It was fervent beyond ordinary admiration, and Guy could only suppose that Lewis was deeply sincere in his belief in his friend's qualities. Guy, on the other hand, thought the whole notion of genius odd, and wondered if it could indeed reside in someone as peculiar and occasionally unpleasant as Ambrose. Did genius consist of clarity of insight and perfection of technique, or was it something else? Was it possible for the morally compromised to possess it?

As the sun rose above the hills, the numinous glow faded from Lewis's cheeks to be replaced by an innocent earthliness. His limpid eyes and smile were no longer an epiphany, but frail and mortal. Guy thought of the tall, fair young men, only a few years older than himself, who had been destroyed in the maw of war. How ignorantly and joyously they had gone to their doom. Not that they could have survived in their transcendent beauty the lesser dooms of middle age and a comfortable job in the City.

'My, but you look thoughtful,' said Lewis cheerily.

Guy asked, 'How badly did Ambrose suffer in the war?'

'Ambrose? Not at all. He joined the Artists' Rifles in 'eighteen and sat it out until the Armistice doing training at Camberley.'

'But you told me that he caught a whiff of gas in France?'

'I did? That's Ambrose for you. One can't help taking him at his own estimation. I must have told you a part of the legend he's created for himself.'

'I see. And is there anything else I should know?'

'That depends. If he's hinted at splendid ancestry and connections, forget them. His mother keeps a lodging house in Ebury Street and his father is a traveller in ladies' hosiery. Admittedly he speaks with the voice of a belted earl, but so does every broken-down actor. I can tell I've shocked you.'

Guy was indeed shocked, though less by the revelation than by Lewis's cruelty in making it.

On their return to the house, Julia said, 'Ambrose has been asking for you. He's in bed, feeling under the weather.'

Guy was not disposed to be sympathetic, but when he went to the bedroom, he found Ambrose in a sweat and coughing violently. 'Guy!' he exclaimed. 'My saviour! Be a dear boy and get your bag of tricks, I'm feeling absolutely beastly.'

'I'll do it,' said Julia. This morning she was subdued and, when she looked at Ambrose, more distressed than was justified by what was, in all probability, a minor infection.

Guy took the other man's pulse and felt his brow, which was a little feverish. Ambrose had been making an effort to write. His bed was scattered with letters to agents and impresarios, and Guy noticed, too, a number of demands from creditors. He recalled his own debt to Signor Truffatore, which Ambrose had still not paid.

Beneath his florid dressing gown and silk pyjamas, Ambrose was a well-made man. To some degree his affectations and air of weariness drew attention away from the fact that he was still young, not more than a year or two above thirty. He still appeared on the stage in his own plays and tried to maintain a studied svelteness. Guy noticed a pair of Indian clubs and a medicine ball.

'Well, Doctor, shall I live?' The tone was flippant, but not the expression in the eyes.

'Do you often have these symptoms?'

'Too frequently, alas. Well?'

'I suspect you have nothing but a cold, but there seems to be an underlying weakness.' Guy hesitated at his own lack of experience. 'I don't know how to put this. Did you ever suffer from consumption as a child?'

'A Solomon come to judgment! What did I say? The lad has talent. Indeed, Guy, I *was* affected when younger, but I have been assured on impeccable authority that I am cured.'

'That's probably so, but there is some lasting damage which means you must be careful of chest infections lest they turn to pneumonia. I can write a prescription, but what I chiefly recommend is that you take things easy in bed for a day or two.'

'Command me and I obey, O Wise One.'

Julia again showed her concern once they had left the temporary invalid's room. She put a hand on Guy's arm and turned him so that her eyes could search his face.

'Tell me truthfully, Polly, how is he?'

'I've told the truth. He has a susceptibility, but he should be all right if he takes care of himself. And you? How are you?'

'I?'

'Are you sleeping well? Forgive me, but I was prowling about last night, looking for a drink of water. I heard you. You seemed to be having a nightmare.'

'Were you spying on me?'

'What an absurd idea – no. of course not.'

For a second it seemed that she was going to be angry. Then she shook her head and answered, 'Just as you say, it's an absurd idea. I'm full of absurd ideas. I simply can't get used to the notion that you are as nice and uncomplicated as you seem.'

'I think I should be offended. You make me sound like a child.'

'No, not that. Children are very wicked. You would be

closer to the mark if you said we were childish.'

'And are you wicked?'

'Very. We are each of us wicked and Ambrose above all. He is the sun and the rest of us merely planets revolving around him.' She smiled. 'What a fey thing to say! Nevertheless it's true. I wish I could convince you of how dangerous we are, and especially Ambrose because he is so very, very clever. But it's too late and the truth is too shameful. Ah, well! *Tant pis!* Kiss me, Guy.'

Guy kissed her, lightly, tentatively, not knowing what was expected.

Margot had an infinite capacity for sleep or basking in the sun. Julia was restless and easily bored. To relieve her ennui Guy broke off from his excavations and, on the following two days, took her shopping.

He exacted a promise that she would do nothing to get them arrested; but, though he kept his eye narrowly on her, on both occasions she returned to the villa with items he could not recall her buying. He mentioned the matter to Lewis, who simply laughed it off.

'Alas, our dear girl is a bold, talented and incorrigible thief.'

'She'll wind up in prison.'

'Too late to worry about that, I fear. Julia already has the convictions of her courage.'

There was no repetition of the kiss, only a flirtatious holding of hands as they walked the streets. Guy did not know what to make of it. Had the kiss marked the beginning of a great passion, it would have been immoral, but – in books at least – could have been excused for its romantic grandeur. In isolation, however, it seemed merely furtive, a shabby betrayal of Elizabeth. The memory remained, as of something unfinished and insidious, and Guy felt defenceless before its incomprehensibility.

Julia had said that she and the others were dangerous and amoral, if not worse. From the pains she had taken to make the point, Guy suspected it was an affectation like so much else. He remembered Byron, of whom it was said that he was mad, bad and dangerous to know. Though his heroic pose must have been bound to the poetry, for the life of him Guy could not see how or why or whether, in the end, it was worthwhile. Rather, it seemed to him cruel, selfish and sad. He concluded not that he was right about this, but that he must be deficient in understanding. That night, quite unlike his usual habit, he said a rosary to Guy of Shoreditch, whose dying words showed him to be equally versed in ignorance.

In the intervals between tennis and swimming, Lewis and Ambrose had settled to work. Tables were brought on to the terrace, and Gianni served cocktails and iced water. Guy thought Lewis was writing poetry. Ambrose was working on his play and, by way of relief, writing the libretto for a new revue. When he did this, he would take out the ukulele and entertain the others with snatches of verse. They were about London shop girls, ladies of easy virtue, and middle-aged women with difficult daughters. They sparkled with wit and incongruous charm when sung in the sultry sunshine under an Italian sky by an English gentleman in a frogged velvet smoking jacket.

One morning, when Signor Truffatore appeared at breakfast with the supplies, he produced a piece of paper. 'A cablegram. A guy I know in the post office gave it me.'

Ambrose announced, 'It's from Jackie in Marseilles. He's pottering about in a boat and will arrive here shortly. Will you stay for coffee, Joe?'

'Like to, but I gotta see a coupla guys,' said Joe, but he did not leave immediately. Instead, he took Guy aside.

'You have a problem?' asked Guy.

'Nope, but *you* gotta problem,' said Signor Truffatore.

'Ah. I see.'

'The money you owe me.'

'I've tried to explain that Signor Carmody is supposed to pay you.'

Signor Truffatore did not seem annoyed. He simply smiled and wagged his finger as if he had caught Guy in a childish lie.

'How much is it?'

'About forty-five thousand lire.'

'Oh? Oh! Good God, that's five hundred pounds! I haven't got five hundred pounds.'

'Whatever. Point is, I got the scratch from some friends–'

'A coupla guys?'

'–and they are old-fashioned about collecting their dues.'

'May I ask how old-fashioned?'

'*Very* old-fashioned.'

Guy decided that he really must have the matter out with Ambrose and also with Lewis, who continually cadged from him while excusing his failure to cash his bankers' draft. He mentioned the matter to Margot, who was uncomprehending.

'Of course Ambrose hasn't any money. He's rich.'

'I'm afraid your logic escapes me.'

'Does it? Then I'm not sure I know how to explain. You see, I've always been rich, and so I've never had any money. One simply borrows. I believe the system is called "credit". I've no idea why.'

'And when do you repay your debts?'

'I don't know that we ever do. They just sort themselves out.'

Exasperated, Guy said, 'But I'm *not* rich!'

'Poor thing,' Margot sympathised. 'My father used to say that the poor should never borrow. I imagine that's good advice.'

The difficulty was that Guy had seen Ambrose's mail, which he left lying about. Some of it was from agents and theatre owners accounting for box-office receipts. *Lighting up Piccadilly* and *Imperfect Tense* had been enormous successes and the reported profits made Guy dizzy. On the other hand, among these items of correspondence were writs and solicitors' letters demanding huge sums. Guy was ashamed at his spying, but his own debts were now so pressing that, if Ambrose did not settle soon with Signor Truffatore, he saw himself fleeing the country pursued by Mafiosi.

Behind it all was a mystery. Guy had visited Ambrose's apartment and seen his motor cars, and, although luxurious, they were well within his means. Nor, among the letters, were there any from bookmakers or stockbrokers recording gambling losses or failed investments. The question was inescapable. Where was all Ambrose's money going?

Guy was strolling into Lerici to buy some tools when he was stopped by a handsome sailor.

'I believe I know you, sport,' said the sailor.

'I don't think so,' said Guy.

'Sure I do. We met once at Uncle Sammy's. Are you still taking the heads off of trumpeters?'

Guy had only a dim recollection of the events of that evening, but he realised who this must be. 'I do apologise. You must be Commander Ferris.'

'I was last time I looked. But skip the "Commander". My friends call me Jackie. And you'll be Guy Polly.'

'Parrot.'

'If you say so. I guess I'm heading in the right direction for Ambrose's place?'

'Yes. I'll come with you, if you like. I can finish my errands later. Did you come by boat?'

'It's moored a little way back there. I thought I'd stretch my legs on land.'

Guy took one of the canvas kitbags the Commander was carrying. It was heavy, but Ferris carried the other effortlessly. He was a large man, rather taller than Guy and long in the leg. On closer examination, his naval accoutrements were confined to a cap and a pair of blue deck-shoes. For the rest he wore baggy white trousers, a shirt of the same colour and a blue neckerchief which gave him a slightly raffish air. His voice, like his movements, was very easy, even in tone with a barely perceptible Yankee drawl and occasional notes or words confirming he had spent a deal of time in England.

Approaching the house, Guy called out, 'Hullo! Look who I've got with me!'

Margot was lounging on some towels spread on the terrace. Ambrose was sitting at a table with his papers and giving instructions to Signor Truffatore.

'You know Margot and Ambrose, but you haven't met Joe,' Guy said to the newcomer, adding jokingly, 'Signor Truffatore has a brudda in Detroit.'

'The name's Cesare,' said Joe sullenly. 'You probably know him.'

'Cesare? Could be. Hullo, Margot. Glad to see you're still looking gorgeous. You look all right, too, Ambrose. Julia here?'

'Inside.' Ambrose looked at Signor Truffatore and said, 'I imagine you've got a coupla of guys to see.'

To Guy's surprise the answer was 'They can wait. I'll take you up on that drink.'

'Very well,' said Ambrose somewhat sourly. 'Guy, be a dear boy and bring some grappa for Joe. Jackie drinks Scotch. Are you still taking it with tepid water *à l'anglaise*?'

'That's right.'

Guy went to get the drink. Ambrose's reception of the amiable American struck him as slightly frosty, and Signor Truffatore's reaction was downright odd. But when he returned he found everyone on the terrace, including Lewis and Julia, conversing apparently normally. The others were putting questions about the voyage from Marseilles, and Jackie Ferris was answering them. Guy had already noticed that he was not prone to volunteering information and his answers were economical, though delivered pleasantly enough. He had a knack of conveying that he found any question amusing and could say more if he chose to.

'I gather you need some money for that boat of yours,' Ambrose said.

'You got it, old sport.'

'Is there any chance that some day you'll be finished with this speed-record business? I merely ask.'

'When I've broken that one, I kind of had a mind to try for the Atlantic sailing record.'

'Dear me, what an active fellow you are. And will that be expensive?'

The Commander gave a throaty laugh. 'I guess so. I was hoping Julia would help out. Julia?'

'I'd love to, Jackie,' said Julia. Guy thought she sounded glum. Ferris tipped his glass towards her in acknowledgement.

Ambrose said, 'You'll be staying a while, of course. The facilities are somewhat primitive, but I've had Maria make up a room for you on the top floor.'

'That's pretty swell of you.'

'Think nothing of it. It's Liberty Hall, dear boy.'

Later that day Guy came across Lewis. He was sitting alone in the saloon with a book of poetry in front of him, but he was not reading.

'Penny for your thoughts.'

'What? Oh, hullo, Guy.'

'You look pensive.'

'Do I? I suppose I do. I was just remembering something about Byron and the Shelleys. Did you know that they kept company with a pirate?'

'They did?'

'Yes. What a rum bunch they were. Much queerer than we are.'

CHAPTER TWELVE

1945

'Are you going to take a look at Tommy's corpse?' asked Jenkins casually over breakfast.

'Not while I'm eating,' said Guy. Afterwards he forgot.

The process of converting the Villa Esperanza into the British Autonomous Hospital was moving apace. Guy had carefully measured out the rooms so that the beds and ancillary functions received their due allowance of space according to King's Regulations. Having thus formed a definite view of the building's capacity and mapped out the location of the various facilities, he was working on a detailed inventory of his requirements.

The mapping exercise had obliged him to study the building thoroughly. Some parts he had no recollection of visiting before, for example the chamber in the small tower reminiscent of a campanile that graced one corner of the building. Also, on the floor above the *piano nobile* was a collection of rooms: a nursery and space for servants, children and guests. As far as he could remember, the only person who had lodged on that floor was Jackie Ferris.

After their brief conversation, Nessuno had vanished. Perhaps to Genoa to find a boat bound for Argentina. It was unreasonable to expect him to stick around until he was hanged. On the other hand, it was a pity he had gone. Guy would have liked to put some more questions.

Memory was a strange thing. Often Guy had revisited places after a lapse of years and found, to his surprise, that the details came back to him as if he had never left. But this was not true of the Villa Esperanza. Although it was vaguely familiar, the details escaped him. For instance, he could not be certain who had occupied the room where Nessuno had made his nest, though he had a notion it might have been Lewis. Moreover he felt a reluctance to discover more. He did not wish to examine this feeling, but thought it was akin to dread.

Jenkins noticed. 'You don't seem to be entirely on the ball,' he said.

'I hope you're not criticising a superior officer.'

'Perish the thought. But you do seem to be letting things slip.'

'For instance?'

'I'm fairly sure that Nick and Jimmy are sleeping together. Do you think we should put a stop to it?'

'I don't see why.'

'Fair enough. And what should we do about Tommy's corpse?'

'I didn't know he'd died.'

'Very droll. I'm referring to the body up on the hill. If you like, I can get rid of it. I don't suppose anyone will bother.'

'What a damn nuisance,' said Guy, without answering the point.

It came up again the following day.

'What does the Captain want to do about they poor bugger whose skelantan we found?' asked Corporal Long.

'Do we have to do anything? Is it getting in the way?'

'It canna stay where it is.'

'Where is it?'

'In the big hole you was havin' us dig oot.'

Guy agreed to accompany the Corporal to the excavations. On the way he remembered something else – another place, one that had, in the past, evoked strong emotions.

'Wait a minute,' he said. 'There's something else I want to take a look at.'

He found the path and it led to the clearing and the grotto. The fountain was still there – not working, of course – but the figures of Hadrian and Antinous had gone, leaving the bare pedestal.

The hole was the cistern. Guy had calculated that the supply of water from the spring was insufficient for the hospital. He intended to divert it into the cistern. which could fill when not being used. His inventory listed a pump and a purification unit. Jenkins had inspected the cistern and reported that, as Guy expected, in the intervening years it had again filled with rubble and loose spoil from the hillside. Guy had deputed Corporal Long and the privates to dig it out.

'It's a damn nuisance, war,' opined Jenkins philosophically. 'Bodies all over the place where one least wants them. Bloody inconsiderate.'

Digging had stopped at a point near the bottom where the upper part of a skull had emerged. The nose and eyeholes were filled with soil. Other bones peeked our here and there.

'Odd, though, that it should have turned up here,' Jenkins continued. 'I don't know that there was any fighting to speak of, and the covering of earth suggests it's been here a while. I suppose the Fascists bumped somebody off and tucked the evidence away. They weren't above such things, so I hear.'

Guy was not certain what King's Regulations had to say on the subject of doubtful corpses. Also, if the deceased had been a civilian it might be a matter for the police (assuming there were any police) or, God forbid, the Americans, who seemed to be vaguely in charge of the area. He gave directions to exhume the remains, which appeared to comprise only bones, and bring them into the house where he could study them and decide exactly what it was he had on his hands.

'Speaking of corpses,' said Jenkins, 'I don't like your idea for locating the mortuary. Too near the kitchen. It could put a fellow off his food.'

For a while Guy toyed with the idea that the skeleton had been overlooked when he cleared the cistern years before. His chief memory was of a large rock whose removal had puzzled himself and old Enzo, until, in the end, the problem was solved by Jackie Ferris and some tackle from his boat. Afterwards they proceeded with the digging, then re-pointed the ancient brickwork so that the cistern was watertight. In the course of these operations they reached the bottom. Guy stood on the stone floor and looked up at a square patch of daylight. Jackie finished smoking a cigarette, flipped it into the hole, grinned and said, 'Congratulations, old sport.' And Fred, who claimed to have masterminded the work, announced, 'I told you I was right.' No, it was impossible that the body had been there.

Jenkins's suggestion of a Fascist crime was not implausible. Nor could an accident be ruled out. Someone – old Enzo, perhaps – wandering the hillside in darkness might have fallen in, though there was a stone cover. There was even the possibility that the long-lost owner of the Villa Esperanza had reappeared and been murdered by his lawyers, who had embezzled the rents. Above all, Guy told himself, there was no reason to suppose any connection between this corpse and the events of that fateful summer, and every reason to believe the contrary. There *had* been a disappearance, a death and a body. But it was not this body. Guy wished he could discuss the matter with Nessuno, by whom all things were known.

The bones were laid out on a trestle table in the saloon and Corporal Long was toasting the deceased with a glass of beer. Guy examined the remains without emotion. Unlike the recently dead, damaged and surprised, still in their fleshly integuments, bones were merely objects.

'Did you find any identity tags?'

The Corporal shook his head. Guy picked up a scrap of cloth. It did not appear to be from a uniform. The corpse was not that of a soldier.

'Is this all?'

Again a nod. 'Will ye have a beer?' asked Long.

The skeleton was incomplete. The pelvis and the long bones of the legs were missing, which made it difficult to estimate the height, or, for that matter, the sex. Guy had no experience of forensic pathology but thought he could have told the sex from the shape of the sciatic notch. In the absence of the pelvis, he could judge only by the skull, the size of the supra-orbital ridge and nuchal crest. Tentatively, he concluded that the body was probably that of a man.

The left forearm showed a healed greenstick fracture. There was no sign of arthritis in the joints. The sutures of the skull were not fully closed. The man (if it were a man) had not been forty years old, possibly much less. Guy would have been more confident if he could have inspected the third molars, but they and most of the other teeth were missing, probably lost in the heaps of spoil removed from the cistern and tipped.

Noticing teethmarks about the bones of the wrist, Guy understood why the skeleton was incomplete. Animals had fed on it, dragging away portions to their lairs. Foxes or the descendants of a starving yellow bitch he had once known. The horribleness of this image lay not in the feasting carrion-eaters but in the implicit loneliness. Buried in the sentiments of his Catholic upbringing was the idea of the communion of the dead with the living, and the assembly of saints before the throne of God. The solitary, unmourned dead were a challenge to these comforting myths. Guy was thoughtful but not too distressed. The death of a stranger is rarely distressing. At best it is bleak and to be forgotten.

Jenkins ambled into the saloon smoking a cigarette and glanced at the table. 'The fellow was on the short side, wasn't he?'

'He's got no legs.'

'Poor chap. How did he die? I suppose losing his legs

might account for it.'

'They were removed after death, by animals.'

Jenkins seemed to doubt this, perhaps because he suspected that Guy's pretensions to any skill were as fraudulent as his own. 'Righty-ho. If you say so. How did he die, then?'

'I don't know.'

'Ah.'

'There doesn't appear to be any damage to the bones, apart from an old fracture. He might have suffered soft-tissue damage.'

'Or disease.'

'That, too.'

They stared at the bones for a while. Then, Jenkins said, 'Well? What do we do with him?'

'I've no idea. What do King's Regulations say on the subject?'

'Search me. I'm afraid you've caught me out there. I never had much use for them.'

Guy decided to sleep on the problem, but found he could get no rest. In the small hours he took a torch and returned to the saloon.

Corporal Long had laid out the remains in approximate order except for the hands and other small bones, which were gathered into a pile. Guy picked them over and began idly to arrange them. He was left with the hyoid, which showed a fracture. The meaning of this escaped him. He returned to bed.

'I've been mulling it over,' said Jenkins next day, 'and I think we should dump this problem in Thunder's lap.'

Guy had no better solution.

The difficulty of making telephone calls remained; though Corporal Long, in his enterprising fashion, had devised an unorthodox system which appeared to work. While Guy was hesitating over a formal approach to the

Americans to use their facilities, Long had fraternised with his fellow NCOs and gained access to their mess. This was housed in a former dance hall in La Spezia. It was, by the bleak standards of the British Army, lavishly equipped.

'Do you mind if I use your telephone, Corp?' Guy asked.

The mess was organised by a Corporal Pulaski, who went under the honorific of 'Corp'. He was young, as most soldiers were, and carried himself with athletic beefiness. Corp came from Detroit and, in a momentary lapse when Corporal Long had first introduced Guy to the mess and filled him with American beer and hamburger, Guy had enquired if Corp knew Cesare Truffatore.

'Everyone knows Cesare,' said Corporal Pulaski and rubbed the side of his nose enigmatically.

'The telephone?' Guy repeated. 'I can use it?'

'One hand washes the other.'

Guy was not familiar with the expression, but had an idea that it related to dealings between Corp and Corporal Long which were not wholly connected with the British Autonomous Hospital.

The telephone was a fine instrument and at certain times of day could be used even to make calls to the United States. Its drawback was a rather public location, close by the bar. Also, tonight there was a band playing, a quartet of Negro servicemen. With a disconcerting frisson of déjà vu, Guy noticed that the trumpeter had no head.

'A beer, Guy?' Corp lounged on the corner of the bar, within earshot.

Guy was both disarmed and dismayed by the Americans' informality and wished, at times, that he were Jenkins, who would handle it with a more democratic spirit. He could not think of a way of dispensing with Corp's genial intrusiveness.

'Colonel Box? Parrot here. I apologise for calling so late, but we're still having trouble with telephones.'

Swift to gain the upper hand, the Colonel asked,

'Where the hell are you? It sounds like a dance hall or a knocking shop.'

'You must be getting some interference on the line.'

'If you say so, but Glenn Miller music is a rum sort of interference.'

'It's probably from a radio somewhere.'

Guy noticed, with a shameful pride, that, during his years in the Army, he had acquired a facility for lying. His latest effort was admired by Corp who gave a thumbs-up sign.

'We have a little problem here,' he told Colonel Box. 'We've found a corpse in the hospital grounds.'

'Then you'd better bury the beggar.'

'Well, yes, of course. Sooner or later he will have to be buried.'

'Good! That's that sorted. I don't know why you're troubling me with a little matter of hygiene.'

'I thought it went rather beyond the question of hygiene.'

'Does it?'

'I think so. We are speaking about a corpse. Shouldn't someone be informed?'

Colonel Box had a rooted objection to informing anyone about anything; with the possible exception of battle orders, it was more important to keep secrets from friends than from enemies. After a moment's hesitation, he asked, 'You didn't happen to kill the poor blighter yourself, did you?'

'Of course not,' said Guy, offended.

'What about Jenkins or that little Scotsman who murdered the Fascist official?'

'It was never proven. In fact he was made up to sergeant.'

'That means nothing. With murderers one has to hang them or promote them.'

'I can't say. However, Corporal Long didn't murder this fellow. He died long ago.'

'Before the war?'

'Most likely.'

Relieved, Colonel Box said, 'Well, if it all happened before the war, I don't see that it's our business at all. The British Army isn't responsible for clearing up other people's messes.'

'May I have that order in writing?'

'No, you bloody well can't!'

The call finished, Corp asked, 'So, Guy, what are you going to do?'

Guy was too tired to be evasive. 'My Colonel says I'm to get rid of the corpse.'

Corporal Pulaski took this news surprisingly badly. 'Bastard,' he muttered.

'Oh, it's not so bad as all that,' Guy answered, curious as to why he was comforting the other man.

'Bastard!' Corp repeated more loudly. 'Get rid of the corps! Doesn't he know that the corps are the backbone of the whole goddamn Army?'

When he returned to the Villa Esperanza, Guy found that the bones had been removed from the table in the saloon. He asked Jenkins about them.

'Tommy took them,' said Jenkins.

'Did you order him to?'

'I've rather given up on orders as far as Tommy's concerned. He did it off his own bat.'

'Do you know what he's done with them?'

'Not a clue.'

There was no point in pursuing the subject. Corporal Long had taken the jeep and gone with Nick and Jimmy to some dubious rendezvous in town. So long as work on the hospital proceeded, Guy no longer cared what the men did in their spare time, though he lived in dread of a visit from the American military police. He went to bed.

He had taken a room on the uppermost floor. The low ceiling and small window reminded him of his bedroom as a child, and the place was free of the associations of the first-floor apartment where once he had slept. Taking off his clothes and listening to the creaking of the rafters as the house settled down after the heat of the day, Guy remembered that Jackie Ferris had not been alone up here. Madame Hecate had also been given a room. Guy recalled how grateful she was. 'Such kindness!' she said meekly. The kindness had been Ambrose's, and Guy believed that, for once, his actions had been entirely disinterested. Madame Hecate had been a poor creature, abandoned by circumstances until Ambrose took her in. Only now did Guy suspect that, in her quiet way, she had divined perfectly what was going on. Had she not tried to issue a warning?

In the morning Guy put Madame Hecate out of his mind. He doubted – or at least half-doubted – that she was as wise as he supposed. One of the frustrating aspects of his self-conscious innocence was that he was always attributing to others insights he did not himself possess. It was this that disabled him in his dealings with Corporal Long. Had he learnt that the Corporal had made a pact with the Devil, he would have been inclined to credit the rumour. Admittedly the man was only a corporal, but Guy suspected that was simply because it suited him and that he could have been a general if he had so chosen. Guy decided to search him out at the first opportunity and settle this affair of the disappearing bones.

'Where are they?' he asked sternly.

At his ease the Corporal answered, 'Dinna fash yesel'.' He waved a hand toward the sea. 'They've gone where naebody will ever find them. And guid riddance, too.'

'You had no orders to dispose of them,' Guy persisted.

'I had nae orders to keep them,' Long answered reasonably. 'What did Thunder – I mean Colonel Box – have to say?'

'He told me to get rid of them.'

'Well, there ye are. Nae harm done. I knew that's what he'd want.'

Guy wondered if Long had eavesdropped on his telephone conversation, but that was impossible. Of course, he might have got the information from Corp – but that could only have been later, after he had already thrown the bones away. The horrible idea came to Guy that Corporal Long was telepathic. If he was, Guy's position was truly hopeless.

He tried to salvage his dignity. He said, 'The point, Corporal, is not whether any harm has been done, but the fact that you acted without orders.'

'Permission to speak out of turn, sir?'

Guy hesitated, fearing some frightening truth. 'Oh, very well, permission granted.'

Corporal Long smiled. He offered one of his Indian-made Victory cigarettes. He said, 'The fact is, Mr Parrot, that the job of officers is tae carry out orders. And the job of corporals is tae use their initiative.' He winked.

Guy put this point to Jenkins when they went for a run in the early evening.

'There's a lot of truth to what Tommy says' was the answer.

They fell to discussing what they would do on return to civilian life. Guy said he would go back to his general practice and to Elizabeth. This had been true until recently, but the memories brought back by the Villa Esperanza had cast a cloud over all his plans. How could he face the future with confidence, when he did not understand the past? Again he missed Nessuno, who held the key.

'And you?' he asked. 'Back to the bank?'

'No thanks.'

'What, then?'

Out of breath, they stopped. Guy looked toward the sea. The houses of Porto Venere had turned purple in the

155

sunset. The grey American warships were indigo riding on plum-coloured water.

'You must promise not to laugh,' said Jenkins. 'While we've been here, Tommy and I have got to talking. He's thinking of setting up a little scaffolding business once we're home. It should do well because of all the reconstruction that's needed. We've discussed forming a partnership.'

'Do you know anything about scaffolding?'

'Absolutely nothing. Of course, Tommy would be the brains of the business.'

'Of course.'

'And I'd be the front man – to glad-hand the customers, that sort of thing. I have a little capital.'

'It would be a risk.'

'Don't you ever take risks, Guy?'

Guy considered the question seriously. 'No, I don't suppose I do.'

Any hope of forgetting the bones ended when they came to Guy in his sleep. He wanted to know the identity of the dead man and the reason he had died and been left in the disused cistern. Mentally he reviewed the remains, dredging his memory of anatomy classes at Bart's.

The hyoid bone was fractured, which was unlikely to have happened post mortem since the other bones were intact. His mind's eye placed it in the skeleton and he pictured how it might have got broken. There was an answer and, by this act of imagination, it came to him quite quickly.

The dead man had been strangled.

CHAPTER THIRTEEN

1930

Commander Ferris was an easy man, content to fall in with whatever the others were doing.

In the evening he took Guy's seat at the poker table. This suited Guy, who habitually lost and preferred to chat with Julia or dance with Margot. He had grown bored with Fred's stories, though these now assumed a nautical cast.

'Before the battle of Jutland,' began one gem, 'I says to Admiral Jellicoe, "As far as sinking the German fleet goes, you've got *no* chance." Afterwards *he* says to *me*, "*Fred*, you were *right*." '

'You don't say, old sport,' answered Ferris, scooping another pot.

Lewis proposed to Guy that they go swimming at Fiascherino in the cool of the morning. Guy went to Julia's rooms to invite her. She was working at her writing table.

'Oh, hullo, Guy,' she said with a bright smile. She was wearing a dress of white linen that absorbed the muted colours of daylight, reminding Guy of a painting by Vermeer. Her hair was drawn back in a loose silk turban, leaving her forehead unnaturally large but pale, curved and faintly erotic. Guy was stirred to remember the kiss she had given him, and wondered if it was a challenge or invitation to which he had failed to respond. He wondered, too, which of the several Julias had kissed him: the spoiled socialite, seductive and slightly vulgar; the mature woman who hinted at a dark past; or the fey innocent who seemed to be present this morning? Each in her own way deeply attracted him, and he feared them all. And yet he was fiercely happy to be here.

'Lewis and I are going for a swim. Would you like to come?'

'What about the others?'

'Ambrose is unwell. Margot has some serious sleeping to catch up on. And Jackie has gone up the hill with his binoculars; he didn't say why, but I suppose he's watching birds.'

'I'm afraid I can't.'

'Why not?'

'I'm writing my story.'

Guy had forgotten about the stories. In fact he had rather hoped the subject had gone away.

'Why? Surely it wasn't your idea?'

'No, of course not. But Ambrose insisted. He's punishing me.'

'What for?'

'I don't know. For not being Ambrose, I suspect.'

'That sounds odd, if I may say so.'

'Not if you regard it as a sin – which Ambrose does.'

Julia offered a cigarette, lit her own, sighed and, in that gesture, made the painterly scene vanish.

Guy asked, 'What will you write about?'

'Oh, the same old stuff, you know: Byron and the Shelleys. Don't groan. I want to find out what happened. How *did* Percy die?'

'He drowned in a sailing accident.'

'Perhaps.'

'Perhaps? Well, if you say so. Personally, I don't damn well care.'

Guy mentioned this conversation to Lewis when, later, they were lying on the sand. Lewis had insisted on bringing Gianni with them to carry towels and deckchairs and fetch beer from the bar. He was now standing a little way off, staring impassively out to sea.

'There's something eerie about that child,' said Lewis,

'as though he's waiting for Death. I imagine he'll die beautifully.'

'What a horrible thing to say.'

'Is it? The Romantics thought Death was beautiful. Romance is about Death, not Love. It's something to be courted and won.'

'You're speaking of Death in the abstract.'

'Not necessarily. Shelley couldn't swim and was a fool with boats, yet he insisted on sailing. Byron was sick, but he abandoned his mistress to go to Greece, ingratitude, disease and the grave. Think of poor Chatterton killing himself. *That's* who Gianni reminds me of. I wonder if he writes poetry?'

Guy looked again at the boy who was standing by a dinghy. Was he all-knowing or all-ignorant? Reassuringly, he had raised one foot to scratch the other with a toenail. Turning back to Lewis, Guy said, 'I hate all this business about Byron. Especially the matter of murder.'

'I know what you mean. The atmosphere at the villa has at times been rather creepy.'

'So you've noticed?'

'I'm reminded of those ghost stories where nothing much happens, but there is a chill in the air.'

'I thought Jackie Ferris got a very frosty reception. Fortunately it's eased off a bit.'

'I don't put that down to ghosts or murders. In my experience holidays are often tense at the beginning. Here!' Lewis had lost interest and was calling to the boy. He threw a stick into the water. 'Show us your paces. Go get it!' Gianni sprang into life like an automaton switched on. 'I should have asked if he could swim,' Lewis remarked carelessly.

They watched the boy. The stick had not gone very far, but a current had caught it and was taking it out.

'Speaking of Jackie,' said Guy, 'how well do you know him?'

'Only gossip and what I've read in the papers. I didn't actually meet him until that night at Uncle Sammy's. I rather like him, even if he is a blackguard.'

'Is he? Then why does Julia give him money for his boat?'

'Oh, the rich have an affinity with blackguards. They keep them as pets. Or possibly it's the other way round.'

The boy was swimming strongly. It was difficult to see him in the sunlight glinting off the water.

'I suppose we must pour our own drinks,' Lewis observed. He fumbled in the hamper.

'How do things stand between you and Margot?' asked Guy.

'Now *there's* a frank question.' Lewis paused, then pulled a cork, poured and offered Guy a glass. 'What shall I say? We rub along. You'll have noted that it isn't exactly a *grande passion*. But one can't expect that of Margot. She's only half a person.'

'What do you mean?'

Lewis tapped his chest. 'No heart. They're all the same. She comes of a very sinister family.'

'The Davenants?'

'No, those are Raymond's people. I mean the Cyrils.'

The boy had now disappeared completely in the reflections. Guy began to grow concerned.

Lewis explained, 'The founder, William Cyril – I'm speaking of Henry the Eighth's time – did very well out of the Dissolution. That's when they acquired Fletchitt from the Carthusians. His son, also William, poisoned people on behalf of Sir Francis Walsingham; which is the Cyrils' notion of public service. A third backed Parliament against the Crown and, for his pains, picked up a baronetcy and a fortune from speculating in Irish land. However, he was wise enough one day to slip over to The Hague to welcome Charles the Second as his king and collect the reward of an earldom. From then on the family has continued in rapacious obscurity, opposing every measure for enlightenment or relief of the poor in the last two hundred years. Margot's elder brother, the present Earl, is a rabid hater of Jews and reputedly backs Odo Milne and his New Politics. Her younger brother, Lord Ballyhugh, is the Great Cham of the Bank of England. He holds to a chilling economic theory which requires closing every factory in Britain and firing every worker, all in pursuit of "sound money" – whatever that is. Do I make myself clear?'

'What about Margot's husband?' Guy asked. 'Doesn't he object to your … relationship?'

'Raymond? Not at all. There was never any sentiment there. It was simply a question of money. Raymond married Margot for it – a transaction perfectly acceptable to the Cyrils, who can't conceive of any other reason for wedlock. From their side it's all right to marry into "trade" occasionally, in order to replenish the family coffers. Raymond is much older than she is. He did well in the war: South American copper or tin or something. However it proved to be fairy gold – perhaps it was gold? He lost the lot in a revolution or a stock-market crash.'

'What does he do now?'

'Lives on credit in Hollywood and sleeps with actresses. There you have the measure of Margot's depth. Raymond finds American starlets more satisfying emotionally.'

'Why are you telling me this?'

'Because,' said Lewis, 'if I ever get bumped off, old man, you need look no further than Margot.'

Guy was still worried about the boy. The sea and sky were painful with white sunlight. Shading his eyes, he could see nothing of Gianni, merely a glimmer of distant sails and a cruiser steaming quietly up the Gulf.

'I suppose we'd better rescue him,' remarked Lewis, casually treading his cigarette into the sand. 'We can take the dinghy.'

'Do you know how?'

'I used to fool about in boats in the vacation.'

They pushed the dinghy into the water and clambered in. Lewis raised the sail and took the tiller. He warned Guy to keep his head low and keep a lookout. Slowly the boat drew out and Lewis let it catch the current, thinking to follow the direction in which the boy had been taken. Guy decided he had sat too long in the sun. He was dizzy and his neck burnt.

'Why did you have to throw that stick?' he asked Lewis.

'I didn't think Gianni would go after it like a gundog. Talk about something else.'

They had gone out half a mile, further than was likely for the boy. Lewis turned the boat and began to beat back towards the shore.

In his anxiety Guy babbled, 'What do you know of Julia? Are she and Ambrose lovers? I see no sign. She has her own room.'

'You'd better ask them. I thought you'd decided that Ambrose was a pansy?'

'I don't know. But if they aren't lovers why is Julia here?'

'I suppose she must do something to pass the time while Hector is in Tangiers buggering Bedouins. I got the impression that you and she were becoming rather thick.'

'I like her,' said Guy, though 'like' was the wrong word and he was not sure of the correct one.

'She can be appealing – rather like Astarte or some other moon goddess, the object of a mystery cult. Of course, there is no mystery other than her husband. She likes to be pitied: fancies herself a Woman with a Past, like a character from Pinero. If you do like her, you shouldn't enquire too closely. On inspection, the Past is usually something mundane or disappointing, such as adultery. Ah, there he is!'

Gianni was floating on his back about fifty yards away. His eyes were closed; his arms and legs moved only fractionally. It was impossible to tell if he were in distress.

'Take my hand,' Guy said as they pulled alongside.

Gianni did so without sign of thanks or relief. 'No stick,' he said simply.

'Forget the damned stick. Are you all right?'

The boy nodded. He shook the water from his black hair and squatted in the bottom of the boat. Lewis set the sails to return to the beach.

'Lewis and I have had the strangest time,' Guy said when he next saw Julia. She was sitting with the others in the shade of the loggia reading whatever she had written that morning. 'Lewis threw a stick into the sea and Gianni went after it. He was caught by a current and might have drowned.'

'Is he all right?'

Guy was pleased to see some genuine concern.

Putting down his knitting, Ambrose said, 'What do you all think of going to Venice for a few days? Jackie?'

'Count me out. I'll hang around here a little longer and then push off back to France.'

'Where shall we stay?' asked Margot.

'Oh, somewhere – there's always somewhere.'

'I've got a pal,' said Ferris. 'Mikey Malvivente. He has a palace someplace. I could call him and fix it for you.'

'A member of the Venetian nobility, is he?' asked Ambrose.

'I think he's Sicilian. I know him from Chicago.'

To Guy's surprise Margot revealed another facet of her extensive social acquaintance.

'I do believe I've met him. My cousin Esmond, who lives in Canada, did some business with him in the importing line. I'm speaking of the time before Esmond retired.' She added lightly, 'He got himself shot.'

The subject faded and Guy was left uncertain if they would go to Venice or not.

That evening Guy walked alone up the hill. There was a

scent of wild leeks in the air. He stopped first at the cistern, where he still needed to erect an A-frame in order to remove the boulder. Then he pressed on higher until the pines gave way to oak and chestnut. In a clearing, he found Jackie Ferris sitting with a pair of binoculars to his eyes.

Guy sat beside him. 'Many birds?' he asked.

'Some.'

Guy had seen none. Sometimes great tits sang with stubborn repetition but not now. Already the bats were out.

Without removing his binoculars, the Commander said, 'Light me a cigarette will you, old sport?' Guy did so. Ferris continued evenly. 'Do you know your friend Truffatore spies on you for the police?'

'Joe?'

'The fellows he meets in town – I know the type.'

Guy was shocked. 'Should we give him the sack?'

'Nope.' The Commander put down his glasses, murmuring, 'The light's gone.' He smiled at Guy. 'There's no point in getting rid of Joe. After all, you're doing nothing wrong – are you?'

'Absolutely not!'

Ferris rose and dusted down his trousers. 'You ever drink a Screwdriver, Guy? Do you want I should make you one?'

'Later, perhaps.' Guy let the other man go down to the house while he took the path aside to the grotto and the statues of Hadrian and Antinous. Julia was already there.

'I've been to see Gianni,' she said. 'He's perfectly all right, thank God. I couldn't make out whether he was ever really in danger. He's a strange boy.'

'That was considerate, Julia.'

'I'm not a complete beast.'

'I never thought you were.'

She extended a hand and he held it. Together they examined the statues quietly.

After a while Julia said, 'Do you think they move?'

'The thought had occurred to me.'

164

'I wonder what they cost?' She glanced at Guy. 'I don't have money in mind. But all art costs something. I wonder who, in this case, paid the price?'

'The customer, I imagine.'

'Oh, no,' said Julia with a note of firmness. 'Where art is concerned, the customer rarely pays.'

'I don't understand.'

'You will … but not tonight,' she added more brightly. She gave him his second kiss. This time it was lingering and exploratory. Although Guy kept his arms by his sides, his hands necessarily held her waist lightly and she pressed her body to his. The kiss, which began so well, ended drily in a thin-lipped smile. Julia pushed him away and said, 'You don't want me to fall in love with you, do you? You're probably wise.'

'Actually, I think it's that I don't want to fall in love with you. It would be very easy to.'

'Because of Elizabeth?'

'Among other things.'

Julia stood pensively. 'You say the sweetest things quite unintentionally. Would it really be easy to fall in love with me?'

'Oh, yes,' Guy answered.

'Then why don't you?' She seemed genuinely curious.

'Because you frighten me.'

Julia giggled, but not mockingly.

Guy went on, 'I'm very conventional about love. I think it's a serious matter. Already I've hurt Elizabeth. I don't want to hurt you.'

'Why should you care? Aren't I capable of taking care of myself?'

'If one is in love, I think that's the last thing one is capable of doing.'

'I see. How very moral. Do you have *any* original thoughts on the subject of love?'

Guy smiled. 'No. In fact, I don't think there are any.' He had lost her hand and now found it again. 'Let's go and join the others. You can tell me about your story.'

They also had to explain the matter to Commander Ferris.

'It's a murder mystery, Jackie dear,' said Ambrose.

'Is that so? And who got rubbed out?'

'A fellow called Percy Shelley.'

Ambrose gave some general background. Percy had fled England with Mary and their child. Byron was in Italy. He had a mistress, Mary's half-sister Claire, whom he increasingly despised. In due course Shelley drowned at La Spezia.

'Those are the bare bones of the affair. Guy, in our first essay at the subject, proposed that Mary was in love with George, a powerful motive for which there is some evidence. After Percy's death, she and Byron continued on very intimate terms – I don't say as lovers (one never knows), but at least on terms of spiritual intimacy, if that expression doesn't sound too disgusting. So, dear boy, I repeat: one must allow that the motive for murder was there.'

'I guess so.'

They were drinking Screwdrivers to the Commander's recipe.

Ambrose was suitably enthused by them.

'Margot picked up the baton from Guy. She came out with it and said, in terms, that Mary and George planned to bump off Percy so that they might slake their lustful desires. Also, she suggested that Percy and Claire intended to kill Mary.' Ambrose glanced at her. 'Correct me if I'm wrong. As I understand it, Claire's motive in removing Mary was to get rid of a rival for George's affections. Percy's reasons are less clear, which seems to me a technical weakness in the plot. However, none of this seems to matter, since we know for a fact that Mary was *not* killed; so the suspicions thrown up against Claire and Percy seem to be a red herring, as it is called in the murder mystery trade.

'Finally,' said Ambrose, 'we have the character of the Hotel Manager.' He winked at Guy in memory of his performance. 'I have great hopes of him. He may turn out to be a version of the famous Butler Wot Done It. Admittedly, there are problems with such a solution, in that there is no historical evidence for the existence of the Hotel Manager. However, the authors of crime novels are notorious cheats.'

A bemused Commander Ferris nodded thoughtfully.

'Julia will now further enlighten us,' said Ambrose.

Returning with Guy from the grotto, Julia had explained something of her story.

'Lewis has become quite pedantic. He insists that we should treat the theory of Shelley's murder with proper seriousness.'

'Do you intend to do that?'

'No, of course not. The idea is completely absurd. However, Lewis has succeeded in confusing me by drawing attention to the facts of the case. Tell me, have you ever heard of Edward Trelawny?'

Guy had not.

'That's a pity,' Julia said doubtfully. 'Where should I begin?'

'At the beginning?'

'I'm not sure I can do that. There are an infinity of beginnings, even if there is only one ending.'

'I began with the evening at Diodati when Byron and the Shelleys told ghost stories and Mary came up with the idea of *Frankenstein*.'

'That's what I mean. Was that event really the beginning? Does it explain what happened? Lewis has been reminding me of the dates. The incident at Diodati occurred in 1815. Percy, Mary and Claire returned to England in September that year, leaving George in Italy. They didn't return to the Continent until the following spring and the group met again only in August 1818. By then George was estranged from Claire and would have nothing to do with her. He never met her again, and at the time of Shelley's death Claire was living in Florence. She was nowhere near the scene of our murder mystery and may be excluded as a suspect.'

'I see,' said Guy. He supposed he ought to respond in the same spirit. 'That makes things look pretty black for George, doesn't it? There aren't many suspects left, assuming that we also exclude Doctor Polidori for lack of motive –'

'He wasn't at La Spezia either.'

'– and the Hotel Manager as a figment of Margot's imagination. Or am I missing something. Who was this fellow Trelawny?'

'A pirate.'

'Ah. Lewis did say something about a pirate.'

From a point in the sky, shooting stars fell.

'I've never seen them before,' said Guy. Julia was standing, her arm brushing his, shivering slightly. 'In England the weather is so cloudy.' He wondered, 'When Shelley died, were there shooting stars or comets in the heavens, heralding the fall of heroes and the death of kings?'

'Sometimes you can be touchingly sentimental.'

'Did the moon turn to blood when George died at Missolonghi?'

'I doubt it. I'm afraid George wasn't in the least Byronic.'

'Apart from being called Byron.'

'Apart from that.'

Surf was breaking invisibly on the beach, as if the stars were extinguishing themselves with a hiss.

Julia said, 'I don't see George as a hero – his expedition to Greece was a farce and he died obscurely from a trivial disease, robbed by his companions. I see him as a child. He spent two years in Venice collecting a menagerie of horses, dogs, peacocks and harlots. His *palazzo* was no more than a giant nursery. And, if one thinks of his life rather than his verses, one realises that his notion of the freedom of the human spirit was, at bottom, the freedom of the playpen. His romantic furore was a mere tantrum.'

Guy had little knowledge and few opinions concerning Byron.

In ones and twos the stars were still falling into the sea as Julia changed the subject back to Edward Trelawny. She said that the adventurer and pirate had joined Shelley at Pisa in January 1822. When Shelley died in July, Trelawny was present.

CHAPTER FOURTEEN

George and the Pirate

by

Lady Julia Carradine

George was bored. All day long the Turkish Army had done nothing, or as near to nothing as made no difference.

First it had eaten its breakfast of bacon, eggs, sausages, toast and marmalade. Next one part had smoked a pipe as it read the newspaper, while the other retired to the bedroom to get dressed. Between rooms, the barbarian generals discussed their plan of campaign. Should the Turkoman horde play tennis as it had done the day before? Or should it go sightseeing? George wished it would get down to massacring innocent women and children. That was what any self-respecting horde ought to do.

The Turkish Army comprised four persons, Grand Pasha Percy, Mrs Pasha, Mary and a Mr and Mrs Williams, who had come to stay. George considered 'Williams' a coarse and vulgar name, far beneath his own aristocratic 'Byron'. He supposed the bazaars of Constantinople were full of Williamses, members of a slavish race. He was still contemplating this when the enemy retired from the field. Whether to wreak havoc in the byways of Pisa, or to return with a few souvenirs of fake *maiolica* pottery, George neither knew nor cared.

He decided he would write poetry. He knew Percy kept some paper in the drawer of his desk. However, the drawer was always locked against prying fingers.

'But I'm not pryin',' George told himself. 'I live here, an' them as lives here is entitled to wot's in the house.'

Also the paper belonged to the Grand Pasha and could be regarded as legitimate spoils of war.

The edge of one sheet was visible at the tip of the drawer. George tugged it and most of the sheet appeared before it tore. He regarded the ragged result.

'Mos' Pomes' is written on old paper, an' mos' old paper is tore,' he said aloud to encourage himself. Noting his muddy fingerprints, he spread dirt from his hands all over the page. It achieved, he thought, a pleasing appearance of antiquity.

Next, George looked for pen and ink. They lay on top of the desk. In a spirit of excitement, George spilt some on to the paper and rubbed it in. It added to the evidence of age. 'I bet 'Omer 'isself could've wrote on this.' he concluded with satisfaction.

He retired to the breakfast table. It offered room for his elbows. Elbows were always in the way of writing poetry. They had a habit of knocking over inkbottles. He also removed his grass snake, Southey, from the top pocket of his jacket in order to give it some exercise. The snake was a temporary pet, useful until he could save up enough pocket money to buy himself a peacock, or, better still, an ape.

Now equipped, George began to write. In short order he wrote a poem about a corsair, then another about a magician. He included various episodes of rapine and wild passion. Then, thinking that the events of the poems should take place in savage and romantic scenery, he added descriptions of places he had been to on holiday.

After half an hour he found the spring of inspiration had run dry. He had added a war poem to his collection, but was now experiencing writer's block. War, however, was on his mind. He decided he must make preparations to face the Turkish Army on its return.

George had long ago concluded that nine parts of warfare consisted in the right costume. It was his opinion that, for so long as the Turks wore white flannels or a

171

morning dress, they would be no match for a suitably caparisoned Greek.

In Percy's study was a volume of coloured plates depicting the folk garb of the Balkan peoples. Here George found a picture of an *evzone* wearing a red stocking cap, baggy-sleeved blouse, short frilly skirt, white tights, and shoes decorated with red pompoms.

'S'truth!' whistled George. However, inspection confirmed that the person was indeed a man. His initial impression was that Greek soldiers were soppy. But, on reflection, he acknowledged that the sight of hundreds of swarthy ruffians emerging from the mists like a line of ballet dancers in tutus was calculated to strike terror into the infidel heart.

Percy wore splendidly patterned stockings for golf. George decided that one would do nicely as a cap. In Mary's wardrobe he discovered a blouse of *crêpe de chine* and several petticoats which he cut to size with Cook's scissors. Tights were a problem, but George found a pair of peach-coloured stockings in fine silk. Finally, there was the question of pompoms. They were surprisingly easy to come by, because Percy had bought a Harlequin costume for Carnival. Flushed with success, George pulled them off. He felt that the resulting tears to the costume were scarcely noticeable.

On the return of the Turkish horde, the brave Greek *evzone* lay in wait behind the sofa.

As the Grand Pasha's forces entered the drawing room, George leapt out with a yell of 'Thermos flask!' He understood this to refer to a battle in which the Spartans had fought the Persians, and so Greek enough for his purpose.

To his disappointment, however, there was only one other person in the room, a tall fair-haired stranger in a linen suit who was smoking a cigarette.

Raising an eyebrow, the stranger said unconcernedly,

'You must be…? '

''S obvious, isn' it?' said George truculently.

'Help me.'

'I'm a Greek soljer.'

'Of course. And who are you fighting?'

'The Jane an' Sarahs,' George answered truthfully.

'I see,' said the stranger. 'Who are they?'

The question distracted George. Previously he had given little thought to the Jane an' Sarahs, but now it occurred to him that Turkish troops must also enter battle wearing women's clothes. With a shudder he concluded that cross-dressing must be listed among war's peculiar horrors.

The stranger went on, 'I guess I should introduce myself. I am the Bashibazouk Trelawny. Pleased to meet you, old sport.'

This game response made George brighten up. 'You're my pris'ner,' he said, adding gallantly, 'If that's all right with you?'

'It sure looks like it.'

At that moment the door opened and Percy entered with Mr Williams. He addressed the Bashibazouk Trelawny.

'Are you making yourself at home, Eddie? The ladies have gone to change. Good Lord, George! What *have* you been doing?'

'Why on earth are you dressed like a girl with a dirty face?' asked the Pasha's slave, Mr Williams, a bald man of sinister cast.

'I'm not a girl,' George objected strongly. 'I'm an *evzone*, an' this Jane an' Sarah is my pris'ner.'

'You're wearing my golfing socks,' said Percy.

'Only one,' George retorted, insisting on accuracy.

Before the conversation could proceed further there was a scream, and a moment later Mary came into the room, followed by Mrs Williams.

Mary exclaimed, 'George has been in my room and – *George*!'

'He's a Greek,' said Mr Trelawny. 'I'm a jannisary.'

The full force of George's appearance as a terrible *evzone* was not lost on Mary. She blanched and showed signs of fainting. It was most gratifying.

In the end a treaty was concluded. George apologised for taking plunder in excess of the laws and customs of war, and the Bashibazouk Trelawny paid two shillings as ransom for his freedom.

That evening they gathered in the lounge again. George had washed and wore civilian clothes.

Mary, who was growing used to living with Greek heroes, was her ordinary self again and asked, 'What else did you do while we were out?'

'Wrote Pomes,' said George.

Percy elaborated, for Mr Trelawny's benefit: 'George writes about war. Have you written a war poem, George?'

He received a nod in reply.

Mr Trelawny said, 'Well, then, are you going to read it, old sport?'

George nodded again. He felt under a poetic gloom. Imagination was a dark burden, and rhymes were the very devil when they would not come right. However, he was enticed by the hope of another two shillings from Mr Trelawny.

The sheet of paper was stained from the morning's efforts and had got mysteriously crumpled. His writing was reduced to squiggles and smudges by mud, ink, jam and Southey. However, he squinted at it and, with the aid of memory, began to recite grandly.

> ' **"Song for Dead Boys"**,
> by Master George Byron Gordon,
> Palazzo Lanfranchi.
> Pizza,
> Tuscany,
> Italy,

> Oorup,
> The World,
> Near the Sun,
> Milky Way,
> The Ooniverse.'

He paused and noted, with pleasure, the rapt attention. His voice filling with emotion, he pressed on.

> 'What ding dong hears the dyin' cow?
> – Only the wham bam of the how-
> Itzer and the bullet's whizz
> Say that Life is such a Swizz.

> 'No itchin' powder; no more laffs or fun;
> No marbles since Lord El Gin stole the lot –
> No corks to put inside my best pop gun;
> No bugles since the bugerler got shot!

> 'What torch will light my way when underground?
> I eat my carrots so they help my eyes,
> 'Cos dampness is no good for batterize.
> The girls can stay away and make no sound,
> Plait daisy chains and go early to bed;
> Or, if they like, can cry 'cos I'll be *DEAD*!!'

'Wonderful!' exclaimed Mr Trelawny, whose tears amply proved his sense of grief.

The following morning, from his bedroom, George saw a sailing boat moored on the river. Recalling his poem about corsairs, he wondered if pirates had paid a visit during the night.

Sadly a full complement of Turks appeared at breakfast, dashing George's hopes that the pirates had slaughtered one or two and merely broken off for a snack before polishing off the rest. Revising his dreams of adventure, he thought it might be for the best that the others were still alive. A spirited resistance offered the chance of heroism.

'There's a boat outside,' he remarked casually across the table.

Percy turned from his newspaper. 'It belongs to Eddie,' he said.

''S that so?' George asked excitedly. 'Are you a Capting?'

'Kind of, I guess, old sport,' came the answer.

George's horizons expanded into new possibilities. The pirate was already within the gate and the others clearly did not know. The prospects for murder and mayhem were improving.

He debated the choices open to him. On the one hand, he could betray the bold buccaneer. A brisk fight with cutlasses should suffice to dispose of him. On the other hand, he could enlist with the Captain as an apprentice pirate. George had often considered the piracy trade as a career, but recognised that a period of training was probably desirable.

'If I wanted to be a pirate –' he asked Captain Trelawny '– an' I don't say as I *do* – but if I *wanted* to be a pirate, would I have to go to school? I mean a *pirate* school, not an orn'ery school.'

'I don't think so,' said Captain Trelawny.

The Captain was keeping his plans to himself despite George's attempts to wheedle them out of him.

'Jus' s'posin' I was a pirate,' said George, 'an' wanted to attack this house, wot would I have to do? Jus' s'posin, o'course.' He granted the Captain a large, meaningful wink.

'Got something in your eye, old sport?'

George wondered if he had. He decided to indicate his alliance with the buccaneering interest. While the Jane an' Sarahs were out he cut one of the black diamonds from

Percy's Harlequin costume, strung it and wore it as an eyepatch when he next saw Captain Trelawny.

'Why are you wearing that?' asked the jolly tar.

''Cos o' my eye,' George answered airily. 'It's sick, jus' as you was sayin'. I 'spect it'll die an' fall out, an' then I'll have to wear this patch for ever.'

'Ah.'

George practised life as a one-eyed man. When he squinted to aim his popgun, the world went dark. 'Odds blood!' he muttered, with an effort at a piratical curse. He had evidently blanked out the wrong eye.

Mary noticed the patch at teatime.

'Why are you wearing that ridiculous thing?' she asked.

'I'm goin' blind,' said George pitifully. 'I'll have to go round with a white stick an' a dog. A big fierce dog,' he added, to avoid any indication of weakness. 'I'll have to work as a beggar 'cos that's the only job for a boy wot's got only one eye. *Unless*,' he said pointedly to Captain Trelawny, 'there's other jobs a one-eyed boy can do. I 'spec there are. At sea, for instance. At sea you can have one eye *an'* wear a hook 'stead of a hand.' He began to wax enthusiastic. 'An' a wooden leg.'

However, the Captain did not answer.

Next morning George found himself looking at some paintings. In one some soldiers were massacring babies while a man and woman rode off on a donkey towards a palm tree. George could see the point to this sort of art.

Contemplating Trelawny, he decided that the Captain had no intention of sharing his booty with a young apprentice. Very well. If that was the case, it was up to George to play the heroic part and stop the pirate's evil designs.

'George has been behaving very well these last few days,' Mary commented as they took coffee in a café by the Arno.

George was sitting demurely. Plans for murder and the

knowledge that he was Doing Good had given him peace of mind.

Mr Williams put down his pipe, grinned and said, 'Eye got better, has it?'

'Yes, thank you.'

'Given up the idea of being a beggar?'

'Yes,' said George. 'I'm going to be a saint.'

From an otherwise dreary book, George had learned that St Dominic had established the Holy Inquisition. The notion of being a saint *and* a torturer was appealing. If George could kill a notorious pirate, he felt it would stand him in good stead when he applied to join the monks.

''S a very interestin' job, bein' a saint,' he observed knowledgeably.

George's plans to kill Captain Trelawny went forward by an indirect route.

'Sabbertaj!' he wrote in the notes he was keeping. He added more exclamation marks and searched for a rhyme to use in the poem he would write later.

In a chest in one of the empty rooms of the palazzo, George found a saw. That night he sneaked out to the Captain's boat and sawed most of the way through the shaft attaching the rudder to the tiller. A little pressure and it would snap, leaving the boat to drift at the mercy of the currents. The Captain would drown.

Morning came, another fine day. George could have wished for a storm.

'I do wish you wouldn't look so angelic,' said Mary. 'The effect is quite sickening.'

'I'm bein' Good,' answered George resentfully. 'I'm s'posed to be Good, aren't I? Wotcher want if I'm *not* to be Good?'

'I *do* want you to be good,' said Mary soothingly. 'I just wish you wouldn't *look* so good.'

George waited patiently for Captain Trelawny to appear. It was his habit to sail in the mornings. With luck he would be dead by lunch.

When the Captain came to breakfast, however, he seemed distinctly unwell and refused food. 'Gyppy tum,' he explained.

'Will you be sailing?' asked Percy.

'Not today, old sport. Too out of sorts.'

'Mind if I try my hand?'

'Be my guest.'

George turned pale and nervous. He felt a tide of panic at the thought of Percy sailing. Percy, who could not swim!

Mary noticed. 'Are you feeling poorly, too?' she asked.

'No,' said George. He looked at Percy and muttered, 'I wun't sail if I was you.'

'Why not?' replied Percy.

George searched frantically for an excuse.

'Cannibals!'

'Cannibals?'

'Yes. All Eyetalians is cannibals. 'S a well-known fact. 'S dangerous to sail alone.' This seemed a likely description of the habits of Italians and George warmed to it. He remembered the paintings. 'They eat *babies*!' he affirmed with a shudder of horror. 'I've seen 'em doin' it in the pitchers.'

Percy, however, was unexpectedly brave. He said, 'Thanks, Eddie. I'll take you up on that offer.'

George's mouth fell open. Before his eyes he could see the hapless Percy sailing away blithely to his doom. Already a storm was brewing and the waves were lashing at the frail craft. Already poor Percy was mangled and dashed against the rocks and reefs of the Spanish Main.

'George!' said Mary sharply. 'It's rude to eat with your mouth open.'

CHAPTER FIFTEEN

1930

Who were the Williamses?' asked Guy. 'You never mentioned them to me.'

'I forgot to,' said Julia. 'I've no idea who they were, though no doubt they were as sinister as the rest of that crew. Lewis gave me their names, so I dropped them in in the interest of verisimilitude. They actually did exist.'

They were sitting under the awning outside an hotel on the shore front of Porto Venere. It was an uncomfortable situation because Guy found his eyes unable to adjust: one moment staring at sea and sunlight where Fred was gambolling on the rocks, and the next moment masked by the shadow of the awning.

Ambrose had offended the management by wearing a striped bathing costume. He lifted his gaze from his knitting.

'Do you know,' he sighed, 'it seems to me that our mystery has become less about murder and more about socks. First, in Margot's play, George is obsessed by the fear of losing his socks. And now, in Julia's story, he wears them on his head as a cap. In the characterisation of George I detect an implied rebuke of myself. By the way, have you noticed that Fascist policemen, like dogs, go to sleep in the midday sun?'

The observation was not strictly true. A policeman was sheltering from the heat under an aleppo pine.

Julia said, 'You're only rebuked if you're vain enough to compare yourself with Byron.'

'Perish the thought, dear. I'm not nearly vicious enough. I haven't the energy.'

With this remark the conversation turned to lazy silences punctuated by random comments that Guy ceased to follow. He was watching dust devils stirred from the roadway by a slight breeze and listening to the soothing ping of lanyards against flagpoles.

Jackie Ferris's voice brought him round. 'I don't get it. Why the children's story?'

'Julia can hardly be held responsible for the deficiencies of American education,' commented Ambrose.

Ferris was not satisfied. 'The stories are fun, I guess. But I'd like to cut the fancy stuff and get to the facts. How much of what Julia said is true?'

'Ask Lewis.'

'Lewis?'

'Oh, I know some of the facts, but not all of them.'

'Come on. Give.'

Ambrose insisted on more drinks before he would allow Lewis to proceed. To please the hotel, he put a tie round his bare neck.

Lewis began: 'Byron got himself involved with a family of Italians called the Gambas, and a Carbonari plot and a Neapolitan uprising. I'm speaking of the confused revolutionary politics of 1821, not of the present condition of peace and prosperity attributable to Il Duce.

'The Shelleys were already in Pisa, staying at the Tre Palazzi di Chiesa. An amiable but unremarkable couple called Edward and Jane Williams had rooms there, as did another fellow called Medwin. Claire was with them for a time, but left for Florence as soon as Byron arrived.

'The Gambas got into trouble with the authorities in Venice and fled to Tuscany, taking George with them. They turned up in January 1822, far too many to stay with the Shelleys and so they took the Palazzo Lanfranchi.'

'Who was Trelawny?' Ferris asked.

'One of Medwin's friends, ex-Navy and something of a romantic and adventurer. He arrived at about the same time as Byron and took a shine to Shelley. By the way, Julia, you made a mistake. The sailing boat belonged to Byron not Trelawny, and it was quite a large vessel, not the oversized dinghy you implied. However, George did put Trelawny in charge of her, so, in a sense, she was his.'

'And what happened at Pisa?'

'Nothing very much. There was some sort of brawl with the local soldiery, and then, in April, the group broke up to spend summer on the coast. The Shelleys came here to La Spezia with the Williamses, and Byron settled somewhere south of Livorno. Trelawny used to sail between the two.'

Ferris turned to Julia. Guy, who had been watching Fred, could not see the American's face beyond its general shape, but his voice sounded strangely serious.

'If all the stuff in your story happened at Pisa, and Shelley or Percy or whatever you call him died later and someplace else, what's the point, huh? What's with Trelawny? Do you have some sort of grudge against him?'

While Julia hesitated, Ambrose answered. 'Trelawny was present on the fatal day when Shelley cast out to sea, but declined to join him on the boat.'

'Oh?' said Ferris. 'So *you* know something about this business, do you? Are you all trying to hide something from me?'

'It's only a story,' Guy prompted gently. 'We're only telling it for fun.'

'Just as Guy says, Jackie dear,' said Ambrose. 'And, indeed, you have a point. Why should Byron wish to kill Trelawny? One can only speculate. Pirates, in their nature, make enemies. Julia has introduced a new twist to the tale – an intriguing possibility. What if Trelawny *had* been on the boat? Do you follow the implications? Perhaps friend Percy was not the object of the murder plot? Perhaps he was its *unintended* victim?' He sighed and, after a moment, to Guy's surprise asked, 'Julia dear, was the Cook in your story a man or a woman?'

'I've no idea.'

'It could have been a man?'

'I suppose so. Cooks often are. Why do you ask?'

'A suspicion – the merest suspicion. Lewis, you say that George was involved in a Carbonari conspiracy?'

'Yes.'

'Hmm. I see.'

'You see what?'

Ambrose closed his eyes and smiled. 'I was thinking,' he said, 'of Byron's household: the cooks, valets, stable boys, ape-keepers and general riff-raff whose names never figure in the histories. And then one considers the period, so full of Italian revolutionaries and the Austrian secret policemen who chased them. It's possible – indeed it would be remarkable if it were not the case – that spies from one or the other side, or both, were present during all these events.'

'I suppose so,' Lewis agreed slowly. 'But what are you driving at?'

'The solution to our murder mystery. I wonder if the Cook and the Hotel Manager were not, in fact, one and the same person. Who do *you* think, Guy dear? After all, it was you who got inside that particular role. I don't say that he was the murderer, but I still have great hopes of the Hotel Manager.'

When Guy next saw Jackie Ferris alone, the latter was bird-watching from a spot near the cistern.

Guy indicated the A-frame and the boulder. 'You mentioned having some tackle which would help me move this thing. Could I borrow it?'

'Sure. Ask me tomorrow when I go down to Lerici to check the boat out.'

'Will you be staying long? I don't know how serious Ambrose is about going to Venice.'

'I've got business in Marseilles, but don't let me stop

you fellows. Mikey Malvivente won't care if you borrow his place.'

Guy settled on a rock. He offered a cigarette.

'Excuse me for asking, but how do you come to know everyone? I don't mean to be offensive, but you don't seem their type.'

'You'd be surprised. Not that I'd say I know everyone. You and Lewis I met at Sammy's. I ran into Ambrose at a party for the first time about two months ago. We got talking and he invited me here.'

'And Margot?'

'I did some stuff with her cousin Esmond in Chicago.'

'The cousin who got shot?'

'Uh huh.'

Guy turned his eyes to the silent trees. 'Birds good here?'

The Commander put down his glasses, shook his head and smiled. 'Nope. The Italians are smart. They take 'em in nets and cook 'em.'

'I wonder why you bother.'

'What else is there to do?'

Guy had no answer and, in any case, had a different matter on his mind. 'About

Julia…'

'You're sweet on her.'

'How did you first meet?'

'Her husband, Hector, is an old naval man, like me.'

'I gather he … prefers other men.'

'That so? I never heard it. Why don't you talk straight with me? You want to know if the way's clear for you?'

'I…'

Ferris laughed. Guy was growing used to cruel laughter and this was among the cruellest, though the other man seemed to notice the effect and softened it.

'If you want my advice, go get the girl. Hector's someplace in Africa and I don't know anyone else who's staking claims. Julia and I are friends, but there's nothing between us except she wants a share of the glory if I take the speedboat record.'

Guy decided not to press the subject, but was left wondering if Ferris were a part of the past that Julia chose not to reveal.

The others had gone into town. Guy and Ferris lunched alone on the terrace. The Commander ate thoughtfully and at the end of the meal said, 'Ambrose wants me to tell a story.'

'Oh? Well, I'll look forward to that. You must have a lot of tales about sailing or the war or –'

'Not that. I've got to talk about Byron and … whatshisname? Percy.'

'Ah.' Guy put down his napkin. He was uncertain of the correct response but ventured, 'Why don't you tell him you won't do it?'

'Why should I say that? You were right when you told me I don't fit in with this crowd. But I'm an easy-going type and where's the harm?'

'There's no harm, I suppose. In that case what's your problem?'

'Only that I don't know anything about those characters except the little bit that Lewis let slip.'

During their last early-morning swim, Lewis had expanded to Guy on the subject of the two poets. He also mentioned that, after the rescue of Gianni, he was minded to get himself a small boat for the sake of amusement. Guy saw no harm in passing on the information.

'You should understand that there isn't the slightest evidence that Shelley was murdered. The whole notion is a conceit that Ambrose seems determined to pursue. Everyone is agreed that Shelley died in a sailing accident.'

'I get you. So?'

'Where to start? With background, I suppose. I'll take Shelley first. He was the heir to a baronetcy – so he was a sort of noble. As I recall, he had a wife, but he deserted her to run off with Mary Wollstonecraft and her half-sister Claire to Europe. That's where they first met Byron, by Lake Geneva.'

'Who was…? '

'Byron? Oh, he was a noble, too. He had a wife and left her, had an affair with Lady Caroline Lamb, got into debt, became involved in a scandal about his relations with his sister and finally fled abroad. Not that this has anything to do with Shelley's death, so far as I'm aware.'

'Go on.'

'They all met again at Pisa, except for Claire, who was in Florence. That was the subject of Julia's story. By that time they'd collected a string of hangers-on. Byron was mixed up with some Italians, and the Shelleys were sharing a palazzo with friends. Lewis told you all this.'

'And?'

Guy was surprised the American found the subject interesting, but Ferris pressed him with a question. 'What's with the Williamses and Medwin?'

'Absolutely nothing. Jane was very pretty and rather dull, and Shelley was perhaps over fond of her. Edward had been in the Navy. He and Shelley probably spent their time talking about boats. I don't remember Lewis saying anything about Medwin.'

Guy wondered if the silence as to Medwin was important. But how could it be, if the whole basis of the stories was nonsense?

Ferris prompted him. 'Guy?'

'Sorry, I was just thinking. No matter. Where was I?'

'Trelawny – he kind of interests me – how does he figure?'

Guy did not know. Julia had suggested Trelawny might have been the true object of the murder plot, but that made no sense at all. Still less was there any evidence. He offered what information he had.

'Trelawny was a sailor like Edward Williams. He met the Shelleys for the first time in Pisa and formed an attachment to Percy. In fact, after Percy's death he wrote a memoir idolising him.' Hurriedly he added, 'I'm not suggesting there was anything improper between them.'

'That's okay. But carry on. Trelawny sounds all right. If he was a sailor, how come he let Shelley drown?'

'He didn't.'

'He didn't?'

'Not if you believe his account. Trelawny was very experienced. Byron had his own ship, the *Bolívar*, a largish square-rigged vessel (I have to rely on Lewis for this part). The *Bolívar* couldn't be sailed single-handedly, and Byron made Trelawny his captain. In addition, Shelley had his own boat, called the *Don Juan*.'

Trelawny had had his doubts about the *Don Juan*. Or had he? It occurred to Guy how far the historical account relied on Trelawny's version of events, which could not be tested. Had he in fact ever told Shelley of his concerns about the boat's safety? But why should he not? Ferris went back to the house to get a bottle of grappa. By the time he returned it seemed to Guy foolish to give any credibility to the murder story by adding speculation.

'You'll have a shot?' Ferris asked, pouring the spirit into two whisky glasses.' Okay, you were saying that Trelawny had doubts…'

'Yes, according to Lewis. The *Don Juan* was very fast and carried too much sail, so three men weren't enough to handle her. Trelawny suggested hiring an experienced Genoese sailor, but Williams refused. Also, she rode high in the water and had to be heavily ballasted. She had no deck.'

The American pushed back his chair and whistled.

'Is that important?' Guy asked.

Ferris was chuckling. 'Go on, go on. I'm loving it.'

'You could let me in on the joke.'

'Not a joke. But you can never figure on how stupid people will be when they fool with boats.'

'I suppose so,' Guy admitted. Getting no reaction, he

went on. 'A few days before his death, Shelley sailed the *Don Juan* to Livorno with Edward Williams, a fellow called Roberts and a boy as crew. He was visiting Byron and a journalist called Leigh Hunt and one or two other friends. On the day of the accident, Byron invited Shelley to stay over, which, if true, seems to let George off the hook, since he didn't want Shelley to sail. However, Williams was anxious to get back to Jane.

'Trelawny – again, if one believes him – was doubtful about the return journey. He offered to accompany Shelley in the *Bolívar*. If he had done, he could have rescued the others when the *Don Juan* went down in the storm. However, he had trouble with the port authorities, who wouldn't allow the *Bolívar* to leave. By the way, this incident puts paid to Julia's notion that Trelawny might have been the intended victim. He was far too cautious to sail in the *Don Juan* and anyway didn't need to, since he had another vessel.

'Williams was still for sailing home, even without Trelawny in the *Bolívar*. This seems to have been the crucial moment. Trelawny insists he pressed Shelley to postpone. There were clouds on the horizon and he could see the risk that the *Don Juan*, undermanned, carrying too much sail, and riding too high, would be caught in a squall. He says he warned Shelley, but Shelley took Williams's advice. He sailed…'

'And died.'

'Yes,' Guy agreed reluctantly. 'Together with Edward Williams and the boy.'

Together with Edward Williams and the boy, he repeated to himself, only now realising the sad significance of that fact, which seemed to be lost on Jackie Ferris.

'Percy was an idiot,' said Ferris, briskly.

Guy nodded, reminding himself that folly rather than murder best explained what had happened. But that was not the point: which was that history, in its focus on

Shelley's splendid egoism, had failed to grasp the core of the tragedy.

In his folly the poet had killed his friend and an innocent boy, and destroyed the lives of his wife and Jane Williams.

When Ambrose, Lewis and the women returned, it was night and they were jolly as if they had been drinking. Guy could hear them from his room where he was trying to write to Elizabeth by candlelight. They had gathered in the saloon, where he joined them.

'Guy, my dear, we're on for Venice,' Ambrose announced expansively. He waved a piece of paper. 'The generous Mister Malvivente has graciously replied to Jackie's telegram and agreed to give us the run of his palazzo. Do you know, I feel so cheerful that I think I *may* pay Joe Truffatore something on account of his bill.'

Guy was uninterested. His conversation with Ferris and the terrible facts surrounding Shelley's death had left him melancholy, and the debate in his mind was not whether to go to Venice but whether to throw over the others and return to England. He felt trapped by a foolishness which, though more petty than the poet's, was equally selfish. If, that is, he loved Elizabeth. The trouble was that he no longer knew. His eyes searched out Julia who also seemed subdued.

'You're very late,' he commented.

'Wonderfully observed,' boomed Ambrose.

Margot giggled. 'We've been arrested.'

'Yes?'

'Yes, and it's every bit as delicious as you reported. The food was excellent, and Inspector Porrello was charming. Such an odd little man. And such super moustaches.'

'What did you do?'

'Nothing,' said Lewis. 'It seems that we are to be arrested on general principles. Porrello admitted as much.

He enjoys our company and pulled us in for a chat. I was reminded of my housemaster, an avuncular character who once invited me to his fireside to discuss self-abuse, unnatural practices, cold showers and my captaincy of the first eleven. Come to think of it, I had that same unearthly feeling, as if the beast were about to spring from behind the smile and devour me.'

'Yes, Porrello does have that effect.'

Jackie Ferris had been in his room in the mansard and had not heard the others return. Entering the saloon, he said, 'I'm out of Scotch and came looking for a bottle. So, how did it go with you folks?'

'Jackie dear,' said Ambrose welcomingly, 'we were just entertaining Guy with a description of our latest arrest.'

'The police picked you up?'

'You mustn't feel jealous at the privileges of the upper classes. I'm sure your turn will come.'

'Thanks but no thanks. I had enough of the law when I was in Chicago.' He poured himself a drink from the decanter.

'As it happens,' Ambrose continued, 'you were with us in spirit. Inspector Porrello was very interested in sailing and, according to Lewis, quite knowledgeable, too.'

'Is that so?'

'He was most interested in your exploits. A "fan" – I think that's the expression. He wanted to know why you're here. Why are you here, by the way?'

'You know the answer to that. Julia and I have business to discuss.'

'I told him you were interested in bird-watching.'

'You should stay out of my affairs,' Ferris answered curtly. Almost immediately he seemed to regret his sharpness, for he raised his glass in a toast, grinned and proposed, 'To hell with policemen – what do you say?'

There was no answer, because at that moment everyone was distracted by a noise from the next room, a fumbling at the door handle which seemed to go on for a considerable time until the door was opened and a stranger entered; at least someone Guy did not recognise. Ambrose, on the other hand, rose to his feet with a smile on his face. He went to the door and gently took the arm of a thin, white-haired old lady who was struggling to carry a large old-fashioned bag decorated in crewelwork.

'Madame Hecate, dear!' he exclaimed, as if she were deaf. 'Please do come in and let me introduce you to those you haven't already met.'

The old lady hesitated, but, with encouragement, was brought to nod in the direction of Guy and Commander Ferris. She had a sweet expression and a pair of piercing cornflower-blue eyes.

CHAPTER SIXTEEN

1945

In the relaxed atmosphere of the British Autonomous Hospital, as it slowly took shape at the Villa Esperanza, Guy found himself dropping in on a conversation between Nick and Jimmy, the two privates. They were talking of their plans now that the war was over, and by the time he caught their drift he was too far involved to withdraw without embarrassment.

'Nicky here is an enlisted man,' said Jimmy.

'You are, aren't you, Nicky? You can tell Mr Parrot.'

''S right,' agreed Nick.

'He's still got a couple of years to go. I 'spect they'll demob me in a month or two,'

'What will you do?' asked Guy.

'Volunteer for another stretch, so's me and Nick can stay together.'

Guy assimilated this information slowly, his concentration distracted by the sharp antics of one of the many small lizards that inhabited the house.

Jimmy continued insouciantly, 'The problem is fixin' it so me and Nick come out of the Army at the same time. Of course, one of us could come out first and arrange things nice like. You know, wait for the other.'

Guy had never paid much attention to the two privates before. Nick was a large, bearish man. Jimmy was fair and small-made, even pixyish. Both were barely more than youths and had mild, genial temperaments.

To be polite, Guy asked if they had anything specific in mind.

'We thought we'd open a shop somewhere,' said Nick.

'sellin' fancy goods, china, little brass ornaments, things like that.'

'People are goin' to want nice things, what with livin' through a war,' contributed Jimmy.

'Well, I hope you find an answer to your problems.'

'Oh, love will find away, won't it?' Jimmy laughed, then put a hand coyly to his mouth. He said to his friend, 'We shouldn't be sayin' this in front of Mr Parrot. He could 'ave us up on a charge.'

'No, that's all right,' Guy said hurriedly, wishing he were elsewhere. 'I like to see people happy.'

The subject of peacetime plans dwelt on his mind. He discussed it with Corporal Long.

'Have Nick and Jimmy told you about theirs?'

'They two buggers'll be fine,' the Corporal answered cheerfully.

'You don't mind how they are?' Guy asked.

'It's no my business,' said Corporal Long, adding as an afterthought, 'So long as they dinna make it compulsory.'

Something had been worrying Guy. 'I've been meaning to mention it' – he hesitated – 'Tommy. I gather that, now the war's over, you and Lieutenant Jenkins intend to set up as partners in some venture?'

'It's no against King's Regulations. I've checked.'

'Yes, of course, I'm sure you're right. Strictly it's none of my affair.'

'But...?'

'As you say, "But..." ' Guy found himself floundering between tactlessness and his kindly concern for Jenkins. 'I hope you'll be easy on him. It's plain to me that you're a sight brighter than he is. I shouldn't like to see him hurt.'

The Corporal eyed him narrowly. 'I'm glad tae see ye've learnt somethin' yersel'. There's nae need tae worry. I'm always guid tae my friends.'

Guy took this as a statement of moral purpose and was content.

*

Two trucks arrived bringing beds and other equipment. They also brought mail, though there was much to be done before anyone had the leisure to read it.

Among the orders and official circulars was a letter from Elizabeth. She did not know where Guy was, and, after rattling around Headquarters and other earlier postings, it had taken a month to arrive. It read:

Dearest Guy,

I should begin by saying, as always, how much I miss you, but I've said it so often over the last years that I'm almost frightened to write it again in case it sounds like a dutiful formula. I suppose there are fresh ways of speaking the old words 'I love you', but I suspect that those who find them are forever falling in and out of love and therefore ignorant. Love is often humdrum and secure, and only when its routine is broken do we understand it. So I give you news, and you must search it for what is in my heart.

Father was very poorly over the winter with bronchitis which I was frightened might turn into pneumonia. I did mention this in my last letter, but I don't know if you got it since I received no reply. He has become quite frail and very deaf, but his mind is still acute. Recently he had an article published on 'The Epidemiology of Venereal Disease among the Indigent'. He was given a prize (a very small one), of which he is suitably modest. Auntie May has also won a trophy – for rearing a pig!

The practice holds up under Dr Maybrick. In fact, it has grown because of the number of younger doctors in the Army. Now that your return is likely in the near future, he is beginning to look for positions as a locum elsewhere. But I think you should offer him a partnership since there is work enough for two.

Auntie May and I went to London to collect the pig prize from Princess Margaret Rose. Annie took care of Father. While we were there we went to the theatre to see 'Imperfect Tense'. It was revived two years ago and has played non-stop to full houses, and is an even greater sensation than when it first appeared. Isn't that odd? I thought it would be terribly dated. Wit and triviality seem very much the notions of twenty years ago and rather inappropriate for wartime. But I suppose people will always want to be taken out of themselves. What struck me was that it seemed to be the very image of its time. The play and the period can be mentioned in the same breath and are the same thing.

Remembering that you once knew Ambrose Carmody, I enclose a photo I clipped from the Manchester Guardian. It shows him with Lord Mountbatten. I believe it was taken in Burma, but I can't be sure because I've lost the accompanying article. It's strange what happens to one's friends. Another of his plays, 'She Paid the Price', was also revived last year, but didn't do nearly so well. Too gloomy, I suppose, and rather old-fashioned.

I'm wittering on – saying everything except the things I want to say. They are in my heart not on my lips. And I don't know when, if ever, I shall get to pour them out to you.

I pray to God to keep you safe. I tell myself that you are, even though I have had no letters from you for three months. I love you, Darling.

Always thinking of you,

Elizabeth

Guy folded this letter carefully and put it with the others, bound with an elastic band. Beside them were the scraps of his own uncompleted letters. He had been unable to write since he first heard again of La Spezia.

Jenkins had had a letter from his wife. 'She's set up home with a building society manager.'

'I'm sorry.'

'No need to be. There'll be a divorce and I shan't have to pay maintenance.'

Tommy had got a County Court summons. Nick had a letter from his mother. Jimmy had one from a sailor he'd met in Portsmouth on embarkation leave.

'Is this yours, old chap? You must have dropped it,'

said Jenkins, handing over the newspaper clipping. 'Lord Mountbatten. Pal of yours, is he? Has no one got a parcel? That's a pretty poor show, isn't it? I suppose they were stolen. That's the usual way. Did I ever tell you of the one I got that had been opened? Someone had swiped the cigarettes, but the obliging fellow left a note and a dirty picture, saying it would probably do me more good. It did, too. Absolutely filthy!'

Guy had forgotten about the newspaper picture but looked at it now. It had been clipped without the caption so it was impossible to say when or where it had been taken, except that it was on board a ship and four men were sitting round a table in the wardroom, involved in earnest discussion.

Ambrose was in uniform – a surprise in itself. Guy was vague about naval ranks, but supposed from the exquisite cut and various badges that the wearer was an officer of some status, though it was difficult to imagine Ambrose doing anything more onerous than organising concert parties. Whatever the case, he had fallen into the spirit of the thing and looked appropriately solemn. He was smoking, but held his cigarette in a manly grip instead of in his usual holder. Beyond that he could tell nothing. Guy remembered Ambrose's difficulty in coming to terms with the last war, a manifestation of anger, resentment and guilt, perhaps, which came out in his savage parodies of the war poets. The various accounts of Ambrose's service had been contradictory. For that reason Guy had never fully understood the playwright's behaviour. Indeed, he wondered if Ambrose himself had been aware of his own oddity. At all events, he had presumably come to terms with the part, which perhaps explained his seriousness in the photograph. With a long-running success in the West End and a respected position in the Navy, it seemed that life had treated Ambrose well since the events of fifteen years ago. Guy did not expect justice and was rarely disappointed.

The generator failed that evening and they had to make do with candles and lanterns. Guy retired to his room, took out Elizabeth's letter again, read it and dozed in the flickering light while taking occasional sips from an enamel mug filled with Corporal Long's wine. Like all her previous letters, it was filled with a tender banality. Reading it, no one would suspect that the ghost of Julia stood between them, but Guy knew that the simple sincerity of Elizabeth's language was a reaching-out towards him. He asked himself if she had ever felt defrauded. Of course, he had tried to give her the full measure of his affection. He thought he had succeeded. But his love seemed to him a damaged thing, a pale, limping sentiment. If he could have any wish, it would be to recover love so that he could give it whole and entire to his wife. Behind all its commonplaces, that was what Elizabeth's letter asked for, and Guy would freely grant it if only he could find it bright and new once more.

In the morning Jenkins remarked that Signor Nessuno was infesting the place again. He had found empty bottles and food scraps in one of the fellow's nests. Guy ordered a search but they had no success.

Guy wanted to find someone. Bearing in mind Colonel Box's strictures against official contact with the Americans, on his next day off he decided to make an informal approach to Corporal Pulaski.

The latter, however, had something on his mind. 'I'm not sure I want to help a bunch of dopes who think they can run this man's army without the corps.'

Guy remembered their previous misunderstanding. Inventing on the spot, he said, 'Oh, you needn't worry about that. There's been a change of orders. In fact I'm going to recommend that Tommy be made up to sergeant again.'

Mollified, Corp offered to buy a beer. 'Okay, so what can I do for you?'

'I don't know that you can. Fact is, I'm looking for someone.'

'Uh huh? Name?'

'Porrello, Ercole Porrello. He used to be a police inspector, though he must be retired by now. He may even be dead.'

Corp was in a magnanimous mood after Guy's concession in the matter of saving the breed of corporals from extinction.

'This Porrello,' said Corp, 'if he was a police inspector, he'd be a Fascist, am I right?'

'I hadn't thought of that, but I suppose he must have been.'

Corp thought for a moment. 'Shouldn't be too difficult. Our boys have a list of anyone who used to be in the Party. Your fella should be on it. Leave it with me.'

With the last consignment of supplies had come a telephone and the equipment to connect it. Guy used it only occasionally, since he had no desire to speak to Colonel Box and, in any case, it was largely occupied by Corporal Long, who had organised a bookmaking syndicate with his fellow NCOs at Headquarters. Two days after his conversation with Pulaski, Guy received a call from Corp. It was brief and gave him the address he had been seeking.

La Spezia, like so many towns along this coast, was built on the narrowest of plains. To north and east rose a range of sandstone heights, the lower slopes terraced for olives and vines, with chestnuts and pines above. Beyond lay the valley of the Magra and still further heights until, some ten miles from the coast, reared the Apuan Alps. The Inspector's house – farm, Guy supposed – lay on the further side of the river where the hills continued above Castelnuovo di Magra.

Guy hired a boy to give him directions. He found him lounging by the station. A cheerful idleness, rather than despair, seemed to be the Italian response to defeat. The boy was completely ignorant, but he was obliging and had a smattering of English and the confidence to ask others the location of Signor Porrello's home.

Castelnuovo was little more than a village with some medieval ruins. Beyond it the road rose in a series of sharp bends through dense woods of maritime pine penetrated by stony paths. A kite or buzzard – Guy could not tell which – hovered on the rising thermals. Dusty and soporific, the land dozed like a dog.

By now Guy had collected as guides the boy, an aged hunter with a shotgun, an old lady carrying a basket of eggs, and a priest who wore a black biretta and a dirty soutane. They seemed dreamily content with the journey and quietly traded eggs for birds and shrugged or laughed when Guy asked for directions. Once at the house, they vanished except for the boy, though Guy could see nowhere they could have gone to, merely slopes of pine and chestnut baking in the sun.

'Signor Porrello?'

In a shallow declivity a small house built of fieldstone with a tiled roof sheltered among a few olives. A vine covered much of the front, spilling over some trelliswork. A fig grew on the shady side. On the other an agave threw a huge phallic stem into the air. A system of wooden frames covered with wisteria provided shade to a vegetable plot.

The old man wore a straw hat with a broad rim and a linen suit although he was working his garden. Age had contracted him as if he were crouching.

Noting Guy, he said, '*Buon giorno*, Signor Parrot. As you see, I am farming my land. I have an apartment in the city but under the conditions of the time … I am not at heart a peasant.' The word 'peasant' was distasteful to him.

Somewhat numb with surprise, Guy stammered, 'You know me?'

Porrello wiped his hands and offered one. '*Si*. Naturally. You English lords and ladies are not so forgettable.'

'But that was fifteen years ago.'

The policeman removed his hat and applied a large handkerchief to his domed skull. He retained his waxed moustachios, which were an improbable black.

'I remember people and things. It is my business. And your friends were so strange, so like the rulers of the earth as one would like to imagine them. But please, you are my guest. I must offer you something.'

He brought a jug of wine and water and a plate of olives. They sat under the shade of the vine. The boy had disappeared into the brush to take slingshots at thrushes and earn his dinner.

For a while Signor Porrello was content to make small talk about the war. He was delighted at the Allied victory, referring to 'we' and 'our' as though Italy had always been on the side of the victors. If he had a Fascist past, he wore it lightly.

'But that is not why you are here. You wish to talk about what happened all those years ago, the death of Signor Lockyer and everything that went with it.'

'Did you have any doubts about the accident?'

'I did not see the body, though the doctor swore to a drowning. And then' – the old man opened his hands and examined the nails – 'the body was buried.'

'That was Signor Carmody's doing. We did consider cremation.'

'Like your Lord Shelley…'

'Yes. He was burnt.'

'…who was murdered.'

Guy was not concerned with Shelley, though it was odd how the subject would never go away. Now that it had been raised, he was curious as to Signor Porrello's opinion.

'Do you have any evidence that he was murdered – I

mean Shelley?'

'No. It is too long ago.'

'Ah.'

'One merely has questions – about circumstances that are suggestive.'

'Such as?'

'Why did he set sail from Livorno on the day of his death?'

Yes, that was the question. Still Guy was surprised to hear it again. Madame Hecate had first raised it, though Guy had not understood its significance. Then Lewis mentioned the point in the notes he wrote before the accident.

'How are your friends?' asked Signor Porrello at last. Guy thought he had gone to sleep in that brief interval. Elizabeth's father was forever dropping off in conversation. But he had aged more severely than the Italian, who seemed scarcely to have changed.

'Signor Carmody is in the Navy. I don't know what he does.'

'I am sure success attends him,' Porrello said darkly.

'Lady Davenant was killed in an air raid.'

'I am sorry.'

'I haven't heard from Madame Hecate, not since a letter I got some years ago. I suppose she's dead.' This remark seemed tasteless. Guy added, 'She was much older than you.'

'Not so very much, but I acknowledge you are probably right. And the others?'

'I imagine you read in the newspapers about Signor Ferris?'

The old man nodded.

Guy sometimes wondered if the fate of Jackie Ferris were a mystery or not, and whether it was in any way connected with the events at La Spezia, though it was difficult to see any scope for a connection. Ferris had left the Villa Esperanza some time during the expedition to

Venice that Ambrose had insisted on. There was a telegram saying he had arrived safely in Marseilles, where he went to ground for six months. Then, so it seemed, he one day decided to take his boat for a sail in the Gulf of Lions. There, in a flat calm sea, he disappeared, leaving his vessel to be found by a bemused Algerian tramp steamer. Boats had proven to be unlucky. They lay behind Lewis's accident, Jackie's vanishing and, not least, the death of Shelley.

The boy was a crack shot. He returned with a thrush and a blackbird strung by their feet. He engaged in a lively conversation with the old man, too fast for Guy to follow, then helped himself to a cup of wine and water and scoffed some of the olives.

Porrello was an affable, if faintly sinister, old fellow with a doubtful history. Guy remembered it had been a pleasure to be arrested by him. The old man said, 'You have a trusting nature, Signor Parrot.' Turning to gauge the reaction, he went on, 'It is not a sin, merely an inconvenience. I know this boy. He is a thief from a family of thieves, though lately they have stolen from the Germans and so are patriots.'

'Good Lord, I had no idea!'

'It does not matter. He is an honourable thief. You are his friend, and he would not steal from a friend – though it is wise not to tempt him.'

'Thank you for telling me.'

'Also, he has your wallet, which he took from you in the first minute, before he became your friend. You must give him a reward for finding it. He would be embarrassed to return it for nothing.'

It was proposed that they walk. Guy's host said it was a panacea for the afflictions of his age. The rocks and the impenetrable woods confined them to the path, but this twisted so much that new vistas were forever opening until, with a sigh of '*Basta!*' from Signor Porrello, they settled in the shade of a low bush. From here they looked down over pines and across more terraces into the valley of the Magra, which shimmered with blues and buffs. The old man mopped his scalp again and glanced at Guy with a smile both frank and curious.

'You are a civilised man,' he said at length. 'You come all this way to see an old Fascist policeman (yes, I admit I was a Fascist) and exchange pleasantries politely, though it is clear there is something you want of me. I think I know what it concerns, since there is a person you have not mentioned. I mean Lady Carradine, whom, with your charming English informality, you called Julia.'

Guy nodded. Now, at the crux, he was distracted by the landscape, the tender light in the valley and the sharp patterns of the sun-smacked rocks. Beauty was not sufficient to explain the emotion evoked by the panorama of the earth, since beauty could be a cold and glittering thing.

'I should like to see Julia again,' he said. 'Can you help me?'

CHAPTER SEVENTEEN

1930

'We came across Madame Hecate when she was labouring under some local difficulties,' said Ambrose. '*Noblesse oblige*, and I felt we must help her out.'

'I was under arrest,' explained the old lady with some embarrassment, as if it were presumptuous of her to claim the honour. 'I appreciate that nowadays it's very smart to be arrested, but in my youth it wasn't, oh dear no.'

'I see,' said Guy, who did not. Indeed the notion was wildly incongruous. Madame Hecate seemed the most inoffensive of old ladies as she sat in her tweed hat with its little feather, her jacket of the same material, her tartan skirt and sensible shoes. 'May I ask, how did you come to be arrested?'

'By a most unfortunate combination of circumstances. I was travelling to Florence with a friend, Miss Pargiter, when she suddenly died – oh, there's no need to be polite and look shocked. For the young, the death of old people is scarcely worth noticing; for the old, it is simply something one gets used to. As I say, my friend died and, as one does, I put grief aside and set about tidying up her affairs. I had done this satisfactorily and was returning to England by train, when my passport and money were stolen by a most charming young man.'

'What rotten luck!'

'Yes. And, of course, I have only myself to blame. I knew at once that he was a bad sort. I'd caught him at Pisa trying to open my suitcase, though he said he was merely replacing it in the rack from which it had fallen. He apologised most handsomely, but that only reminded me of young Albert, whose father was a locomotive driver and most respectable, and who became a stockbroker. The sons of working men who become stockbrokers rarely come to any good, don't you think? At all events, there was a scandal and Albert had to replace some money and go to Australia. But, you see, Albert wasn't a pickpocket, and that made all the difference.'

'We found the dear lady in chokey,' Ambrose continued. 'Inspector Porrello didn't want to keep her there, but his hands were rather tied since she had no money or papers. In the end, he agreed to release her into my custody if I would stand bail for her good behaviour.'

'And very kind it was of you, too,' the old lady acknowledged graciously. 'Inspector Porrello was most sympathetic, even though he is a Fascist, which I suppose shouldn't be held against him since I'm sure there must be some very considerate Fascists.'

'Is Madame Hecate really your name?' asked Julia.

'Oh, no, my dear,' the old lady smiled. 'That would be silly, wouldn't it? It's the name I use in my profession. In addition, I have a "spirit" name, which I'm not allowed to disclose, if you'll forgive me. My real name is Westmacott, Miss Agnes Westmacott. Not a distinguished name at all. Certainly not as lovely as "Lady Julia Carradine", if I may be permitted to say so.'

Julia blushed. 'How mysterious – to have three names. And what *is* your profession?'

'I'm a medium, my dear.' Madame Hecate ignored a stifled 'Humph!' from Lewis. 'I know: it's a very odd thing to be, and I'm sure I should prefer otherwise since it isn't everywhere considered nice. But one is given certain talents, and taught to accept them as a blessing, even though one doesn't always feel blessed. I understand that Mr Carmody is a playwright. I'm sure that at times he must find that very inconvenient, both to himself and to his friends.'

'You speak very truly,' observed Ambrose thoughtfully.

'I once went to a medium,' put in Margot. 'She produced a smell which she claimed came from the Other Side. But I fancy it was the fried onions she had eaten with her dinner.'

'There are a lot of frauds,' admitted Madame Hecate, 'and you are right to be sceptical. You may think me a foolish old pussy. However, I should hate it if you thought I were dishonest.'

'Let the thought perish!' said Ambrose, unintentionally affirming the general belief that their guest was a foolish old lady.

Madame Hecate was given a room in the mansard next to Commander Ferris. At breakfast Ambrose explained something of their presence at the Villa Esperanza.

'For the most part we're here on holiday, though for my sins I am working on a new piece and Lewis is fooling with poetry.'

'How very nice,' said Madame Hecate, who this morning was wearing a high-necked blouse and a fluffy cardigan of pink wool.

'Jackie is a sailor. He potters about in boats and does some bird-watching. Bird-watching? How implausible life seems.'

'And how do you amuse yourselves?'

'We're very dull dogs, I'm afraid. La Spezia offers all the pleasures of Portsmouth. Porto Venere may be recommended for its swimming and a certain quaintness. Otherwise we read, play tennis and tell stories. By the way, Jackie, how is your story coming along?'

'It's doing fine,' drawled the American.

Madame Hecate was interested in the stories.

'Of course, in my childhood there was no cinema, and one could go dancing only if chaperoned. Life is so much freer now, which I'm sure is a good thing, though one occasionally wonders. I used to read to my brother –

wholesome books, Stevenson and Captain Marryat. What do you read?'

'We don't read,' said Julia. Her voice was low and rather bleak.

Guy thought she looked unwell. 'We make up stories.'

'Really? How terribly clever. I have a nephew who writes. What are your stories about?'

'Murder,' answered Julia and abruptly she rose and said she must go to her room.

The response was so sudden and her action so out of place that Guy, in his surprise, followed Julia into the house without knowing why. She did not proceed directly to her room, but stood in the hall sobbing.

Guy put his arm round her.

'What is it?' he asked. 'What's wrong?'

Her face, when it turned to his, was filled with anguish and she buried it in his shoulder. Guy hesitated, not knowing if he were friend or lover.

'Julia … darling,' he murmured gently. 'Surely you can tell me?'

She shook her head. 'It's all happening,' she said, so softly that Guy could scarcely hear. 'It's all happening, and I'm too weak to stop it.' She added more, all of it inaudible, then sharply wrenched herself away. Her face, which Guy had grown used to thinking of as a 'Vermeer' face, looked torn and ugly, and she snapped angrily. 'Stay away from me, Polly! For God's sake stay away! Leave! You can't help. You're being deceived.'

With that she ran away. Her shoes clattered across the tiles. A door opened and closed. In the silence Guy could hear her breathing, though she was in a room on the other side of the door. Puzzled and upset at his own incomprehension, he returned to the terrace, where the others were discussing murder in the cool morning sunlight.

'I'm sure there's no harm in it,' Madame Hecate was saying, 'but I don't entirely approve of murder stories.'

'Why not, dear lady?' asked Ambrose tolerantly.

'Because stories are so very much an expression of one's character. One need only think of Dickens, who was clearly an amiable and sociable man, and De Quincey, who wasn't. Talking of murder turns one's mind in that direction. I don't say that one will necessarily become a murderer, but the contemplation may stimulate the desire and suggest means by which it may be accomplished. I don't hold to the modern view that one's secret passions should be uncovered and allowed to find expression. On the contrary, they are secret largely because they are disgraceful, and should be firmly suppressed. The result may be personal unhappiness – even madness – but one should not foist one's problems on to others.'

'That's a harsh doctrine,' Lewis commented. 'And if it were true, the police courts would be full of respectable lady novelists.'

'I wasn't speaking of authors in particular. The poor things have a living to make and so have no choice in the matter; and, naturally, one doesn't believe a word they say. But *your* situation is quite different. Nothing compels *you* to talk about murder, and the fact that you choose to do so may not be without significance.'

'You are a very shrewd person,' said Ambrose, which made Madame Hecate become flustered.

'Well it's very kind of you to say so. And it's true I have lived a long time and seen a great deal of wickedness. But in your case I may be mistaken. Yes, well, let us hope that I am.'

On Sunday, Guy went to mass after first taking confession. Because of his limited command of Italian, he mentally listed his sins in Latin. This inadequacy of language made him reflect on the inadequacy of the list itself. It seemed not so much to describe his sin as to give a set of markers by which to steer toward some darker recess of the soul. Markers that were unhelpful, even useless, like those strangers who give directions by naming unfamiliar public houses along the route.

The fact was that, like the Saint of Shoreditch, Guy was afflicted by Doubts now made more acute by, of all things, the stories of Byron and the Shelleys. In reflecting on Percy's drowning and George's death of disease at Missolonghi, it came to Guy how unnecessary these events were: how avoidable by the exercise of even moderate prudence. Had it rested there, this innocent and commonplace insight would have meant little, but, with Jesuitical rigour, Guy pressed it into service to examine the life of Christ. There, too, it came to him with force that he was faced with just such another case. That Christ's death, rather than being essential and redemptive, was equally unnecessary: an elaborate Divine gesture, having a doubtful purpose, like the unfortunate present given by a rich relative one does not desire to offend.

Assuming – as Guy did assume – that it was Jesus' intention, by His example, to bend Mankind to the will of God, then He had made a fine start with the miracles: feeding multitudes and walking on water being a thoroughly effective way of convincing sinners by the drove. It seemed odd, then, to change tack and submit to crucifixion. For, although the Resurrection might signify a triumph over Death, good plain immortality would have been an argument still more triumphant and less open to the quibbles of the sceptical.

At bottom. it seemed to Guy. Christ's death was neither compelled nor desired by Men, but appeased the Deity's own obscure need for sacrifice. Sin was human and oddly democratic and compassionate, and, had the position been fairly explained to the sinners chosen by Jesus to be His followers, Guy suspected they would have answered, 'Don't you worry about us, lad. You leg it and we'll take our chances.'

Guy was well aware that these speculations hardly amounted to a theological position. Rather, they reminded him of the questions put to a bored teacher by a bright but annoying thirteen-year-old. Nevertheless they remained unresolved to cloud his conscience.

Guy went to the Church of S. Pietro at Montemarcello.

Fred offered to drive him. 'I can wait outside. I'm not a left-footer myself.'

Guy declined. The long walk would serve as penance. He invited Julia. It was in his odd moments of Doubt that he became particularly devout: his need for God being more acute; and it was this that made him speak.

'What a prig you can be,' she answered acidly. Guy sensed that he was unforgiven for seeing her in her distress.

Montemarcello was situated on a hill with a view of Porto Venere on the one side and across the Magra valley on the other. The streets were steep and narrow and a faded pink wash covered the church.

The confessional was dusty. The priest smelt of tobacco. As Guy began, he was interrupted in English.

'C'mon, let's make it snappy.'

'You speak English?'

'Yeah, yeah.'

Taken by surprise, Guy asked, 'Do you have a brother in Detroit?'

'You know my brudda Mario?'

'No. No, I was just guessing.'

'Uh huh. So why are we discussing Mario? Let's cut the small talk. What d'you got for me?'

Pressured to be brief, Guy said simply, 'Father, I have been guilty of cowardice.'

'Cowardice?'

'Yes.'

'That's a sin?'

'What? Yes, I think so.'

'You sure? It's not on the list of the whatchumacallems – the "Thou shalt nots".'

Guy considered the Ten Commandments. 'I think it's implicit.'

'That so? You sure you wouldn't like to confess to some of the stealing, killing and coveting stuff?'

'I haven't done any of that.'

'Cowardice? Okay, you're the customer. Whaddaya say? Ten Hail Marys to be on the safe side?'

'Thank you.'

''S all right.'

After receiving absolution, Guy asked if there was a suitable offering he could make to the church.

'You got American cigarettes?' said the priest.

Descending from the village to the road, Guy noticed an ancient motor car and, beside it, Signor Truffatore with two men who were smoking cheroots.

'Hullo, Joe,' said Guy. 'Are these your friends?'

'Just a coupla guys. Listen, we gotta talk.'

Guy allowed himself to be drawn aside.

Joe was solemn and a little agitated. 'It's the dough,' he said.

'I understood Ambrose to say he intended to pay you?'

'Nope, not a dime.'

'But I've already explained that it's not I who owe you the money. Why don't you speak to Signor Carmody?'

Joe shrugged. 'It wouldn't be nice.'

'I see. What, then?'

'I told you I had to borrow.'

'I'm sorry about that.'

'These two bozos' – Joe nodded in their direction – 'work for the guy I borrowed from.'

'Ah.'

'So they gotta rough you up a little. Nothing personal. Afterwards we go get some breakfast.'

It was agreed that, for everyone's convenience, Guy would be assaulted locally. From the road a path led upwards through a pine wood. These were not the small aleppo pines of the shore, but tall and dark. Between them grew a thick undergrowth of woody heather and bramble. Spurge and Herb Robert filled the clearings.

Guy felt light-hearted. Climbing the path, he had glimpsed the distant Alps beyond Carrarra and this view, his earlier view of the Gulf in morning sunshine, and now the flowers at his feet had caused him to experience a quiet epiphany, and he decided he would as soon be beaten up today as on any other day. Smiling, he took his coat off.

'Let 'em hit you a coupla times,' Joe suggested helpfully, 'and maybe bust your nose.'

Guy was not certain he wanted a bloody nose, and, when the first of his assailants approached, he faced him squarely and struck out with a short jab to the left. Another to the right followed. Neither blow was powerful, but the other man was surprised, fell over, hit his head and lay groaning.

The second hoodlum was more cautious. He came on with his arms open, wrestler fashion, as if to grapple. Guy remained out of reach and delivered a cut to the chin and then a blow to the belly. The man was winded rather than disabled, but seemed to lose interest in his task and went to help his colleague.

'Where did you learn that stuff ?' Joe asked.

'At school. I say, I do hope they're not hurt.'

'Forget about 'em. They'll tell their boss they worked you over good.'

'Right. And what will you do now?'

'I guess I'll talk to Signor Carmody after all.'

'That's the ticket.'

'What? Oh, sure. Now let's get breakfast.'

Refreshed after their efforts, Guy and Signor Truffatore drove to Lerici and loaded the car with sacks of cement and a box of coloured glass globes which Ambrose had requested for the purpose of holding candles. Guy was feeling invigorated and on their return to the Villa

Esperanza he searched for old Enzo and explained to him that it was his intention to make good the ancient brickwork in the cistern. Once that was done, he saw no reason why he should not get the fountain to work.

At luncheon the conversation was about the excursion to Venice.

'I see no cause why we all shouldn't go,' said Ambrose generously. 'Except Jackie, who has business in France. I include you, too, Aggie dear,' he added for the benefit of Madame Hecate, pinching her hand with a note of playful indecency.

'I'm sure that's very kind of you,' answered the old lady.

Julia remained morosely silent, though by daylight her melancholy had lost its tragic tone. Rather she seemed like a girl frustrated by the plans of grown-ups. Their talk had lost some of its artificial brightness and they spoke as if Venice were a holiday from the gloom that occasionally afflicted them at La Spezia. The jolly note was struck by Ambrose, who announced that the arrangements for his New York production were well in hand and he was writing with enthusiasm.

In the mid-afternoon Guy was sitting comfortably in the shadows at the bottom of the cistern, eating a piece of bread with one hand and trowelling mortar with the other, when the face of Jackie Ferris appeared over the rim.

'How are you doing, old sport?' asked the Commander.

'Fine. I hope to be finished by evening. And you? Still bird-watching?'

'You better believe it.'

'Good show. And your story? Making progress?'

'Sure. I'm not so good on the historical stuff, but Lewis has been filling me in. And giving me hints on the writing, too, which is pretty swell of him.'

Guy clambered out of the hole to obtain more mortar.

Ferris was sitting on a rock, smoking. 'I guess you're used to the arty crowd,' he said.

213

'No, not especially. In fact I find them disconcerting. I imagine you do, too.'

'They're certainly different. Sometimes they act like they're the only folks that matter. Same as Shelley and the other fellow – George.'

'I suppose you're right.'

'And you don't know whether to love them or hate them for it,' Ferris added thoughtfully.

'If I get back in the cistern, will you hand me the board with the mortar on it?'

Guy climbed down. Ferris carried the board over and together they manoeuvred it.

'Do you remember saying that Signor Truffatore is a police spy?' Guy asked.

'Uh huh.'

'Well, I don't think he is. I rather think he's just a petty gangster. He wanted to beat me up because of some money Ambrose owes him.' Guy did not mention he had seen off the two hoodlums. His success struck him as a fluke and he was embarrassed by it, as if he had somehow cheated.

'You don't say, old sport? That's interesting. So who is the spy?'

'I don't know. I mean, I don't believe there is one.'

'There's got to be,' affirmed Commander Ferris.

While Guy worked, the American continued to make small talk. Guy did not know why he should be the object of the other man's confidences except that he was not a member of what Ferris continued to call 'the arty crowd'. Guy detected behind the Commander's assured exterior a note of personal anxiety and his careful manners began to seem assumed. Of course, if he were indeed a bootlegger, he would have had few opportunities to acquire the social graces.

Ferris said, 'When Julia and Ambrose were in New York they didn't care a damn about art. Ambrose used to drink with Morty Lowenstein at his speakeasy. Morty put up the money for Ambrose's show and, believe me, the only thing he was interested in was the gross box office.'

'I didn't know you met Ambrose in New York. I thought you met him at a party in England?'

Slowly, Ferris lit another cigarette.

'Did I say that? I must have meant that the party was the first time in a long time. Are you about finished? Let's go to the house.'

'We're letting our standards slip,' said Ambrose at his most imperial.

While Guy dressed for dinner, he heard outside the thrum of a ukulele and the sirens of distant ships. Gianni had set the coloured globes round the perimeter of the terrace with a candle in each forming a trail of light like the phosphorescence churned up by a passing liner. Julia and Margot were talking carelessly about Christian Science and the Bahai Faith: was there anything to them?

Guy offered Madame Hecate an American Martini.

'Thank you, my dear. Is it very strong? Normally I drink only the occasional sherry and, at Christmas, a glass of port to the health of the King.'

'Let's say I wouldn't drink two of them.'

'Is the recipe Mr Ferris's?'

'Yes.'

'He is a strange man, isn't he? And his bird-watching seems so *unlikely*. I'm reminded of Charlie, our postmaster's son. He claimed to be a bird-watcher but was caught peering into ladies' windows at night. No, not very nice. He went to Aberystwyth and became Welsh.'

'I think Jackie – Commander Ferris – intends to tell his story tonight.'

'I'm sure that will be very nice for you,' said Madame Hecate sceptically. She pulled her pink cardigan round her and seemed to hunch inside it. Guy thought of a cat which will crouch soft and fluffy within its fur while keeping a wary yellow eye on all around it.

Over dinner Ambrose waxed expansive concerning

Venice. Guy began to share his enthusiasm. La Spezia had both disturbed and excited him and he was looking forward to fresh novelties with these extraordinary people. Only Julia seemed troubled and reluctant to leave.

Full of wine and good humour, Ambrose declared, 'Jackie, dear boy!'

'Yes, old sport?'

'Gianni, clear the plates and bring cigars. Lewis, pour the brandy. Now, Jackie dear, it's time for your little turn. *Thrill* us, do.'

'I'm not sure I can do that, but I'll try my best,' Commander Ferris said with a smile.

'I ask no more. But where are we in our tale?'

'Shelley was murdered,' recalled Lewis. 'We're all agreed on that.'

'I'm not,' murmured Julia.

'Well, at least for present purposes we are. Shelley was murdered. George and Mary seem the most likely suspects…'

'And the Hotel Manager,' chimed in Ambrose.

'As you say. But all of this is the merest suspicion. So far we haven't addressed the evidence in any detail. With all respect to Julia, her suggestion that Shelley was accidentally killed by George in a plot to murder Trelawny has absolutely nothing to support it.'

'Hear, hear,' said Ambrose and he fixed the American with a decidedly foxy stare. 'So there you have your task, Jackie. No more beating about the bush. We want the case and the evidence that will stand up before the beak. Do tell us. 'Oo was it wot done the 'orrible deed?'

CHAPTER EIGHTEEN

The Last Poet

by

Commander John Dexter Ferris

Some people I recall by an image of the day we met. I think of sunlight glinting through palm fronds, a splash of colour on a beach towel, a sparkle on a cocktail glass. Now and then a woman arrests me with a frank and appraising gaze or the dazzle of a smile, and these things remain like unkept promises when we agree to go our ways.

Percy Shelley fixed himself for ever when he first spoke.

'Let me guess,' he said. 'Do they call you Ted or Eddie?'

They call me Eddie, though I've never thought much about it and only Shelley made my name sound like the key to a mystery.

'I don't see the difference,' I told him.

'Oh, there's a whole world,' he said. But he never told me what it was. Or maybe he did when he said, 'I must introduce you to Edward Williams. He's a "Ted". You'll like his wife, Jane, too. She's a fine girl.'

Shelley was a poet. I can't say if he was great. He wanted to be, and Mary needed him to be, and once he was dead everyone agreed that he was. In his life he was a failure, which is why he was always on at George Byron to clean up his act in the poetry department. Byron was a great poet – or, at least, he was a great showman, which may amount to the same thing.

My father wanted me to get in on the bond-selling

racket, but the war intervened and I became a sailor. When it was over, I drifted around and finally fetched up in Italy where George Byron hired me to skipper his boat the Bolívar.

The world is full of fools, but sailing fools are the worst, because they can get themselves killed and you too. Both George and Percy liked to mess with boats and knew something about them. But they had no sense of the sea. I don't think they caught on to its real existence, its dominating and relentless physicality. Their sea was a poet's sea, an interior thing, lodged somewhere in the whorls and recesses of the brain. They looked at it but didn't live with it. It wasn't wife and lover to them. Or the friend with a comforting smile and murder in his heart.

During that early spring in Pisa we had fun. That was George's opinion and for me it was true because I take my fun in uncomplicated ways. With George, he had to say it to believe in it.

'Swell party, don't you think?'

'Just dandy.'

'Seen Percy?'

'He's in the...' I couldn't remember the name of the room. The rooms of *palazzi* have names as if they are movie sets: the Green Room, the Gothic Room, Main Street and the Western Saloon.

'He's smashed.'

'We're all smashed.'

'That's true,' George murmured with a note of pride. He didn't exactly shuffle his feet like a kid waiting for a penny, but he did his best. His gimp prevented him from doing better.

'Cigarette?' he asked.

'Sure.'

We went to the window and smoked. I thought he was going to say a lot about the evening: the air, the light, the sad gay mood. But he didn't. He just murmured, 'I like getting drunk during the day.'

'Why not?' I answered.

'Who were all the people? Did I invite them?'

'Bums – they were all bums.'

He smiled, 'Not Mister Lowenstein. I borrow money from him. I may have disreputable friends, but I insist on reputable creditors. It's so much safer.'

'Not Lowenstein,' I agreed.

In the room the waiters, in white ducktails, were clearing the remains. Their chief, a fussy little fellow in a black jacket, minced round them, pressing them on with short, sharp handclaps. He woke the boy who was sleeping at the piano.

The boy stirred. He looked the college type in white flannels stained with beer. His face was long and oval and he wore round, rimless spectacles, which he couldn't find though they were on his nose. He was drunk, but sober enough to feel ashamed.

'Sorry,' he mumbled.

Byron stared at him and the boy recoiled at the threat, but George was simply distracted.

'So you play, kid?' Tiredness made the words sound flat and cruel. The boy took them as an invitation and began to pass his hands lightly over the keys. Once he found his voice, he sang like a black man: like an old Negro, who rocks on the front porch, cracks peanuts and drinks moonshine.

'You're good, kid,' said George, and then forgot about him as though he wasn't good at all.

The waiters were about done, but the floor was still strewn with broken crackers, cigarette butts and big pieces of ice. The ice was from a sculpture of a swan and had stood on the table surrounded by crabs and lobsters.

Mary was lying flat out on an ottoman with her feet bare and a pair of silver slippers under her head as a pillow. At the sound of the piano and the boy crooning, she opened her eyes and gave a smile of dreams and wonderment.

I pulled her by the hand that was draped off the ottoman with the fingers stroking the carpet.

'Let's dance,' I said.

She stood up with a lingering backward glance, sighed and fell towards me with her hands lightly over my shoulders and mine round her waist where the silk of her dress moved like water.

'Percy?' she asked.

'Search me. He took on a load. Maybe he's sleeping it off,' I said.

Then the door opened and he came in.

He looked as though he had been in a fight, but plenty of drunks do without actually fighting. He rummaged in the ivory box on the table and came up with a cigarette. He lit it.

'I was with Jane, watching Ted play poker with the Gambas,' he said defensively.

'No one suggested differently,' I commented, trying to keep the thing light. And I knew what George and his pink perfect suit reminded me of as he framed itself against darkness. It was the smouldering sun behind a storm cloud.

As spring wore on, the circus moved to the coast. Shelley and Mary went to La Spezia taking the Williamses with them. George Byron decided on Livorno, though he kept up his place in Pisa. Whatever there was between Shelley and Byron was too intense to survive prolonged company.

I stuck to the boat and sailed between the two, watching each grow restless and fractious and wondering where things would lead. There was a sense that we were all about something and we'd better get it over with. I think this was especially true of Mary.

The place at La Spezia was a mistake, pokey and crowded. The summer heat wore everyone down. Mary looked exhausted by being a woman, by motherhood, by love. Jane was perky but out of mood with the time. She doted on Ted, who was a sailor like me and hadn't much time except for boats.

Percy was a mystery as George was a mystery. But George was following a career. He had decided to be a bad man and was thorough about it. He was like your regular alcoholic, practised in it, never sober and never in danger. Percy was the fellow who lives quiet but once in a while goes on a binge so wild and crazy that someday he isn't going to come home. Mary could see it but knew she could only have him all of a piece. That was okay by the bright light of day, but there were times, I suspect, when, foreseeing the disaster, she wished for it so that she could love Percy completely.

This was Leigh Hunt's opinion, which he told to me one day when we were playing billiards. Hunt was a journalist and he often spoke as if he had put the words together in his head and was trying them out for an article. He said that, for Percy, women were mysterious and as luminous as moonlight. He was one of Shelley's friends but George Byron had an idea of financing his own newspaper and Hunt had come to Italy with his wife and children to talk over the deal.

There may have been something to what Hunt said. But, as if he had suddenly grown tired of change, Byron seemed settled on his latest girlfriend, Terri. I don't think it was a case of moral fidelity. It was as though he had tried the infidelity game and decided it wasn't worth the candle.

I took five hundred lire off Hunt and he was sore.

'Jeez, it's hot!' he groaned, and ran a finger round the collar of his cheap shirt. 'I play better when it's cool.' He looked around for the pitcher of beer, but it was empty. 'Did you know that the heat does something to the table, warps it or something? And the ball are bigger.'

'Not that I can see.'

'They're bigger,' he affirmed aggressively.

'Go get some more beer. You want I should stick the balls in an ice-bucket?'

He glared at me as I tossed the cue ball from one hand to the other, calculated his chances and decided he'd get the beer. As he went out, George came in.

'Is it hot?' I asked. 'Hunt says it's hot.' I was sweating myself, but George, in a beige tussore suit, looked as cool as they come. He didn't appear to notice my question. Instead he looked around the room, taking it in like he had never been here before. I didn't care much for the place, especially by daylight with the dust and cigar smoke when it looked like the wreck of an empire.

Lighting a cigarette, George asked, 'What do you make of Hunt?'

'He's a piker.'

'Aren't you … a piker, too? Here for the use of my boat?'

Maybe I was, but I admit I wanted to hit him. That was how the atmosphere affected us all. We were all slightly crazy with heat and hangovers, and suspense was in the air. Loaded to the gills with highballs, we sailed, played tennis or golf, or mooched about the city spouting a lot of phoney stuff about *quattrocento* paintings. I was sick of it and yet I couldn't leave. Somehow George and Percy had taken me prisoner and I could only wait and watch to see how it would all work out.

Percy drifted in with Ted Williams. They had put away some whiskey and were carrying glasses, and Shelley's face was glowing serenely. Though I disliked Hunt, I thought again of what he said, and it came to me that such serenity did not come from drinking but was the mirror of Mary's luminosity. Back home at the Villa Magni she might have lost it so that Shelley in frustration spent his days mooning over Jane Williams; but here away from Mary she still shimmered for him.

Percy threw himself on to a chair and Ted stood behind,

gripping the chair back, both grinning like dopes. There are moods, times and places, and the room stank of smoke and stale beer, and the sun seemed to have tipped in a bucket full of dust.

'I just saw Leigh,' said Percy.

'I hope he still isn't sore at our game,' I commented.

George looked at me sourly. 'Every time that bum loses, he chisels me for cash.'

'So *I'm* supposed to lose?'

'Forget it,' said George and looked away as though he was studying Higher Things, which was a way with him.

Percy was off his stride but he said, 'Since Leigh and his folks seem to be settled in, it's time Ted and I were heading home.'

'I'd prefer you to stay,' George answered.

Ted chipped in, 'I promised Jane to get back home as soon as possible, and you know how it is when you stand up a dame.'

'What's in a day or two?'

Ted persisted, 'I really gotta get back.' He looked ready to stand on the point, but George had lost interest.

'Give Mary my love,' he said to Percy.

'What does that mean?'

'Whatever it usually means. It's too hot to argue,' George added; though, as I've said, he was the coolest of all of us.

'You should be careful what you say,' Ted contributed. I don't think he was looking for trouble, but he had the drunk's habit of mixing where he wasn't wanted under some notion that he was clarifying matters and making things easy. 'A fella once said that about Jane and I socked him. I mean socked him – right here. On the other hand, he wasn't a close friend. That makes a difference. A friend can say stuff without it being taken the wrong way.'

'Then I guess it's all right,' said George, 'since we're all friends.'

*

Percy's boat was on the quayside at Livorno by the old fortress. She was called the *Don Juan* and was a sleek racer, two-masted with a bunch of gaff-rigged sails. I thought she might do fine on a lake with a crowd of other fellows around to lend a hand, but even then she might get blown over by one of those cross-winds that come howling out of a valley. When Shelley took delivery of her two months before, I warned him she was no good for the sea. On the way down, four of them had crewed the boat: Shelley, Ted, Williams, some kid I forget, and Roberts, who was another Navy man. But Roberts didn't propose to return, and they were only the three that day at Livorno. Williams had never bought my idea of hiring an Italian to make up the number.

'Stay on a few days,' George Byron proposed. He could see Ted Williams hopping to leave. So, passing it off as if a girl had turned down a date, he said, 'It doesn't matter. I guess if you've got to go, then there's nothing to say.' And then he looked annoyed as though Shelley was sticking around too long.

The weather had been on and off for a few days. Today it was flat calm and the coasters were taking their chances to make a few miles before it closed in again, as it can do suddenly in those waters.

'What do you think, Eddie?' Shelley asked me. We could see the same thing. To the north-west, beyond that calm sea and calm sunny sky, was a patch of cloud. It was nothing and everything, a faint opalescence like a bruise on a woman's cheek, masked by powder and framed by a pair of dazzling eyes and a smile.

'Why don't you take the *Bolívar* to go with him?' George suggested. He sounded bored and wanting to get rid of us all.

I said, 'That's fine by me,' and collared one of my men and asked him to make the *Bolívar* ready.

Shelley looked at Williams, who shrugged and tapped

his watch. 'Do you have the ship's papers?' he asked me, and I said I could get them.

One of my boys brought the ship's papers and I strolled over to the office. Joe Truffatore, the harbour-master, was there with a little fellow. This little fellow wore a dove-grey suit and a homburg and spats to match. One hand was covered in a tan glove, skin-tight, and the other hand held its mate and a malacca cane with a shagreen handle. He sported moustaches, waxed and perky as a smile.

'Hullo, Captain Trelawny,' said Joe.

'Hi, Joe,' I answered democratically.

'What brings you here?' he asked.

'Nothing in particular,' I told him. 'Just shooting the breeze.'

I looked at the clock.

Joe looked at the papers I was carrying. 'What d'you got there?'

'Just papers.'

'You leaving port?'

'Who's your friend?'

Joe shifted uncomfortably until the little fellow in grey nodded. Then he said briefly, 'Name's Porrello. He's a cop.'

'That so? Pleased to meet you, Mister Porrello.'

'My pleasure,' said the little fellow.

The office had a window giving on to the quay. I could see the ship's monkeys running around and stock still, in the middle of them, Shelley, Byron and Ted Williams. I say 'still', though I guess they were talking. But they looked like three statues, there on the quayside, in the sunshine, with the world running round them.

'Sir Shelley is sailing,' Joe remarked. 'He came for his papers.'

'Uh huh,' I agreed, and asked Porrello, 'What brings you here?'

He didn't answer, but smiled. I liked Porrello's smile. It

was that of a man who knows he isn't fooling anyone.

Joe tapped the barometer. 'What d'you reckon to the weather?'

'It may last.'

'I wouldn't like to be caught in it.'

'You won't be.' I reminded him and we passed the ball backwards and forwards a few more minutes. Every time I looked outside, the group of statues had taken new positions. Only once did I see movement: Ted Williams shaking his watch.

Joe Truffatore knew I wasn't there for the sake of my health. He had to figure I was looking to leave port and was calculating how much squeeze to apply. It was driving him crazy.

'Are you sure you ain't doin' nothin' with those papers?' he asked at last.

'Don't be stupid, Joe,' said Porrello loudly. 'Can't you see Captain Trelawny doesn't want anything from us?'

'Why'n hell's he here, then?' Joe complained.

'I'll go,' I said.

Immediately Joe Truffatore took the other tack, asking, 'Why leave?' petulantly as though he was going to miss the last reel of a film.

'Let it pass,' said Porrello. He placed his hand on Joe's which Joe had lifted but didn't know why. 'Goodbye, Captain Trelawny.'

'See you around, Mister Porrello.'

I left the harbour-master's office and walked back along the paved quay where the stones retreated in parallel lines toward a false horizon behind which lay the water. Shelley and the other two became slowly animated.

'Any luck?'

'No. Some problem with the papers.'

Ted Williams stubbed his cigarette and immediately lit another. He took a hip-flask from his pocket. 'Care for a shot? Did you offer Joe anything?'

'There was someone with him.'

The flask passed from hand to hand. I took a large slug.

'Hey, steady,' said Shelley. 'Anyone would think *you* were risking the voyage. Any more thoughts on the weather?'

The stain of cloud was still on the horizon, spoiling the clear blue day. It hadn't moved but that meant nothing. A shift of wind and it would blow in sudden. I shook my head and Shelley said that, in that case they'd better leave.

I took his hand and held it a moment, forgetting to let go as I tried to puzzle out what I'd done. The notion played in my head that, if I was to tell him, he'd understand: that it would make no difference to his sailing. He would understand and explain to me why I did what I did. Because that's what poets do, if they do anything at all.

However, the moment passed. Ted Williams was already dropping down the ladder into the boat, where the boy was acting the man by wrapping his lips round a bottle. I remembered that drunks were often lucky and saw them sailing through the storm as tight as drums and laughing their heads off. And maybe there wouldn't be a storm.

They cast off. George waved, turned to me and said, 'What do you think? Will there be a storm?'

'God knows.'

'I'd better go back. I gotta speak to Hunt.'

'Throw the bum out.'

'Maybe.'

We waved again. Percy Shelley waved back. Williams was setting the sail and the boy was at the helm. Behind them the wide open sea glittered all the way to La Spezia and Mary.

Hunt was right. Mary was the point of luminosity, the westering sun that beckons the traveller in the evening. Shelley sailed for La Spezia with that sun in his eyes, not knowing that he would never reach it, since it lay beyond the furthest horizon. It died in the storm that closed the day. Yet for him, though nor for me, there would be another day: calm, blue, and bathed in imperishable light.

CHAPTER NINETEEN

1930

Ambrose smiled wanly. 'What a dangerous fellow you are, Jackie dear, I should be frightened to go sailing with you.'

One by one the coloured lights on the terrace expired, but on the table was a paraffin lamp brought by Joe Truffatore only that morning. It burnt steadily over the American's notes.

'I liked your depiction of Mary,' said Margot brightly. 'So elusive. What did you call her? Luminous? I should like to be luminous.'

Julia said very softly, 'I was touched. You showed a side of your character I never suspected.' Guy had noticed that, during the telling, she had seemed to withdraw into shadow as if not wanting to hear. But now her voice held notes of both surprise and unwilling admiration. It had been Guy's previous impression that Julia disliked Ferris, though this seemed incompatible with her supplying him with money for his sailing. Then, at that word 'luminous', he had searched out her face and seen in it that very quality. Thus he knew that the story was in part directed at her and that the American was in love with her. Perhaps they had been lovers and had quarrelled, which would explain Julia's sense of obligation and her present distaste.

'Lewis gave me some ideas,' Ferris admitted.

'I didn't suggest that Trelawny was such a swine,' Lewis protested.

'That was my idea. Julia suggested that Trelawny was maybe intended as a victim. I just wanted to set the record straight. Trelawny was the most dangerous of the lot of them. He wouldn't have waited to be killed. He was a sailor and he knew how to act.'

Lewis was doubtful. 'You've given him a sentimental streak.'

Madame Hecate had sat throughout working at a piece of lace. She put it down and remarked in a cool but hesitant voice: 'I think I understand Commander Ferris perfectly. Sentimentality can be such a cruel thing. A sentimental murderer feels compassion for his victim, and that excuses his act by covering it with virtue. The murder itself then becomes merely a regrettable matter of necessity and not an expression of evil. Oh no, one is very much mistaken if one considers these people to be less than human. Monsters are frequently sentimental.'

This sombre observation flattened a mood which was in any case chilled by the tone of Ferris's tale. Ambrose called for drinks.

Gianni brought them and they fell to small talk about Venice.

'I'm not sure I shall go,' said Lewis.

'Feeling unwell, dear?' asked Ambrose sympathetically. 'Gyppy tum or something?'

'A good night's rest may cure it. I'll see how I am in the morning.'

'Well, drink up. That will cheer you. Meanwhile Jackie can explain something of his conclusion that Trelawny was the murderer. I think I see the motive. The captain was smitten by Mary, which seems plausible enough. He was also very much taken by Percy – a fact I'm also prepared to grant since in later days he wrote a hagiography of our man. How such admiration leads to murder we must leave to psychologists, but the breed of poets is a queer thing and one must sacrifice them or sacrifice to them. And there *is* a sort of perfection in Shelley's death. Yes, I think we can allow the motive.'

Ferris searched for a cigarette, lit it and lounged back in his chair with the lamp illuminating only the lower half of his face.

'What do you want to know?' he asked in his even American drawl.

'The evidence, my boy. We're tired of hints and speculation. We want to "nail" the villain, as the saying goes. We want the "lowdown". Facts, dear boy, facts.'

Guy leant forward. He glimpsed the others doing the same except Madame Hecate, whose fingers seemed only to work faster. How intense they were! Guy could not explain it to himself when he knew that there could be no evidence against Trelawny, that Shelley's death was an accident, and that in any case it didn't matter. And yet Ferris seemed convinced that he had something.

'Trelawny lied,' said Jackie Ferris. 'And I can prove it. Which boat was based at Livorno?'

'Don't be a tease, Jackie,' complained Ambrose.

'The *Bolívar*,' said Lewis curiously.

'Since when?'

'April, I think. Shelley drowned in July.'

'And the *Don Juan*?'

'Shelley took delivery of her in May.'

'Had she been to Livorno before? Not that it makes much difference.'

'I don't think so.'

'Exactly,' said Ferris with a grin. He relished the pause. 'I've got to go on? Well, maybe it takes a sailor to see it. You have to get into the situation. Trelawny is berthed in Livorno. He's an experienced Navy man. He's been there three months or so, sailing in and out of Livorno up and down the coast. He knows the system so far as it concerns his paperwork. Hell, he probably drinks with the harbour-master and the customs guys. I know I would.

'So July comes. Both ships want to leave harbour. Williams gets his papers stamped for the *Don Juan*. Trelawny can't fix them for the *Bolívar*. Why not? He's done it before and he knows the people. What's so special about Williams that he has no problem? Why is today different from any other day and why is it so difficult for

231

Trelawny, who knows the ropes, but not for Williams, who doesn't?'

Listening to Ferris, Guy wondered if he was an arrogant man. An arrogant lover, dangerous and sentimental? Some rain in the late afternoon had carried humidity into the warm night. This, he supposed, explained the prickling of his skin.

Lewis was avid for more. 'Gosh,' he said, 'I do believe you've got something there.'

'What a sleuth you are,' agreed Ambrose, admiringly. 'I follow your argument, but, for completeness, tell us your conclusion.'

'Trelawny lied. There is no way that Williams could have got his papers for the *Don Juan* and Trelawny fail to get them for the *Bolívar*. The only explanation is that he never tried. He saw the storm in the offing – he admitted as much – and decided to let Shelley and Williams take their chances in a boat he knew wasn't seaworthy. The lawyers can argue whether that amounts to murder, but in my book it does. Trelawny killed Shelley as sure as if he'd put a bullet in his head.'

'I do believe you're right,' Ambrose said, and sighed with disappointment that the mystery was solved.

In the far west an electric storm flashed silently over the purple sea. On the terrace of the Villa Esperanza the stonework glimmered with an intermittent yellow light. The air remained warm, still and damp. Margot spoke first, proposing that, since they were now finished with murder, they should play cards. Julia enquired how Lewis was feeling. Jackie Ferris, contented at his success, smiled, stretched his limbs until they cracked and made a remark about retiring to bed.

'Aggie, dear,' said Ambrose considerately to Madame Hecate, 'you must be tired.'

The old lady had been sitting quietly and gave a start at being addressed.

'Oh, don't concern yourself with me,' she answered in a fluster of modesty. 'At my age sleep is not so important. I was merely thinking.'

'What about?'

'The death of poor Shelley and how clever Commander Ferris is to see through the events of that terrible day. I must admit, he raised aspects I had never considered. It is so useful to have the point of view of a sailor. It forces one to think. Thank you, Commander Ferris.'

'You're welcome, ma'am.'

'No, truly, I *do* thank you.' She hesitated. 'But, does it not strike you how foolish Captain Trelawny was?'

'In what way?'

'Why, to tell an unnecessary lie! The business of the ship's papers – if it were indeed as odd as you suggest – would have struck his contemporaries as odd, too. Do you see? How much easier it would have been for him simply to ignore the risk of the storm. Such things are so difficult to predict and, at worst, he might have been accused of an error of judgment. And even that is unlikely, since Williams was prepared to hazard the weather. To *emphasise* the danger of the storm would run quite counter to any plan of murder. By the way, it *was* Trelawny who emphasised the danger of setting sail that day. By his own admission, in his book, he volunteered to escort the others in the *Bolívar*. If he hadn't done so, he would not have needed the ship's papers and could have avoided telling a foolish lie to explain why he could not obtain them.'

'My dear lady,' exclaimed Ambrose, 'I have quite underestimated you!'

'Oh, dear me … oh, I am sorry. I did not wish to put myself forward. And what Commander Ferris has said is such a very good explanation of matters, even if there are some difficulties.'

'Damn right it's good,' said Jackie Ferris forcefully. 'Maybe Trelawny was an idiot to get himself into a situation where he had to get the ship's papers stamped.

But that's where he found himself, and the fact is that he lied about not getting them, or else how do you explain that Williams had no problem?'

Madame Hecate was evidently unused to displays of temper. Guy, too, thought Ferris's behaviour inappropriate. The old lady waited, coughed discreetly, then continued.

'One does not know; one can only speculate. But I believe your error lies in assuming that Trelawny's situation was advantageous as regards the port authorities. However, I very much doubt that was the case. You see, the *Bolívar* belonged to Lord Byron, and he was keeping very doubtful company – freemasons and revolutionaries such as the Gambas. I take it for granted that his comings and goings were most closely watched by the Tuscan police. So, if I am right, the harbour-master at Livorno would have had no authority to release the *Bolívar* without the permission of his superiors, a permission that was not available since the proposal to put to sea arose only at the last moment, when the risk of a storm had already become apparent. In contrast, no such difficulties confronted the sailing of the *Don Juan*. Shelley and Williams were merely visitors to Livorno, and Shelley had displayed little interest in Italian politics. The two cases are in no way comparable, do you see?'

Jackie Ferris was generous enough to laugh. 'Okay, lady, you got me.'

'Never mind,' Ambrose consoled him. He asked Madame Hecate, 'I believe you have other reasons for discounting Captain Trelawny as our murderer, am I right?'

The old lady nodded and smiled. She said, 'Captain Trelawny reminds me of my great-uncle Ernest. Did you know that the Captain modelled himself on Byron's Corsair? He was a vain man with a romantic disposition.'

'And Uncle Ernest?'

'Not dissimilar, though I think he imitated Robert Louis

Stevenson, rather than Byron. It suited him to be considered a very dangerous and ruffianly character. He went to the East and did very well in the tea trade and took a Chinese wife and had Chinese children – which was not at all respectable. In the end he was tempted by an expedition to Borneo, where he was eaten by Dyaks – at least, I think it was Dyaks. My point is that it is very hazardous to consider oneself a dangerous character. One may be in a very difficult position when one discovers the self-deception.'

In the morning Margot announced, 'Lewis is still complaining about feeling seedy. Be a sweet, Guy, and persuade him to get out of bed and come to Venice with us. He'll listen to you. You're his friend. I'm merely his mistress.'

'Sorry, old man, but I feel dreadful,' said Lewis.

'Are you running a temperature?' Guy did not think the other man looked particularly feverish.

'Some sort of stomach bug. It'll pass, but for the moment I don't feel I could move.'

'Will you be all right?'

'Jackie is sticking around for a couple of days before he returns to Marseilles, so I shouldn't come to any harm.'

Julia was the most upset. Unreasonably so, in Guy's opinion.

'He isn't ill, he's faking it!' she said angrily and pleaded, '*Please* make him come, Ambrose.'

'What do you think, Guy?'

'I took his temperature and there's nothing wrong there. His abdomen is tender. I gave him some kaolin and morphine to settle his stomach. Jackie is here, and Joe Truffatore will be looking in, so I don't think he's in any danger.'

'But is he fit to travel?'

'It's usually well to leave that sort of decision to the patient,' Guy ventured uncertainly.

Julia turned on him scornfully. 'What an utter fool you are!'

Guy did not see her again until the cars were packed and it was time to leave. But to satisfy himself he checked his patient again. Lewis was in bed and Jackie Ferris was sitting with him, smoking a cigarette and chatting.

'I guess it's time to say goodbye,' the American said cheerily. 'I'll be in London again in the fall. Maybe I'll see you there.'

'That would be nice,' Guy agreed. They shook hands. 'What about you?' he asked Lewis. 'You can still change your mind.'

'To be frank, I'll appreciate the peace and quiet to work at the old poetry. Ambrose can be entertaining, but he does wear you down. You must have noticed. Still,' he added, taking Guy's hand and fixing him with the frank gaze of their carefree student days, 'it's nice of you to be concerned for me, Polly.'

'You're sure you'll be all right? You seem very down in the dumps,'

Jackie Ferris intervened. 'If Lewis is on his feet tomorrow, I'll take him out in the boat. There's nothing like sailing to take you out of yourself. And don't worry,' he winked slyly, 'I'll make sure our boy doesn't drown.'

Guy travelled with Ambrose and Madame Hecate in the Bentley. Fred drove Margot and Julia in the Alvis. The arrangement was proposed by Ambrose, who had taken a shine to the queer old lady and treated her half mockingly, half protectively. Guy still could not make her out. At moments she seemed a bumbling inoffensive creature, preoccupied with the contents of her crewelwork bag and inclined to forgetfulness. At others she seemed intense and alert, quietly judging the world through her clear blue eyes and finding it lacking.

Julia continued in her morose silence. The intimacy which Guy had found so inexplicable had vanished equally inexplicably. If he had been more self-assured, he might have been angry or indifferent in the face of this caprice. Instead he was puzzled. For no reason that he could fathom, she had called him a fool. A self-assured man would have dismissed the accusation, but Guy did not. He could only meditate humbly on the nature of his folly and of Julia's sorrow, and find no answers.

They drove by Parma and Mantua, where Ambrose wanted to see the monuments of the Gonzaga dukes. The road was dusty and bordered by meadows and fields of wheat and maize, save here and there where ranks of vines grew among pollarded mulberries. They found a quiet spot among the latter and picnicked in the shade, dozed and woke under the gaze of a jolly peasant who had wine and cheese to sell. Ambrose took out his ukulele and Margot, displaying another of her oddities, sang a music-hall song in a cockney accent. Fred followed with a long comic monologue, and Madame Hecate was persuaded to recite some Tennyson.

That night they dined at a small restaurant with a view of the Ponte dei Molini and the Lago Superiore at a table placed outside among tubs of lemon bushes. A radio played dance music and a polite youth in uniform collected money for a Fascist charity.

'Tonight, no stories,' announced Ambrose. 'Unless Fred has a tale of how he gave sound advice to Signor Mussolini.'

'I never met Signor Mussolini.'

'Don't be literal, Fred.'

'I mean I didn't actually *meet* him,' Fred murmured darkly.

'At all events,' Ambrose went on, 'we seem to have exhausted Byron and Shelley. More's the pity. I thought that Jackie's sinister story was very promising and was quite prepared to believe Trelawny bumped Percy off. Alas,' he bowed to Madame Hecate, 'you thoroughly scotched that theory. I am coming to the depressingly uninteresting conclusion that the fellow died in an accident after all.'

'Well...' began Madame Hecate hesitantly. Feeling all eyes turn to her, she stammered, 'Yes, well, it *could* be an accident, I suppose. It is so difficult to know the truth, and I'm sure it's the best – the most charitable interpretation of the facts.'

'You have doubts?'

'Doubts? Oh, yes, one always has doubts. As I say, the truth can be so difficult to ascertain, especially when one cannot ask those questions which would clarify matters. On the other hand, there are quite circumstantial accounts of that tragic day and – of course, one may be wrong – they seem to answer the problem very clearly.'

In his tiredness Guy almost missed this last remark. He was shaken awake by Ambrose demanding, 'No, no, Aggie dear! You can't leave us in suspense. Are you saying that Shelley actually *was* murdered?'

Madame Hecate scanned the others with her innocent blue eyes, and in a quiet voice said, 'Well, that is what the evidence shows, isn't it? You do see it, don't you? Oh dear! It seems I have misunderstood the purpose of your stories. I had assumed that you were merely testing alternative theories in order to reject them. I had thought you *knew*.'

'Not at all,' said Ambrose in some confusion.

'No, I see that now. What a difficult position you place me in. One does not like to speak ill of the dead, and it isn't as if any of this mattered any more. And, you know, I may be just a foolish old lady. I *may* be wrong.'

The reputation of the dead and the possibility of error seemed to pain her. She murmured, 'Oh dear,' several times.

'No, Mr Carmody, you have been very kind and hospitable – more than I deserve, I'm sure. But you must not press me.'

'Surely you don't propose to leave us without an answer?'

'Well, no, I...' The old lady sighed. 'How shall I put it? There is a question that one must deal with. It is really so simple, though one's thoughts become clouded by the fact that we no longer think as people did a hundred years ago. Honour, for example, was held in very high esteem and men used to go to extraordinary lengths to defend it. Do you understand now?'

'Not at all.' Ambrose smiled. It seemed he had concluded that the old lady was only wandering vaguely among her thoughts. He had turned to ask Fred to pass the wine when she spoke again.

She said, 'The question is – *why* did Shelley leave Livorno that day? Answer that and you will answer everything.'

CHAPTER TWENTY

1945

'If that fellow Nessuno shows his face, you must catch him and lock him up until I've spoken to him.'

'Righty ho, Guy,' said Jenkins. 'Though what you want with an Italian tramp is a mystery to me.'

'Just do what I say,' Guy answered.

As Jenkins was about to leave, Guy remembered there was something else he wanted to ask: why the hospital he was so carefully establishing at La Spezia was beginning to disappear.

He had noticed it in small ways at first. After one of the early deliveries of supplies had arrived, he had Corporal Long show him round the inventory so that, by physical inspection, he could compare it with the manifest. Certain items were missing, which at that time he put down to clerical error or pilferage en route.

His doubts as to this explanation began when a large generator arrived and the smaller, but still useful, machine it replaced simply vanished.

This morning the contents of an entire ward of six beds had evaporated like mist – so completely that Guy, opening the door in the course of his inspection, assumed that the room had always been kept vacant. He was telling himself that it was handy to have such unexpected additional space, when the incongruity struck him and he returned with the naive hope that the furnishings would miraculously reappear.

'Can you explain it?' he asked Jenkins, wishing he sounded more stern.

'I can, but it'll come better from Tommy,' Jenkins

answered evasively.

Corporal Long was summoned. Guy required Jenkins to stay and hear the interrogation. 'And tell Nick and Jimmy not to hang outside the door, giggling. Haven't they got anything to do?'

'Well, no, actually. I don't like to mention it, but haven't you noticed that we haven't got any doctors, or nurses – or patients?'

'That's none of your business.'

'No, I suppose not. Still, it's odd, isn't it?'

On reflection Guy agreed it was odd. But the oddities of the Army were a species of normality.

Corporal Long was smiling and at ease. After putting the facts to him, Guy asked bluntly, 'Have you stolen all those beds and things?'

'No, sir,' said the Scotsman stoutly.

'But you do know where they are?'

'Yes, sir.'

'And you took them?'

'Yes, sir.'

'I see.' Guy was not certain whether the Corporal's confession was helpful or not. 'May I ask...?'

'They're all at yon Italian hospital in town. They was all they poor weans with nowhere to lay their heads and –'

'You gave all our equipment to some children?'

'An' old folks. I didna exactly *give* the stuff away. It's more of a loan.'

'I see. No, I don't see. Why on earth did you do it?'

'They was very grateful – if you take my meaning. An' we've nae use for the stuff, seein' we've nae patients.'

'But ... I mean ... that's hardly a matter for you. And how do you know that patients won't start arriving tomorrow?'

'We'd need some nurses first.'

'Yes, well, after the nurses, then.'

'And doctors.'

'Doctors, too.'

When Corporal Long did not reply, Guy felt the last tenuous residue of his authority slip away. The trouble was that he liked the little Glaswegian and had no desire to see him in the glasshouse on a charge. He also doubted he could keep hold of him long enough to bring one.

'Permission to speak, sir?' said the Corporal.

'What? Oh, very well. At ease.'

'Well, sir, it's like this. The Army disna know we're here.'

'Pardon? Are you sure?'

'Aye.'

'How do you know?'

'Because the telephone link to Corps disna work. They buggers have moved on somewhere and havena left a forwarding address.'

'Good God!' said Guy.

Guy went to see Signor Porrello again at his small farm in the hills. He was working among his vegetables and carrying an ancient percussion-lock rifle on a sling over his shoulder.

'Going hunting?' Guy asked him.

'No.'

'Oh. Then why the gun?'

'To defend myself against the Communists who want to kill me.' The Inspector smiled. 'Please, don't concern yourself. I am an old man and my death is not important – except to me. Come now, we will take a drink together.'

They went into the cool interior of the house. It had an earthen floor and an open fireplace for cooking and was in the neatest order. The shutters were closed and Signor Porrello lit a lamp. He produced a bottle of wine and a jug of water.

'Well?' he began. 'You have returned to pursue your enquiries concerning Lady Julia?'

'Yes. I should like to see her again.'

'May I ask why?'

Guy wondered if he should tell the Inspector about Nessuno and the bones discovered in the cistern. Fearing their terrible significance, he decided not to.

'I am trying to remember what happened all those years ago.'

'You don't remember?'

Guy shook his head. 'Some of it is clear, but some isn't.' He looked up into a pair of intelligent, kindly eyes. 'After Lewis's – Signor Lockyer's – boating accident, I became unwell.'

'Really?'

'Yes. I had ... a sort of nervous breakdown, I suppose. I was ill for about a year. My fiancée – that is to say, my wife, Elizabeth – helped me to get over it. I'm all right now, except that some of my memories are unclear. They get mixed up with stories we were telling. For example, I'd forgotten that Commander Ferris disappeared. Not that there's any connection, since it was months later that he drowned – I suppose he drowned? – and by then I was already unwell, which is probably why I forgot.'

Signor Porrello considered this explanation sympathetically. He sighed.

'You were not fortunate people. And yet you seemed to be so intelligent, so beautiful, so rich. At our little police station we admired you intensely. If we were bored with our poor Italian criminals, someone would suggest, "Let us arrest the English." And sometimes we did.'

Guy smiled at the shared recollection and shook his head. 'We were very foolish, Signore, and paid the price. You know about Lewis and Commander Ferris. Lady Margot married Sir Odo Milne, and died last year after spending the war in prison.'

'Sir Milne was often in our newspapers. He was said to represent the true spirit of the English.'

'I believe he thought he did. He and Margot were married in Berlin. Goering attended the wedding. Even before the war, that was a mistake.'

'You have not spoken of Lady Julia.'

'No.' Guy paused. 'I should like to see her first.'

They descended from the calm, sunny, dusty hills and into the town. The streets were full of American military vehicles, though whether arriving or departing Guy could not tell. The noise and bustle of the conquerors contrasted with the sleepy slyness of the watchful Italians. Gangs of the latter were shovelling the rubble of ruined buildings. Guy could not recall if La Spezia had been bombed or shelled; or perhaps the buildings had collapsed of themselves, as Italian buildings occasionally did. The air was russet with brick and concrete dust and smelled sourly of petrol exhaust. A convoy of Americans, which had evidently lost its way, was struggling through the streets of Migliarina. The soldiers were dirty and brashly handsome, the relaxed symbols of militant democracy. He recalled that Lewis had once said that Mussolini and Hitler were the heirs of Byron, Shelley and the whole Romantic tradition: a proposition that Guy found memorable but incomprehensible. As he and Signor Porrello waited for the Americans to pass by, Guy shuffled this intellectual small change, recognising that it represented only the remains of larger ideas, like coins given indifferently to a beggar.

The cemetery of Montemarcello was at a little distance from the village and the crest of the hill, where the road to Bocca di Magra snaked through pine brakes in its descent to the valley. The landscape unfolded across the river to distant tree-clad heights, each topped by a small town, and still further to the Apuan Alps, visible as a grey shimmer.

Under the deprivations of war, the cemetery had fallen into dusty neglect like a North African town whose crumbling monuments compete in sun and shadow with a rundown souk.

'Come, come.' Dapper Signor Porrello's purposeful mincing walk led Guy between stacked tombs barren of flowers. The dusty cypresses rotated with each twist of the path. The dusty sun blazed in a flat pink sky.

'I wasn't certain,' said Guy as the old man paused, 'that Julia was buried at La Spezia. In fact I couldn't be sure she had died here. The newspaper said Italy, that was all. Did she never return to England after that summer? I'm sorry – there's no reason for you to know.'

'It was my job to know,' answered Signor Porrello. 'No, she never left Italy.'

'Was she alone?'

'Mostly. I arrested her occasionally, for old times' sake. And sometimes when she was drunk and in danger.'

In a spot without beauty, a place surrounded only by other tombs, was a simple earth grave, plain except for a stone and a framed photograph, as was common in Italy, and an inscription.

Lady Julia Victoria Carradine

1905-1936

'She Paid the Price'

'I wondered at the quotation,' said Signor Porrello dryly. 'It is so *intentional*; so brutal. I am used to the polite pieties.'

Guy remembered a remark he had made earlier. That they had all paid the price of their summer at La Spezia.

'I should have brought flowers.'

The old man shrugged. 'In the heat they die quickly.'

'I…' The remark remained unfinished. Guy had no sense of what was appropriate. He was used to the sad, damp cemeteries of England. Here the statement 'dust to dust' was physically emphatic and shorn of obvious melancholy.

He examined the photograph. It was a studio portrait using artful shadow and filled with factitious mystery, as if Julia had been a *femme fatale* in a cheap film. Yet, partial though it was, it was truthful. In one aspect Julia's life could be interpreted as a pose over which she had lost control.

'She was very beautiful,' commented Signor Porrello.

'Luminous,' said Guy, thinking of Vermeer. He glanced at the old man. 'Was she very unhappy?'

'Yes.' Signor Porrello considered his next remark. 'She was not beautiful always. She was very often drunk, and when she was she became ugly and, in time, would have been an ugly woman with an ugly voice. I was reluctant to bring you here, Signor Parrot, because you have a kind heart and I see that such pain and waste distress you. Do you have a good wife?'

'Yes,' said Guy, surprised at the question.

'Lady Julia was not a good woman. I am telling you what you have always known. She was sinful and unhappy in her sin.'

Guy was shocked but found himself nodding. 'You are a wise man.'

'No,' said Signor Porrello sharply. 'I am a clever policeman and a foolish old Fascist. I have no wife or children, and the system I served has betrayed me. I am not a wise man. Now, shall we go?'

On the return to the car, Guy felt at ease enough to smoke a cigarette. The light playing on the rectilinear structures made the cemetery a place of sunny abstractions. 'I suppose this is grief,' he thought. He wondered if war had made him indifferent to the conventional insignia of death.

'Who came to the funeral?' he asked.

'Her husband, Sir Carradine.'

'Hector?'

'You sound surprised.'

'Yes … well … I didn't know he cared for her. It was always said that he was a homosexual.'

Signor Porrello chuckled.

'Is that funny?'

'Yes. You see, Sir Carradine was not alone. He was in the company of a most charming Arab lady and two children who resembled him very closely, except for their dark skins.'

'Ah.'

Guy supposed that in Hector's circles it was preferable to be considered a pansy than to admit to being in love with a member of another race. Still, he had come to Julia's funeral. Evidently Hector had understood and forgiven everything.

'And the inscription?'

'Also Sir Carradine.'

'That surprises me. It comes from the title of one of Signor Carmody's plays.'

'It is a cruel title.'

'Yes.'

The play had been put on three years before the war, in fact in the year that Julia died. Ambrose was the leading man, though the piece was generously written for the leading lady, Annabelle Croft. At the time critics had praised it for taking the author's writing to new depths of feeling and it enjoyed a long run in the West End. However, Guy remembered, Elizabeth had said in her letter that an attempt to revive the play had failed. One earlier critic, out of step with the rest, had called the theme 'Edwardian'.

Signor Porrello was still curious. 'What was the play about? I ask only because the epitaph seems significant.'

'I didn't see it. I haven't been to any of Ambrose's things since that summer. I...'

'Because of your illness? I understand.'

Distracted, Guy found he had taken a wrong turning. They were driving along the Passagiata Constantino with sea and palm trees on their left and a westering sun. The light was in his eyes, bringing back memories of sunbathing and Julia's tender caprice as they two scampered among the narrow streets of Porto Venere. All of it gone, with the price paid and a closing of accounts. Presumably Hector had meant something like that.

Guy found the road to Sarzana and returned Signor Porrello to his farm. He accepted a glass of wine and some cheese and asked if he could help the old man in the way of provisions.

'No, please, it is not necessary. At my age I eat very little.'

Guy nodded and they shook hands formally.

'Come again if you need help,' said Signor Porrello.

'Today has helped.'

The old man looked sceptical.

Guy took a step towards his car. Then, thinking he had withheld too much, he turned and said, 'About the play…'

'Yes?'

'I do know the general idea, though not the details. The heroine is a woman of thirty or so, who has a secret in her past – a crime or shameful incident. Her lover is a writer who has exhausted his inspiration. The woman tells him her secret and, as she knew he would, he uses it in a book. The result for her, of course, is disastrous. She is recognised and loses everything.' Guy hesitated, wondering how this explanation was being received and whether it was material to anything. He added, 'I believe she kills herself.'

Signor Porrello nodded sympathetically. Seeing there was no more to come, Guy repeated his farewells and got into the car.

He had never seen Ambrose's play, rarely thought of it. But the use of that brutal title as Julia's epitaph shocked him. The price paid by the heroine (if that was the right term) and by Julia was self-evident. But for what had they paid? Guy supposed it had been for their past sins, but this conclusion seemed crudely moralistic, appalling and unworthy. Had something else been purchased by their sacrifice?

Guy stopped the car. He was still in the hills. Below

him the valley was in shadow. To the south, splashes of pearl and wine lay on the surface of the sea. To the west, the big yellow sun hung low in a sky of dusky roses. He began to weep in ignorance and humiliation.

The headlights of his car caught a girl on the terrace of the Villa Esperanza. She froze, put her hands over her face in surprise, then dashed away into the darkness. Equally surprised, Guy stopped the car, got out and set off in pursuit. He gained only a few yards before shadows enveloped him and the girl was lost to view. He was left with the impression of someone pretty, with short blond hair and wearing a light dress of printed cotton. Her presence was so unaccountable that almost immediately Guy began to doubt that he had seen her at all; she was, perhaps, no more than a spirit of the house.

In the saloon, Lieutenant Jenkins and Nick were playing pingpong on one of the trestle tables, using a line of empty beer bottles as the net. Corporal Long was studying some papers.

'Eighteen-sixteen. Oh, hullo, Guy. Spent a productive afternoon, have you?' Jenkins enquired. 'There's grub in the kitchen. Bully beef and stodge. What's the stodge, Tommy? No idea? Me neither. Anyway, it's stodge in one of its many varieties. Eighteen-seventeen. Damn!'

Later the two officers drank mugs of strong sweet tea on the terrace, where no lights shone except the stars.

'On such a night as this…' said Jenkins.

'Go on?'

'There isn't any more. I only remember half-lines of poetry. "Into the valley of death rode (or possibly charged) the six hundred" – or was it three? I meant merely that it's a lovely night.'

'I used to drink cocktails here by the light of lanterns,' Guy mused.

'Really? Were you troubled by moths?'

Guy walked to the edge of the terrace, where the ruined

balustrade provided uncertain protection against a fall. He picked up a few small stones and threw them one by one, hearing each click on the rocks below.

It was a lovely night. *On such a night as this …* he and Julia had stood in silence, arms about each other's waist, looking out over the shadow of the pine trees. On such a night as this, he had danced a barefoot tango with Margot. The memories of that summer were not wholly evil. On the contrary, until the last disastrous revelation, Guy had never felt so happy – so vital.

'I gather you accept Tommy's explanation about the vanishing beds,' Jenkins ventured cautiously.

'Why didn't you stop him?'

'There isn't any stopping him, is there?'

'Probably not.'

'And in any case,' Jenkins said consolingly, 'since this Labour lot got in power, it's probably perfectly legal to rob the state blind. I believe it's called Socialism.'

Guy sat down again with his tea.

Jenkins asked, 'What do you think of the notion that the dear old Army seems to have lost us?'

'A couple of telephone calls should sort that out.'

'Do you think so?' He sounded disappointed.

'Don't you want to go home?'

'Can't say I much care. My wife and her bloody lover will no doubt want to throw me out of the house. And even this dump is preferable to sitting in a bank.'

'We must leave some time.'

'I daresay.' Jenkins leant over and whispered, 'But, speaking confidentially, Tommy has some deals going that will give us the capital to start our scaffolding business.'

An owl flew over, white and silent. From the remote waters of the Gulf came the faintest piping as a launch or jolly-boat returned to its ship. Tonight, inexplicably, the unquiet memories – and gaps of memory – were stilled. Tomorrow they would no doubt return.

Poor, sad Julia. Guy had forgotten to ask how she died.

Of drink and misery, he presumed. It was too horrible to contemplate. He sighed and lit a cigarette.

As Jenkins rose to leave, Guy enquired, 'Have some nurses arrived today?'

'What an extraordinary question! Why do you ask?'

'When I came back tonight, I noticed a girl – here on the terrace.'

Jenkins breathed an uncomfortable 'Ah!' and added reluctantly, 'I've been meaning to talk to you about that.'

'Tommy hasn't opened a whorehouse, has he?'

'Good God, no! I say, though, that doesn't sound a half bad idea.'

'No.'

'No? Righty ho, Guy, if you say so.'

'And don't mention the idea to Tommy, or he'll do it anyway, whatever I say.'

'Okey-dokey.'

'Good. Now, what were you saying?'

'Just a small thing. A request from Jimmy. I told him I'd put it to you. Feel free to say no. I don't mind, though there seems no harm in it.'

'Go on. Spit it out,' Guy said, a little impatiently.

'Jimmy was wondering, would you mind awfully if he wore a dress when not on duty?'

CHAPTER TWENTY-ONE

1930

'Is Venice always so quiet in the summer?' Guy asked. 'I thought it would be full of visitors.'

After visiting the church of San Giorgio dei Greci, he and Julia were taking lunch at a restaurant in a quiet courtyard shaded by vines.

'It's the Depression. When Hector and I were here, the place was heaving with Americans. Are you bored, darling? There's a bar I know, a louche little place in the Calle Vallarosso. It's frequented by Yanks, writers and other drunks, but quite gay. We could take a gondola. It's too far to walk in this heat.'

Since they were inspecting churches, Julia was wearing a lace fichu across her shoulders and a simple dull red dress and sandals. She looked like a girl come to visit her fiancé's bourgeois parents, and, too, a little like one of the bold-eyed Mediterranean women beloved of Victorian genre painters.

'It suits me that Venice is empty,' she went on. 'I love the feeling that one has arrived after a very long and riotous party. Do you know the sort? One comes too late, after the theatre or something equally dull, and expects to be welcomed to join in the fun. And instead there is nothing but the remains of food, empty bottles, cigarette stubs and paper streamers. The hostess has gone to bed, the hired waiters are putting on their coats, and one realises that the night has gone and there is nothing to be done except take tea and a sandwich with a fruit porter in Covent Garden. It's so deliciously melancholy. The party is over and we shall never see Venice in her glory.'

However, Julia was not in the least melancholy. That mood had passed somewhere on the journey away from La Spezia. Since their arrival in Venice two days before, she had been making shy and contrite advances to Guy, who resisted them only by his own shyness.

'Shall we go?' he asked. To avoid her gaze he made a show of reading his guide. 'Did you know that Vivaldi lived quite close by? We could look at the house if you like. I don't think it's open to the public.'

'Wouldn't you like to have lived at that time? Think how wonderful it would have been to hear the great castrati, Farinelli, Il Tedesco and the others.'

Guy called for the bill in Italian, but the waiter appeared to speak another language. They went outside, where Julia took Guy's hand and gave it an affectionate squeeze.

'I do like walking with you, Guy. You make everything seem so … fresh.'

'Do I? I'm not sure what to make of that.'

'Take it in the nicest possible way.'

'All right. And I like walking with you because you make everything seem so mysterious.'

'I don't like mysterious.'

Guy smiled.

'I'm being serious,' said Julia. 'Mystery is only one step away from furtiveness.'

'Are you furtive?'

'I have been – must be. At least to a degree. But – do believe me – I'm trying to put all that behind me.' She kissed Guy's cheek and laughed brightly.

Uncertain of directions, they found themselves in a narrow calle that proceeded under a covered way into a small square. In the shadow of the arch, two men were talking. One was short and sported a loud ready-to-wear suit. The taller man was extremely good-looking and very well dressed, so that Guy, vaguely recognising him, thought he might be a well-known actor. In a languid but bad-tempered voice, he was saying, 'Where the devil has Harry got to?'

Guy felt a tug on his arm.

'Come away,' Julia urged him, a little frightened. 'Oh, God! What's *he* doing here?'

They turned on their heels and Guy found himself dragged around a corner. Julia seemed angry.

'Is something wrong?' he asked.

'What? Don't tell me you didn't recognise him. Bloody Odo! But why should you? You've probably only seen his picture in the papers. Have you got a cigarette?'

Guy lit one and passed it over. Julia adjusted her lace shawl so that it covered her hair.

'How do I look?'

'Lovely. So that was Odo Milne we just saw. I thought he looked familiar. We met once, briefly, at Uncle Sammy's.'

'Damn him! Why has he turned up in Italy of all places?'

'I take it you don't like him.'

'He's an appalling man and more than a little insane. Do let's go on. Anywhere away from here.'

Guy allowed himself to be led. They took a crooked path and crossed several bridges across some narrow, fetid canals until at length, Julia, a little breathless, halted outside a crumbling gothic palazzo.

'Are you going to tell me what this is about?' Guy demanded. 'Is this one of your mysteries?'

Julia laughed a little hysterically. 'Odo! Oh no, there's no mystery where he's concerned.'

'Then tell me.'

'What's to tell? I once got somewhat tipsy and was unwise enough not to slap his face when he made a pass at me. Since then I've made it clear that I think he's a toad. But Odo's problem is that he's used to women fainting at his feet, and he can't take rejection. He's decided that I'm only playing hard to get and has convinced himself that he's madly in love – as distinct from merely mad.' By now she was largely recovered. 'I'll be all right after a brandy.' She sighed. 'Really, the whole affair is too grisly for words. If I were sensible, I'd sleep with him once so that he'd lose interest.'

'You can't do that.'

'Of course not. I'd be violently sick. But that's enough. We'll have a drink and talk about films.'

They found a hole-in-a-corner bar and took shelter in the shady interior. Some workmen were taking a snack and at a small table was a man with red hair, cut *en brosse*, sitting uncomfortably. He looked up at the newcomers and said pugnaciously 'I *know* you.'

'Excuse me?' Guy answered.

The pugnacity was repeated. 'I said: I *know* you. The face, not the name. I've *definitely* seen the lady before,' he added slyly as though suggesting an impropriety. 'It's Lady Julia Carradine. And *you're* not her husband. *He* lives someplace foreign and has wogs for boyfriends.'

Guy bristled. 'Are you spoiling for a fight?'

The other man stood up. He was short, stocky and vaguely familiar. The prospect of violence did not seem to disturb him. Guy felt Julia's hand on his shoulder.

'Don't let him trouble you,' she said wearily. 'He's one of Odo's houseboys.'

'Not a houseboy,' the stranger contradicted firmly. Seeing Guy was prepared to stand his ground, he changed his stance, grinned and held out his hand. 'Pleased to meetcha. Name's Harry Arthurs. I'm South-East Regional Leader for the New Party. Sir Odo's our Chief. You haven't seen him, by the way, have you? We was in some bleedin' church an' I went out for a fag an' lost him.'

'We saw him looking for you near Vivaldi's house.'

'Who's he when he's at home?'

Guy was about to give directions when he realised he did not know where he was.

Harry asked, 'You heard of a place called Florian's?

The Chief said that if we was ever lost we was to meet there. The Chief's always prepared.'

'Such a Boy Scout,' muttered Julia.

'We're heading that way,' Guy offered. 'We'll take you.'

Outside, Julia asked, 'Why do you have to be so nice?'

In Saint Mark's Square a few tourists were taking photographs and buying bad paintings. A troop of Balilla, the Fascist youth organisation, was performing callisthenics to a drumbeat. Sitting outside Florian's were Ambrose, Madame Hecate and Margot among a group of smartly dressed officers. Evidently Sir Odo Milne had seen them, for he had joined their table.

The South-East Regional Leader clicked his heels and gave a form of salute. With a flicker of disgust, Ambrose waved a hand and said, 'Guy dear, I believe you know Odo slightly.'

Guy nodded and offered a hand. Milne grasped it firmly.

Margot was slightly drunk and indifferently flirtatious. She caught Milne's attention by placing her hand on his and saying, 'Odo darling, you were about to tell us what's brought you to Venice.'

The Chief's eyes crossed Julia's before returning to Margot. 'I believe I was,' he answered with a winning smile. 'I'm here in Italy to interview Signor Mussolini and study the Italian solution to the labour question and the operation of the corporate state. I want to see how we can adapt it to England.'

'Is that Government policy?' asked Ambrose.

'I'm not in the Government,' Milne replied curtly. 'I resigned the whip a month ago. It was in the papers.'

'Alas, we don't get the papers in La Spezia. It's one of the few blessings.'

'Well, I have.'

'Pray tell.'

'There's nothing to tell. The whole system in England is rotten to the core and in hock to Jews and bankers. The nation is completely enervated and desperate for leadership. All the best sort were killed in the war and the racial stock needs to be revivified.'

'Are you in the revivifying business?' Ambrose enquired.

'If the People will have me.'

'Ah, yes, the People, bless 'em.'

Milne continued for a while longer, speaking with lucidity and a politician's single-mindedness until everyone except Margot grew bored. Guy caught Madame Hecate's eye and the old lady smiled and gave an almost imperceptible shake of her head. Then Margot spoke. Guy could not tell if her enthusiasm were false.

'Odo, darling, you have the most enchanting way of explaining things. What are you doing this evening? We thought we'd dine and go dancing at the Hotel Danieli. I don't know if there's a nigger band, but I'm sure they have something just as good. Why don't you come? Bring your charming friends.'

When Sir Odo and his companions had left, Ambrose rasped,

'Margot, why did you invite that idiot this evening?'

Wide-eyed, Margot answered, 'But he's delightful! And you do know that it's considered very chic to sleep with Fascists.'

That evening, as they danced, Guy said, 'You should be grateful to Margot. She seems besotted by Odo and he looks as though he's taking an interest.'

'What a glamorously gruesome pair they make.' Julia stifled a laugh. Tonight she was gay, a little drunk and very beautiful. Her cheek rested against Guy's.

'Why haven't you made love to me?' she whispered.

Guy had drunk too much to be unduly disconcerted. 'Only a few days ago you were behaving very coolly towards me.'

'Was I?'

'You called me a fool.'

'That can be a compliment. Sometimes we use words in a very special sense.'

'It didn't sound like a compliment. In fact you seemed generally out of sorts. Angry about the damned murder stories and concerned for Lewis. Oh! Sorry, darling. Did I miss a step?'

'No, no. It was my fault.'

Guy glanced at the tables. 'I hope Odo decides quickly who it is he wants to seduce. Harry's looking daggers at me. I wonder if Lewis is feeding my yellow bitch? I haven't given her a name yet. Any suggestions?'

'I don't want to talk about Lewis.'

'I was speaking about my dog.'

'Shall we sit down a moment?' said Julia, suddenly weary.

Their seats were with Ambrose and Madame Hecate, but at the next table Margot was talking extravagantly.

'Murder, darlings! Foul and beastly murder!'

'Is that so?' said Sir Odo.

'Definitely. We have it on the authority of Madame Hecate, who got it from an Indian Chief on the Other Side. Percy Shelley was brutally done in. However, Aggie won't say who it was that done it.'

'That's not very sporting.'

'No, it's dreadfully bedint, but what can you expect?'

Ambrose leant towards his partner and whispered, 'Don't be offended, dear.'

'I'm not,' answered Madame Hecate. 'We mediums are used to being abused. Though I should explain that I have received no revelations on that particular subject. The Departed are rather reticent on the circumstances of their deaths. Rather wisely so, I think, or those of us who have

258

not yet passed over might become distressed.'

'Let the dead bury the dead, eh?'

'Just so. I am more concerned with the living. I worry for Mister Lockyer. I do wish he had come with us.'

'You're frightened he might go sailing with Jackie Ferris?'

'I believe it would be very inadvisable,' said the old lady thoughtfully.

That night, sleeping fitfully in the heat, Guy heard soft footfalls. The handle of his door turned and the door might easily have opened, but did not. The footsteps went away.

In the morning Sir Odo Milne appeared outside Malvivente's palazzo. He was in a large motor launch with Harry, his fellow thug and a crew of smart Italian sailors. Pennants and Fascist flags flew from the launch, and it was the noise of the motor that was heard over breakfast.

Ambrose went to the open window and looked down from the balcony.

'Oh, God! Il Duce has arrived. Why can't the man use a gondola like a civilised person?'

Margot got up excitedly from the table and waved. 'Bravo, Odo!' she cried, and explained, 'He promised me he'd put on a show today. The Italians are out to impress him. They see him as our next Prime Minister, once the present crowd drown in their own filth.'

'Lord help us,' murmured Ambrose. He looked back into the room. 'I wonder if Byron had to put up with this from his revolutionaries?'

Julia was more cheerful. 'I do so like to see young love in bloom,' she said coquettishly to Guy.

'Margot and Odo?'

'I look at them and hear birds singing. Isn't it curious how the old romantic magic works for them just as it does for real people? By the way, I'm still waiting for you to make a thorough-going pass at me.'

'You're a dreadful hussy.'

'I haven't said I'll give in.'

No, she hadn't. Guy wondered if it was she who had been outside his bedroom last night, and, if so, what restraint had prevented her from opening the door. Further contemplation was halted by a racket of bugles and drums from Sir Odo and his crew.

'Where do you think we're going?' Guy asked.

'I don't know. No doubt Odo intends to overawe us.'

Milne was standing at the prow of the launch, nursing a glass of champagne in one hand and a cigarette in the other. He was wearing a navy blazer and white flannels, and on his breast was the elaborate star of some foreign order, possibly Italian. His face, framed by immaculately cut black hair, was undeniably handsome.

'Don't you think he looks Byronic?' Julia observed grudgingly. 'I mean in the vulgar sense. Not that there is any other sense as far as I'm concerned.'

'I admit he's good-looking.'

'Mussolini, too, and that German fellow, Herr Hitler. The future seems destined to be ruled over by Byronic men. What a beastly thought! Ah well, let us go and be dazzled by whatever Odo has in store.'

What Sir Odo Milne had in store was a tour of the familiar sights of Venice, with the variant that, at each location, other visitors were absent, and the role of guide was taken by an Italian captain in a handsome uniform.

'How frightfully sinister,' Ambrose remarked as they wandered the gloomy halls of Saint Mark's. 'Having the place to oneself, one feels like part of a conquering army. Do you suppose Odo notices, or is he too caught up in his own grandeur? I say, is that a cat?'

Under the Dome of the Ascension, in front of the iconostasis, a stringy cat was quietly licking its genitals.

'Do you suppose it's a symbol?' Ambrose asked.

'What of?' said Guy.

'I've no idea. The universe seems full with symbols. I sometimes fancy God keeps a few spare ones up His sleeve. Symbols with nothing to symbolise. I don't know why He does it, except to hint that His entire dreary creation has an ineffable purpose. Frankly it's a cheap trick I've often used myself to fool the punters with intimations of profundity. I do hope there's not much more of this. I need a drink, a large pink gin.'

Lunch was taken in a small, shady *piazzetta*, at tables set around the usual antique stone cistern. By courtesy of Signor Mussolini, the Italian Army provided waiters and a string quartet.

Julia whispered, 'Ambrose hates it that Odo is the centre of attention.'

The musicians were playing Mozart and Odo Milne was tapping his knee, keeping time as if it were a march, while his eyes ranged about the square. Ambrose brooded over his glass of gin and yawned.

'Ambrose and Odo both seem very restless,' Guy remarked.

'Yes. My comparison with Byron was just. His behaviour seems inexplicable unless one supposes Byron was continually bored and fretful if people weren't always looking at him.'

'At least he was a great poet.'

'But a terrible lover, I imagine.'

'Do you think so?'

'I don't see how anyone so self-absorbed could be otherwise.'

Guy smiled and shook his head. 'That sounds like the consolation that the less successful give to themselves to disguise their envy.'

He was shocked when Julia kissed him.

'What was that for? Are you laughing at me?'

'No. No.' Julia sighed and looked wistful. 'Oh, Guy Parrot, what an infuriating and lovely man you are!'

The air in the *piazzetta* was balmy. Filled with good food and wine, Guy had difficulty staying awake, especially when Sir Odo Milne began to expand on the lessons to be learnt from the great Italian experiment. Julia, too, seemed to be dozing. Her head rested on Guy's shoulder. It was a mention of Byron that pulled him from his reverie, where he had been thinking of Elizabeth.

The two poets were a subject which would not go away. Guy almost wished he could be as casual with women as they had been. Compared with their fierce passion, his own kindliness and belief in fidelity seemed insipid virtues – indeed scarcely virtues at all: more the by-products of sloth or cowardice; not active moral feelings but rationalisations that explained the inactivity of a tepid nature. Whatever Julia might suggest, he could not be certain that the Romantics, in their fervent attack on life, were wrong. And their error, if wrong, was glorious.

Guy wanted to love – but out of passion, not duty.

Sir Odo Milne said, 'One need only consider *Manfred*. In it Byron surely prefigures Nietzsche's Superman?'

Guy gathered that this discussion had been going on a while. The waiters were clearing the table and the musicians had undone their uniform jackets and were smoking.

'Yes, yes,' Ambrose muttered quarrelsomely, 'Byron was a Fascist; Newton was a Fascist; no doubt Jesus Christ was a Fascist. Why do we always want historical support for our own moral conceits?' He groaned. 'Oh, God, I'm spending too much time tippling in the sunshine! Odo, dear boy, do for once forget politics and answer the question in hand. Did Byron bump off Shelley?'

'I didn't know that Shelley was murdered at all, by Byron or anyone else. I understood he died in a sailing accident.'

'Of course! We all know that – except for dear Madame Hecate, who believes Shelley was indeed murdered but ain't letting on whodunit. However, let us exercise our imaginations. Let us suppose that Shelley was murdered...?'

'Why?'

'Because we might learn something from the fiction.'

'I don't see how.'

'Saints preserve us!'

'Ambrose, I do believe you're drunk,' Margot said merrily. She leant over to Milne, stroked his ear and coaxed him, 'Darling Odo, do show us that you're something more than a boring politician. I'm sure you could tell a story if you put your mind to it. I'm sure you could do anything,' she drawled, 'if you put your mind to it.'

Flushed with wine, Ambrose intervened crossly. 'Margot, you really shouldn't impose on Odo. I fancy his forte is ranting rather than story-telling. And, as it happens, I have been quietly preparing my own piece.'

'Have you?' enquired Julia. Her voice was sharp with suspicion rather than amusement.

'Yes, I have, dear girl. I can't say I have any light to throw on the mystery of Shelley's murder. However, it seems to me that we have abused the character of Byron.'

'Is that possible?'

'As I say, we have abused him and it falls to my lot to redeem him for the noble, selfless fellow he truly was.'

'Are you being ironic?'

'Perish the thought,' said Ambrose.

CHAPTER TWENTY-TWO

The Lovelorn Lord

A Sublime Work of Romantic Genius
by
Mr Ambrose Carmody

'I don't suppose your brother would lend me money, would he?' snarled Colonel George Leigh.

'I don't know,' answered Lady Augusta Byron Leigh hesitantly.

'I don't see why he shouldn't,' the Colonel retorted mockingly. 'He's a writer and so must make plenty of tin from his scribblings.'

He put a glass of finest brandy to his cruel lips and Augusta shuddered.

Her husband was no longer the handsome Beau she had married.

Clad in silks and satins, beruffled and bejewelled, Colonel Leigh enjoyed a dreadful reputation even in the worst Dens of London.

The marks of Evil living marked his countenance with signs of Vice.

Milne, the loyal and faithful Butler, entered bearing a bottle of superb Napoleon *cognac* on a silver salver.

Although a member of the lower orders, the ancient retainer was almost one of the family and had dandled Augusta on his knee when she was a child.

How she bitterly lamented those dear dead days and longed to see again his ruddy good-natured face and twinkling eyes.

But today the Butler was glum and shared a look of sympathy with his beloved mistress.

'I'm going to my room,' said Colonel Leigh, disdaining any politeness to his servant. 'I'm not to be troubled unless the Duke of Wigan or Lord Maltravers call.'

Augusta shuddered. The Duke of Wigan was known as the Wicked Duke, and the reputation of Mad Bob Maltravers was a byword for infamy.

She recovered herself by going to the French window and looking into the garden of the ancient, noble house. The grass was so green and the sky so blue and the verdant trees cast shadows over the pretty flowers.

Feeling more cheerful, her thoughts turned to her brother, Lord George Byron Gordon.

Because their family was of such ancient lineage, George had been sent away to a famous Public School as was the custom among the Upper Classes.

The result was that Augusta scarcely knew him.

She had heard that he had fallen into bad company in London. But she could not believe that this could overcome his sweet nature or those principles which many generations of aristocratic forebears had bred into him.

Still, she would see!

At four o'clock, she was in her *boudoir*, sipping a luxurious and expensive cup of tea brought by an East Indiaman from the East Indies, when there was a knock on the door and the faithful servitor announced Lord Byron.

The newcomer was tall, slender, with a very manly figure and a shock of black hair and raven-black eyes. He extended a hand.

'How d'ye do, sister,' he drawled in accents of the Capital. ''Tis pleasant to see you after so many years, to be sure.'

Augusta took the proffered hand and pressed it to her lips.

'I am glad to see you, too, brother,' she said shyly.

'And I hope … that you will enjoy your stay here. Though I doubt it can compare with … London.'

'London?' was the weary reply. 'I am grown tired of London. For the present I am done with the World and it with me.' His handsome mouth was drawn in a cynical smile touched by bitterness.

He wore a wine-coloured, close-fitting tailcoat set off with perfect white cambric *jabot* and cuffs, and tan-coloured Inexpressibles that set off to perfection his elegant legs.

'Where is Colonel Leigh, your husband?' he asked. 'Ain't he going to greet his guest?'

Just then the sound of raucous laughter came from the Study.

'He is entertaining friends,' said Augusta.

Byron raised an eyebrow. 'Oh? And might they be people I know?'

'I cannot … say,' answered Augusta, reluctant to admit her husband's degradation. 'They are the Duke of Wigan and Lord Maltravers.'

''Tis pretty company your husband keeps.'

'If you know them, perhaps you are in no position to criticise,' replied Augusta in spirited defence of a man who was her husband even though worthless.

'Nay!' Byron shook his head. 'Though I admit to being a Sinner, I am not so far gone in Sin that I would count such rogues my friends.'

'Then how do you know the Duke?'

'An affair of honour. I cannot speak of it. Maltravers was his second and played the blackguard. They may be Aristocrats, but they are not Gentlemen.'

It was a fine speech, but Augusta recognised the admission that, if her brother was not an absolute villain, he was only one step above.

Yet, in that sentiment she detected a glimmer of Hope.

*

That night Augusta could not sleep.

Her heart was near to breaking as she repented her unfortunate marriage. If only her husband had not fallen into the clutches of the Wicked Duke!

Augusta knew little of politics but had heard it said that, if the Prince Regent were to die, the Duke of Wigan would stand within a heartbeat of the Throne.

That night her husband told her that the Duke and Lord Maltravers were to leave for London in the morning. But she did not see Lord Byron who passed the day riding his fine stallion, Satan.

Augusta watched his return, erect on that high-tempered creature and felt a strange excitement. He looked so wild and free.

He asked her, 'Do you know how long the Duke intends to remain hereabouts? It is not like him to stay away from Wigan Castle during the Hunting Season.'

'Why!' said Augusta with surprise. 'Did you not know that the Duke and his Lordship were to depart this morning?'

'What!' exclaimed Byron fiercely. 'D —n me but I have been wasting my time if this story be true!'

'I assure you it is.'

Immediately it seemed as if for Byron she no longer existed.

'I cannot tarry!' he shouted, digging his spurs into Satan. 'I must post haste to London before it is too late!'

'But…' stammered Augusta.

It was no use. With her brother's cruel words ringing in her ears, she was left Deserted and Alone. And her heart felt as if it would break, though, she told herself, she could not possibly be in love.

The following evening, while Augusta was at dinner, she was interrupted by Milne.

The good, faithful old fellow was in a state of high excitement. 'Lord save us all, your ladyship!' he exclaimed. 'But what a to-do there is! 'Tis the latest report from Lunnon Town and terrible news it is, too.'

'Yes, yes...' Augusta urged him.

'Well, it seems that last night the Duke of Wigan – a fine and noble gen'leman – was dining at the Reform Club with the Prince of Wales, when a mysterious Stranger called him out. They went together to Hampstead Heath – a wicked place – and fought a duel. And,' the poor old man sobbed, 'the wicked villain – whoever he was – killed His Grace the Duke stone dead. Lord have mercy on us!'

'Oh, no!' cried Augusta and, with horrible presentiments, she fainted.

Augusta passed the following day in a swoon of agony.

Was it a coincidence that Byron had pursued the Duke to London and that His Grace had been killed that very day?

Surely George was not a common murderer?

Already Augusta foresaw Scandal and Shame falling on the ears of their family's fair name.

She was grateful for the arrival of blessed night and a hope of calm.

She was still in her *boudoir*, soothing her nerves with the luxury of drinking chocolate brought by a West Indiaman from the West Indies, when she heard a tap at the French window.

She asked in a whisper, 'Who ... is ... it...?'

The window rattled furiously.

'Let me in! Let me in! It is I, your brother George.'

'George!'

An exhausted, dishevelled figure fell into the room.

'Thank God!' Byron cried. 'I knew I could count on you.'

Augusta said nothing.

Her heart went out to Byron. No longer was he the arrogant Beau, languid and cynical, but a poor hunted creature.

Yet the dark fire was still in his eyes and she knew, that, once rested, he would return to being the same superb man that, in the depths of her soul, she admired.

'What ... has ... happened?' she asked. 'Tell me. I ... can bear ... the worst.'

'I have killed the Duke!'

'Ah!' she cried and sank to her knees.

Byron revived her with a glass of champagne. He explained. 'Although I am a poet, I have another – more secret – profession which I cannot talk about except to say that it is known to the Prime Minister, Mr Pitt the Younger. To protect against the catastrophe of the Duke becoming King, I have followed him to foil any Plot to murder the Prince.'

'Good ... Lord!' Augusta put a hand in horror to her lips.

'Two nights ago, I learnt from your husband in his cups that the Prince was to be poisoned at the Reform Club. The cowards!' Byron exclaimed.

'That explains why I left you so abruptly, my darling,' he continued, but Augusta only half heard him in her daze.

He had called her his "darling". Surely not!

He was her brother! But how could she explain this strange tenderness towards him? This lightness of her heart as if the sun were rising and birds singing?

Not recognising the revelation of his own secret longings, Byron said: 'I returned to London and informed Mr Pitt the Younger. The Government cannot intervene openly against one of the Blood Royal, and he said I should have to take responsibility for any action. "Your reputation will be wholly destroyed, but the future of the Country is at stake." It was a sombre moment, but I felt I could not refuse.'

'But ... to ... murder!' stammered Augusta.

'It was not murder!' Byron retorted angrily. 'I had still the unresolved quarrel. It was the perfect excuse for a duel. I called the Duke out. Fortunately I got to the Reform Club before the Prince was poisoned.'

'Thanks be to God!'

'Aye, thanks to Him!' Byron confessed thoughtfully. 'Well, you know the rest.'

Turmoil raged in Augusta's bosom. The horror of his tale chilled her, yet she glowed at the memory that this stranger had called her … darling!

Then something else occurred to her.

'My husband! He, too, must be … a Traitor!'

Byron gazed on her with kindly, loving eyes.

'Nay, fear not,' he said. 'For the sake of your goodness and loyalty – which, God knows, the vile wretch does not deserve – his part in this sorry affair will remain hidden.'

'Bless you!' Augusta cried from her soul and fell weeping at Byron's feet in gratitude at his generosity.

She knew now with certainty that she was beloved and felt the thrill of magic and enchantment at this knowledge, for she, too, loved him with a deep, wild, perilous love.

But theirs was a forbidden love, and Byron was too noble to press his suit.

'I must flee the country,' said he in forthright manly fashion.

'Oh no!'

'Nay, 'tis so, my dearest. In the interests of my Country my reputation must be destroyed. But, fie for that bagatelle! That is not my concern. Rather I fear that that hound Maltravers will be in pursuit, and I have no desire to have still more Blood on my conscience.'

'You … are … too … generous … to … that … brute. '

Byron clasped her to him and kissed her until it seemed that sparks flew like fireworks from her troubled soul.

Then, abruptly, he pushed her away.

'No! I cannot! The bidding of my heart is against Morality and Duty. Ah, sweet one!' Byron fell to his knees and drew Augusta's hand to his lips.

'W-what can I … do … to help?' she stammered.

'Come with me to Dover!'

These were the days when Old England was at its best and Kent, known as the Garden of England, was at its loveliest.

Everywhere along the road the Spring flowers were in bloom, and the rosy-cheeked peasants were picking ripe hops and apples.

In due course they arrived at Canterbury.

They found an inn in the shadow of the ancient Cathedral built by Thomas Becket, the Saint, and that evening they dined by candlelight in a private room.

They ate the finest of foods and drank Champagne.

Then there came a knock at the door.

Byron opened it.

The landlord entered. His once jolly face was sombre and he wrung his cap in his hands.

'Beggin' your Lordship's pardon, there is a person below – a villainous-looking fellow, no True-Born Englishman I'll warrant, although he claims to be an Aristocrat and my better.'

'Maltravers!' snorted an astonished Byron with an oath.

Scarcely had the good innkeeper finished speaking when Lord Maltravers and two ruffians burst into the room.

Maltravers was dressed from head to toe as the perfect Beau and Dandy, yet his eyes were cruel.

'So!' sneered the visitor, striking his thigh with a riding crop, 'I find you sheltering like a coward behind a woman's skirts.'

Staring Maltravers out of countenance with his majestic eagle's eye, Byron answered soberly, 'I am as you find me, hoping to spare your villainous life by avoiding an encounter. But you find me willing to settle this Affair like a Gentleman. Or do you and your cut-throats propose to play the part of common footpads?'

At this the two ruffians looked uneasy.

'Beggin' your Lordship's pardon,' said one, 'but my friend an' I thought you was only a common person, not Quality. Seein' as 'ow this is an Affair of Honour we dun' want to become involved. We are 'onest English robbers, not foreign riff-raff. So we'll just stand by and see Fair Play is done.'

Maltravers blanched.

Byron nodded.

Such men, true Hearts of Oak though twisted by unfortunate circumstances, were the same fellows who manned the Armies of the Iron Duke and cast fear into the hearts of England's enemies.

'Very well,' said Maltravers with a scowl. 'Let us decide this matter with our blood.'

The two men descended to the big courtyard of the old coaching inn. They faced each other, each a fine virile figure, and drew their swords.

The fight began.

Augusta could not look.

Her heart was torn with agonies at the thought that her beloved might die.

Then there came a cry and she opened her eyes.

Maltravers lay upon the ground, clutching his arm from which poured Blood.

'Mercy, for Pity's sake!' he pleaded.

Byron studied him coldly. He extended a hand to aid the Vanquished.

At that moment Maltravers took a Dagger from out of his sleeve and would have stabbed his foe.

But the chief ruffian stamped upon the blackguard's hand and, regarding him with contempt, said, 'Nay, we can't be doin' with any Froggie tricks like that. Your Lordship was beat in a fair fight.' To Byron he said, 'Dun' you worry, Lord B. My friend an' I will see this fellow does no more harm.' He added with a wink, 'An' then p'rhaps we'll give up the robbery trade an' take the King's Shilling.'

'Thank you, my good fellows,' said Lord Byron and shook their hands heartily.

'I thank you, too,' said Augusta. Her heart overflowed

at their reformation and she pressed a gold Sovereign into each of their hands and shed a grateful tear.

The following day Augusta and her Beloved arrived at Dover, where he would take a ship to the Continent.

Augusta felt like a wanton. As their fingers touched, her bosom heaved and her body thrilled with transports of ecstasy.

At last, as the galleon was about to sail, Byron spoke.

'Oh, my dearest,' he said. 'You are my only True Love and I feel cleansed and redeemed. I must go now to a far country and may never see you again. The true circumstances of this Affair may never be known. I shall depart into exile under a cloud of Infamy, which, my darling one, may also touch your reputation with Scandal. Yet still we shall know the Truth.'

'What … is … the … Truth?' asked Augusta, fighting her tears, and yet filled with pride at her lover's Sacrifice.

'The Truth,' said Byron, 'is that ours is the most wild, passionate and sensuous of Loves, and yet at the same time the most pure, chaste and Perfect. For our Love were the Heavens made, for us the Angels sing. For this the World turns on its axis. Every creature under Heaven and every animal and blade of grass rejoices for us.'

'Yes! Yes!' exclaimed Augusta, fearing that she would swoon at the beating of the heart within her woman's breast.

'Go!' she said. 'Go! Though your exile may be for ever, it will not be eternal. For, as surely as there is a God in Heaven, He will have mercy on us, and in that place where there is no Sin we shall surely be joined as one in Love!'

'Aye!' said Byron with a parting sigh, 'and thrice Aye! And until then, you must think on me as you sit a-sewing at the inglenook or tending to the Poor. Think always on poor Byron. Your Lovelorn Lord!'

CHAPTER TWENTY-THREE

1930

Guy was bored with visiting churches, and bored, too, with religious paintings which seemed to be the curse of Italian art. He had no taste for Mannerism and Baroque. Instead his instinct for a domestic life drew him to the Dutch, and any longing for drama was satisfied by portraits of fierce burghers dressed in black who held on to their money and stared at the artist with a ruthless gaze.

For beauty he had Vermeer and Julia.

'Left here,' said Julia, consulting the guidebook.

Guy took a dutiful turn. They were strolling through Cannaregio, one of the city's sleepy backwaters. Elsewhere Venice seemed to indulge in a sinister gaiety. Here it did its washing and quarrelled with its wife. Laundry hung from windows and balconies among occasional pots of wallflowers.

'Was Ambrose being satirical when he gave us his tale? Odo seemed distinctly annoyed. He didn't like being relegated to the role of the Butler.'

'Odo is a snob where art is concerned. He considers Ambrose to be the author of vulgar comedies. He doesn't share Lewis's faith in Ambrose's genius.'

Something occurred to Guy. 'Given Ambrose's desire to lay Shelley's murder at the door of menials such as the Hotel Manager and the Cook, there's a good case for Odo being the murderer. Do you follow? It was the Butler that did it.'

'You shouldn't read anything into our stories.'

'Shouldn't I? I thought that was partly the point. It's obvious even to me that Ambrose is Byron and Jackie

Ferris is Trelawny the pirate.'

Julia looked at Guy thoughtfully and her eyes glazed as if she did not wish to see him. 'We've told a great many lies about Byron – and about each other.'

Guy tried to oblige by changing the subject. 'Is Ambrose a genius?'

'Oh, yes.' A sigh without enthusiasm.

The diversion had taken them into the old ghetto, a place of tall, ancient tenements, small squares, the occasional synagogue and ever-present cisterns. Guy wondered if the cistern at the Villa Esperanza was now filling with water as he hoped.

Byron had stayed in Venice, filling his palazzo with monkeys, women and Italian revolutionaries. Guy tried, but could make no connection between this and his own prosaic appreciation of the city as it slumbered in the summer heat.

Julia slouched in languid dissatisfaction. Even in her obscure miseries, Guy found her lovely. More than any other woman – more than poor Elizabeth – she infatuated him with her intense otherness: her possession of qualities that utterly resisted his comprehension. If he allowed himself to fall in love with her, what would such love be like? Could there be a love in which there was no meeting of minds but only an encounter of passions?

When Julia next spoke, it was to say suddenly, 'I don't want to talk of bloody Byron or bloody murders. I'm sick of the whole business – everything.'

Then, suddenly, she was in tears and Guy was holding her in his arms as he might a child, stroking her hair and soothing her.

'Oh, Guy, Guy, you sweet, silly man. No matter what I say, you keep stumbling onward into danger. And why? Simply because you have a kind and loving nature.' She pulled back slightly and looked at him, her eyes bright with moisture. 'How mysterious you are. Goodness is always mysterious – far more so than evil. Oh, God, my nose is running. Have you got a handkerchief ? Here I am, making a declaration of love, and my nose is running. How pathetic!'

'Here.' Guy gave her a handkerchief.

'Thank you.' Julia blew her nose. 'You're a gentleman,' she murmured. 'There! I've said it. I'm head over heels in love with you, Guy Parrot. I shouldn't be, and you should run a million miles away and it doesn't matter at all. Oh God, I'm crying again like a snivelling schoolgirl. It's disgusting. Do you love me?'

'Yes.'

'You don't sound sure.'

'I'm sure I love you. I'm just not certain that I should.'

Julia laughed. 'Oh, that's easily answered. You shouldn't. I can promise you only pain and unhappiness.' She looked away into the square, which was three parts filled with shadow. A pious Jew was crossing it towards the synagogue. 'What an unlikely place for romance. I can see I've made a mess of things. Let's forget we've spoken about love and simply continue as friends.'

'I want to be more than your friend.'

'You do?'

'Yes.' Guy held her more closely. He kissed her high, pale forehead and tentatively his lips moved across each of her closed eyes, her nose, her cheeks, her neck until at last they fastened on her lips, which smiled beneath his.

'Madame Hecate has yielded to my entreaties,' announced Ambrose, 'and I've prevailed upon her to give us a séance.'

'That sounds very jolly,' commented Guy, who was feeling light-headed since the events of the morning.

They were at Florian's, taking coffee at a table in the square. Ambrose sat next to Madame Hecate. Sir Odo Milne and Margot, who today both glittered with beauty, were absorbed with each other. Under the old lady's cool eye, Guy and Julia smiled furtively.

'I don't think "jolly" is the right word,' observed Madame Hecate with gentle severity. 'I was reluctant to accede to Mr Carmody's request since I am aware that séances are often the object of mockery.'

'My dear lady!'

'Please don't protest, Mr Carmody. You know it to be so. But you have been very kind and generous towards a foolish old woman, and it would be ungrateful to refuse.'

'That's settled then.'

Strolling back to the palazzo of Mikey Malvivente, Guy found himself alongside Madame Hecate. Feeling he ought to make conversation, he apologised for any impression of levity he might have given.

'Oh, no,' said his companion, 'there's really no need to say that. You obviously have no experience of séances and, since you are a sensible young man, are naturally sceptical.'

She was looking ahead at Julia, who was very gay and talking animatedly to Ambrose.

'You remind me,' the old lady continued, 'of a nice young person I knew. His name was Roger – a very solid name – a solicitor.'

'Really?'

'Yes. He fell in love with a young woman. She was of the same age but troubled and far more knowledgeable about the world, since she had worked in the theatre.'

'I see. And what did they do? Run off to India together?'

'No. They had a tragedy. Afterwards Roger married a nurse and had two children, but I don't think he was ever entirely happy. You see, there are some natures that never get entirely over an unhappy love affair.'

'I'll bear that in mind.'

'Will you?' asked Madame Hecate sceptically. 'Roger didn't.'

As he was dressing for dinner, a knock came at Guy's

door. It was Julia, still in the summer dress she had worn all day.

Guy smiled at first in his normal good-natured fashion. Then, rather alarmingly, it seemed that a series of involuntary movements and reactions were pulling him and he found himself gazing tenderly at this woman.

'Hullo,' he said. 'Are you not proposing to change?'

'Later.'

'Oh?' He looked at his watch. 'Am I early? Did we agree seven-thirty or eight?'

'Eight.'

'Oh, I'm early then?'

'Yes.'

Guy sat down on the bed. Julia took a chair and sat upright on it like a very pretty secretary attending an interview.

'What –'

'I –'

'I'm sorry. You were saying?'

'No, please, Julia. You speak.'

She gave a shy giggle that Guy had not heard before, but liked.

'I knew you were different, Guy. With any other man I'd know how to behave in a situation like this.'

'You've had other situations like this?'

'I … no, on reflection I don't suppose I have.'

'But similar ones?'

'That question makes me feel like a tart.'

'Does it? I didn't mean it to.'

'Don't worry – darling. I shall have to get used to calling you "darling", shan't I?'

'You've called me "darling" before.'

'That meant nothing. Now the word will sound different.'

Julia took out a cigarette. Guy offered her a light from an elaborate table lighter in the form of a scantily clad young woman. Mister Malvivente's taste in bedroom furnishings reminded Guy of the set for a Hollywood musical with some small pornographic additions.

'I hadn't realised that being in love made one so nervous.'

'Haven't you been in love before?' asked Guy, slightly relieved.

'I thought I was, but I suspect it was merely sexual excitement.'

'Not even with Hector?'

'Least of all Hector, though don't mistake me. He's a very good sort. Among my kind of people, sexual attraction is very smart, but love is regarded as a private vice. Or so I realise now.'

'What kind of people are yours?'

'Trivial and amusing.'

'Are you getting cold? I am.'

The window was open to ventilate the room. Guy closed it. When he turned, Julia had removed her dress and was standing barefoot in a pink silk slip.

'Don't look so shocked,' she said gently.

Guy tried not to. He told himself that he had seen Julia equally clothed – or unclothed – when bathing. But then she had looked neither fragile nor vulnerable, or had her skin been so pale or her face so empty of expression.

She twisted a foot nervously on a small rug.

'You're wondering what this means and how I feel,' she said. 'It means I'm in love with you. And I feel frightened. You?'

'I'm in love, but I don't think I'm frightened. Puzzled. I'm often puzzled.'

'Puzzled? That's one odd thing to be.'

'Isn't it? I think so, too. It puzzles me.'

Julia laughed and Guy stepped towards her. He took her in his arms, kissed her, picked her up and deposited her lightly on the bed. He knelt over her as her arms encircled him and drew him to her until they were kissing again.

As Guy dressed a second time for dinner, Julia said, 'Shall you write to Elizabeth?'

'Yes, of course. Why not?'

Julia had put on her dress, which was rumpled and gave her a *gamine* air.

'I see,' she sighed, and, without irony, added, 'what a gentleman you are.'

'Am I? I mean, shouldn't I write?'

'You are asking me?' Julia smiled faintly as if exhausted. 'I'm in no position to give moral advice, though explaining the situation to Elizabeth does seem to be the decent thing to do and...'

'Yes?'

'Probably a mistake.'

Guy felt both happiness and certainty slide away from him. *I am puzzled, therefore I am.* This Cartesian syllogism seemed to be a condition of his existence.

'What on earth are you getting at?'

Julia brightened. 'Are you getting angry?'

'I ... yes, I rather think I am. Were you lying? Don't you love me?'

'Poor Guy. So honest to the core. Yes, I do love you.' Julia shook her head, smiling sadly. 'I *do* love you and I am trying to be unselfish which, believe me, is difficult. I agonised over whether to let you fall in love with me, and I'm afraid the other Julia, the wicked one, won.'

'But surely, if you love me...?'

'Stop there. This is beginning to sound like the dialogue from one of Ambrose's plays. I should hate that, because it always sounds so unfeeling and implausible, though...'

'What?'

Julia was standing now, turning on her elegant legs as she smoothed the skirts of her dress. She appeared very calm.

'Oh, I was merely thinking that, in these intense situations, if people can overcome their natural tendency to mumble, they simply borrow words from bad novels and cheap songs. The alternative of speaking from the heart would be too painful or too incoherent, or both. Don't press me, Guy. Write to Elizabeth if you wish. I must go back to my room and change out of this dress.'

Julia was halfway out of the door before she thought better and returned. She gave Guy a brief but not unfeeling kiss.

'Darling Guy,' she whispered regretfully. 'How terrible it all is.'

They gathered for cocktails in the saloon. Sir Odo was examining the decorations and possessions of the absent Mikey Malvivente.

He commented. 'Our host's taste seems to owe more to Cunard than the *quattrocento*. I'm reminded of the last time I was on the *Mauritania*, or perhaps in the foyer of one of the more lavish London cinemas.'

Ambrose asked, 'Aggie, dear, which would you prefer? Shall we hold the séance before or after dinner?'

Madame Hecate's natural disposition to flutter was exaggerated by her dress, which was black, hung with sundry diaphanous fichus and extravagantly patterned with designs of an oriental character.

'How kind of you to ask,' she said. 'Yes, how very kind. Before dinner, I think.'

'Really? You surprise me. I should have thought afterwards, when we are more relaxed and in the mood.'

'Relaxed? How exactly you put it. However' – the old lady blushed – 'the difficulty is that, after a good meal, instead of going into a trance I have a dreadful propensity to fall asleep. I am sure you don't want to watch me snooze while under the misapprehension that I am waiting on messages from the Other Side.'

'No, that would be most unfortunate.'

'Indeed it would.'

To distract himself from the turmoil of his thoughts

concerning Julia, Guy enquired what arrangements were necessary to make contact with the Spirits.

'Do you have a guide? An Indian or Chinaman?'

'Yes, I have, though Chloë – that's her name – is neither Indian nor Chinese. In fact she's from Peckham.'

'Peckham?'

'Peckham,' affirmed Madame Hecate, adding seriously, 'I do assure you that it is every bit as spiritual as Xanadu. Chloë died in one of the cholera outbreaks of the last century. I can't be more exact because she doesn't like to talk about it. She was – is – eleven.'

Margo was solemnly interested. 'Will you go into a trance? The mediums I visit go into a trance at the drop of a hat.'

'I know dear. And produce the smell of fried onions – you mentioned it – and possibly liver and bottled stout as well. You will forgive me if I have my own preferences.'

'Which are?'

'Initially, at least, I shall try table-rapping. That small tea table should do. Please bring it over, Mr Parrot, and some chairs, too. That will do nicely. Please don't snigger, Sir Odo.'

'Was I?'

'The Spirits don't mind, but I do. It's very rude.'

'That's put you in your place,' observed Ambrose and he bestowed his kindest expression on the medium. 'Do we have to do anything? Hold hands?'

'That would be best.'

Madame Hecate sighed and breathed in deeply. 'Chloë? Is that you, dear? Are you there?'

Guy waited expectantly.

'Chloë, dear?'

'Yes, do come on, Chloë,' said Julia.

'Hush, please.'

'Sorry.'

' Chloë, dear?' Then more sharply: ' Chloë!'

Guy found himself willing the old lady to succeed, but

the trembling he felt in the table was only the pressure of his own fingers.

'I can see this isn't going to work,' said Madame Hecate regretfully.

'Does anyone care for a smoke?' commented Sir Odo.

In the interval another round of cocktails was prepared. Guy went on to the balcony. Julia was standing there, staring down into the canal where a party of Americans, lit only by lanterns, was passing in a gondola. Their voices rang clear in the night air.

'Don't stick your hand in the water, Henry, it's dirty.'

'Put a sock in it, Emily.'

'Are you telling me to shut up?'

'Listen, honey –'

'You're telling me to shut up!'

'Whatever.'

'I said don't put your hand in the water.'

'Jesus Christ, Emily!'

'I don't like men who swear. I didn't marry a man who swore.'

'Put a sock in it. A whole drawerful.'

The floating lanterns moved on.

Julia had a shawl over her shoulders. She pulled it closer and let her head fall against Guy's shoulder. 'Do you suppose that's our message from the Other Side?'

'Quite possibly. I wonder what it means?'

'It's the part that gets edited out of love stories, along with cocoa and warm underwear. Do you think it might be us?' She sounded earnest. 'Can you honestly see it, Guy? Can you see us – you with a pipe and *The Times* and me, a doctor's wife, warming your slippers or whatever it is doctors' wives do? I don't know what they do do.'

Guy tried to imagine. 'I suppose so. Love is taking what comes, isn't it?'

'Is it? Is it really so feeble? So mundane? How can anybody conceivably want it?'

From inside Ambrose called, 'Come on, you two.

Aggie's ready to pull out all the stops. We're going to summon the Spirits as if at the Last Trump.'

Madame Hecate, however, seemed less certain.

'I wonder if I might have a biscuit and a glass of water? Going into a trance does tend to unsettle the stomach. You should also understand that the results are often unsatisfactory, even faintly absurd.'

She relaxed into her chair and closed her eyes, though whether she went directly into a trance was doubtful, since she continued to nibble her biscuit. The Americans meanwhile had returned and their shrill, exasperated, voices drifted through the open window.

'What do you mean: you're broke?'

'For Chrissake, Emily, that's what I've been trying to tell you! I went down in the Smash. I'm all washed up. The apartment, the car, the summer cottage: they've all got to go.'

'I don't understand. How did you pay for this trip?'

'Aw, honey, I knew you had your heart set on it, so I borrowed from Morty Lowenstein against my insurance.'

'You did that for me?'

'Sure. You're my baby doll, ain't you?'

'Henry … you're still trailing your hand in the water.'

'Put a sock in it, Emily, and give your boy a kiss like you used to.'

They stood about, smoking and making desultory conversation while Madame Hecate breathed deeply and seemed to slumber. The moon, which streamed through the open window, passed behind a cloud and there was talk of turning on more lights and whether this would affect the old lady's efforts.

Guy looked at Julia, who was shivering slightly; the room did seem cooler. She said, 'Considering that this is ridiculous, why do I feel frightened?'

Ambrose answered evenly, 'The ridiculous is frequently sinister. It reminds us of our pathetic condition.'

'I think we should stop.'

'That would be to give in to our fears and confirm them.'

'I tell you I'm frightened.'

'Guy?'

'It is a silly business, but I think we should continue.'

'There, Julia, you have a medical opinion.'

'I merely think that it would be kind to humour the old lady,' said Guy, uncertain if that really was what he meant. He had taken to heart Ambrose's assimilation of the ridiculous and the pathetic. The conversation of the Americans, so intense and yet amusing to the detached listener, had saddened him though it had ended on a note of hope. He wished the room were not so dark or Madame Hecate not so evidently sincere.

Madame Hecate twitched.

'Hullo?' said Ambrose. 'I detect signs of life – or do I mean afterlife? Aggie, dear, are you all right? How does the expression go? "Is there anybody there?" '

'*Murder*!' exclaimed Madame Hecate.

'Aggie!'

However the old lady was still sleeping, or else in a trance.

Guy went quickly to her side and took her pulse. 'She seems to be okay.'

'*I don't know if I can go through with it,*' said Madame Hecate in a low, troubled voice.

'With what, dear?'

Concerned, Guy asked for light. Julia said, 'No, leave her. She's in a trance.'

'She is, too,' said Margot, adding with airy knowingness, 'I've seen it before. I wonder if she'll produce ectoplasm? I do hope so. It's disgusting but absolutely fascinating.'

'Do be quiet, Margot!'

'I'm only trying to help.'

'*How still he looks.*'

'Who looks?'

'*Oh, God, but the price has to be paid?*'

'Is that a quotation? It sounds like Pinero.'

'*The weight! How can a corpse weigh so heavy?*'

'It doesn't sound as though the speaker is dead,' said Guy. 'I can't see how it can be a ghost.'

'I don't like this,' said Julia, and suddenly she turned on the lights and ordered peremptorily, 'Guy, wake her up!'

'I'm not sure it's safe to do so.'

'Of course it's safe. She's only pretending, the old fraud!'

'Ambrose?'

'I'll do it,' said Sir Odo Milne, firmly. He put his cigarette in his mouth and gave Madame Hecate a sharp slap on the face. 'Come on, old girl. Time to wake up. You've had your fun.'

The old lady did not seem to resent the blow. Her blue eyes slowly opened and she looked about her in bewilderment. Then she smiled.

Julia made a cup of tea for Madame Hecate and stood, white-faced, as the good-natured creature sipped it and observed, 'You all seem rather put out, if I may say so. I do hope it wasn't a disappointment. So often it is. The concerns of the Departed are not ours, and much that we would wish to know cannot be revealed.'

'It was … interesting.' Ambrose commented.

'Oh, good.'

'But whoever it was that you got in contact with seems to be very much alive.'

'Dear me,' said Madame Hecate gravely.

Ambrose proceeded to explain, while the old lady listened attentively. Occasionally she shook her head.

'You may be right. The Departed are normally reluctant to speak of the act of Death.'

'But is it possible for the living to speak through you?'

'Oh, yes. It rarely happens, but yes it is possible. When someone is very distressed and not in conscious control, the spirit can sometimes range free. I imagine that the person – whoever he or she was – was dreaming.'

'Then it certainly wasn't one of us.'

'Or day-dreaming.'

Julia put the question to which everyone wanted an answer. 'Has there been a murder?'

Madame Hecate did not reply immediately but studied her cup of tea.

'Not necessarily,' she said at last. 'The murder may not have happened yet. It may be merely in contemplation, in which case the murderer's own conscience may prevent the crime. Let us hope so.'

She looked up at Ambrose with an expression of innocence that Guy found disconcerting.

She said, 'I suggest, Mr Carmody, that we return to La Spezia. I confess that the well-being of Mr Lockyer does concern me.'

CHAPTER TWENTY-FOUR

1930

The Villa Esperanza was deserted except for the yellow bitch, which shrank between the cypress and the palm on the terrace.

'Hullo, girl,' said Guy coaxingly. The dog crept forward on her belly, her tail wagging intermittently with doubt and pleasure.

The main door was unlocked and everything in order. Fred began to unload the cars. Ambrose went inside, calling 'Jackie! Lewis!' The women complained of being tired and, in Margot's case, regretted that Milne had remained in Venice to sort out Fascist business and the New Order.

'Not a trace of anyone,' said Ambrose, returning to the terrace. 'It's like the *Mary Celeste*, if one assumes – which I admit is unlikely – that the jolly sailors on that vessel ate *prosciutto crudo* for breakfast and washed it down with orange pekoe tea. In short, there's every sign that someone has been living here, though no one is at home.'

'I wonder where Maria and Gianni are?'

'I shall have words. With Joe, too. It's very inconvenient to have no staff.'

'Has anyone been murdered?' enquired Margot lightly.

'Not that I noticed, though I confess to being more concerned with the catering. When Fred comes down from dropping off the bags, you might ask him if he's stumbled across any corpses. Turning to more serious matters: since we are evidently not expected, I suggest we dine in Lerici, where I noticed an enticing trattoria.'

'And if someone has been murdered?'

'Then we shall have to make do with sandwiches.'

Lewis appeared towards the middle of the afternoon while the others were taking refuge in the loggia against the glare of the sun. He was cheerfully sunburnt and walked with a jaunty swagger. He called out, 'Hullo everyone. I'll be with you in a couple of shakes.'

When he joined them, he was wearing white ducks and deck-shoes stained with brine.

'As you see,' he said, 'I've been having a jolly time sailing.'

'Does that mean Jackie's still here?'

'Jackie? No, I imagine he's in Marseilles by now. Oh, I see what you mean. The sailing. I've hired a boat. I told you I had a mind to. It's a little thing moored at Lerici. Really it's only fit for taking spins in the Gulf. I took it to Tellaro this morning to try out its paces.'

'We were thinking you might have been murdered,' said Margot.

'Not me. I'm right as rain. You must be confusing me with Percy Shelley. I say, is that gin and tonic in the jug? I'm dreadfully parched.'

Given Lewis's mood of mild afflatus it seemed tactless and rather absurd to tell him that, as a result of a séance, they had become concerned he might be dead. The subject of how he had spent his time did not come up again until evening, when, as Ambrose suggested, they dined in Lerici.

'So, tell me, dear boy,' said Ambrose, 'how long were you unwell?'

'Two days. Jackie was a brick and put off returning to France until I was on my feet again. In fact, he even volunteered to take me out in his boat in order to clear the cobwebs. We were going to buzz around the Cinque Terre.'

'And did you?'

'Sail with Jackie? This is good veal, isn't it? Better than

England. No, as a matter of fact I didn't. I had … I don't know how to put it … a feeling that it was probably a bad idea. I suppose Jackie's sinister reputation was at the back of my mind. Can't think why, because I scarcely know the fellow; and afterwards I felt a bit of a swine for refusing, but you know how it is. To be fair to Jackie, he didn't press me. If he had, I'd have some grounds for suspicion, but, as I say, he didn't. Next thing was he pushed off to France.'

'And did he arrive there?' Guy asked.

'I've no idea. He mentioned dropping me a line, but I haven't been checking my post. Speaking of which, did you write to say you were returning early?'

'Yes,' said Ambrose.

'Well, there you are. I didn't know. Once I was on my feet, I decided to amuse myself. I gave the staff a holiday and went to Lucca, where I holed up in a very pleasant *albergo* and whiled away a few days sightseeing and writing poetry. That, by the way, is why there was no one to meet you at the house. I've been getting by very well on my own.'

Guy next bumped into Lewis the following morning after the latter had returned from an early swim.

'I've got something to show you, old fruit,' said Lewis.

'Oh? What?'

'A secret. But I promise you'll like it. Wait a tick while I change.'

On his return Lewis proposed that they go up the hill.

'To the grotto?'

'I say, you haven't been already, have you? That would spoil my surprise.'

'Hadrian and Antinous haven't run off together, have they?'

'Hadrian and Antinous?'

'That's what I call the two statues.'

'Is it? I call them "Laurel and Hardy". Still, there's no accounting for tastes. No, as far as I know they haven't run off. What makes you think they might?'

'There's a mystery about them. They seem somehow alive.'

'I don't know about that, but I agree that Hadrian and Antinous are good names. The way they touch and look at each other, there's something uranian about them. George would have approved.'

'Byron? Would he?'

'Indubitably. If he wasn't chasing women, George liked to bugger young boys. When he died at Missolonghi he was madly in love with a Greek lad. So there are your Hadrian and Antinous, if you like.'

In the clearing by the grotto, the two statues maintained their quiet conversation. The shadows of leaves, falling on them, rippled in the faintest breeze, each movement suggesting a quickening of flesh.

'Did you tidy the place up?' Guy had noticed that the clearing was largely swept of pine needles.

'In the fleeting hour between verses.'

'What are you writing about?'

'Byron, what else? Don't pull faces at me, Guy. I can't get the beggar out of my mind.'

Guy offered a cigarette. They stood for a while smoking and gazing outward over the trees to the Gulf and Porto Venere where the campanile of S. Giorgio and the Genoese fortress shone brightly and the pines and cypresses were still green before the blue shimmers of noon. Byron had swum from Porto Venere to visit Shelley at Lerici. Shifty guides showed tourists the cave from whence he started. The visitors did not know what to look for and studied the empty cigarette packets strewn about the floor as if they were clues.

'I thought we were finished with that business,' said Guy. 'Jackie came up with the only halfway plausible theory as to Shelley's murder, and Madame Hecate thoroughly scotched it.'

Lewis smiled in wistfulness or embarrassment – Guy

could not tell which – and said, 'I can't help it if the fellows fascinate me.'

'That may be so, but you – all of us – seem to be fascinated by the wrong thing. We talk of nothing except Shelley's murder. But that's simply a conceit we invented to entertain ourselves. Surely the important subject is what he and Byron wrote? And we never talk of that at all.'

Lewis was amused. He put a hand on Guy's arm.

'I have a confession to make. Although I write verses and work in publishing, there are times when this literature thing is completely beyond me. I've no idea where the true beauties lie or what any of it means. Is it any different for you?'

Guy admitted that it wasn't.

'There you have it, then. We're all in the same boat. We get our wisdom by misunderstanding the work of great authors – bad ones, too, for that matter.'

Guy looked around the swept clearing. The basin of the fountain, too, had been emptied of leaves.

'Have you shown me what I'm supposed to see?'

Lewis said, 'I see you're bored with Byron. No, I'm not finished here.' He disappeared behind the statues. 'There isn't a tap as such, just a tile placed in the pipe to act as a shutter. It leaks a little but works well enough. The water in the cistern is good for about two hours before the pressure falls, and it takes a day to refill. But not bad, all in all.'

Lewis returned. He and Guy faced the two statues. Lewis said with some feeling, 'This is the reward for all your hard work.'

'I –'

He was interrupted by the sound of water. It was low at first, like a stream over stones, and became visible only as a trickle at the feet of the statues that trailed down the pedestal into the basin. Then, as if a blockage had been overcome, it suddenly burst forth: high arcs of water that rose to the height of the figures, only to break into droplets, each one catching its portion of sunlight and spinning it before it fell. The effect was not magical – Guy discarded that word – it was too real: too intensely physical. He could hear the water, see it, feel the drops on his face. Lewis was laughing. That was it. It was joyous. The water was flowing, the jets sparkling and in sheer joy the two men held hands and capered in a circle round the fountain, hooting and yelling, round and round, now nearer now farther, close enough at times for their outstretched arms to pass through the jets, then back a little so that the fountain and the statues became a single form of expanding life.

Hadrian and Antinous looked at each other tenderly and smiled.

Lewis proposed that he take Guy for a spin in his boat. The others were busy. Margot was writing one of the love letters with which she harassed her husband's solicitor. Ambrose and Julia were driven by Fred into La Spezia to shop and collect mail from the general post office.

'I'm hoping for something from Jackie,' Julia explained.

'Your concern does you credit,' said Lewis.

'I think Lady Julia has good reason to be concerned,' Madame Hecate observed, and she explained, 'Memories of poor Shelley make one fearful that the Commander may have encountered a storm or other mishap at sea.'

'I suppose so. Will you join Polly and me in my boat? I'm sure we could squeeze you in.'

Madame Hecate smiled knowingly. 'I won't, thank you. I've grown rather frightened of boats.'

Guy knew nothing of sailing.

'No matter,' said Lewis. 'I'll handle the sail and you take the tiller. I suggest we go to Tellaro – I know the way. It's a pretty little fishing village with a jolly legend involving Saracens and an octopus. The main thing is to stay clear of the warships or we'll have some explaining to do. If Jackie really has got into trouble, it'll be for spying on the Italian fleet.'

'Jackie isn't a spy.'

'Isn't he? I rather thought he was. He was always sailing up and down the Gulf, making very free with his binoculars. Naval men often are spies. Many of my friends are spies. It's very good form.'

They went out about a mile. From here Porto Venere with its tall painted houses shone brightly. Patches of oleander formed splashes of colour among the aleppo pines. They found themselves among half a dozen other small boats, which gave Guy some comfort.

'Speaking of Shelley,' Lewis began.

'We weren't speaking of Shelley.'

'Humour me, Guy. Speaking of Shelley, I can see that Jackie's solution to the murder mystery is no good. But to my mind that doesn't dispose of all the questions.'

'Such as?'

'Why did Shelley set sail from Livorno to return to La Spezia? Let's put it another way. Why did Percy ignore Trelawny's warning of the risk of a storm?'

The question called forth a sharp recollection.

'Funnily enough, Madame Hecate asked exactly that. We were chatting over dinner in Mantua. She said the answer was the key to the whole business.'

'And?'

'Nothing. She didn't explain. She simply muttered something about conceptions of honour in days of yore.'

From mid-channel they put about and headed for Tellaro.

Lewis asked, 'Do you know why Shelley sailed that day?'

'No, and I don't much care. I imagine he was anxious to see his wife.'

'I doubt it. By that date Mary and Percy had fallen out of love and Percy was making eyes at Jane Williams. Mary's children had died of disease and she was depressed

– I believe the modern term is neurasthenic. *Nil nisi bonum* and all that, but she can't have been much fun to live with.'

'In that case I don't know. Perhaps something had happened in La Spezia, an emergency.'

'Again I rather doubt it. I've never heard it suggested. If there'd been a problem at La Spezia before Percy sailed to Livorno, I imagine he wouldn't have gone. After all, he had no important business except to make peace between Byron and the Hunts, which could easily have waited.'

'I give up,' said Guy.

Lewis sighed. 'So do I. Shelley's actions are inexplicable, and the more inexplicable the more closely one examines them.'

At Tellaro they put into a small cove at the foot of the rock on which stood the church of S. Giorgio. The village, like others along that coast, was compounded of shady alleys rising steeply from the shore. Guy was tired and proposed that they take a drink.

Sitting outside a small bar, Lewis enquired, 'How are things between you and Julia? I detect the blossoming of love, you poor idiot.'

Since the séance Julia had been distracted by concerns first for Lewis, then for Jackie Ferris. Guy was beginning to think she regarded love as an aberration. For an hour since his return, he had thrown himself into writing a letter to Elizabeth, but in his confusion nothing would come right. He wondered if he had rejected her not for another reality but for a mere glamour, a blighted hope. Against his deep belief in fidelity, Julia opposed an inability to make any commitment.

'By the way,' Lewis went on, 'I know all about Margot and Odo.'

'I'm sorry.'

'Don't be. It's something of a relief. She and I had a heart-to-heart talk about it. It went along the lines of Margot: "I've fallen in love with Odo, so it's all over between us." Lewis: "Righty ho, old girl, I'll clear off." A poetic moment that rent the heart in twain.'

'You take it very well.'

'I have to. If I kick up a fuss, Margot is quite capable of knocking me on the head.'

'You have a low opinion of her morals.'

'I have a healthy respect for her ruthlessness. Which reminds me, I should drop a line to Raymond. If Margot has set her sights on marrying Odo, Ray had better give her a divorce. I wouldn't give tuppence for his chances if he says no.'

'Aren't you forgetting that he's well out of reach in America?'

'Mere oceans are as nothing when one steps between Margot and her prey.' Lewis looked at his watch. 'I think it's time we pushed off home.'

Where the dark mass of pines rolled down to the shore, they swayed their bulk in the evening air like a seal going to water. Lewis and Guy, having drunk a bottle of wine and some grappa, sailed on tipsily. The sky was alive with swallows.

On such a night as this … Guy dreamt of Julia, though night had not quite fallen. Lewis's tale of Margot's exotic love life had half persuaded him that his own aspirations for a calm marriage were far from usual and even more bizarre. He loved Julia and would strive to adjust to her moods. His steady affection for Elizabeth had – apparently – been no more than friendship and he would write and tell her so.

'Penny for your thoughts,' said Lewis. 'Or possibly a lira. Say something to amuse me.'

'Oh, very well. Have you noticed that we talk only of the death of Shelley?'

'I thought you didn't want to talk of Shelley?'

'I'm amusing you.'

'All right. Go on.'

'We talk only of the death of Shelley, as if no one else were involved. Yet Edward Williams and the boy. they died too.'

'I hope you're not going to suggest that either of those two was the object of the plot. That's the sort of cheap device that brings crime fiction into disrepute. Let's stick to reality.'

'But the murder of Shelley *is* fiction.'

'That remains to be seen. There are fictions and fictions. The trick is "suspension of disbelief", as it's called in the trade. I can believe in Shelley's murder. Small boys, on the other hand, are run over by motor cars but never slaughtered in novels. As to Edward Williams, he's such a grey character one could kill him five times over without eliciting a flicker of interest.'

Some distance ahead, the grim castle of Lerici loomed purple on its rocky head and here and there the first lights appeared and other boats made silently for home. *On such a night ...*

'My point,' said Guy, 'is that we think only of Shelley and never of the others. Or, to look at a different aspect, what does anyone know of the Greek war of independence except that it caused Byron's death? Do you see? It's as if we adopt their egotism.'

'They make us,' answered Lewis. 'That's their particular genius.' He fell silent for a while, save for muttering about wind and trim, and Guy allowed his gaze to drift to a stretch of still water which the dying sun had gilded with aimless splendour.

At length Lewis said, 'Have you ever considered the havoc wrought by artists? The fortunes squandered, the friends betrayed, the women abandoned?'

'The deaths of Edward Williams and the boy?' Guy contributed. 'Go on.'

'I pay a few bob for a book and a couple of pounds for the theatre and fancy that's the price for whatever the artist has produced. But that isn't so at all, is it? The true cost is borne by those whose lives are ruined so that Byron, Shelley and their like can provide us with our hour of entertainment and reflection.'

'Viewed like that, the whole business of art sounds disgusting,' Guy agreed.

'Doesn't it? Ah, well! Not a thought on which to return to Ambrose, our own dear *maestro*.' Lewis beamed and reached into the bottom of the boat for the remains of the grappa.

The next moment, Guy found himself drowning.

'A drink?' Ambrose offered genially. 'You fellows look rather wet. Hadn't you better change before dinner? You're smiling. Are you drunk?'

'A little,' Guy admitted, adding, 'Lewis has just saved my life.'

'How very decent. In the circumstances I suggest whisky rather than gin.'

'I was helping myself to some grappa and let go of the tiller. We nearly capsized.'

'My, my. Well, bottoms up and then get changed. You may tell Uncle Ambrose of your adventures later.'

But later, when they gathered in the saloon for dinner, the episode of Guy's near-drowning seemed one of foolishness and incompetence and best forgotten. And Ambrose had other things on his mind.

'I've got two pieces of good news. The first, and to my mind more important, is that I've found Maria and persuaded her to cook us a good meal. Julia can tell you the second. Here she is.'

Julia entered at that moment and Guy, whose emotions were still heightened by what he considered a brush with death, thought that she had never looked more lovely. She shone with gaiety and, as she advanced, Guy hoped she was about to kiss him. Instead she went to Lewis, took both his hands in hers and bestowed her most dazzling smile.

'Jackie's safe,' she said. 'We've had a telegram from Marseilles sent yesterday. He apologised for not writing sooner, but he caught your tummy bug and was laid up. Not that it matters. The point is: he's safe.'

Lewis glanced at Guy and shrugged. 'Well, that's a relief,' he said flatly. 'Though I don't know why you should get so excited. I always told you he was all right.'

'And aren't you pleased, too, Guy?' asked Julia, at last giving him the promised kiss.

'Yes, of course,' he answered, which was true since he bore Jackie Ferris no ill-will.

Yet the incident seemed to confirm that Ferris and Julia had once been in love. And Guy wondered if Julia still was.

CHAPTER TWENTY-FIVE

1945

'We've got a small medical emergency,' said Jenkins.

'I hope not,' said Guy.

The hospital continued to disappear around him. The contents of the wards were now largely gone. The operating theatre had vanished when still in its crates. In proof that the Army had lost Guy and his men, no more supplies had been received, but the monotony of a military diet was relieved by Corporal Long, who foraged and traded in ways Guy did not care to examine.

Signor Nessuno had not returned and likely never would. The skeleton found in the cistern remained unexplained.

To escape from his troubles, Guy found himself frequently going over that hoary old problem, the murder of Shelley. He had solved it fifteen years before and was still persuaded of the correctness of his solution, though whether it was of any importance was another matter. The death of poets seemed insignificant in time of war.

Why did Shelley sail from Livorno to La Spezia on that day?

It was a good question. Guy smiled.

'Did I say something funny?' asked Jenkins.

'No, no. Forgive me. There's nothing funny about medical emergencies. What's this one?'

'Jimmy has been bitten on the testicles by a lizard.'

'Ah.'

'Do you want to examine him?'

'Good God, no! I'm sure he's telling the truth. How did it happen?'

'Are you laughing, Guy?'

'Absolutely not.'

'I could understand if you were, but the fact is, it's dashed painful – so Jimmy says.'

'Right, yes, if you say so. But how did it happen? Call it curiosity on my part.'

'I'm not sure. I thought it was tactless to enquire too closely. If it helps, I gather it happened out of working hours, when Jimmy was wearing his dress.'

'Of course. That would explain it, except…'

'What?'

'Well, if it were a regular hazard of wearing a dress, one would expect a lot of difficulty in the Highland regiments.'

'Gosh, I hadn't thought of that.'

'Cigarette?'

'Thanks awfully.'

They smoked a while in silent contemplation of hordes of Scots with lizards hanging from their nether parts, until at last Jenkins said, 'I'm not certain the two cases are similar. I can't imagine any creature taking a Scotsman's balls in its mouth.'

Independence Day saw an invitation from Corporal Pulaski to dine at the American mess. Guy was assured that the presence of a British officer would not be resented and there was a free place since Jimmy was in bed nursing his injury.

'I don't know what you gave him,' said Jenkins. 'Lizard ointment, testicle cream. Either way, it doesn't seem to be doing the trick.'

'It's an antiseptic,' Guy told him. 'Give it time.'

'What about this new wonder drug, penicillin?'

'I haven't got any.'

'Couldn't you ask the Americans?'

'I'll think about it.'

An opportunity arose later that evening. After dinner the assembled NCOs and guests were transported in trucks and jeeps to the Passegiata Constantino where an alfresco party continued under the palm trees while the American vessels in the Gulf fired a salute followed by a display of flares and thunderflashes in lieu of fireworks. A band played.

Corporal Pulaski had taken a shine to Guy and plied him with drink until his eyesight began to fail.

'Why haven't your bandsmen got heads?' Guy asked. He was getting used to headless musicians and the subject was now relegated to mere curiosity.

Corp popped the cork on another beer and examined the band, who had converted their march to a dance step. 'God damn it, but you're right!' he exclaimed.

'I am?'

'You sure are.'

'Good Lord! In the past people have always told me I'm wrong.'

Guy was warming to Corporal Pulaski and, after an exchange of photographs, felt able to put his question. 'Have you heard of the new drug?'

'Penicillin?'

'That's the fellow. Look, is there any chance you could get me some?'

Corp whistled. ''At's a tall order. Whaddaya got to trade?'

'Trade? I was hoping you'd do it as a favour for a friend.'

'For a pal, huh?' Corporal Pulaski considered this curious proposition. He grinned and gave Guy a dig in the ribs. 'You're a kidder, am I right?'

'If you say so.'

'Tell you what I'll do. I'll talk with Tommy.'

The crowd began to thin. Those left were mostly

chatting with the local tarts. Guy felt unwell and went to be sick in a bush.

'A little umpty-poo, are we?' asked Lieutenant Jenkins, who had appeared from nowhere. 'I got rid of my dinner about an hour ago and have been a lot better since. This is Anna, by the way.' Anna was a snub-nosed girl with freckles, who looked no older than fourteen.

Guy raised his head. 'Where is everyone?'

'Gone sailing.'

'Sailing?'

'Jolly-boats, bumboats, launches, everything they can put in the water. It looks enormous fun. I thought I might join them.'

Jenkins pointed to a flotilla of small craft swarming into the Gulf in a gunpowder fog broken by flares and flashes. Watching them, Guy experienced a quickening fear and an irresistible need to do something.

'You mustn't! It's dangerous!' he shouted – or thought he did; his later recollections were vague.

'Cup of tea? How are you this morning?' Jenkins asked.

'Terrible,' said Guy, and he enquired hesitantly, 'Did I make a fool of myself last night?'

'In a manner of speaking. You ran up and down the shore telling the Americans to get out of the boats or die.'

'I see. And how did they take it?'

'Rather well. They thought it was an example of British humour and cheered. But you were being serious, weren't you?'

'Yes,' said Guy, but he did not explain his reasons, which were too absurd. Instead he proposed to examine Jimmy's testicles and visit Inspector Porrello.

By the time he arrived in the hills beyond the Magra valley, Guy was feeling more refreshed, a state that would have continued if someone had not shot at him.

The bullet flew high and hit a chestnut tree. From a puff of black powder smoke, Guy judged it came from a thicket of bramble. He drew his own Webley revolver with uncertain confidence. Another shot came from the enemy. Again it comfortingly missed its mark.

Guy called out, 'Hullo! Look, I don't know who you are, but I'm a captain in the British Army! *Sono capitano nel esercito Britannico*!'

The pause that followed was longer than had taken his opponent to reload and at last a quavering voice replied.

'Is that Signor Parrot?'

'Yes. *Si.*'

'Are you alone?'

'Yes.'

The undergrowth rustled and Inspector Porrello appeared. He was wearing a homburg hat and one of his natty suits, both stained and snagged by thorns, but, though his face was grim, his moustache retained its usual splendour. He trailed his ancient hunting rifle and advanced cautiously. Only at the last step did he relax and assume his pleasant, knowing smile.

'Signor Guy,' he said, 'how can you forgive me?'

'I have a sausage for you.' Guy hoped this response was adequate.

'You are too kind. Come, come. It is not safe here.'

'The Communists?'

'*Si.* They want to kill the Fascist monster.'

'I am sorry.'

Signor Porrello shrugged.

Together they mounted the jeep and drove the last stretch of winding path. With the advancing summer the neglected vines and olives grew more ragged. Only the old man's vegetables, shaded under their trelliswork, flourished.

'You have some reason for your visit, Signor Guy?'

They sat outside the house where they could look out for Communists. The rifle lay across the old man's lap.

'I think I shall be leaving La Spezia soon,' Guy answered.

'Your work here is done?'

'To tell the truth, it never seemed to begin.'

'I mean your other work – your real work.'

'What is that?'

Guy was unclear if the response were directly an answer or not.

'Did you ever discover who murdered Lord Shelley?' asked the Inspector.

'Oh, that. I think so.'

'So you will go home to your wife?'

Guy nodded.

Wisteria and bindweed grew on the trellis. A great tit was shouting from the chestnuts. These things or something like them had been here when Shelley stayed at La Spezia. From this physical connection Guy wondered how valid it was to impute a moral one between the poet's death and the events of fifteen years ago. Home in Didsbury, Elizabeth managed the practice, the children and the rationing. Did she do so unwittingly under the shadow of Shelley? That life and art were bound together was a truism. What Guy had not previously appreciated was how difficult it was to grasp even those things that were self-evidently true or wise. Yet, did the drama of life not stem precisely from the failure to understand the obvious? The storm lay on the horizon and the fools would always sail towards it?

'May I ask you a question, Signor Porrello? You may not be able to answer.'

'Go ahead.'

'Was Commander Ferris a spy?'

'We believed so.'

'I thought as much,' said Guy and wondered what to make of that information. He hesitated before asking, 'Did the Italian Government have him killed?'

'It is possible, but I doubt it. You must understand, I was not in the counter-espionage section.'

'His disappearance was very mysterious.'

'It was theatrical. An abandoned boat and no sign of disturbance. We would have sunk the boat.'

Guy agreed that was odd. Jackie Ferris had been alone on the boat. He was a strong man. It seemed impossible that he should have been murdered without evidence of the fact.

To Guy's surprise, Signor Porrello went on, 'Do you know, my friend, that the boat in which Commander Ferris disappeared was not the same as that in which he left La Spezia six months before? That boat was never found.'

'Surely you're mistaken? He sailed to Marseilles in it.'

'No. The boat did not reach Marseilles.'

'It must have. We received a telegram from Jackie.'

'I know.'

'How?'

Guy had never known the old man show embarrassment, but he did so now. He confessed, 'We had an informer at the Villa Esperanza.'

'Joe Truffatore? I knew it! Jackie said so.'

Signor Porrello shook his head, laughing. 'No, no. It was Maria, your cook. Giuseppe Truffatore was a nobody, a petty criminal. Unfortunately, neither he nor Maria was at the villa when the Commander left. So the only evidence we have is the telegram.'

'Are you saying it was a forgery?'

'It was genuine. It was sent from Marseilles on the date stated – at which time you and your friends were at the Villa Esperanza. How Commander Ferris got to Marseilles is a mystery, though his boat is recorded as leaving La Spezia. Nor do we know what he did in the following six months until he hired another boat and finally vanished. Perhaps we ought to have discovered the truth, but for as long as he remained in France, he was of no interest to us.'

Jimmy had hobbled from his bed to a chair on the terrace. He tried to stand when Guy arrived, but abandoned the effort.

'Hullo, Mr Parrot,' he said with an attempt at cheerfulness.

'Hullo, Jimmy. Where is everyone?'

'I'm on my tod. Tommy and Mr Jenkins have gone into town with Nick and the two-tonner.'

'Have they stolen more of the hospital?'

'Ha, ha, Mr Parrot! What a card you are!'

Guy no longer cared. He offered to get the private a beer. On his return he commented, 'That's a nice dress you're wearing.'

Jimmy brightened. 'You don't mind? It makes me feel better while I'm poorly.'

'No, I don't mind at all. I'm just surprised you're wearing it after what happened.'

'The way I see it is that I'm not likely to get bitten on the nuts twice.'

'You're probably right. Where did you get it, the dress?'

'I made it myself.' Jimmy was proud of the fact. 'Me and Nick bought the material together when we was on leave in Rome. He likes me in pink.'

'I once knew a man who knitted socks.'

Jimmy considered the point. 'It's not the same, is it?'

Guy heated some dinner from Army rations. He found a bottle of wine. When Jimmy said he wasn't up to climbing the stairs to the saloon, Guy set a table on the terrace and lit a candle.

'How romantic. You are good to me, Mr Parrot.'

'That's all right.'

'Wine, too.'

'Go steady with it.'

'This is a nice place, isn't it? I was telling Nick something I learnt at school. Shelley the poet used to live here. Did you know that?'

'Yes,' said Guy, and added, 'He was murdered.'

Jimmy had nothing to contribute to that subject, except to say,

'Was he? What a shame for his old mum and dad.' He was tired but had no desire to go to his room nor to talk very much. He and Guy sat together by candlelight staring over the Gulf. Half an hour must have passed before Jimmy spoke again.

'I owe you an apology, Mr Parrot.'

'You do? What for?'

'Something slipped my mind. That Italian tramp, Nessuno, called.'

'When?'

'This afternoon. He was drunk but nice enough. We had a beer together. Was that all right?'

'That was fine. What did he have to say?'

'I couldn't really make him out. He said something about being fed up with everything and ready to be hanged. He's a sad bastard, isn't he?'

'Yes, very.'

'He spoke English, which surprised me. In fact I thought he was English – or American. It was hard to tell, with him being near dead drunk and me with one eye on him and one on my balls.'

'Did you get the impression he'd come again?' Guy asked.

'Oh, yes. He said he was going to give himself up.'

At last Guy found his copy of the *Manual of Military Law*. He took it onto the loggia and studied it over a cup of coffee while the day brightened into a pale pearly grey. Lieutenant Jenkins found him there.

'Did you get a good price for the hospital?' Guy asked.

Jenkins was a little taken aback. 'Are you feeling all right? Tommy absolutely assures me that we can get it all back if we need to. Even so, you're being damn decent about everything.'

'Coffee?'

'Thanks. My head's a little wobbly. Hullo, what's that you've got? King's Regs? Dull stuff and, please God, we shan't need them much longer.'

'I've been reading the bit about stealing hospitals. Apparently the Army's against it.'

'I thought they might be. But as I say –'

'Don't bother,' Guy interrupted. 'It doesn't matter. I shall be going to prison anyway.'

Guy had also studied the *Manual* concerning the harbouring of fugitive war criminals, the organising of an illegal bookmaking operation, the disposal of the skeletons of murder victims found in cisterns, the permitting of a private soldier to wear ladies' garments, and the consequence if said private were bitten on the genitals by a lizard. It seemed that the Army was against such things, too, though the draughtsman had lacked the imagination to conceive of them in detail.

Guy added to his crimes the fact that he had befriended a former Fascist official.

'Look on the bright side,' said Jenkins.

When Corporal Long next appeared, he seemed a little sombre. Guy took him aside.

'I've got a couple of requests to make, Tommy,' he said.

The Corporal cast a more than usually cautious eye on him.

'The first concerns Jimmy. I'm not happy with his … injury. It seems to have got infected despite the antiseptic and an injection I gave him. The Americans must have penicillin at their hospital. I've asked Corp to get me some. He'll be in touch with you.'

'Yon Corp is a crook,' said Tommy acidly.

'Is he? Yes, well, I suppose he is. But, if you could do your best, it'd be appreciated.'

'And? You said there was a second request.'

'I'd be awfully glad if you could get the hospital back. I have a feeling we're going to need it one of these days.'

'Captain Parrot, sir. There's a telephone call for you, sir.'

'You're being very punctilious this morning, Tommy,' said Guy, who was feeling amiable after a good night's sleep. 'Who is it?'

'Colonel Box, sir.'

'Ah. So we've been found, at last?'

'It looks like it.'

'So all good things come to an end.'

'Och, it's nae so bad,' said Corporal Long dropping his pretence of soldierly formality for a moment, 'so long as we're here and Thunder's doon there.'

'Captain Parrot here, sir,' said Guy into the telephone.

'Parrot!' boomed Colonel Box. 'Reports! Not had any! Where the hell are they?'

'We lost our communications. It seems you moved … sir.'

'No excuse! I want them tomorrow! Understood?'

'Of course, sir. Will that be all, sir?'

'No, it bloody well won't! Your man, Corporal Long.'

'Sir?'

'Tell him he's to stop that gambling syndicate of his. I've had to can Captain Hale for buggering with the mess funds, and my batman, Daisy, has lost his shirt and doesn't know what to tell his mother.'

'Very good, sir. Anything else?'

'That stiff you found.'

'Yes?'

'Still got it?'

'Not exactly.'

'Oh? Pity that. Fact is, I let slip in my cups that you'd found a dead body, and the Provost-Marshal pricked up his ears and started taking an interest. I'll have to see what I can do to put a stop to any enquiry.'

'Thank you, sir,' said Guy gratefully.

'You can keep your thanks,' Colonel Box retorted. 'I know a shambles when I smell one. I'll be seeing you on Sunday.'

310

CHAPTER TWENTY-SIX

1930

Madame Hecate obtained a new set of papers and a banker's draft from a friend in England. She announced her intention to leave La Spezia and return home.

'Must you, dear lady?' asked Ambrose.

'Indeed I must. In fact, I have pressing reasons to go.' She did not say what they were.

Guy had taken to visiting the grotto in the mornings. Each time he set the fountain to flow for half an hour. He never recaptured the feeling of surprised transcendence that accompanied the first occasion. But it was not wholly lost, rather transformed to a muted miracle like the repetition of spring.

Coming up behind him, slightly breathless from scaling the slope, Madame Hecate said, 'I hope I'm not disturbing you, Mr Parrot. May I call you Guy? We are friends, I trust?' A leather box joggled on her hip.

'You have a new camera?'

'A souvenir. And so very useful at the oddest moments.'

Guy smiled at the old lady's eccentricity. 'Surely it would have been better to buy one at the beginning of your holiday?'

'May I sit down? Isn't this a lovely spot? And in spring it must be filled with violets and celandines. As to the camera, you must bear with me. Though I may seem very foolish, I have my reasons.'

Madame Hecate took a seat on the bench inside the shallow hillside opening that formed the grotto itself. When she had adjusted her skirts and her hat with its

311

jaunty feather, she patted next to her in sign that Guy should also sit down. They both gazed across the clearing at the two statues caged by water.

'Hadrian and Antinous, aren't they?' said Madame Hecate calmly contemplating the pair. 'Such a disreputable relationship for a Roman Emperor. I suppose it is a redeeming quality that there was love between them. But ill-considered affection does have a habit of leading people into most unsuitable liaisons.'

'I don't think one should moralise,' Guy remarked uncomfortably.

'No, no, I quite agree. But I was speaking of circumstances and character, not morality. The Emperor should not have loved the boy because it made him look absurd. The point is obvious and I imagine Hadrian's advisers told him so. Alas, there are times when we believe we are exempt from the normal course of events. One tries to advise. I have tried to advise the others.'

'You do horoscopes?'

'Oh dear, no. So many charlatans claim to know the future. I merely predict from observation and a certain knowledge of the world.'

By that Guy supposed that she took her prejudices and elevated them to universal laws. She was looking at him with her mild blue eyes as though this criticism were familiar to her.

'I believe,' she continued hesitantly 'that you are in love with Lady Julia?'

'I don't think…'

'…that it's any business of mine? No, it isn't, except insofar as one has a duty to prevent unhappiness where one can. You *may* make Lady Julia happy, but I am confident that that troubled young lady will cause you nothing but misery. You should marry your fiancée, Elizabeth. She seems a very nice person.'

'I'm not in love with Elizabeth,' said Guy firmly. He

rose from the seat and washed his face at the fountain. The old lady, still perfectly composed, called out, 'Because you are in love with Lady Julia? My dear boy, it is a popular superstition – quite contrary to all the facts – that one cannot love two people at the same time.'

'And if I choose Julia?'

'Then you will be unhappy.'

The old lady stood up and joined him. Distractedly she murmured, 'With age comes poor circulation. Sitting on stone benches makes one's … parts … numb. Where was I? Ah, yes. As I was saying, it's a question of character. You have a talent for the quiet, faithful love that leads to domestic happiness. Lady Julia is a woman of intense momentary passions and, if I may be so bold, her talent is for self-dramatisation. The two of you will never agree. Consider for a moment. Since you have known her, though your emotions have been stirred, have you known an instant of peace?'

Guy turned on her. 'Is peace the only aim in life?' he said angrily.

The old lady seemed to pity him.

'It is certainly a most *sensible* thing to desire.'

An hour later Guy was standing on the terrace next to Ambrose as Madame Hecate departed in the Alvis.

'Well, that's that,' Ambrose said with a note of sourness. 'What a formidable old harridan!'

'That's an odd thing to say. I thought you were fond of her?'

'So I was. But I have discovered that a nasty mind lurks behind those fluffy cardigans.'

As Ambrose stalked off, Lewis enquired of Guy, 'Did Madame H treat you to one of her homilies?'

'Yes.'

'What about?'

'I prefer not to say. And you?'

'I got both barrels. The upshot was that Ambrose is a bad influence on me and I shall regret my friendship with him.'

'That's a cruel thing to say.'

'True, though, apart from the bit about regret. I've always known that Ambrose is a bad lot. The trouble is the fellow is a genius, more's the pity.'

'You could be wrong.'

'For God's sake don't say that!' Lewis paused. Then he laughed. 'I think I shall get drunk. And afterwards I must complete my poem.'

'About Byron?'

'Yes – damn him.'

Guy took his drink and went to find Julia. She was sitting between a pair of columns in the loggia where it opened to the sky with a line of swallows' nests. The birds swooped in, then, seeing humans, broke off and swept away with complaining twitters.

'Hullo, darling,' said Julia quietly.

'You didn't say goodbye to Madame Hecate.'

'We had a private conversation.'

'What Lewis calls one of her "homilies"?'

'Yes.'

Julia rose from her chair. She took Guy's hands in hers and examined his face curiously. Then, with great deliberation, she placed a kiss on his cheek. She sat down again.

'Aggie has told Margot that she must marry Odo Milne.'

'What a terrible prospect.'

'She's a very practical woman. Although Odo is a swine, he and Margot will find a grisly happiness together and rear a brood of monsters.'

'And you?'

'Apparently I'm to give you up.'

Guy lit two cigarettes and passed one to Julia.

'Will you? Give me up?' he asked.

'I've not decided.'

'Do you love me?'

'Yes. But don't confuse things. I have to make a calm decision, and it seems love doesn't count.' She flicked her cigarette irritably. 'I'd like to know what *does* count! Madame Hecate's version of happiness seems a very chill affair involving sitting in the inglenook listening to the wireless, Horlicks and bedsocks. She says that's what you need. Is it?'

'It's not what I want.'

'I said "need" not "want". Madame Hecate was very precise on that point. Don't you absolutely hate it when people tell you perfectly commonplace things that you'd rather ignore? It makes one fear that there's nothing profound or passionate in the universe and that in the hereafter we shall be everlastingly pestered by angels telling us to dry properly after a bath or risk athlete's foot.'

Although Julia's erratic mood made the moment inopportune, Guy had to speak.

'If we are to continue … seeing each other, I need to know something. I don't believe you've told me the truth about Jackie Ferris.'

The look that greeted this was malevolent. 'Am I to be treated to more of your bedint notions of morality?'

'I'm sorry, Julia, but I have to know.'

She stubbed her cigarette viciously and looked away to the sky and swallows. When she spoke again, it was with a calm briskness as if delivering a report in which no one – least of all she – was interested.

'About five years ago, Ambrose and I were in New York for one of his early plays, *Future Surprises* – you may have heard of it? The production was financed by Morty Lowenstein, who was, for want of a better word, a gangster.

'Jackie was in the Navy during the war and found himself at a loose end afterwards. When Prohibition came, he started running spirits in small boats from Canada.

315

That's how he came to know Morty and happened to be in New York while we were there.

'How much of this do you want to know? If you hadn't realised from Jackie's story, he's an educated man – Princeton, I think. When he met Ambrose he became ... infatuated I suppose, like Lewis. I'm not speaking of sex, which was quite another thing. But he could see Ambrose's genius, which everyone can, except you and Odo. His mind was in a romantic haze, and he followed us everywhere' – Julia softened – 'which was quite touching. And we became close.'

Guy asked, 'Were you in love with him?'

He was no longer troubled by the brutality of the question. Since speaking to Madame Hecate he had been torn by an incoherent anger. Julia could see it and, from her eyes, was pleading for him to stop. He waited for an answer.

'Let's say that we became lovers. I was already estranged from Hector, if that's what worries you.'

'Poor Hector.'

'Yes, poor Hector. He's a very good man and deserved better than having his reputation torn to shreds.'

'Go on. How long did this affair last?'

'As long as we were in New York. About three months, I suppose.'

'And then?'

'I don't want to talk about it. Not even to you, Guy. There was a quarrel and recriminations. It should be enough for you that we parted.' Julia bridled. 'Look, where is this conversation going? You must accept me as I am, Guy. I've never claimed to have a virtuous past and God alone knows what the future holds. I've warned you. Doesn't that show I love you? That I'm capable of at least a small degree of self-sacrifice?'

'Are you still in love with Ferris?'

Julia looked shocked, as if this question above all was

incomprehensible. 'Have you understood nothing, darling?'

'It seems not.'

Julia breathed, then said vehemently, 'I *loathe* Jackie Ferris!'

Skittering across the terrace was one of the lizards that infested the cracks in the stucco and the rocks around the house. Ambrose and Lewis watched it with silent intensity. It was noon and they were drunk.

Used to this breed of sinner, Fred said prelatically, 'Look at the pair of them. Three sheets to the wind and none the happier for it.' A bottle of Gordon's gin stood on the table. 'They've had too much of the General and no mistake. Speaking of which, Mr Parrot, I once said to Field Marshal Haig (who was a whisky man) that he should watch his grog. And he said, "*Fred*, you're *right*!" and went on to win the war. Mr Parrot…?'

Everything was spoilt, Guy decided, and he suspected it always had been. La Spezia seemed possessed of an infection for which there was no cure. He glanced up to the loggia but saw only the bright columns. Julia Astarte was still there, cold and unforgiving in her moon-wrapt loneliness, and he knew that, unless he could transform himself, there was nothing before him except the prospect of Elizabeth, Didsbury, and a future that announced itself like a bronchitic patient at the surgery door.

'*God knoweth what it means, for I am sure I do not.*' The prayer of those martyred for unfathomable causes in the sure and certain knowledge that pain was the only Real Presence and resurrection to eternal Horlicks their modest hope for an afterlife. In self-pity, Guy muttered it, then took a bottle of brandy and went to bed.

He woke some two hours later at the sound of voices. He went below and found, on the terrace, the two women, Ambrose and Lewis awake but crapulous, and a genial

Inspector Porrello with two policemen in uniform.

'Speak to the fellow,' groaned Ambrose. 'If we're to be arrested, you may inform him we have no objection. If executed, so much the better.'

'Signor Parrot.' The Inspector smiled and doffed his hat.

'*Buon giorno*, Inspector. Signor Carmody wishes to know if we are to be arrested.'

'Do you wish to be?' said Signor Porrello, adding waggishly, 'We like to oblige our foreign visitors.'

Guy tried to respond in kind but found his legs were waywardly inclined.

'Forgive me if I sit down. I'm a little … tired. What brings you here?'

'Your American friend, Commander Ferris. He left La Spezia some days ago in his boat.'

'Yes, but he's perfectly safe. We've had a telegram from him.'

'No doubt. However, that is not my affair. My request is to examine his room.'

'His room? Do you have a warrant? No, forget I said that. I … Ambrose, any objection?'

'Search away,' said Ambrose wearily.

'Please show me,' Signor Porrello asked politely.

Guy led the Inspector and his colleagues to the second floor. The door to Jackie Ferris's room was unlocked and the room itself open to dusty sunlight. The bed had been stripped and the bedclothes folded or rolled and placed on the paliasse. Beyond that the room contained a commode, a marble-topped washstand and a painted chest of drawers, all shabby but serviceable. The floor was of boards, partly covered by cheap matting.

Guy enquired, 'Should I go or stay?'

'We shall be a little time.'

'You will? Ah, yes. All right, I'll be downstairs.'

On the terrace Lewis was snoozing. Ambrose pronounced languidly, 'I always said that Jackie was a sinister fellow. I wonder what he's been up to? Smuggling, I fancy. I ask myself: what does one smuggle into Italy, and is there any money in it? Guy, dear?'

'I've no idea.'

'He was probably in cahoots with Joe Truffatore, who knows a fellow crook when he sees one. Which reminds me, we haven't seen Joe since we got back from Venice.'

Lewis opened an eye. 'I paid him off before I went to Lucca. You may recall saying you didn't want him back.'

'Did I? More fool me. Joe probably knows the etiquette of bribing bobbies in this part of the world.'

'Signor Porrello is honest,' said Guy.

Ambrose regarded him sceptically.

Signor Porrello and his men returned. Ambrose extended both hands, fists down and close together.

'Okay, Guvnor, it's a fair cop.'

'Please?'

'Do I take it we're free? What a relief!'

Signor Porrello looked at Guy, who suspected he was being singled out as trustworthy.

'Did the Commander leave anything with you? An envelope? A package?'

'Not with me.'

A chorus of denials and headshakes came from the others.

'May I ask what this is about?'

'No,' said the Inspector, lightly.

With night came bats and moths around the lanterns. The air was damp and tepid and smelled of resin. The pines soughed and crepitated.

Over dinner Ambrose announced, 'I think we should plan for our return to England. Shall we say in a week's time? I'm tired of La Spezia and I think it is tired of me.'

'Why wait a week?' asked Julia.

'I'm expecting some cables from New York.'

Margot said, 'I may go to Rome. Odo has an audience

with the Duce.'

'Have you told Raymond of your new *amour*?'

'I've had a letter from his solicitor. He wants to marry me – the solicitor, I mean, not Raymond whom I'm already married to. I don't know whether the man is obtuse or humorous. What do you think?'

'Marry him. Guy, dear, what will you do about your yellow bitch?'

'Nothing.'

'Desert her?'

'What else can I do?'

Ambrose looked at Julia. 'It seems our Guy is a man of fickle affections. First Elizabeth and now the yellow bitch. His commitment is that of cheap sentiment. Guy, you should take up bigamy as a career if medicine ever fails you.'

Guy was too dispirited to protest vigorously. Julia did not defend him.

'I don't deserve that remark,' he answered, feeling nevertheless that it might be justified. He was spared anything further by Lewis's appearance from the house, recovered from his binge.

'Don't ask how I am. I'm feeling very chipper, thank you very much.'

'You look like a man who's come to a decision.' said Ambrose.

'I have. I'm going to sail the boat down to Livorno and say farewell to Shelley before we all go home.'

'Are you sure that's wise?'

'Perfectly. Shelley and company did it in a day. I shall allow two. I'll send a telegram to say I'm all right, and I'll be back within the week, weather permitting.'

Lewis sailed to Livorno and, as promised, sent a telegram to confirm his arrival. At the end of a week he had not returned and the journey to England was postponed. Three days later Inspector Porrello delivered a message from the authorities in Viareggio concerning a body.

There had been no storm.

CHAPTER TWENTY-SEVEN

1930

At Viareggio children of the Balilla played ball games on the beach. Ambrose prowled the sand, fanning himself with his hat. He looked tired and dispirited like a seedy copra trader cast up in the tropics.

He said, 'It was Trelawny who arranged Shelley's funeral. That fact in itself lends an air of romance, since Trelawny was an odd character in an odd age. His family was quite well known in the West Country. He joined the Navy but deserted and – if he's to be believed – commanded a Malay pirate ship for a time before marrying a beautiful Arab lady whose life he had saved. After Shelley's death he followed Byron to Greece, joined forces with a partisan chief with the unlikely name of Odysseus, and married the fellow's daughter. I mention these facts because one could not invent Trelawny and expect to be believed.

'In those days the quarantine regulations of Italy were very strict and Shelley was buried where he was found. Then Trelawny persuaded the Tuscan authorities that the poet should be cremated in the fashion of the ancient Greeks. It was done here, on this beach. No, no, Guy, I don't swear to the exact spot.

'Our pirate had an iron frame made on which the corpse was placed. It was sprinkled with incense, honey, wine and salt – the salt would have made the flames burn blue. Was it really Shelley? There was no flesh on the hands or face. However, I cast no aspersions.

'Byron, Leigh Hunt and a squad of soldiers attended. It

was high summer and the affair took a long time, so I imagine that much of the intended effect was lost. The soldiers would have slouched on their weapons, stretched on the sand and dozed, while occasionally asking their officer for permission to relieve themselves. I see Byron and Leigh Hunt muttering about Trelawny's absurd pretensions and sloping off for a smoke. On the first day only the body of Edward Williams was burned.

'On the second day – by which time, no doubt, everyone was thoroughly bored with having to put on a decent face and the soldiers like as not drunk – they attended to Shelley.

' "I restore to nature, through fire, the elements of which this man was composed; everything is changed but not annihilated; he is now a portion of that which he worshipped." The words are Trelawny's. I fancy Byron sniggered at their banality and Leigh Hunt noted them down for his newspaper and got them wrong. At all events, our bold buccaneer pranced about the pyre for hours on end, chanting this nonsense and pouring libations.

'Finally the corpse was reduced, if not to ashes, to something too disgusting for the horrible spectacle to continue. Trelawny reached into the pyre and removed the heart. Not surprisingly, the idiot burnt himself. The object was placed in a box and sent out to Byron's boat.

'Byron, Leigh Hunt and Trelawny pushed off to a nearby pub.'

Ambrose sighed. 'I don't claim to speak for you, Guy, but I was rather fond of Lewis. I think we should give him a decent burial and write a sober letter to his parents.'

At the civic mortuary, Ambrose and Guy identified the body. It lay covered save for the face, which was badly damaged. The scalp was bound in cloth to hide the removal of part of the skull during the post mortem.

'How long was he in the water?' Guy asked.

'Six to ten days,' said the doctor. 'The body had floated

and there is extensive decomposition of the trunk.'

'It doesn't look like Lewis.'

'It doesn't look like anyone I know,' said Ambrose.

The clothes were Lewis's and contained his passport and a volume of Keats's poetry.

'How did he die?' Guy asked.

'He drowned,' said the doctor. 'There was foam in the trachea, bronchi and lungs, signs of cadaveric spasm in the hands, and haemorrhaging of the middle ear.'

'He was a very good swimmer,' said Guy.

The doctor shrugged. 'If he fell into the sea, perhaps through a gust of wind, the boat may have swung and struck him, causing unconsciousness. The injuries to the face and back of the head are clear.'

'I'm glad Julia and Margot didn't come,' Guy remarked as they walked to the harbour-master's office. 'Do you think it really was Lewis?'

'I've no idea, but I can't think why it shouldn't be.'

'Neither can I.'

The harbour-master's office was opposite the entrance to the Darsena Toscana.

'I don't know what you expect to find out here,' said Ambrose. 'As I understand it, Lewis put into Livorno, not Viareggio.'

'The record may have been brought here for the enquiries.'

It showed that Lewis had arrived at Livorno on the day of his telegram. He had sailed twenty-four hours later. In both cases he was alone. The corpse had washed up on the tenth day after his departure. No trace of the boat had been found.

On the beach the Italians and a few resident English disported themselves. Most tourists were kept away by the effects of the economic depression. Ambrose recited the facts of Shelley's funeral.

'If I were of a suspicious turn of mind, I should say that Trelawny was getting rid of the evidence.'

'Trelawny seems to have been infatuated with Shelley.'

'We always kill the things we love. I believe Wilde said that or something like it, though in our case murder seems to be precluded by the fact that Lewis arrived and left alone. Nevertheless, I am open to any theory you may have.'

'Jackie Ferris.'

'Jackie?'

'We were all at La Spezia, but Jackie remains unaccounted for. He has a boat. He could have encountered Lewis at sea.'

'True, but, disregarding for the moment the lack of any evidence, why on earth should Jackie kill Lewis, or vice versa for that matter? They scarcely knew each other and, from what I observed, seemed to be on perfectly good terms.'

'They could have quarrelled while we were in Venice.'

'In which case why did Jackie not knock Lewis on the head there and then? That would be consistent with a quarrel. Lewis gave no hint of disagreement except an understandable reluctance to go sailing with Jackie, and Jackie's telegram was couched in very friendly terms. No, Guy dear, we have allowed our heads to be turned by all this talk of murder.'

Julia helped Guy to pack Lewis's belongings. Ambrose undertook to write to Lord Lockyer and to make any necessary arrangements with the British authorities. The Consul arrived from Livorno, a jolly man with a bibulous complexion and a ginger moustache.

'I'm glad to see you've got on with things. It makes my job a lot easier when people get on with things. Getting on with things seems to be the British way.'

'I'm glad you think so,' Ambrose told him.

They sat on the terrace drinking gin. The Consul was in no hurry to leave. He drove a small Morris saloon and was very proud of it.

'A propos of nothing in particular, I've had an enquiry from the Americans. They've lost one of their chaps and wondered if I might help. Commander Jackie Ferris – the sailor fellow who's been in the papers? A little bird told me he'd paid a visit to La Spezia.'

'He's in Marseilles.'

'So I heard, but the Yanks can't find him there.'

'Really? Well, I shouldn't worry. He's very good at getting on with things.'

'You're probably right. It's a shame about Mr Lockyer. I met him briefly, you know.'

'You did?'

'He wandered into my office, just to let me know he was in town. He was right to be careful, and I can't help people if I don't know they're around, can I? He seemed … I think the word is "preoccupied". Any idea why?'

'None at all,' said Ambrose. 'Have another drink.'

'I don't mind if I do. And then I'll be getting on.'

'Margot should be doing this, not I,' said Julia, though in fact she was of little help.

Guy folded Lewis's shirts and packed them. He looked for his friend's shaving kit, which was with a set of brushes in a leather case. But, of course, Lewis had taken it with him and it was presumably at the bottom of the sea.

'What is she doing?'

'Planning her wedding to Odo. In her enthusiasm, it may take place before her divorce from Raymond.'

'Will you go through the drawers?'

'If you like.' Julia threw her cigarette out of the window; it described a bright red arc against the night.

'There's something here.' She had found a page of rough notes. She spared them a glance before throwing them at Guy. 'They're about bloody Shelley!'

Guy picked them from the floor and sat on the bed.

'You're not going to read them, are you?' Julia said disdainfully.

'Pass me the candle,' Guy answered and unfolded the paper on his lap.

The Murder (?) of Shelley

Victims

(1) Shelley!!!

(2) Edward Williams.

(3) The Boy – name?

Suspects

(1) Mary – In La Spezia at time of death.

(2) Jane Williams (?) – ditto.

(3) Claire – In Florence. In any case, she was fond of Shelley.

(4) Byron – He pressed Shelley to stay at Livorno. Did he? No evidence to contrary.

(5) Leigh Hunt – No motive? No opportunity?

(6) TRELAWNY!!! – Could Jackie be right about him? Still the likeliest out of the whole bunch.

Case for the prosecution (according to Jackie)

- *T knew the 'Don Juan' was a dangerous boat.*
- *T knew a storm was in the offing.*
- *T says he was prepared to accompany S in the 'Bolívar'.*
- *The 'Bolívar' could not sail.*
- *There is no reason why the 'Bolívar' could not sail. T should have been able to clear her papers.*

Case for the defence (Madame H)

– *T would be a fool to draw attention to the storm.*
– *Ditto if T offered to sail in the 'Bolívar'.*
– *T had no notice and could not clear the 'Bolívar'
with the police.*
Motive? T had a jealous infatuation with Shelley.

(7) Others?

– *The Hotel Manager?*
– *The Cook?*
– *The Butler Wot Dunnit?*
– *Et cetera, et cetera!!!*
BLOODY NONSENSE!
YET WHY DID SHELLEY SAIL INTO THE STORM?

'Well?' said Julia. 'Is the answer there?'

'No. There's nothing we don't know already.'

'What a surprise.' Julia pulled an envelope from the drawer. 'This is for you. It has your name on it.'

Guy pocketed the envelope and went on with the packing.

Julia asked, 'Aren't you going to read it?'

'I know what it is,' Guy told her. 'Lewis was writing a poem about Byron. Do you want it?'

Julia wrinkled her nose. 'I think I'd rather have Odo's babies.'

'I propose that we leave tomorrow. There should be no difficulty. I've had enough of La Spezia and, to quote Tennyson, "I'm half sick of Shelley, said the Lady of Shallott". If anyone wants me, I shall be in my room.'

With that, Ambrose quitted the terrace, leaving the others to finish their coffee. A little later he returned to ask, 'Has anyone seen my socks? I was packing and seem to be missing a couple of pairs.'

'Is that a clue?' asked Julia dully.

'To what, dear girl?'

'I don't know. I'm talking rubbish. I wish Lewis was here.'

Ambrose shook his head. 'It's all very sad. Did he ever finish that poem he was writing?'

'Guy has it.'

'Oh dear. Lewis had no talent in that direction. Too derivative.'

'Good night, Ambrose.'

'Ah, yes. By the way, is there any milk left? I should like a cup of cocoa. Don't trouble yourselves, I can make it.'

On such a night as this ... Fred found Ambrose's socks.

'I shall miss Lewis,' said Margot as if this were unexpectedly decent of her and worthy of praise.

'Will you call on his father?' Julia asked. 'I'm sure he'd appreciate it.'

'Would he? I never thought of that.'

'What's he like, Lord Lockyer?'

'Rather a cheerful old villain. I tried to get him to give my cousin Esmond a job as his representative in South America. He refused. He said a one-legged man was not a good advertisement in the boot and shoe business.'

'Esmond only has one leg?'

'He lost the other when Morty Lowenstein shot him.'

'What does he do these days?'

'I believe he's a spy. It was a choice between that and being a bishop in the Church of South India.'

Guy decided on a last visit to the grotto and the statues of Hadrian and Antinous. The yellow bitch followed at a distance, though by lantern-light her colour was green.

The fountain was not playing. The cistern was exhausted and refilling from the spring. The two figures whispered endearments that were audible in the swish of pines. Guy listened to their conversation and heard

Shelley's name repeated in the susurrations. Sometimes their eyes deviated from their intimate exchange and bestowed on Guy the look of sinister kindness that is given to children who are not to be told the truth.

'Guy! Guy! I can't see you!'

He picked up the lantern and waved it. Julia stumbled into the clearing.

'I knew you'd be here,' she said breathlessly, 'but I got lost and I've been wandering around in the dark. Kiss me, darling.'

Guy did so dutifully but took no pleasure in a sad, spoilt embrace.

Julia detected his reluctance and sighed. 'Something horrible has happened, hasn't it?'

'I don't know what.'

'Neither do I. Jackie has gone away and Lewis is dead. Ambrose is in one of his Olympian moods, like Zeus disposing of mortal fates – though I can't see how he can have disposed of anyone, can you?'

'No.'

'He was in Venice when Jackie left and here when Lewis drowned. In any case, Jackie is alive and well somewhere in France and Lewis's death was an accident. And yet everything feels wrong.' She looked at the statues and remarked, 'You've always been impervious to Ambrose's charm, haven't you?'

'Yes.'

'Lucky you. Ambrose belongs to that class of men, like Shelley and Byron, who fascinate others. I think Mary must have had Byron in mind when she conceived of Frankenstein. Men who aim at truth and beauty but unwittingly create monsters out of dead people.'

'Dead people?'

'Oh, yes. That's their secret. They live so intensely that they offer life to those who have died inside. Think of poor, pathetic Claire, in thrall to Byron. Trelawny dedicating his life to a biography of Shelley with all its absurd pretensions as to his own importance. Even Mary, absorbed in collecting and publishing her husband's work at the expense of her own. All of them became vivified by borrowing other lives in a vampire existence.'

'Polidori wrote a vampire story,' Guy remembered.

'So he did,' said Julia.

'I'd forgotten.'

'That's not surprising. He was a ridiculous little man and not very important.'

They returned to the house hand in hand.

'Shall I come to your room tonight?' Guy asked.

'No, not tonight,' Julia replied. Guy felt slightly relieved.

He returned to his room and began packing, a task ignored earlier when he had Lewis's things to attend to. By his bedside was the envelope with his name on it, a fact which only now struck him as curious, as though Lewis had known he would not return from Livorno. He opened it and removed several sheets of paper, of which the first was a brief letter addressed to him. It read:

La Spezia
15 August 1930

Dear Guy,

The fact of your reading this should tell you all you need to know. I don't expect I shall see you again. You will find enclosed my contribution to our evenings' entertainments, which I had planned to deliver in person if unforeseen circumstances had not dictated otherwise. I make no claim for my skill, but the poem collects all the facts of 'the case' that seem to me relevant. To me they say nothing but they may speak to you. I do not know who murdered Shelley or if he was murdered at all, and I wish that we had never, in our heartlessness, raised the question. As you may suspect, your trust and kindness have been abused. Please forgive all of us.

Your friend
Lewis

Guy turned to the poem and spent half an hour reading it several times. It was crude in execution, repulsive in its conceit, and savage in its judgments. Guy was frightened by it. Yet Lewis was his friend, and for that fact he cried.

The storm raged, but below the surface of the water was a calm ocean flickering with light and shadow. Here there was no horizon but only an immediacy that absorbed all Guy's strength and consumed every breath. He was drowning, but he did not know whether it was the storm or the calm that was killing him.

The hunting call of an owl woke him. He reached for matches and lit a nightlight. Now bare of his possessions, the room offered its indifferent composure. Guy lit a cigarette while remembering, with the dull chaos of sleep, where he had misplaced his collar studs and, also, that he knew who had killed Shelley. He decided that he would wear soft-collared shirts during the journey home. The cigarette finished, he rose, retrieved the studs from the washstand where they had been obscured by the basin and put them in his collar-box. That done he sat down again and pondered his muddy reflections before deciding that he should tell Julia the news.

He took the candle and crossed the bedroom. He passed through the small withdrawing room on the further side and into the saloon. The columns and other painted architecture briefly confused his senses, but at last he found another door and entered the large reception room beyond which lay the apartment occupied by Julia. Here he paused and considered returning to bed. He wondered if the present revelation was one of those compelling enlightenments that come in sleep but prove on examination to be worth nothing. Shaking his head, he admitted himself to the outer room of her suite and rapped on the bedroom door.

Julia and Ambrose were in bed together. This was unexpected, and in his half-awake state Guy contemplated apologising and going away, and indeed got as far as saying he was sorry.

Ambrose stirred. He turned and leaned on one elbow.

'Good Lord, it's Guy,' he said mildly.

Julia was asleep and emitted only the word 'Guy?' in a puzzled voice before also turning, yawning and opening her sleep-dazed eyes.

Ambrose nudged her. 'Julia, my dear, we have some explaining to do. If not, then Guy is going to think me the most awful cad. Dear boy, nothing that you see impugns our own darling's love for you. You must see that.'

He smiled, and his eyes were unfathomably benign.

'Julia dear, this is Guy. It's time you two were properly introduced. Guy, this is my sister.'

CHAPTER TWENTY-EIGHT

1945

'Jimmy's going to die if we don't get some penicillin,' Guy explained. 'I've put in a request and have half a promise that some may come when Colonel Box pays us a visit, but I suspect that may be too late. I was pinning my hopes on Tommy's getting it out of Corporal Pulaski. But Tommy seems to be avoiding me.'

Jimmy was lying feverish in a lone bed, stranded in an empty ward like a lifeboat at sea.

'You'll have noticed, too, that the hospital hasn't come back.'

'Yes. I feel awfully bad about that,' confessed Jenkins.

'I don't like to pull rank, but you and Tommy really shouldn't have stolen it.'

'What can I say? I thought we were only borrowing.'

'And is it going to come back? The Colonel will be here tomorrow.'

'It doesn't look like it.'

'Why not? I was told that there was an arrangement.'

'Oh, there was!' Jenkins affirmed vigorously. 'Tommy sold everything strictly on the understanding that we could buy it back at the same price. You see, Tommy had a scheme. He was going to take the money and double or treble it by beating the Yanks at poker.'

'Do you mean he lost my hospital in a *poker* game?'

'That seems to be the top and bottom of it. The trouble is that Corp cheats.'

'Cheats?'

'Yes, terribly. I'm sure that Tommy would have won in a fair game.'

A little later Jenkins said, 'I suppose this business will put paid to my career at the bank. They take a dim view of stealing hospitals and are rather expecting me to tip up after I've been demobilised, not five years later or whenever the Army decides to free us.'

Guy reflected on the likely term of imprisonment for stealing substantial Army property, not to mention his other crimes, and five years sounded like a sentence imposed by a liberal judge in a kindly frame of mind. He made a decision.

'Don't worry. I'll take the responsibility. I'll claim I sold everything.'

'You will? Oh, what a brick you are, Guy! You're being awfully brave about it.'

'I am?' Guy contemplated the novelty of his heroism, albeit in a disreputable cause.

Jenkins' gratitude was tempered. 'Mind you, I don't know what Tommy and I are going to say. The hospital did rather vanish from under our noses.'

'You'll think of something,' said Guy.

Jimmy's condition deteriorated during the day. Guy went to see him.

'I've brought you a present,' he said.

'Oh, that's sweet of you. What is it?'

'A porcelain figure – Capo di Monte. I thought it would make a start when you and Nick open your shop. I bought it in the market.'

'Give it to me.'

Guy handed him the piece. Jimmy caressed it with his fingers.

'Capo di Monte! Now ain't that posh, Nick?'

Nick nodded. 'Mucho posh. You're a sentimental thing, aren't you, Mr Parrot? I don't mind. Me and Nick love schmalz. Life's never been the same since Shirley Temple grew up, has it, Jimmy?'

'On the go-o-od ship Lil-li-put,' sang Jimmy.

'Lollipop. It's *Lollipop*. He always gets that line wrong. Half the time I think it's pure mischief. I've had three years of him getting' it wrong, ever since we met up in Alexandria when he was in love with a stoker and I helped him get over it.'

'His ship was called *Lilliput*,' said Jimmy.

'No, it wasn't, Mr Parrot, it was called the *Jersey Lily*. He was Welsh – the stoker.'

'The Welsh are a dark and passionate race,' Guy recalled.

'I don't know about that. He was a mean and graspin' bugger. Jimmy was a virgin and that bloke made promises about undyin' love that was somethin' shockin'.'

'We've always been faithful to each other,' Jimmy groaned with emotion.

'Well, there was that American sailor, the one in Portsmouth who wrote letters,' Nick corrected him tactlessly.

'Just a lapse,' said Jimmy.

'And that chap from Fulham who held out the dream of a florist's shop he already owned. That was hard, Mr Parrot. You can't compete with someone who owns a florist's shop.'

'I came back to you.'

'That you did, love,' Nick agreed tenderly. 'It was only a weekend in Cairo and a bottle of scent,' he explained to Guy. 'Everyone's entitled to a mistake. What people don't understand about real love is the stamina it takes.'

'You're right,' said Guy thoughtfully.

'I know I'm right. It came to me one night in a blindin' flash when I was paintin' Jimmy's verrucas.'

Guy decided he could not stay any longer. These days the least display of affection, no matter how banal, moved him to tears. He was a sentimental man and recalled Madame Hecate once saying that sentimentality was a cruel thing, thus proving that universal truths were rarely universally true. Behind him the exchange continued.

'I love you, Nick.'

'Course you do.'

'Do you love me?'

'Silly thing. Now, blow your nose.'

Guy heard no more.

During the night, Jimmy died.

A telephone call confirmed that Colonel Box would arrive late that day. Leaving Corporal Long and an emotional Nick to wash and dress the corpse, Guy decided to pay a final visit to Inspector Porrello.

'I know you haven't asked for anything,' Guy said, 'but I've brought you some coffee.'

The Inspector broke with his usual air of amused sagacity and was almost childishly grateful. 'Real coffee! I no longer believed there was any such thing left in the world.'

They sat outside the cottage in the shade of the vine. Guy told the old man about the stolen hospital, the love affair between the two privates, and the bones discovered in the cistern.

'That is most interesting. How old were the bones?'

'I can't say. I can't even swear they belonged to a man. I don't make any connection with my last stay at the Villa Esperanza, because there were no bones when I dug out the cistern.'

'Can you be certain?'

'Yes. I went down as far as the old floor and sealed it to prevent leakage. It crossed my mind that Old Enzo might have fallen into it one night when he was drunk.'

'No. He died in bed four years ago.'

Guy debated whether to disclose the unworthy thought that Signor Porrello or some of his Fascist colleagues might have deposited an unwanted body.

'Do you have any ideas?'

'It is too soon to draw conclusions from such new information.' the old man answered meditatively.

Guy needed to walk. The prospect of his arrest made him restless and he wanted the whole business over with. He did not know what he would say to Elizabeth. He wondered where the Army would imprison him. In Italy or quite possibly in Egypt. The innocent would no doubt have preference over the guilty in the competition for transport to England. He walked further up the hill, where the oaks and chestnuts were beginning to ripen and early falls of nuts and acorns were scattered on the ground.

Signor Porrello made coffee.

'You shouldn't have. It was meant for you.'

'Did you know that you are the only person who comes to see me?'

'Haven't you any relatives?'

'A sister in Milan.'

'If you've got any letters for her, I can post them. I can check if there are any for you. Where would she send them? It may be that the mails aren't operating.'

The old man dismissed the offer with a wave of the hand. 'You have been kind to me, Signor Guy. I should like to help you.'

Guy smiled. 'I rather doubt you can. I shall be going to prison.'

'You say that calmly, like a man who does not want to go home to his wife.'

Guy was shaken by the other man's perspicacity. For a while it had been true that he did not want to see Elizabeth, though he had never been sure of the reason except that it was connected with the events at La Spezia. Sometimes, it seemed that his life since that summer of fifteen years ago had been like attendance at a séance in which engagement with the present was halted by rapt attention to the voices of the past: voices which promised but never delivered a revelation. He was tired of it – had always been tired of it – but the path he must take in order to escape from this savourless existence had never been clear to him.

Signor Porrello sipped his coffee and blinked at the

sun, which now lay just above the pine tops.

'I must be leaving,' Guy told him.

'To be arrested? Truly your capacity for duty astonishes me – I speak frankly.'

'I'm being arrested because I haven't fulfilled my duties.'

'Your moral scruples are too complex for an old Fascist. But, please, wait a moment. I have given some thought to your affairs and you may find them useful. They concern Commander Ferris.'

'Jackie?' Guy glanced at his watch, calculated the duration of his return journey, and waited.

'I have told you that your friend did not return to Marseilles in his boat.'

'He must have travelled by train. I can't imagine he hired a car.'

'In which case he must first have put into a port. His boat would then have been found. But it was not. You should also consider his passport. It would bear an exit stamp cancelling his Italian visa on leaving La Spezia. How, then, did he re-enter Italy? How did he pass the Italian frontier into France?'

'Another boat may have met him at sea.'

'And the original vessel was scuttled? But why, Signor Guy? Why? If Commander Ferris wished to change his destination and disguise the fact, it might be comprehensible. But that is precisely what he did not do. He intended to sail to Marseilles. and the telegram announcing his arrival was sent from Marseilles.'

'We were all in La Spezia when it was sent,' Guy reminded him.

'But Commander Ferris did not send it,' said Inspector Porrello, smiling gently. He drank the remains of his coffee and placed a hand on Guy's shoulder, murmuring, 'My friend, my friend, how you have been deceived.'

The birds fell silent. A storm was forming over the far sea

to the west. The valley of the Magra was filled with a bright yellow light under a dark sky. Its floor was punctuated by low knolls topped by pine and cypress and these dark islands seemed to glide across the floodplain between a flotsam of farms and villas.

A group of men, half a dozen or so, to all appearances peasants or hunters, was filtering from the margin of the nearest trees into the abandoned olive grove.

'You must leave, Signor Guy,' said the old man with quiet urgency. 'Go further up the hill. Hide and wait. They have no interest in you.'

'My cap and jacket are in the house.' Guy was already opening the door when he heard the Inspector telling him to leave them.

It was not clear to Guy, even later, that he ever decided to stay and defend the old man. The first shot was fired as he crossed the threshold and the term 'decision' seemed a word applicable to another class of event but not this one. True, he bolted the door to the rear by which he might have escaped, but his action was unreflecting.

Signor Porrello returned fire. His ancient rifle required loading at the muzzle and the insertion of a percussion cap in the firing mechanism. Having no time to repeat this operation, he retreated to the cottage and closed the front door behind him. He glanced at Guy and muttered, 'Foolish, foolish.'

Guy habitually kept his revolver empty, having no use for it except, perhaps, to shoot off his foot. He loaded it while the old man took up position at the single firing point he had made by knocking out a plank from a window shutter. Guy manned it while the Inspector went through the cumbersome process of reloading. The attackers had gone to ground among the olives and did not seem disposed to attempt a direct assault across the relatively open vegetable garden.

Signor Porrello asked, 'How many bullets have you got?'

'Only six, I'm afraid.'

'Never mind. They may go away.'

'Has this happened before?'

'Two or three times. They are sensible men and have no desire to be killed.'

'Have you killed any?'

The old man chuckled. 'The fact is, my eyes are poor and I cannot even see them.' He loosed off a shot and Guy took his place.

'And then?' Jenkins asked some time later, when he and Guy were in Genoa waiting for a troop transport.

And then a breeze stirred the wisteria that draped the wooden frames over the vegetable garden and a mistle thrush announced the storm with a melancholy song.

'It began to rain.'

'I didn't ask for a weather report.' Jenkins was bored and testy because the Movements Officer had created difficulties over his papers.

'There was a great deal of silence and we had time to think about the weather.'

'If you say so.'

'It reminded me of summer in England.'

'Oh, don't tell me about it. I know what you mean.'

Though the rain fell hard, it was only an outrider of the storm. The hills that barred the further side of the valley from La Spezia and the sea disappeared in mist. The wind gusted like a steam engine through the woods.

In a prurient tone Jenkins asked, 'Kill anyone? You can tell me. It won't go any farther.'

'Not a soul.'

'What did you do?'

'Waited for the rain to pass. Signor Porrello and I chatted. The Communists smoked.'

They were short of cigarettes and those they had were passed hand to hand.

Guy said, 'If it hadn't been for the rain, I think they

might have gone home.'

'I don't see that?'

'It forced them to take shelter. And having nothing better to do, they shot at us.'

'Put like that, they don't sound very serious.'

'Oh, they were serious. They simply saw no reason to hurry.'

The rain paused and the attackers revised their tactics. A party of three infiltrated left, beyond the arc of fire from the window. On that side of the house was another room – the cottage comprised only two. Guy and the old man heard the sound of rifle-butts beating at the shutter. Since Guy was better armed to deal with any attempt to rush the house from the front, Signor Porrello went into the second room. The rain fell again. Guy could hear it drumming on the tiles and the old man barricading his side of the door so that Guy could not get in.

'I don't understand that part about the barricading,' said Jenkins, but by now he was losing interest. A party of sappers was playing football on the quayside, using kitbags for goalposts and a helmet as ball.

'Whoever was in that room when they broke in was going to be killed,' Guy explained.

'Gosh! Were you frightened?'

'Puzzled.'

'Puzzled? That's a damned odd thing to be.'

'I've often heard that said. Sometimes I wonder if it's a Catholic thing.'

'Sorry, you're over my head.'

'There was a saint, Guy of Shoreditch…'

'Relative of yours?'

'Quite possibly,' Guy conceded, but Jenkins was lost in the game.

'Offside! Did you see that, Guy? Definitely offside.'

*

There were two shots: the loud bark of the old man's rifle and the sharper crack of a modern weapon. Guy placed his revolver on the floor and called, '*Sono capitano inglese qui! Capitolo!*' doubtful from experience that this would mean anything to his captors. He debated lighting a cigarette but thought the action capable of misconstruction.

A voice replied in heavily accented English. 'Put your gun down, English captain.'

'Yes, right, I've done that.'

The barricade was removed and the door opened. One man, who must have clambered in by the window, entered. He cast a glance at Guy, went to the other window and shouted something to his friends.

'How is the old man?' Guy asked.

'Dead.'

'May I see?'

A shrug.

Guy went into the other room and found Signor Porrello lying against a wall. He had a chest wound, and his eyes were wide open. The look of fear on his face suggested that he had met death without any particular wisdom or resignation; at the time a mildly surprising fact. Guy returned to join the Communists, who were wet, tired and a little elated. They were working men in shirtsleeves, waistcoats and caps, except for their leader. He was a man of thirty or so, exceptionally handsome in a dark way, and wore a stained suit and a felt hat. His particular quality was stillness. Whereas the others, recalling from time to time that they had succeeded in their efforts, produced spasms of backslapping, he moved calmly between the few objects of furniture and searched each. Guy, ignored, squatted on the floor and ventured to light his cigarette. At last he attracted attention.

'You, English captain. Name?'

343

'Parrot. I'm a doctor,' Guy added, thinking that qualification might disincline the partisans to kill him.

'Par-rot,' repeated the leader. 'Other name?'

'Guy.'

'Guy Par-rot.'

'That's it. Doctor Guy Parrot.'

'*Si, si, Capisco*. I know you.'

'No, I don't think so.' Guy was curious at the cocktail-party direction taken by the last remark, which was made without enthusiasm. Acknowledging that it was a small world, he still thought it unlikely he was acquainted with any Communist *banditti*.

'Par-rot ... Lock-yer. Other man?'

He knew of Ambrose?

'Carmody?'

'*Si*. Car-mo-dy. I say I know you.'

'So you do.' At a loss, Guy wondered if he should offer a hand.

'*Mi chiamo Giovanni Malatesta*.'

'Malatesta? Look I'm sorry if – Malatesta?'

'Gianni,' said the Communist leader.

'Gianni? I ... Gianni? '

'I am pleased to meet you again, Signor Par-rot.' The man did not smile. Gianni had never smiled.

'Good God,' said Guy.

Guy drove down from the hills bearing with him six murderers (as he supposed he should consider them, since the war was over). It was not possible to cover the Jeep, and when the storm broke over them they were soaked. In La Spezia the American Military Police, swaddled in rain capes, directed traffic round heaps of rubble which were barely visible in the fugitive light. He deposited his passengers, who slipped away into the night without farewells.

The high road towards Montemarcello was dark and partially blocked by mudslides. To the right, the waters of the Gulf flickered with reflected lightning. A wild boar, driven out of the shelter of the trees, trotted alongside for a while before bolting off across the front of the Jeep, making Guy halt. Ahead a patch of sky glowed an improbable orange and Guy supposed it was a fire caused by the storm striking among the pines.

As he approached the last turn of the road, a figure in khaki battledress sprang from the shadows and waved.

Guy halted. 'Daisy?'

'Mr Parrot, sir. I was hoping you was the fire brigade.'

'I'm not sure there is a fire brigade. Is the Colonel here?'

'Large as life and hopping mad, what with a gorgeous FANY to keep him company and no bed for the night.'

'Why no bed?'

'The fire, sir. Do you mind if I get in?'

'If you like. I'll run you back. What fire?'

'At the Villa Sprinter.'

'It's on fire?'

'That's the general idea.'

They drove on until the headlights picked out an Army Humber parked to take such cover as was to be had from the trees.

'In there,' said Daisy, 'last I seen. Watch your step, Mr Parrot.'

'He's in a temper, is he?'

Daisy whistled.

Guy walked gingerly between the puddles, came to attention by the side of the vehicle, and saluted. A driver sat in front and two people, presumably Colonel Box and the FANY, occupied the rear. One of the misted windows was wound down.

'Parrot, sir. Reporting for duty.'

'About time,' came the answer. 'Seen that?'

Guy looked up the hill where the palms and cypresses of the terrace were silhouetted against the fire.

'I have now. It looks bad, sir.'

'Is he always this funny?' said the FANY sourly.

Colonel Box's head emerged from the window looking oversized like that of a glove-puppet.

'Are you aware, Parrot, that you have achieved what the Hun never managed?'

'Remind me, sir,' said Guy.

'Don't get clever with me. You've burnt down my bloody hospital!'

CHAPTER TWENTY-NINE

1945

'We were lucky the storm put the fire out,' Guy remarked as he and Jenkins walked among the ruins of the Villa Esperanza. With the rain had come a fall of cones, and some of them remained miraculously unburnt. Guy picked one up, intending to keep it as a souvenir. 'The entire hillside could have caught ablaze. I gather that sometimes happens in summer.'

'It's been damned uncomfortable having to bivouack in the open. I notice that Thunder overcame his prejudice against Americans and found a nice billet for himself and his FANY.'

'Consider it a penance.' But Guy decided that this observation was too Catholic for Jenkins's taste. Changing the subject he asked, 'What do you think caused it?'

'Lightning? Tommy also hinted at an electrical fault with the generator.'

'You don't think Tommy…?'

'Absolutely not,' Jenkins said firmly. 'There isn't a shred of evidence.'

'Damned convenient, though.'

Jenkins grinned. 'It certainly took Thunder's mind off things. And who's to say that everything we stole isn't here' – he waved a hand at the wreckage – 'transformed?'

The Real Presence become a Real Absence? In his relief Guy had a feeling that miracles were in the air, a sentiment that prompted his next question.

'Didn't it strike you as odd that we found *two* bodies?'

One could be accounted for. It was Jimmy's,

discovered on his bed where they had left him – an event that caused Nick to break down. The second was a mystery. Considering the lies that had once been indulged in, there was a case for its being Shelley's, transported from one funeral pyre to another – a poetic case, admittedly.

Jenkins was cautious in committing himself. 'Thunder was content to accept that the "spare", so to speak, belonged to that fellow we found in the cistern.' On that basis Colonel Box had disclaimed responsibility and allowed it to be discreetly buried. 'Personally, I could have sworn Tommy threw those old bones into the sea, though today he claims that he only planned to.'

'There was flesh on the corpse.' A loose term for a horrible reality quite unlike flesh. Guy looked at Jenkins to see what he would make of it.

'That rather clinches the point, doesn't it? My own theory is that it's that old tramp, Nessuno. He was lurking again and could easily have slipped in out of the rain.'

Guy agreed. 'That seems plausible. But I wonder why he was naked? At least, I think he was.'

'How do you make that out?'

'I would have expected metal objects to survive – buckles, identity tags, buttons perhaps.'

Jenkins gave a theatrical shudder. 'It doesn't bear thinking of. Thunder and lightning and Nessuno capering about in the altogether.'

On that Gothic note, they returned to the terrace, where a sobbing Nick was cooking breakfast on a Soyer stove.

Jenkins's theory about the second corpse held good until the following day, when Guy encountered Nessuno.

In the morning Colonel Box had paid a flying visit before disappearing with Daisy and the FANY to headquarters, there to explain the destruction of a hospital that had always been regarded as his pet project. Guy was under orders to empty the site of anything salvageable and then follow with the Jeep and the two-tonner. Since anything of value had been earlier misappropriated by Corporal Long, this was an easy task, which he delegated to the Scotsman and Nick under Lieutenant Jenkins's negligent eye.

In the clearing by the grotto, a figure was sitting on the pedestal from which the two statues had departed as if one of them had slipped away for a smoke and the other was taking five minutes' break from an eternity of calm immobility. Nessuno sported a seersucker suit and straw hat, both greasy and worse for wear, but his manner betrayed a certain shamefaced jollity.

'Hullo, Guy.'

'Hullo.'

'I wasn't sure I'd catch you, but thought you'd come up here before leaving. It is rather pretty – sad, too – isn't it? Pity about your hospital.'

'Corporal Long – I believe you met him – burnt it down.'

'How enterprising. I always thought he was a useful chap.'

Guy joined Nessuno on the pedestal and sat looking down upon those ruins still remaining above the treetops; they were still smouldering gloomily.

'Are you sober?'

'As a judge. There isn't a great deal to be said for it. Do you know, I was drunk from 1930 to 1941? I call that impressive.'

'What happened in '41?'

'The Italian Government cleaned me up and found a use for me – as you well know. In favour of Fascism, I will say it gives a chap a purpose in life. Especially when he's feeling low and at something of a loose end.'

'I gather Julia also drank?'

'Awesomely. She and I lived together for a while on Hector's money: a generous fellow, Hector. We couldn't agree. I got drunk during the day and she at night.

Afterwards we kept in touch, and since she died I've tried to tidy up the grave from time to time. She did love you, in her own way. She felt dreadfully guilty about what we all did.'

'Lewis…'

'Yes, Guy?'

Lewis's voice, coming soft and beguiling from the wreckage of Nessuno, was poignant and Guy, troubled by ancient affections, lost his thread, if he'd ever had one.

'We found a skeleton in the old cistern.'

'Ah. I thought you might.'

'It's Jackie Ferris, isn't it?'

'Yes.'

'And whom did we bury at Viareggio?'

'Joe Truffatore.'

'Joe?' Guy found himself actually shocked.

Lewis apologised. 'I admit to being rather sorry about killing Joe. There was something attractively louche about him. My only consolation is that he wasn't a good man – in fact, he was a bit of a villain.'

Guy remembered what he wanted to ask. 'After the fire, we found a spare body in the ruins of the house. Is he one of yours?'

'You seem to take a very dim view of my character,' Lewis protested, slightly indignant.

'May I remind you that by your own admission you're a double murderer as well as a traitor?'

'Oh, I see what you mean. Put like that, I do sound somewhat evil, don't I? Golly! It isn't an epithet that one readily applies to oneself.' After a moment's meditation Lewis said sombrely, 'I don't recommend evil. It hasn't made me happy. My defence is that what I committed was unselfish evil. What do you think of that, Guy? One hears all the time of unselfish love. But unselfish evil? I did it all for Ambrose. You knew that, didn't you?'

'I suspected as much.'

'When I say "for Ambrose", I really mean for the sake of his art.'

Guy nodded wearily, and they sat a while in silence.

'Have you got any cigarettes?' Lewis asked. Guy gave him one. On reflection, he passed over the pack. 'What luxury!' Lewis sighed appreciatively. 'Victory? Is it an American brand?'

'Indian, I believe.'

'Excellent, all the same. I suppose you want me to tell you all the whys and wherefores of my murdering Jackie? Joe was in the way of an afterthought. I wouldn't have killed him if it hadn't been for that bloody Hecate woman.'

'I should like to know.'

'Thought you might.'

With a cigarette dangling from his lips, and dressed in his shabby seersucker suit, Lewis reminded Guy of someone else as he reached into his inside jacket pocket, searching, it seemed, for a document. A Levantine shipping agent Guy had run across in Port Said: a man who, for the duration of hostilities, sold pornographic pictures to English soldiers.

'What have you got there?'

Lewis held several sheets of paper covered in pencil scrawls.

'I wrote it all down. Here you are, Guy, take them. They cost me an awful lot of effort.'

'I had a nervous breakdown,' Guy said, making a vague connection. 'After I discovered about Julia and Ambrose. I knew someone had been murdered but not who or how or, indeed, why.'

Lewis was still holding the papers. 'We all went to the dogs after that summer. All except Ambrose. I also exempt Margot, who isn't human. Is it true that Raymond met with an accident when he said no to a divorce? Please, Guy, do take these!'

Guy took them and began to read.

La Spezia
July 1945

Hullo, Polly,

To begin ... to begin ... in the beginning.

It all began ... where? ... when? At the birth of stars? At the first crawling of a blind thing from the primordial ooze? I can assure you that it did not begin at Uncle Sammy's, although that may be your recollection.

Let us start at school, mine and Ambrose's, if we are not to get unduly metaphysical. Why at school? Because that is where Ambrose presented himself in his first theophany to the bedazzled eyes of a twelve-year-old: as bright as Lucifer on the day when he was beloved, and as terrible in his potency.

Do you follow me, Guy? 'We are speaking of hero worship, adoration, uttermost infatuation. But – lest you misprise me – not of unworthier matters. In short, we deal in beggary not buggery; for I was simply a supplicant who hoped that when the Prince of Morning wiped his anointed brow a few drops of that precious chrism would fall upon me.

From another point of view, I blame swimming.

Imagine, then, Ambrose at the age of seventeen, superb in his godlike splendour: witty, gay, inventive, alluring in his insouciance, and careless of his own talents. Imagine this creature, surrounded by worshipful boys and unrestrained by the intimidated masters only too aware of the limitations of their own creeping pedantry. Imagine: and there you have Ambrose in his glory!

As to swimming, he took the Arbuthnot Prize (ten bob and a silver pot), which I won, in sheer emulation, five years later.

Who could resist him? Certainly not Julia. I leave to the alienists any enquiry into their earliest coupling, but their incestuous liaison was established before I ever knew Ambrose (for what it is worth, I blame an absent father and the furtive atmosphere of his mother's lodging house). It was – and still is – a matter of perfect moral indifference to him. Indeed, I understand he more or less boasted of it in a tale be told in Venice. How brazen of him!

Who knew? All the world who cared to – a point which brings me to a lacuna in Ambrose's perceptions. He could not understand that the suspicion of sin is merely cause for a frisson of entertaining gossip: but that sin, once proven, stirs English hypocrisy and demands reproof and the expulsion of the sinner from decent society. Think of poor Oscar Wilde.

Failure to understand this distinction meant that Ambrose thought he was safe from reproach and this led him into carelessness.

Hector found out. Ambrose had the decency to leave the poor husband to the joy of his honeymoon, but afterwards resumed his usual relations with Julia. Of course, the discovery put an end to the marriage, though Hector was a gentleman, made no scandal, and always treated Julia with such consideration as remained from his ruined affection.

I assume you know something of Jackie Ferris. When Ambrose was in New York, borrowing money from Morty Lowenstein to finance a show, Jackie fell head over heels in love. With whom? Unquestionably with Julia – in the conventional sense. But between Jackie and Ambrose I fancy I also hear crackles of uranian fire sparking across the luminiferous ether. I imagine it confused Jackie no end. At all events he joined the ranks of bemused spectators of Ambrose's genius. He glimpsed – dimly, no doubt – the sacerdotal role of the Artist as hierophant mediating between this world and a higher one. He saw the Godhead, but did not appreciate that to worship Art is to worship Moloch and that the price of his favour is sacrifice.

(Did I tell you that Ambrose swam the Bosphorus? So did I. I must not forget.)

Let us come down to cases. Jackie discovered that Ambrose and Julia were lovers. Worse, he had evidence – letters or photographs (or possibly both – as I say, Ambrose was careless and never entirely certain). In measure as his earlier admiration was great, so his revenge was severe.

He became a blackmailer. This reflects rather badly on his character, but he was moving in circles where differences were usually settled with a gun, and so he probably regarded his behaviour as displaying moral restraint. Through supposed gifts from Julia, he took Ambrose for every penny he had.

Which brings us at last to La Spezia. Ambrose was completely broke and at his wits' end. Jackie was relentless and unforgiving. Exposure and ruin were certain for as long as he lived.

The plan, in essence, was simple. Ambrose and Julia would go on an excursion to Venice, while I disposed of Jackie. I, of course, was above all suspicion: a stranger to him and having no possible motive. Your role, my poor abused Guy, was to be the disinterested witness who would draw all suspicion away.

The execution was somewhat more complex.

My first inclination was to go sailing with Jackie, knock him on the head, and pop him in the water under pretext of an accident. However, quite apart from the fact that this would draw attention to me, there was an insuperable practical objection: namely, that a small boat is a confined place in which to commit murder and Jackie was a hefty fellow so that, if I fumbled, it was just as likely that he would kill me as that I should kill him.

Murdering Jackie on land bad the great advantage that I could select the best opportunity, but it, too, was not without problems. Firstly, I would have a body to get rid of. And, secondly, there was a boat moored at Lerici which was supposed to sail to Marseilles in accordance with Jackie's announced intentions.

I do not like to think of the actual killing. Truly, Guy, I do have a conscience. I shall say only that we went for a walk, I hit him on the bead, and then I strangled him with one of those socks Ambrose was forever knitting. (Ambrose was right on that point. This tale is as much about socks as about murder.) Jackie was in a very cheerful mood and suspected nothing, which I account a blessing. Madame Hecate once said, a propos some relative, that he considered himself a dangerous man and found himself in difficulties when he discovered his error. I think this was true of Jackie, He had no conception of how much more dangerous Ambrose was.

I could not dispose of the body at sea. I had no means of carrying it from the villa to Lerici or of loading it on the boat in public view. I put it in the cistern and weighted it with stones, counting, quite rightly, on the probability that, once we left, the cistern would fill again with soil and rubble. Fortunately, we did not use it for drinking water.

Jackie was cleared to sail from Lerici, and I was confident I could pass myself off as him, because the authorities were fairly lax about people leaving as distinct from entering the country, and provided that no one had reason to investigate my departure. I considered scuttling the boat at sea, leaving Jackie's fate a mystery. Then, on reflection, it seemed altogether too inexplicable that an experienced sailor should simply vanish in clear weather, and the disappearance would be too close in time to his leaving Lerici so that questions might arise and my imposture be discovered. How much better if it could appear that Jackie reach Marseilles.

I did not sail to Marseilles. I was uncertain of my seamanship and did not fancy the risk of passing myself off as Jackie a second time and under closer scrutiny since I would be entering France. As you must guess, I never went to Lucca, I took the train to Marseilles, travelling on my own papers. Once there, I wrote Jackie's supposed telegram and paid a barman to hold it for a week or so and send it once I was back in La Spezia.

Admittedly, if asked, I could not prove I had been in Lucca, and my passport showed that I had travelled to France. But who was going to ask? I was merely an innocent, casual acquaintance of Jackie. And there was the clear, dated evidence of the telegram. How Jackie got to France might become a mystery, but that he had done so seemed undeniable. Any investigation into his disappearance would commence with events after the date of the telegram and I had nothing to fear. So I scuttled the boat five miles out at sea, swam ashore and took the train to France.

Jackie's second 'disappearance' six months later was Ambrose's handiwork. By hiring a boat using Jackie's papers he would prove he was still alive, and by staging a vanishing act finally dispose of him. How exactly it was done I do not know, since I took no part and thought it unnecessary and theatrical. I would guess that he paid someone to sail the boat out and abandon it. Since the question of murder would not arise on this occasion, I imagine he had no difficulty in finding a likely villain to undertake the task. However, you must ask Ambrose – if you dare (which I would not advise). Alas, dear Guy, you will find that explanations are rarely complete.

I swear to you that that was the intended limit of my crimes.

Had it not been for Madame Hecate.

'Mr Lockyer,' quoth she (this was about half an

hour before her departure when the cunning old bitch knew I did not have the time, even if I had the inclination, to throttle her) 'I am reminded of young Albert, the projectionist of our local cinema, who formed an unfortunate – though I don't say improper – attachment to the resident organist, whom he considered an artist of merit. When the organist was blackmailed by the husband of an usherette with whom he was having an affair, young Albert was prevailed upon to subject the husband to a serious assault. He was forced to flee to Lapland.' I don't swear it was Lapland.

By the by, old chap, do you suppose there was ever any truth in the old girl's tales, or did she make them up in the way we did our stories?

But I digress.

Madame Hecate collared me in the shrubbery. She had cabled the authorities in Marseilles to ascertain that Jackie had never arrived by boat. She had bought a camera, sneaked into my room and photographed my passport with its damning entry and exit stamps. She had, in short, seen through the entire scheme, though she had no evidence against Ambrose.

I can't say exactly what she expected of me. She simply appraised me with her fluffy, ruthless complacency and left me to draw my own conclusions. I suppose she may have had an old-fashioned idea that I would do the gentlemanly thing and go into a quiet room with a decanter of whisky and a loaded revolver. However that may be, I saw that, short of slaughtering her 'à l'improviste' (a tempting notion to which you would have been an inconvenient witness and against which she was undoubtedly prepared), I had better make preparations for my own vanishing, preferably with every appearance of fatality.

Thus we come to Joe Truffatore.

He, of course, believed Jackie Ferris was still alive.

I told him we had a plan for a little smuggling and arranged that I would sail from Lerici and pick him up from a secluded spot along the coast.

My difficulty was that Joe and I bore no particular resemblance to each other.

I killed Joe within minutes of our meeting. The poor fellow had his back turned and was getting into the boat when I bashed him and then drowned him. It was necessary to commit the murder as soon as possible, because I could not be seen arriving with him at Livorno and I needed the body to spend as much time as possible in the water to aid decomposition.

I'm sorry, Guy, if this is all rather disgusting. We sailed, the pair of us. I manned the boat and Joe, so to speak, tagged along, trussed by his ankles in the water. At Livorno he remained in the water, and we sailed again and cruised up and down the coast for several days until I was satisfied the sea had done its work. Then I cut him loose on an incoming tide, sank the boat and swam ashore.

So you see how important swimming was?

I don't know what else to tell you, Guy, except that, in my own fashion, I'm sorry – at least for your part. But, you see, Ambrose is a genius and someone has to pay the price of Art.

You do see that, don't you?

Since that time, Signor Nessuno has stayed in Italy. Ambrose confessed everything to Margot and she asked Odo to arrange papers for me through his Fascist friends. Margot, whose life was not above reproach, had no time for blackmailers and considered murder a mere bagatelle. As for Odo, be was probably getting his hand in as preparation for future fatal glories. So my secret has been safe.

I have spent the years drinking

Odd though it sounds, I do believe I must have a delicate conscience.

Guy finished reading and asked, 'Did Julia know?'

'She suspected,' was Lewis's answer. 'Much though she hated Jackie, she didn't want to kill him. Hence her fear – and her relief when it seemed that he'd arrived safe and sound in Marseilles. You look very sad, Guy.'

'You forget that I loved her; or felt something, by whatever name one calls it.'

'Julia did have that effect. I can't explain it, any more than I can Ambrose – or Byron and Shelley for that matter. Some people have the ability to fascinate and others a weakness for fascination. Ambrose, with the deadly eye of genius, knew exactly what he was doing and exploited it. That play of his, *She Paid the Price*, was his monument to Julia and his masterpiece.'

'There you're mistaken,' said Guy.

'What do you mean?'

'Elizabeth mentioned in a letter that it was revived a year or two ago and failed. Too old-fashioned, apparently. If Ambrose is remembered, it'll be for *Imperfect Tense*, which, as I recall, you considered trivial and unworthy of him.'

Lewis smiled.

'Gosh!' he said softly and shook his head, still smiling. 'Just the sort of absurdity that inclines one to believe in God.'

Inwardly Guy agreed. The Argument from Absurdity might not be one of the classical proofs of the Divinity's existence, but it was oddly compelling. To Guy's puzzlement the Universe proceeded not according to the banal rule of Good and Evil, but freakishly, even playfully; and there were no great revelations, merely clues, as if Creation were a rebus compiled by a subtle but not especially benevolent Mind. Such a Creation had no use for spiritual heroes. Saints like Guy of Shoreditch were its true martyrs. Guy – the later Guy – believed in intercession as much as he believed in any other thing, but he acknowledged the unpredictable answers that greeted the most fervent prayers. For the shifty saints of an absurd Heaven wore sanctity uncomfortably. And the work of salvation went forward erratically in a place where even the angels shirked.

'We're leaving tomorrow,' Guy said.

'You seem very easy about my tale of murder and mayhem,' Lewis responded. 'Have you any questions before you go?'

Guy could think of only one. 'Why was your poem so savage against Byron and Shelley?'

'Aren't I allowed to kick against the pricks? I imagine that whoever killed Shelley was infatuated by him, just as I was by Ambrose. But that didn't prevent the murder. You do understand that I hate Ambrose, don't you? I always did.'

Somewhere below, Jenkins was calling. Guy stirred.

'I must go.'

'I have a favour to ask,' said Lewis. His hand prevented Guy from moving unless he used force to shake it off. His expression was perfervid and pathetic.

'What is it?'

'I'd be awfully glad if you didn't turn me in. I appreciate that a couple of murders and a spot of treason are quite rightly disapproved of. But, you see, my mother is still alive. She believes I'm dead and it would be hard on the old girl if I were to rise from the grave one minute, only to be hanged the next. And, of course, people will call me all sorts of names and be generally unsympathetic. She would dislike that.'

Guy looked away. He felt … indifferent, he supposed. Lewis's request related to the past and, although Guy bore its scars, they were just that: scars, evidence of survival, no matter that he might be lame or blind. And was he? Perhaps he was mistaken. When had he last tried to walk or see?

'What will you do?' he asked.

'I've thought of discreetly killing myself. It would be

the right thing to do, wouldn't it? However I don't want to promise it absolutely, since I shouldn't like you to think me a cad if I ran out of courage and fluffed it. I rather think I should – run out of courage, I mean. See, my hand is trembling even now.'

Indeed it was. Lewis looked old and fevered and Guy was at once sorry for him and disgusted by him. But he felt no hatred.

With a sudden access of cheerfulness Lewis said, 'I expect I'll die soon, anyway. So, in several senses, poetic justice will be achieved.' He paused and gazed bleakly through the haze over the Villa Esperanza. 'Like Shelley's funeral pyre,' he muttered and looked at Guy. 'Speaking of poets and Shelley, did you ever discover who killed him?'

'Yes,' said Guy. And explained.

CHAPTER THIRTY

The Strange Death of a Romantic

1931

Behind the hospital was a large garden laid to lawn, and on the lawn sat Guy Parrot reading a novel while convalescing, once more in England. A dozen paces away grew a horse chestnut. A man with a bandaged head was walking in circles round it.

'Are you a German?' asked the stranger.

'No,' said Guy.

'Good. The Germans have terrible eyesight.'

When tea was brought he joined Guy at the table, a beefy man of thirty-five or so, red-faced, with the staring eyes of a heavy drinker. Guy put away his book. Knowing the subdued mood of most of the patients, he waited patiently for an introduction.

'Bolsover,' said the stranger.

'You're from Bolsover?'

'Ha, ha, that's a good one! Seriously, though, Bolsover's my name. Bolsover is bolshie but Harwich is horrid. I'm from Harwich.'

'Guy Parrot.'

The lawn emptied as others took tea inside, but this did not restrain Bolsover from shouting, 'This is Guy Porridge and he's my pal! We were in the war together!' To Guy he said, 'Don't mind me. I find it never hurts to claim to have been in the war. One can get free drinks in some awfully good clubs, which is important if one's down on one's luck. I've had a thin time of it lately because of my eyesight.' However, he was not wearing glasses.

Guy returned to his book.

'Reading, eh?' Bolsover observed slyly.

'If you like I can lend you something.'

'No point. Can't crack the code. I'm only a simple infantry Johnny, not in Intelligence like you.' A tap on the nose and a knowing look. 'Besides, there's my disability.'

'The eyesight?'

'I say, you are sharp! That's why I'm here – the eyes.'

For a while Bolsover was content to share in companionable silence. An aeroplane flew over from the direction of Croydon.

'German,' commented Bolsover levelly. 'Probably an artillery spotter. I'll bet those poor devils in the front line will cop it soon.'

Equally levelly he corrected himself. 'Sorry. Forgot the war's over.'

'That's all right.'

'I'm here by mistake,' Bolsover confided.

'Really?'

'Absolutely. Jerry is supposed to have killed me. I was a clear target but he made a mess of it. The Eyeties have eyesight, but the Hun has none. Blind as bats. That's why I'm here. Fancy a beer? Later, I mean?'

'Alcohol is forbidden.'

'Is it?' Immediately Bolsover lost interest.

Arnold, the orderly, came with medicine and rugs for those determined to stay outside a little longer. In a far corner of the grounds stood an elm where rooks nested. Guy liked to hear them settle before night fell.

'Eyesight tablets.' Bolsover popped a couple of pills cheerfully into his mouth. He adjusted the dressing on his scalp. 'Gunshot wound,' he explained, startling Guy.

'You were shot?'

'Shot m'self.'

'Really?'

'I missed.'

Guy was enlightened. 'The eyesight?'

'Soon as I get that fixed, I'll try again. Then it's back to Blighty for me.'

On wet days patients used the common room. Guy usually took the opportunity to write to his parents and Elizabeth. His mail was placed each day on a baize-topped table by the door. A letter had arrived by the afternoon post.

Bolsover lumbered over. His dressing had been removed and revealed a fleshy trench across his scalp, which, like a Martian canal, crossed another older scar that had never fully recovered and bristled with spikes of ginger hair. To mark his gradual improvement he was growing a sporty red moustache. He plonked a cardboard box on the table.

'What say? Ludo for the lewd ho-ho? 'S that you've got there? A letter? Nothing better! Who's it from?'

'An old friend,' said Guy. Madame Hecate had written. He was surprised by this and equally surprised that such a reminder of the previous summer caused only a pang, not the full attack of anxiety that would have afflicted him only a short time before.

'Shall I go?' Bolsover asked.

'No, there's no need. I'll read it later.'

'Not later but soon. Not by the light of the moon. I'll clear off .'

'I don't want to drive you away.'

'Then I'll set out the game, if that's all the same with you. I'm happy to wait.' He sat down and took the lid off the box of Ludo, leaving Guy with no choice but to offend him or read the letter. He opened it and scanned the first page.

Bolsover placed two white tiddlywinks like cataracts on his eyes, looked at Guy and grinned.

'What's it about?'

'A poet called Shelley,' Guy told him.

The other man coughed in a deep, rumbling fashion like a music-hall comedian.

'You know Shelley?' Guy asked.

'Never heard of him.' Bolsover seemed offended. 'I don't associate with the Irish. They give a fellow a reputation.'

> *Colchicine House*
> *Marple Bridge*
> *Cheshire*
> *18th July 1931*

Dear Mr Parrot,

May I resume our former familiarity and call you Guy? This letter will no doubt come as a surprise, but I learnt only lately that you have been unwell following the events of last year. At first I supposed you had contracted a physical illness at La Spezia and assumed that something in the water or food had disturbed an unaccustomed English stomach. Only afterwards did I discover that your affliction was of the spirit rather than the body, and this disturbed me greatly. It led me to review my own conduct and question if there was more I could have done to avoid the consequences of that terrible time.

You see, Guy, I <u>understood</u>. More, indeed, than it would be wise for you to know even now. Truthfully, I did try to advise, though cautiously, since the advice of strangers – in particular of an elderly lady of no credentials – is not welcome, and it is so difficult to steer people from the path to which they are inclined by their passions. Moreover, your friends possess such fearsome intelligence: a quality which persuades people that they are exempt from the common lot. So, with all that, I proceeded, as I say, cautiously: too cautiously in your case, I fear.

Where to begin? Beginnings are so difficult, aren't they?

One night, during our journey to Venice, we stopped

at Mantua. Over dinner that evening we discussed the death of poor Shelley, a subject I disliked because it was approached frivolously and with no thought for its significance. I was reluctant to express my true opinion for several reasons. One was that, after the great lapse of time, no conclusion could be certain and I did not wish to libel the defenceless dead. Not least, however, was a feeling that the circumstances of the murder (I believe it was murder) had a meaning for your situation: a meaning I did not feel able to discuss before your friends. I blame myself for not raising it with you later, but you were so obdurate in your attachment to Lady Julia. Now...? Well, perhaps.

So let us begin.

Why did Shelley sail from Livorno to La Spezia and into the storm that caused his death? Byron desired him to stay. Trelawny warned of the dangers. Shelley himself seems to have been indifferent whether to go or remain a while longer.

The answer has never been in doubt. Shelley sailed because Edward Williams asked him to. All accounts are agreed upon this. In terms of cause and effect, Edward Williams killed Shelley.

Forgive me if I put more questions, but the answers are so important if one is to decide whether Shelley died as a result of a tragic error of judgement or by design.

Why did Shelley rely upon Williams's advice rather than Trelawny's?

Did Williams appreciate the dangers he was running?

Why did Williams wish to sail?

It is easily overlooked that Williams had been in the Navy and was an experienced sailor. By comparison with the exotic, self-glorifying Trelawny, he was a quiet, steady, family man. Shelley knew both, and if he chose to follow Williams's judgment rather than the pirate's it was because he had good reason to believe the other man was sound.

This background and experience, however, make Williams's error all the more inexplicable. For the unreliable Trelawny was correct in every particular of his warnings: <u>and Williams must have known</u>.

Consider the risks he ran. The 'Don Juan' carried too much sail. She rode too high in the water and needed ballasting. She had an open deck, which increased the danger of swamping. Her crew was too small and only Williams had the necessary knowledge (Shelley was a capricious amateur and the third member was merely a boy). A storm was in the offing, which Trelawny had observed when he volunteered to accompany the others with the 'Bolívar'. These were not hidden mysteries but facts plain to any sailor, and Williams's error was not single but a compound of gross misjudgements – if misjudgements they were. Only a self-confidence that exceeded that of Trelawny, a blindness amounting to wilfulness, or the most pressing reason to return that day to La Spezia could have overridden common sense. There is no evidence of any of these things.

Do you see, Guy?

It is so difficult to imagine the world of 1822, but we must do so. In those days the term 'urgent' did not – could not – have the meaning it bears now, a century later. Transport and letters were so slow that events unfolded, and crises were resolved for good or ill, while those in distant places were ignorant of them; still less could they intervene. An immediate response to an emergency, which nowadays we take for granted, was beyond the capabilities of our forebears, and therefore beyond their imagining.

If Williams had a reason to return to La Spezia, what was it? More to the point, how pressing? What did he hope to accomplish? Certainly no one could have expected his return on any particular day, for the vagaries of travel made such predictions valueless. Knowing this, a delay of twenty-four hours to wait out a storm would have surprised no one. To seek to avoid it at the risk of one's life is almost inconceivable.

No, Guy, there is no evidence of an emergency at La Spezia that demanded Williams's return and it is impossible to invent one. If it had existed, Byron would not have requested that Shelley and his party stay on at Livorno. In short, <u>Williams had no reason to sail</u>.

Am I mistaken? Is the truth hidden behind the unknowable? Perhaps it is not necessary to explain Williams's decision. Perhaps we should recognise the fallibility of human nature and accept that, for all his experience, he simply made a mistake of judgment, gross though it may have been and despite the explicit warnings of Trelawny.

We all have our bad days, do we not, my dear?

How much easier it would be if we could show that Williams's odd behaviour was not confined to a single day but had occurred earlier. For that would indicate premeditation.

More of that on another occasion. Today I am tired and must break off.

Yours sincerely,
Agnes Westmacott

'Interesting letter?' asked Bolsover.

In front of him on the table stood a brown medicine bottle with a cork stopper. It held whisky, which Arnold supplied for a small payment.

'Yes.'

'Does it tell you anything?'

'Nothing I didn't know. Shelley was murdered.'

Bolsover nodded sagely. 'That's the Irish for you. Fenian was he, this Shelley?'

'No. In fact, I don't believe he was Irish.'

'Cunning. And you say you knew he was murdered?'

Guy nodded.

'Hardly seems worth reading, then,' Bolsover commented. 'But you carry on. Don't mind me.'

A second letter was enclosed with the first.

Colchicine House
Marple Bridge
Cheshire
23rd July 1931

Dear Guy,

On reflection I decided against posting my last letter immediately. It seemed unfair to tell part of a story and not the whole. So I must continue.

Captain Trelawny relates a revealing tale of an incident that occurred some time before Shelley's death.

His reservations as to Shelley's seamanship were well known – indeed, he refused to sail with the poet after one occasion when he caught him reading verse while supposedly manning the tiller. This lends credibility to his misgivings concerning the inadequate crewing of the 'Don Juan' (though the point seems to me self-evident).

It was always Trelawny's opinion that the 'Don Juan' required a crew of four. He recommended that Shelley should employ a Genoese seaman. Did Shelley reject this advice? No – it was Williams who did so.

I asked myself: why did Williams refuse? My point is quite simple. The cost of the sailor would have been borne by Shelley. Trelawny's suggestion offered every advantage to Williams and no disadvantage. He had no reason to refuse.

I find this point very telling against Edward Williams. His behaviour was both inexplicable and *dangerous. Moreover, since this incident happened <u>prior</u> to the fatal day at Livorno, it shows that his capacity for ignoring obvious risks and overriding sound advice was not limited to a single misjudgement on the occasion of Shelley's death. Premeditation? I do believe so, for, though one cannot be certain, it seems so highly unlikely that Williams should commit such a catalogue of errors in the face of warnings which he was thoroughly capable of understanding: and all this for no benefit to himself. Unless one supposes that the benefit was the death of Shelley.*

Most certainly there was a benefit in the death of Shelley. A terrible one.

Shelley was seeking to seduce Jane Williams.

'It's a rum business, killing oneself,' proclaimed Bolsover as if it were not in the least odd. 'I can only speak from personal experience, because in the nature of things all the experts are dead. I say, old chap, you don't mind if I rabbit on while you're reading, do you?'

Guy put Madame Hecate's letter down. He found the regular rows of her copperplate handwriting disconcerting and slightly inhuman.

'I'm sorry, you were saying?'

'Suicide. It's rather like going over the top. One screws up one's courage, and once the decision is taken it seems natural: irrevocable. One goes forward because that seems easier than retreating only to face again the anxieties one's left behind.' Bolsover glanced at Guy. 'I don't know how it is with civilians.'

'Neither do I. This is a gloomy topic.'

'Not for me, old man, not for me. Ever since I got my head round the idea, things have been a lot clearer.'

'Then why haven't you killed yourself?'

The question was too obvious to avoid and Bolsover did not seem to mind. On the contrary, he warmed to the subject as if discussing a favourite hobby; which in a sense it was, since he had already made two attempts on his life.

'I go on trying with the old revolver, but keep missing. It's my damned eyesight. The technical side of blowing one's brains out is devilish tricky. After my first attempt' – he indicated the ancient furrow with its ginger bristles – 'I went into hospital and got the eyes fixed. Then I tried again. Not immediately. Between times I had a relapse.'

Guy was puzzled by 'relapse' until he understood that it meant a period during which Bolsover was *not* trying to kill himself.

'What caused it?'

'Oh, sometimes a fellow has a stroke of luck and his credit's good and other fellows are willing to stump up for a drink. That sort of good fortune is bad for morale and saps the will. Suicide is best attacked with bayonet – up an' at 'em, in a manner of speaking – with no opportunity for regrets. I'll watch my step next time. As soon as the eyes are all right, it's so long dull care.'

'I see,' said Guy and returned to the letter.

To understand the force of the evidence better (wrote Madame Hecate), *imagine the facts as I have given them, but suppose that at the last moment Edward Williams found an excuse not to join the 'Don Juan'. Knowing the cause he had for mortal hatred of Shelley and the bizarrely inexplicable circumstances of his behaviour which led to his enemy's death, think how damning the case against him would be. Once this is appreciated, you will realise that what exculpates Williams is not the lack of compelling evidence but the fact of his own death. But if one allows that Williams might be prepared to risk death – might even welcome it – the objection is removed and things look very black.*

That is in fact the position. Williams was willing to risk death. In a sense he was <u>obliged</u> to risk death. Shelley's conduct in attempting to seduce Jane Williams struck directly at Williams's honour. This was *just such a situation in which men of his class and time risked their lives in duels for reasons which seem to us, in this more enlightened epoque, capricious. But, once recognised, the truth of Williams's death is the very opposite of appearances. It is <u>not</u> remarkable that Williams was willing to sacrifice his life. It would be more remarkable if he had not been so willing. He murdered Shelley, but not shabbily or cold-bloodedly. Instead he contrived a situation in which God would decide the event and by a means that appealed to the Romantic sentiments of his peers.*

Thus the case, my dear Guy. It will remain for ever unproven to the standard the law requires; though for our purposes that scarcely matters. I believe it. You may not. But I ask you to bear with my fancy, for whatever wisdom it brings. If you like, treat it as yet another story told by one of your friends.

I do not see Edward Williams as a monster. By all accounts he was a likeable man and Jane Williams a most pleasant woman. Neither was gifted, but they had the misfortune to move in a circle of brilliant men who felt unconstrained by any normal conventions: men who had not only great talents but winning manners and astonishing beauty. Such gifts when combined with eloquence and lack of wisdom are exceptionally dangerous to others who are less endowed. For dull, prosaic truth, the Romantic substitutes an exotic and convincing glamour. For reason: feeling. For careful reflection: passion.

Such is how I imagine the situation of poor Edward Williams, confined as he was to the exclusive company of Byron, Shelley and others like Trelawny who were also in thrall to the pair. I see him in dazzled stupefaction watching them and comparing the intensity of their lives with his own dull existence, which must have seemed scarcely life at all. As with the whole, so with each part: sense, thought, feeling – all were revealed in his eyes to be less than those of a truer, higher humanity, the demigods for whom Creation had been wrought and who, like lords, took possession of it.

I doubt he was in the ordinary sense a jealous man. Such creatures rarely kill the seducer: more often the seduced woman. They are motivated by spite and a mean desire for possession. They negate: they do not affirm.

Negation was not in the mentality of Byron and Shelley. They acted out of a belief in unlimited self-affirmation which they hoped contained in itself a moral purpose. Edward Williams was convinced by them. He saw his own quiet, steady, constant love for Jane only in the shadow of theirs, and at last could not see it in its character of love at all. He did not lose Jane herself. He thought he had lost his capacity to love her. He killed Shelley in order to lift himself to a higher plane where love is proven by extreme action, and thereby he aimed to regain it.

Or perhaps he did not.

My maid tells me it is almost tea time. If I finish now I shall be able to catch the evening post. I confess, my dear boy, that I feel more than usually foolish in trying to understand life from my own limited experience and the observation of a few people around me. However, in the end, I have little else to judge by.

Please accept this letter in the kindly spirit with which I have written it.

Yours sincerely,
Agnes Westmacott

A few weeks after receiving Madame Hecate's letter, Guy left hospital. First, however, he attended the funeral of Bolsover, who had recovered his eyesight. It was a shabby affair and the mourners were limited to a few shifty types from whom the dead man had cadged drinks. Yet, had not the deaths of Shelley and Byron been shabby?

Depressed, Guy returned to the letter and then, in the light of its insights, he studied Lewis's poem again. This time he was able to see behind its facetious humour. He found horror, hatred and hideous envy.

CHAPTER THIRTY-ONE

Lord Byron

A Poem
by
Mr Lewis Lockyer

Bob Southey is his victim; so is Bill
   Of Grassmere, poets of an earlier Age,
With others who are long since o'er the hill,
   And scarcely worth a mention on the page.
But Coward and Waugh escape from Byron's will,
   For George is dead before they take the stage.
Thus may we judge th' injustice of Time's writ:
A latecomer may claim the greater wit.

We may not read the Dead, but we must praise
   Their work, as we are taught to do at school.
Lord Byron has the talent to amaze;
   The rest of us are limited by rule.
Yet, do we have no duty to *our* days?
   How will things stand if Byron is a fool?
His verse, though doubtless fine, will be amiss
If there's no moral core, just wind and piss.

The boy is poor, though not so poor as we
   Who are not noble but must earn our crust.
George comes into substantial property
   By waiting till his elders turn to dust.
So first acquire the money to be free
   To choose to do – or not – what others must.
The rich and powerful fall to Byron's lash.
I'll flay them, too – when once I've got the cash.

George grabs the loot and opens London's doors
    (Not difficult for those with looks and wealth),
And finds the Great and Good are mostly bores,
    Yet does not have the wit to act by stealth,
But gains his wisdom at the breast of whores
    And diets oft – for vanity, not health.
I ought to mention now: among his toys
He takes an amorous interest in young boys.

What am I saying! Byron is a queer?
    Ask Edleston – alas, the dead can't speak.
It's true George likes his girls; but still, I fear,
    In strange and varied ways he studies Greek
(Alpha to Omega – *viz.*, front to rear)
    And any other vices he can seek.
At heart he stays as guiltless as the birds.
What means 'guilt'? Oh, he has a way with words!

He marries Annabella, fair and rich,
    And doomed to be abandoned very soon.
He thinks she is a veritable bitch
    And tells her so upon the honeymoon,
With wishes that she'll drop dead in a ditch.
    Perhaps she will not dance to George's tune?
A wise man justly doubts the views on life
Of one who lacks the skill to keep a wife.

Augusta is the next. She is his sister:
    Belle, witless, pleasant-mannered, married, mild.
It doesn't take George long to find he's missed her
    (And devil take his missus and his child).
His brains are in his balls when once he's kissed her.
    The marriage beds of both are soon defiled.
Family values ought to have their day,
Though swiving sisters ain't the usual way.

The lovely Claire's a relative of Mary.
    George finds her quite attractive at the start.
Though she has every reason to be chary,
    She is (one must assume) a silly tart.
She isn't loved or wed or wise or wary.
    A bastard is the payment for her part.
George proves to be a moral sort of lover:
He takes the child (although he dumps the mother).

Now Caroline's the object of his sin.
    (Alas, I cannot swear as to the order.)
No Lamb but rather Wolf under the skin.
    Love her, swive her, leave her, cross the border:
Another lady goes into the bin.
    Perhaps dear George has found he can't afford her:
Though women, bought in bulk, come very cheap –
And cheaper still once scrapped upon the heap.

The atmosphere of England is too hot
    To hold a man of George's disposition.
Abroad he finds a more congenial spot
    To practise heroism (and coition);
Since Italy's an amorous melting-pot
    And Catholic (so no need for contrition).
For George's feasting at the sexual trough
Ten million British women aren't enough.

To press on with my verse, I turn to Shelley.
    He took a wife, gave her a child, and quit.
Mary became his whore. What's to tell? He
    Was a noble too – a perfect shit,
Quick to put a baby in her belly.
    One wife, one trull, two brats, but what of it?
This is Percy's notion of his marriage:
His darling wife was buried by the parish.

377

"Now where the quick Rhone thus has cleft his way"
    They set up shop in which to ply their art.
Beauty lies in not deeds but what men *say*:
    Freedom of Spirit is th' important part.
What matters it if women have to pay?
    Women are whores, and so not worth a fart.
We love 'em while we can; so do not blame us.
Desertion is a virtue. It don't shame us.

Here George and Percy read Jean-Jacques Rousseau.
    La Nouvelle Héloïse supports their pride.
Such Art! Such Sentiment! Such Wisdom! So
    They track his footsteps o'er the mountainside,
Sigh at his thought and blend it in the flow
    Of Poesy: he is their moral guide.
I see a certain similarity:
The Switzer's brats were raised on charity.

The storm strikes Diodati with its rage.
    George, Percy, Mary, Claire amuse themselves
In telling stories aiming to assuage
    Their fears with tales of devils, ghosts and elves,
And Frankenstein, who's destined for the page
    Of books that show the darkness in our selves.
Before we kill that monster, should we start
By killing those that lie within the heart?

Byron moves next to Venice on a spree;
    Calls for monkeys, peacocks and his trollops;
Spends all his gold on this menagerie,
    Devouring women as if they were collops
Of beef made tasty by adultery.
    In trying vices Byron pulls out all stops.
Concerning apes, perhaps one should not bother,
Though I'd have doubts, were I the creatures' mother.

George falls in with a group of wild Italians,
    And thinks he'll free them from the Austrian yoke.
Great heroes are this gang of tough rapscallions.
    (I fancy they consider George a joke.)
At all events, he pays the price of dalliance
    With them and many similar sorts of folk.
Statesman and artist, as a normal rule,
Don't mix – unless the last's a bloody fool.

He flees to Pisa, taking there his boat
    And motley crew (Trelawny and the rest),
Where Percy still remains a randy stoat,
    Paying his court to Jane, who is the best
Of women. (Now her turn comes up by rote:
    With Percy every girl must pass his test.)
Poor Mary views her husband with a sigh,
Weeps at lost love and sees her children die.

'Tis summer and they set off for the coasts.
    George to Livorno. Percy packs his bags,
Takes Mary and the Williamses, and hosts
    In lordly style his party. There are snags.
La Spezia is poor for one who boasts
    His quarterings and proud ancestral flags.
It ain't no Gothick castle. Percy, glum,
Meets dreadful Death while living in a slum.

Oh doleful Fate! Oh Tragedy! Hey ho!
    (Truthfully, I find the subject funny.
Who tolls the bell for cattle when they go
    Like doomed youths to their deaths? Time is runny
With blood: the poets' … mine. It is not kind. So
    I think I'll live for ever and make money.)
Charon, the ferryman, waits at the moat
For every classicist who cuts his throat.

Now to Livorno. Percy visits friends.
    With him are Edward Williams and a lad.
Mary and Jane must wait until Fate sends
    Its Judgment, partly earned and partly sad.
Why should the poor boy die? He served Art's ends.
    Forget him! He'd have likely turn out bad.
The lad's death does not blemish Shelley's glory:
He's usually omitted from the story.

The wise Trelawny cautions: 'Do not sail.
    I fear a storm.'
Says Williams: 'Do not worry.
    I was a sailor.' Percy means to rail
At God and storms. Such fun! He's feeling merry.
    'I have no fear' – or sense – 'I shall not fail
To welcome Death.' (Me, I don't see the hurry.)
Romantic heroes always welcome Death.
(I think they change their minds with their last breath.)

"Oh storm and darkness, ye are wondrous strong!"
    Oh yes? A pleasant thought when one's in bed.
If I were stuck at sea, then I would long
    For home and wife and comfort. (But I've said
Already that I think Romantics wrong.
    I'd rather leave heroics 'till I'm dead.)
Crash! Bang! Splish! Splash! Forgive me if I shirk
Description – sometimes Readers have to work.

Crash! Bang! Splish! Splash! Ah, onomatopoeia!
    Good God, I'm talking Greek! How marvellous
clever!
The sounds of Nature charm the poet's ear,
    But Percy (who speaks Greek) would rather never
Have heard them, for his bowels gripe with fear
    As he bids to the World farewell for ever.
(I think of the sad boy, the wives. Enough! It
Served that bastard Shelley right to snuff it.)

Days pass, and then on Viareggio's shore
    The drear wreck of a body comes to land.
Both fear and hope resolve, for it is poor
    Young Percy Bysshe whose corpse lies on the strand.
Gone is his fey, bright beauty! Never more!
    Bloated and gnawed by fish and washed with sand.
Mary must weep in dreams. There's the rub. Her
Eyes can find no trace of him in blubber.

Up steps the bold Trelawny. 'Light a fire.
    Worthy of Heroes are the rites of Kings.
Let us burn Heaven and Earth upon his pyre!'
    Shelley, in mortal life, burnt many things.
'Let us chant doleful dirges to the lyre.
    Such was a man of whom blind Homer sings.'
(Digression – listen to the scholar speak.
In those days even pirates knew their Greek.)

Fires are thus lit and turn the corpse to ash.
    Well … not exactly. Bones resist the flame.
Flesh grills and chars; and, well-sauced with a dash
    Of relish, man and pig will taste the same.
Will broiling poets start a gourmet fashion?
    Will drowning bards become a game?
Oh, lucky Critics! Meat is in the shops.
Why should you eat your words? Gorge on my chops.

What should George do? All hail, O brave Hellene!
    Achilles' kinsmen fight the dastard Turk.
George thinks to struggle with them: earn the paean
    Of praise. They have no army but they lurk
In mountains; live in hovels none too clean;
    And spring from shadows; then flee in the murk.
George finds his new friends' manners most alarming
(Though, for myself, I think the fellows charming).

George sits upon the hilltops and is mobbed
    By brave Greeks saying why they cannot fight.
"It's hot!" – "It's cold!" – And all the while he's robbed.
    "It's wet!" – "It's dry!" – or else "It's day!" – "It's
    night!"
He's loose of bowel; he's palsied – how he's sobbed!
    He's sad when sober: miserable when tight.
A boy he loves declines. What frustration!
Even buggery's no consolation.

No hero. No heroics. George grows sick.
    Do faint regrets of Folly touch his mind?
Does Conscience now recoil beneath the prick
    Of Fate? Or, in this sad case, do we find
That Death has soothed his poor soul with a trick
Causing forgetfulness? Death can be kind.

No Hero should depart hence bit by bit,
To die not of a shot but of a shit.

CHAPTER THIRTY-TWO

1945

'Did you ever discover the identity of our spare corpse?' asked Jenkins.

He and Guy were stripped because of the heat, helping Tommy Long and Nick to load the two-tonner. The egalitarian spirit that had grown with the end of the war and their close confinement at La Spezia made this seem quite natural.

'No,' said Guy. 'Though I imagine it's Nessuno, as you suggested.'

'Well, I'm glad that's settled. I was beginning to think that corpses sprouted like weeds in this place. Odd, though, that the fellow was naked. A suspicious mind might think someone was trying to put us off the scent.'

Corporal Long generously offered to complete the loading while the officers had a final cup of tea.

Guy was curious as to the future, Jenkins' and his own.

'Have you thought again about going into business with Tommy?'

'I have,' said Jenkins resolutely, 'and I'm going to do it. I feel ready to take a chance with life.'

'Aren't you worried about his honesty?'

'I admit it did occur to me. But I think you may have misunderstood him. Tommy's a strange chap. His views on morality aren't exactly conventional, but he's not without principles. He believes in keeping his promises and sticking by his friends. That's good enough for me.'

'Well, it's your lookout.'

'In the end it always is, isn't it?'

'I suppose so. Drink up. It's time to go.'

*

Nick drove the Bedford. Jenkins volunteered to act as relief: 'I've always wanted to get the hang of one of these things.' Guy travelled with Corporal Long in the Jeep.

When they reached the highway, Guy noticed that, on this side, the Villa Esperanza had become invisible, burnt to below the level of the trees. They would soon invade the driveway and the ruin would be lost, to be rediscovered in a remote future by walkers who would ponder over the meaning of the remains; or perhaps it would be bought by a speculator who would make something quite different of it.

The Scotsman was in a good humour. He spun the wheel and made the Jeep weave. Guy found himself sharing nervously in the enjoyment.

'Steady on, Tommy. Glad to be going home, are you?'

'That I am, Mr Parrot! By the way, thanks for putting in a word tae have me made up tae sergeant again.'

'It was the least I could do. I thought the extra stripe might help if the Army pays a gratuity on demob.'

Having buried his own mistakes – to some degree literally – Guy had thought he should do something for his men. He recommended Jimmy for a medal in recognition of his selfless attempt to save the hospital from the fire. Since Jimmy had been dead at the time, the reference to his 'miraculous efforts' was strictly accurate.

Nick was tearful when he received the news. 'It's awful good of you, Mr Parrot. Jimmy's old ma will be pleased no end. And he did deserve it, even if not for what you said. He was a brave boy.'

'Was he?' said Guy, for whom it was an agreeable but surprising disclosure. 'How?'

'Well, bein' the way that me and him are you've got to be brave, haven't you?'

There were fewer warships in the Gulf. The summer was at its height, but with the first subtle signs of waning.

The quality of light was changing. The pure blue sky had acquired notes of gold and russet. Porto Venere was hidden in a soft haze.

Guy asked, 'Tommy, did you ever sort out your differences with Corporal Pulaski?'

'Aye,' answered the Scotsman cheerfully. 'He came over for a dram and we settled everything.'

This was news. 'He came to the villa? When was that?'

'The night o' they fire.'

To occupy himself, Guy took out a letter.

'From the missus?' enquired Corporal Long.

'No. It's from an old lady called Madame Hecate.'

'Hecate? Italian was she?'

'I don't think so.'

Her letters were Guy's sole memento of his terrible summer. Occasionally he studied the account of Shelley's murder. Once it had accorded with his own conclusions, but now he was inclined to doubt that the poet had been murdered at all. It was impossible to say.

He suspected that his opinions of Shelley were unfair. The obscurities of any biography and the callous fabrications they had made that summer out of conceit and for amusement had so confused things that any just estimation was beyond Guy's power. Above all, he was conscious that at no time had he and the others ever debated the poet's work. Yet surely it mattered – it was perhaps the only thing that mattered. It was so difficult to tell: in particular, because Shelley's verse was frankly beyond Guy's understanding. Thinking over the point, it occurred to him that the relevance of Shelley's life (and death) was possibly this: that poetic truth was not the logical exposition of ideas but more akin to prophecy; and that its validity was inseparable from faith in the integrity of the prophet. If the latter did not possess *gnosis* – if he were not indeed touched by God – he was no more than a blind shaman mumbling in a cave, and the offerings smouldering on the sacrificial fire were not the price of entry to a higher realm but the pitiful flesh of slaughtered innocents.

Thus Guy was left to choose. Were Byron and Shelley fools, or were they a type of spiritual athlete, falling at the hurdles only to rise and continue the race towards a hidden prize? In his own hylic condition, his state of utter *agnosis*, it was difficult to take on trust the revelations granted to others. Guy remembered the words of the shabby martyr: 'God knoweth what it is all about, for I am sure I do not.' There was really nothing else to be said.

The ruins of La Spezia were before him. But even here was change. The piles of rubble had been moved, swept and ordered. The Americans were disappearing from the streets; the Italians resuming control with an optimism born of experiencing a hundred invasions.

On the floor of the Jeep Guy noticed a small bright object. He picked it up. It was a button from an American uniform.

'Did you drop this, Tommy?' he asked.

'Aye,' said Corporal Long briefly and put it in his pocket.

Guy was curious. 'Does it belong to Corporal Pulaski?'

'Aye.'

'I suppose he gave it to you as a souvenir?'

'In a way.'

Tommy took his eyes momentarily from the road. His bright white teeth flashed merrily.

'Corp didna exactly *want* tae give it me,' he said and paused. 'But I took it all the same.'

A smile of sly charm passed across the Scotsman's face but already Guy had ceased to pay attention. He was thinking of the letter he would write to Elizabeth. No doubt his stubborn tongue would stumble over the words, his imagination fail him, and the reticence of his manner veil his thoughts. Yet Elizabeth knew him thoroughly and he could trust his imperfections to her forgiving care. She would read both words and silences and search out the feelings of his heart. Words were, in the end, only a gloss on the actions and affections of their quiet years together.

Elizabeth knew him thoroughly and would recognise even in his muteness the belated discovery of a passionate love.

READERS' NOTES

Readers may spot that it is impossible that Guy Parrot should have read *Rebecca* in 1930, or that Ambrose Carmody should parody 'Today we Have Naming of Parts', since neither work had yet been written. There are other anachronisms and misstatement of fact. You may conclude that I do not regard accuracy as the essence of fiction.

The Strange Death of a Romantic is the third in a series of novels in which I investigate the central mystery of the Whodunit – the murder itself – to see whether there is something original that can be done with it. What the novel offers is a worked out "solution" to a murder which in fact never occurred. In short, the poet Percy Bysshe Shelley died in a sailing accident and wasn't murdered by anybody. And this book tells you who killed him.

In thinking about this, you may also want to consider some classic conspiracy theories: for example, that the moon landings were faked or that 9/11 was an incident staged by the U.S. Government and the Twin Towers were demolished by explosives rather than the impact of two passenger jets. The common theme is the ability of human beings to construct internally consistent and superficially plausible stories by the selective use of evidence, and the lesson – if there is one – is that we should be cautious about our ability to judge these things.

Stories about stories are a Post-Modernist conceit, and certainly this novel, replete with stories told by the characters, is in some respects a Post-Modernist murder mystery. However, this interpretation is in large degree a product of hindsight. When I was writing the various pastiches and parodies of other writers and styles I was simply having fun. If the book seems light hearted and frivolous, it's because I am. Also I wanted to stretch myself technically and see whether I could manage the three-layered narrative structure (1822 – 1930 and 1945) and try out various different voices.

As far as I know, the book doesn't have a deep subtext and it isn't intended to convey a message about the Human Condition. Guy's feebleness is an exaggeration of my own uncertainties as to What Life Is All About, and his solution is to cling to everyday kindness and the warmth of human relationships – which is also mine. It isn't very profound, is it?

Winston Churchill once said of his rival, Clement Attlee that he was "a modest man with a lot to be modest about." The quip is normally regarded as a magnificent example of a put-down, but in mulling it over in recent years I've increasingly thought that it must be a nice and good thing to be: a modest man with a lot to be modest about. Guy Parrot is such a person, and in my better moments I hope to be the same. However I am always open to being corrupted by lashings of fame and money – preferably undeserved. One shouldn't confuse virtue with lack of opportunity.

Offers, anyone?

Jim Williams

March 2014

Connect with Jim Williams and Marble City Publishing

http://www.jimwilliamsbooks.com/

http://www.marblecitypublishing.com

Join Marble City's list for updates on new releases by Jim
Williams:

http://eepurl.com/vek5L

Follow on Twitter:

http://twitter.com/MarbleCityPub

Other Marble City releases by Jim Williams:

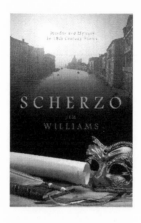

Scherzo by Jim Williams

MEET two unusual detectives. Ludovico – a young man who has had his testicles cut off for the sake of opera. And Monsieur Arouet – a fraudster, or just possibly the philosopher Voltaire.

VISIT the setting. Carnival time in mid-18th century Venice, a city of winter mists, and the season of masquerade and decadence.

ENCOUNTER a Venetian underworld of pimps, harlots, gamblers, forgers and charlatans.

BEWARE of a mysterious coterie of aristocrats, Jesuits, Freemasons and magicians.

DISCOVER a murder: that of the nobleman, Sgr Alessandro Molin, found swinging from a bridge with his innards hanging out and a message in code from his killer.

Scherzo is a murder mystery of sparkling vivacity and an historical novel of stunning originality told with a wit and style highly praised by critics and nominated for the Booker Prize.

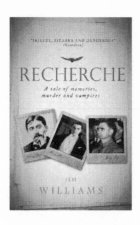

Recherche by Jim Williams

"A skilful exercise, bizarre and dangerous in a lineage that includes Fowles' *The Magus*."

Guardian

You get to be a lot of people when you are a vampire.

Meet old Harry Haze: war criminal, Jewish stand-up comedian, friend of Marcel Proust and J. Edgar Hoover. John Harper encounters him while spending the summer in the South of France with his mistress Lucy, and is entranced by Harry's stories of his fabulous past. Then Lucy disappears without explanation and both John and Harry fall under suspicion.

Yet how are we to know the truth when it is hidden in the labyrinth of Harry's bizarre memories and John's guilt at abandoning his wife? Nothing in this story is certain. Is Lucy dead? Is Harry a harmless old druggie or really a vampire? Deep inside his humorous tales is the suppressed memory of a night of sheer horror. And it is possible that one of the two men is an insane killer.

Tango in Madeira by Jim Williams

A disillusioned soldier looks for love. An exiled Emperor fears assassination. Agatha Christie takes a holiday. And George Bernard Shaw learns to tango.

In the aftermath of World War I, Michael Pinfold a disillusioned ex-soldier tries to rescue his failing family wine business on the island of Madeira. In a villa in the hills the exiled Austrian Emperor lives in fear of assassination by Hungarian killers, while in Reid's Hotel, a well-known lady crime novelist is stranded on her way to South Africa and George Bernard Shaw whiles away his days corresponding with his friends, writing a one act play and learning to tango with the hotel manager's spouse.

A stranger, Robinson, is found murdered and Michael finds himself manipulated into investigating the crime by his sinister best friend, Johnny Cardozo, the local police chief, with whose wife he is pursuing an arid love affair; manipulated, too, by Father Flaherty, a priest with dubious political interests, and by his own eccentric parent, who claims to have been part of a comedy duo that once entertained the Kaiser with Jewish jokes. Will Michael find love? Will the Emperor escape his would-be killers? Will any of the characters learn the true meaning of the tango?

The Argentinian Virgin by Jim Williams

A sensuous novel of erotic fantasy, obsession, jealousy and betrayal set in the dreamlike atmosphere of a Riviera summer in wartime.

Summer 1941. France is occupied by the Germans but the United States is not at war. Four glamorous young Americans find themselves whiling away the hot days in the boredom of a small Riviera town, while in a half-abandoned mansion nearby, Teresa and Katerina Malipiero, a mother and daughter, wait for Señor Malipiero to complete his business in the Reich and take them home to Argentina.

The plight of the women attracts the sympathy of 'Lucky' Tom Rensselaer and he is seduced by the beauty of Katerina. Tom has perfect faith in their innocence, yet they cannot explain why a sinister Spaniard has been murdered in their home and why Tom must help them dispose of the body without informing the police.

Watching over events is Pat Byrne, a young Irish writer. Twenty years later, when Tom has been reduced from the most handsome, admired and talented man of his generation to a derelict alcoholic, Pat sets out to discover the facts of that fateful summer: the secrets that were hidden and the lies that were told. It is a shocking truth: a tale of murder unpunished and a good man destroyed by those who loved him most.

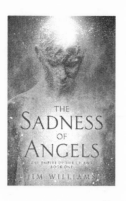

The Sadness of Angels by Jim Williams

Lord T'ien Huang controls the universe through poetry, telepathy and the violence of his insane Angels. His subjects consider him to be God. Emperor of a universe ruled by the Ch'ang, immortal but not invulnerable, his interest is aroused by Sebastian, a novice monk on the remote and wasted planet of Lu, who can see and speak to God. Should he destroy the boy or toy with him?

Sebastian is rescued from the Lord T'ien Huang's avenging Angels by Mapmaker, an ancient Old Before the Fall with a forgotten history of betrayal, and they journey to the snowbound north. They are accompanied by Velikka Magdasdottir, a girl belonging to the Hengstmijster tribe of warrior herdswomen who maintain a veiled harem of husbands.

In the frozen wastes they encounter the remains of the Ingitkuk who rebelled against the Ch'ang in antiquity and lost their witch princess, She Whom the Reindeer Love. Mapmaker knew her, when she died half a millennium ago, as Her Breath Is Of Jasmine.

Will Mapmaker lead Sebastian, the Hengstmijster and the Ingitkuk to their doom against the Ch'ang? Can Sebastian master his own powers? How will they survive against the Angel Michael, thawed and frozen more times than he can recall, with his power to destroy humanity by the billion?

The Hitler Diaries by Jim Williams

A stunning literary prophecy! The international bestseller that caused a sensation when it was published 9 months before the famous Hitler Diaries forgery scandal.

A French aristocrat and his mistress are murdered. A mysterious businessman offers the Fuehrer's diaries to a new York publishing house. Are they a hoax or a record of terrifying truth? A controversial historian and his beautiful assistant are commissioned to find out the answer following a trail that draws them into a terrifying web of conspiracy and slaughter as competing forces fight to publish or suppress Hitler's account of the War and of secret negotiations with his enemies.

But are the Diaries genuine or just a plot to destabilise contemporary politics? A shattering revision of history whose revelation must be prevented at all costs: or a fake, just a sinister manoeuvre in the Cold War?

If the Hitler Diaries are authentic, then who left the bunker alive?

Made in the USA
Charleston, SC
31 July 2014